Close Call

Close Call

Stella Rimington

B L O O M S B U R Y
LONDON · NEW DELHI · NEW YORK · SYDNEY

First published in Great Britain 2014

Copyright © 2014 by Stella Rimington

Bloomsbury Publishing Plc
50 Bedford Square
London
WC1B 3DP

www.bloomsbury.com

Bloomsbury is a trademark of Bloomsbury Publishing Plc

Bloomsbury Publishing, London, New Delhi, New York and Sydney

A CIP catalogue record for this book is available from the British Library

Hardback ISBN 978 1 4088 4104 4
Trade paperback ISBN 978 1 4088 4105 1

10 9 8 7 6 5 4 3 2 1

Typeset by Hewer Text UK Ltd, Edinburgh
Printed and Bound in Great Britain by CPI (UK) Ltd, Croydon CR0 4YY

www.bloomsbury.com/stellarimington

To my brother, Brian Whitehouse
1932–2013

THE SUN WAS SLANTING through the high-vaulted roof of the souk, throwing down shafts of light in which dust motes and thin drifts of cigarette smoke swirled lazily. Miles Brookhaven began to relax as he walked down the long central avenue, breathing in smells of powdery piles of spices, reaching over to touch the shiny purple skins of aubergines, and exchanging a shouted greeting with the stallholder.

He stopped at a food stall on the corner of one of the side aisles where the same old man who'd been there since God knows when had a juicing machine. As he usually did when he took this route, Miles stopped for a glass of fresh orange juice. Against the wall behind the counter a *shawarma* of meat the size of a tree trunk rotated on a long sharp pole. Miles propped one hip on a stool in the corner, from where he could look down the main aisle, the way he'd come, but his eye was drawn to the spit. There was something different. Usually, as he drank, he would watch a short balding man called Afiz, his apron stained by the spattering juices, wielding a long knife of incredible sharpness, peeling shavings of meat off the *shawarma* like strips of wallpaper.

He and Afiz had established a friendly unspoken ritual – Afiz would turn and gesture to Miles with his knife, as if to ask *You want some?* Miles would shake his head and hold up his glass to show that was what he'd come for. Afiz would laugh and turn back to the *shawarma*.

But it wasn't Afiz who tended the spit today. Instead a young man held the long knife. He was tall with a prominent Adam's apple and long black hair tied back into a knot, and he stared at Miles with dark indifferent eyes, then turned away to serve a customer. He had none of Afiz's practised delicacy; instead he just hacked at the meat, which fell in chunks instead of paper-thin slices. That seemed odd, Miles thought as he sipped his juice. Holding the glass in one hand he reached into his pocket for some coins to pay, and it was then he sensed movement, looked up and saw the young man coming towards him, holding the knife in one hand, his eyes glazed and hostile.

Not pausing to think, Miles tilted his glass of juice and hurled its contents straight into the eyes of his attacker. The long-haired youth was caught by surprise, blinking furiously, trying to get the juice out of his eyes. Miles took a step back, and as the young man lunged forward, swiping hard with the knife, he threw the empty glass at his face.

It hit the youth square in the eye. He yelled in pain and dropped the knife, which fell onto the tiled floor of the stall and bounced from its point, erratically, before landing at last, like an offering, at Miles's feet. As Miles bent down and grabbed it, the young man ran out of the far side of the stall.

Miles stared at the fleeing figure and when he turned back he saw that the juice man had fled as well. The commotion was drawing a crowd. Miles understood from the jabber of Arabic that they were wondering what this Westerner was doing, holding that knife. He put it down on the counter and without looking around strode quickly down the aisle towards the exit from the souk. The last thing he or his colleagues needed was the attention of the police.

By the time he'd reached the modern end of the souk, no one in the crowd of shoppers seemed to be taking special notice of him. He slowed to a stroll, forced himself to breathe normally and began to review what had happened. Was the young man just another extremist who hated Westerners? He didn't think so. The fact that he'd been working at the stall where Miles regularly stopped – and that the juice man had fled as well – made it seem more likely that he'd been targeted.

Perhaps the group he'd been working with had been penetrated – but by whom? That was what made it hard to deal with the rebels. Too many conflicting interests; too many irons in the fire. Your enemy's enemy wasn't necessarily your friend. Whatever the explanation, he couldn't go on using the same cover. It was time to move on.

Outside in the bright sun, Miles realised that his hand felt sticky, raised it and found it covered in blood. More blood was running down the sleeve of his jacket, and moving his shoulder made him wince in pain. That swipe with the knife must have connected.

He'd begun to feel faint; best get back to the office fast. He heard a gasp and looked up to see a young woman staring in horror at his jacket. Behind her a little man with a bushy black moustache was pointing at him. The blood was flowing fast down his arm now, dripping from the cuffs of his shirt and jacket onto the paving stones. His vision was blurring, and he'd started to sway as he walked.

Seeing him stagger, the little man put his arm round him, waving with his other arm at a taxi. 'Hospital, hospital,' he shouted at the driver, and as he bundled him into the back of the car, Miles passed out.

2

LIZ CARLYLE WAS SITTING at her desk in Thames
House, the London headquarters of Britain's MI5,
frowning at the pile of papers neatly stacked in the centre
of her desk. She'd just got back from a three-week holiday
walking in the Pyrenees and was wishing she'd stayed
there. A spectacled head poked round the door, followed
by the rest of Peggy Kinsolving, Liz's long-standing
research assistant and now her deputy in the Counter-
Terrorist section that Liz ran.

'Welcome back,' said Peggy. 'Did you have a good time?
You must be fit as a flea. It's never stopped raining here
since you went away.' She waved a hand at the pile of paper.
'Don't worry about that lot. I've read it all and it's just
background stuff. The top one is the only important one –
I've summarised where we've got to in all the current
investigations. You've got a meeting with the Home Secretary on Friday to bring her up to date. If you like I'll come
with you.'

Peggy stopped to draw breath and Liz smiled fondly at
her younger colleague. 'It is actually great to be back,
though I didn't feel that when I woke up this morning. We
had a wonderful time. Walked miles, ate too much, drank

some great wine. Martin is fine, though he's still wondering whether to leave the DGSE and go into private security work. He fancies getting out of Paris and living in the South – his family home was near Toulouse. But it's a big step to leave government service and go private and there's a lot of competition in the private security field – just like here. Anyway, how are you? And how's Tim?'

Tim was Peggy's boyfriend, a lecturer in English at King's College, London University, a very bright lad if a bit of a sensitive soul. Peggy said, 'I'm fine, and so is Tim, thanks. He's still doing the vegetarian cooking course – advanced level now. I hadn't realised it could be so tasty. I'm quite converted.' They both smiled and Peggy went on, 'There's one thing you won't be too pleased about. We've been given an extra responsibility. I was only told about it on Friday. It's a "watching brief" – whatever that is – for under-the-counter arms supplies to the Arab Spring rebels.'

Liz knew all too well what a watching brief was. It meant extra responsibility with no additional resources. Then if anything bad happened you were to blame. She sighed. 'Is there any intelligence that arms are going from dealers in this country to the rebels?'

'Not that I've heard. It's not so much the rebels per se that anyone's worried about; it's the jihadis who've infiltrated them. The Foreign Secretary went to a meeting in Geneva last week and this was on the agenda. There's a lot of concern about al-Qaeda-type groups leaking into the Arab Spring countries. There were some gruesome pictures on TV while you were away of what they were doing to their captives.'

'I saw them on French TV. But I would have thought they could get arms quite easily from the countries who support them.'

'I know that seems more likely. But the conference decided that each country should put measures in place to ensure that no undercover supplies from the EU countries get to these jihadis. It seems to be more of a matter for Eastern Europe than us, but DG told me on Friday that it's been decided that we were to have the "watching brief".'

'Great. But what about Six? I wonder what they have on this.'

'Quite a lot, I imagine. But guess who's running their part of the show – your favourite officer, Bruno Mackay. Bruno rang me on Friday to welcome us on board. Said he'd like to come over to see you when you were back.'

Liz put her head in her hands and groaned. 'Did I just say I was glad to be back?'

Peggy grinned. 'Bruno told me something quite interesting. Do you remember Miles Brookhaven, who used to be in the CIA station here? Andy Bokus's deputy?' When Liz nodded she went on, 'Apparently he was nearly killed a few months ago. He was under cover in an aid charity the Agency had set up in Syria, running a source in a rebel group, and he was attacked in the souk. They aren't sure if his cover had been blown, or if it was just an opportunist attack, but from what Bruno said, it sounded planned to me. Miles needed a series of blood transfusions – they had to get him out of there pretty quickly.'

'Poor Miles. He was a bit naïve when he was here. He tried to recruit me once – he took me on the London Eye in a private pod and plied me with champagne. It was fun, and I enjoyed watching him waste the Agency's money. I wonder if he's grown up.'

'I hope so.' Peggy got up to go. 'I'll leave you to catch up.'

But as Peggy walked out of the door she bumped into

someone coming in. 'Whoops. Sorry, Geoffrey. I was just going. Liz will be delighted to see you!'

The tall, heron-like figure of Geoffrey Fane, a senior MI6 officer, sauntered into the room. 'Good morning Elizabeth. Delighted to see you looking so fit and well. Been on holiday I hear. I hope you had a wonderful time and that our friend Seurat is in good form.'

One of Geoffrey Fane's characteristics, which drove Liz mad, was his inquisitive interest in her private life and his delight in showing how much he knew about it. She would much have preferred him not to know that she was seeing Martin Seurat of the French Military Intelligence Service, the DGSE. But he did know, and she suspected that he had learned about it from Bruno Mackay, who had been the deputy head of MI6's Paris Station when she'd first met Martin.

What she didn't like to acknowledge, though everyone else knew it, was that Geoffrey Fane himself would have liked to be in Martin Seurat's shoes. He was divorced, a lonely man and evidently deeply attracted to Liz, who though she admired and respected his professional skill, couldn't disguise the fact that on a personal level she found him pompous and patronising. What she couldn't – or wouldn't let herself see – was that much of his manner towards her was a cover for his feelings. So he went on calling her 'Elizabeth', though he knew that she preferred to be called 'Liz', and she went on grinding her teeth at the sight of him while everyone marvelled that they seemed to have such a successful working relationship.

Now Fane folded himself elegantly into the chair that Peggy had just left and crossed one long, tailored leg over the other, showing a length of subtly striped sock and a highly polished black brogue. 'I was delighted to learn we'll be working together on the arms supply front,' he said.

'Yes. I've just heard about it from Peggy. I gather we've been given a watching brief and no extra resources, so I don't suppose we'll be doing much active investigation. Anyway, Peggy told me that there's no specific intelligence about any UK arms dealers being involved, and we certainly haven't the time to go looking.'

Fane leant forward in his chair. 'That might have been true last week, but things are moving on. I had a call from Andy Bokus over the weekend. They've just posted a new man into Yemen. An old friend of yours if I'm not mistaken. Miles Brookhaven. I'm sure you remember him from when he was here at Grosvenor with Bokus. I gather he was quite smitten.'

Liz gazed at the languid figure in the chair, clenched her jaw and said nothing. Fane smiled slightly and went on, 'He had a bit of a rough time on his previous posting but he's recovered now. The Agency have sent him to Sana'a to pick up a rather promising contact of the Embassy. Bokus seems to think there may be something interesting to come out for us as well as for the Agency.'

3

MILES BROOKHAVEN'S SHOULDER STILL ached at night if he turned over awkwardly in bed, and now driving the heavy SUV he felt a twinge of pain whenever the car bounced over a rut in the road or he had to turn the wheel suddenly to avoid a pothole. The long knife had slashed the tendons at the top of his arm and the doctors at the military hospital in Germany to which he had been evacuated had told him that they would never properly heal. But, under pressure from CIA headquarters in Langley, the doctors had finally authorised his posting. There was a shortage of experienced case officers with fluent Arabic, and as the Arab Spring spread and jihadis joined the rebels in one country after another, the need for intelligence both from the front line of the fighting and from the countries on the periphery had become urgent.

From NSA at Fort Meade and CIA at Langley to GCHQ in Cheltenham, the eyes and ears of the West were focused on the movement of weapons around the world, and in particular to the countries where rebel groups were fighting governments. It was clear that supplies of some of the most sophisticated weapons were getting through to jihadis.

Yemen was a special focus of attention. Overhead surveillance had shown piles of what appeared to be weapons crates stacked on the dockside at Aden. The photographs had landed on the desk of an analyst in Langley at the same time as a report from the Commercial Counsellor at the US Embassy in Sana'a. The diplomat's report described his meetings with the Minister of Trade, one of his main contacts. The Minister seemed uninterested in developing trade with the US except in one area – weapons. The Minister explained this as the need for his government to be able to protect both its own citizens and foreigners against increasingly aggressive jihadi groups. But the Embassy report pointed out that the same message was coming from the Interior and Defence Ministers – departments where issues of weapons supply seemed a more natural fit.

The other notable feature of the diplomat's meetings with the Minister of Trade was the frequency of his references to 'his' Foundation, set up he said to help the homeless and in desperate need of funds. But research by the Embassy had thrown up no sign of such a charity. It was this last point that had brought the diplomatic cable onto the desk in Langley and which had resulted a few months later in the diplomat being moved to a senior post in another country and Miles Brookhaven turning up in the Sana'a Embassy as the new Commercial Counsellor. He had one brief – to recruit the Minister of Trade.

As he drove, Miles could see the mountains in the west, ranged in a rough semicircle around the city. His health not fully restored, it had taken him a few days to get used to the thin air of Sana'a. This was to be his first meeting with Jamaal Baakrime, the Trade Minister, his recruitment target, and he was feeling rather nervous. In normal circumstances he would have taken months to get to know a target, to assess weaknesses and vulnerabilities before he made his pitch, but he had been told not to hang about with this one but to go straight in and offer him cash for information. If the approach failed he would be quickly withdrawn and posted somewhere else where he could be useful.

He parked on a wide street and walked, turning into a much narrower side street lined by squat government buildings, concrete blocks mostly, put up in the Sixties with US aid money. They were interspersed with a few more recent constructions built as Yemen began to develop its oil resources. Not that Yemen nowadays showed much sign of being oil- or gas-rich. On the streets, even here in the capital, poverty was rife, and as he walked along Miles reflected that if the Minister's charity existed there was plenty for it to do.

Inside the Trade Ministry, a guard with a holstered pistol was sitting in a chair in one corner of the entrance hall reading a magazine. He raised his eyes lazily as Miles came in, then resumed reading. A young uniformed woman behind the front desk took his name, consulted a sheet of paper, then waved Miles to follow her. She led him up the stairs to the first floor, into a large open-plan office where a dozen men and women sat typing, and on into a long corridor with dark little offices on either side, occupied by men sitting behind desks covered with piles of papers.

At the end of the corridor she knocked on a large, closed door. A loud voice boomed out in Arabic and the woman opened the door and ushered Miles inside.

Baakrime's office could have been in a different world. It was roughly forty feet long, lined by picture windows with fabulous views of the mountains. The floors were polished mahogany boards overlaid by a rich sprinkling of fine

Persian carpets. Gaudy oil paintings hung on the walls, scenes from the Arabian Nights, featuring scantily draped female figures.

Baakrime came out from behind a large antique desk, his hand extended. He was a diminutive square-shouldered man, with short black hair brushed back in a lacquered wave, and a thick Groucho Marx moustache. 'It is delightful to meet you, Mr Brookhaven. Your predecessor and I had an excellent relationship,' he declared. 'Come, let us make ourselves comfortable.' He gestured towards a sitting area, where two sofas were adorned by soft cushions covered in coloured damask.

They sat down at right angles to each other. 'Coffee is coming,' Baakrime said hospitably. He wore a light grey suit and a white shirt with a canary-coloured tie. A triangle of paisley silk handkerchief peeked out from the breast pocket of his jacket.

'It's good of you to see me,' said Miles. 'I know you have a full schedule.'

'Nonsense. I always have time for my friends,' said Baakrime. He shrugged his shoulders. 'And you know what they say – if you want to get something done, ask a busy man.'

They chatted for a few minutes inconsequentially. Miles was accustomed to the Arab insistence that all business, however pressing, was prefaced by small talk. The coffee arrived, brought in by a young woman, smartly dressed in Western clothes – a noticeably short skirt and a blouse unbuttoned at the top. Baakrime ogled her legs with unconcealed pleasure and, as she put the tray on the low table and bent down to pour out the coffee, his eyes moved to her cleavage.

When she had left, Baakrime continued chatting idly,

13

asking after the welfare of Miles's family. When Miles explained that he was unmarried, Baakrime asked after his parents. He moved on to describe the location, ambience and menu of a new restaurant that Miles must try, and recommended two holiday resorts on the Egyptian coast along the Red Sea.

When finally Baakrime paused to sip his coffee, Miles said, 'I understand that your Department has a role in the import of arms to your country.'

Baakrime stopped sipping but continued to hold his cup to his mouth. He said nothing for a moment, then put the cup on the table, looking all the time at Miles. He said, 'That is true. It is a trade that interests me greatly. We have, as you know, many threats to our country, both internal and external.'

'Yes indeed,' replied Miles. Then, with the instruction from Langley to 'get on with it' at the front of his mind, he said, 'It is also a subject that greatly interests those who sent me to your country.'

Baakrime didn't reply. Miles hoped that he had picked up the hint he had been offered about who Miles worked for. Then, his eyes slipping away from Miles, Baakrime remarked, 'These affairs can be a little complicated, but I might be able to help you get started on your work.'

Miles's heart gave a lurch. Baakrime had recognised the bait. It was time to see if he would swallow it. He said, 'That would be very much appreciated by my government. You know, data is freely available these days – we in the West with all our computers are positively awash with information. But knowledge is scarce, and can be expensive to find. Don't you agree?'

Baakrime smiled and nodded. 'How true that is, my friend.'

Miles ploughed on. 'My colleague also told me that another interest of yours is the Foundation you have set up to help the homeless in your country. That is such an excellent cause that I am authorised to offer you substantial and regular contributions to help in its work. In fact,' he said, reaching into his pocket, 'not knowing what the bank account details for the Foundation are, I have brought our first contribution of ten thousand dollars with me.' And he put a thick white envelope on the table, thinking that if Langley had got this wrong he was going to look awfully stupid.

But Baakrime rapidly swept up the envelope and stuffed it into his pocket. 'That is so very kind and much appreciated. The Foundation is helping many people, I am glad to say. But the recent upheavals in my country mean more people are suffering than ever before, and we cannot keep up. We find it is better not to operate through the banks. They are not so reliable always. This' – he patted his pocket – 'would be the best way to make your contribution in future. I will ensure the cash gets to where it can best be used.'

You bet, thought Miles, but he merely smiled and nodded.

Baakrime said, 'In return for your generosity to my Foundation, you must tell me how I can best help you.'

Miles decided to strike while the iron was hot. 'We know that Yemen is one of the countries through which weapons are reaching rebel groups. And not just legitimate rebels – but others fighting with them, outsiders. Jihadis, extremists, al-Qaeda supporters.'

Baakrime smiled and shrugged but said nothing.

'What we want to know is the sources of those weapons and in particular any sources in Europe or the United States.'

Baakrime's manner changed from the wily to the businesslike. 'These young men. They think they are all Osama Bin Ladens. They are crude and cruel and defame the name of Islam. They are indeed a threat to us all. I will do what I can to help you, my friend. Come back in one week and I will see what I can find out.'

4

A RAW DAY. VIEWED from the window of Liz's office, the Thames looked battleship-grey, sprinkled with the frothy white lines of waves stirred up by the October wind. To Liz, her skin still brown from her holiday in the Pyrenees, the sun was a faraway memory.

She turned back to the pile of forms on her desk. The Service was blessedly free of much of the bureaucracy that affected the Civil Service, but it strongly believed in annual appraisals of staff, and now that Liz was responsible for managing a team of people, she had to write their performance assessments. She took the task seriously, knowing how important it was to the careers of her team, as well as to the Service itself as a tool for getting the right people in the right jobs. But it was not her favourite pastime. Even though she was now a manager, Liz was still an operational officer at heart. Too much time spent sitting behind her desk made her restless and irritable.

'That looks like fun.' Peggy Kinsolving was standing in the doorway.

Liz looked up. 'I thought you were at the conference.'

'I am. It's the lunch break, so I nipped back to check how that surveillance operation is going on.' Peggy was running an investigation into a group of young men in Camden Town who had just come back from Pakistan.

'Anything happening?'

'No. No movement at all so far. I think they're all still in bed.'

Liz nodded. Peggy had transferred to MI5 from MI6 several years ago. She had been a diffident, shy girl but a genius at research. She would follow a lead like a bloodhound but if you'd asked her to go out and interview someone she would have panicked and frozen with nerves. But over the years, under Liz's guidance, she had grown in confidence and now she was running her own operations, and directing a small team. Peggy had become a skilled interviewer, and had discovered a talent for finding out what made people tick, getting underneath their reserves and breaking down their defences.

But though her personality had developed, her appearance had hardly changed from her days as a librarian. She was a little short of medium height, with long brown hair she tied back in a wispy ponytail. Her spectacles, round and brown, seemed to be too big for her face and were forever slipping down her nose. The sight of Peggy pushing back her spectacles was often the preface to a remark that would begin the unravelling of some knotty problem.

'What's going on at the conference? Any good?' Liz asked. It was a Home Office-run conference aimed mainly at regional police forces, and designed to draw their attention to a nationwide growth in gun crime. Little of the agenda had much direct connection with the work of Liz's team, but she had thought it worthwhile to send someone to register an interest and demonstrate that they were taking their watching brief seriously.

Peggy said, 'Actually it's not been too bad. This after-noon might be quite interesting.'

'Really? What's happening?'

Peggy seemed to be struggling not to laugh. 'Well, it was meant to be a keynote address from the Foreign Office. You remember Henry Pennington?'

Liz groaned. She'd crossed swords with Henry Pennington several times over the years. A long lean man with a large nose that dominated his thin face, he was a panicker. Any indication that something might be going wrong caused him to begin rubbing his hands together in a washing motion and breathing heavily. At such times he was liable to make sudden decisions, which on one or two occasions had landed Liz in difficult situations. She never forgot the time he had volunteered her services as an undercover protection officer for a Russian oligarch, almost succeed-ing in getting her killed in the process.

'But sadly,' Peggy went on, 'Henry's indisposed. So they've put together a panel instead. Some senior officers from the North and the Midlands are going to be talking about their experience of the arms trade. I thought you might be interested.'

Liz thought about this. Her interest was in illegal arms shipments abroad, but there might be something worth hearing and the alternative was the pile of assessment forms on her desk. 'I think I'll come along.'

When they arrived at the conference room in the Queen Elizabeth Conference Centre in Parliament Square the session had already started. The room was three-quarters full and they slipped into seats at one side of a back row. There were three people on the stage, sitting in a semicircle so that Liz could only see two of them clearly. They were discussing the impact of Britain's gun laws, and Liz recognised one of the speakers – a senior policewoman from Derbyshire, notorious for her impatience with junior officers. The man next to her, who was obviously from the Home Office, was praising the government's tough stance on firearms as if one of his political masters were in the audience. He contrasted the UK's ban on handguns with America, where more often than not there didn't seem to be any gun laws at all. The policewoman from Derbyshire agreed with him that the total ban on handguns in the UK was a great thing.

Suddenly the third member of the panel, who Liz couldn't see properly, interrupted. 'Make no mistake, this country has a gun culture too – it's just invisible to most of us. All the government has really managed to do is drive gun sales further underground. We only hear about them when some drug dealer gets shot in Merseyside. Things have got worse in the last ten years, not better. We need to remember that when we congratulate ourselves on not being like the Americans.'

The bluntness of his remarks would have seemed out of place if the delivery had not been so self-assured, and as it was there was a murmur of assent round the room. The Home Office man looked uncomfortable. Liz sat up and leaned over to try to catch a glimpse of the man's face. There was something in the voice that was familiar.

Peggy noticed. 'What is it?' But Liz put a finger to her lips. The man she couldn't see properly was still talking.

It couldn't be, Liz told herself. She could see that the man was dressed in a suit, not a uniform, and from what she could see of him he looked pretty smart for a policeman. The man she was thinking of had always been a bit of a clothes horse.

Then he shifted in his chair and she could see his profile. She recognised the sharp nose and rugged chin. The hair now was thinner than before, but well cut, with only a few flecks of grey. He was still good-looking; whatever you thought of him you had to give him that.

'You look as if you've seen a ghost,' whispered Peggy.

Liz sighed, leaning back in her chair as the Derbyshire woman started up again. 'It's not a ghost,' she said at last. 'Just somebody I used to know. Though it was a long time ago.'

5

L IZ HAD BEEN IN MI5 just eighteen months. She had applied on the spur of the moment, in her last year at Bristol University. She had been thinking vaguely and without much enthusiasm that she might stay on at the university to do research when the chance remark of a visiting lecturer had coincided with an intriguing newspaper advertisement for logical, level-headed and decisive people to do important work in the national interest. She had sent in her cv, such as it was, without much hope of any response, and had been amazed to be called for an interview. After that the recruitment process had ground slowly on until, at the end of it all, she'd found herself a member of MI5, Britain's Security Service.

Although she was still on probation and in the training period, Liz felt settled and comfortable in the Service. Each morning when she left the flat in Holloway that she shared with four other Bristol graduates to take the underground to Thames House, she looked forward to the day.

Even though she'd been at university in a city, she wasn't really a city girl. She had grown up in the Wiltshire countryside where her father had been the land agent for a large estate. He was dead now and the estate had been broken

22

up after the death of the last owner without an heir, but her mother still lived in the octagonal Gatehouse where Liz had been brought up. Susan Carlyle managed the flourishing garden centre that now occupied the old kitchen gardens of the estate.

Liz was enjoying living in London and felt guilty that she didn't go down to Wiltshire more often, as she knew her mother was lonely. Susan Carlyle didn't disguise the fact that she would like Liz to abandon what she thought of as a 'dangerous job' and marry a nice young man, a solicitor or a doctor or something safe. Liz couldn't think of anything she wanted to do less.

Between them Liz and her flatmates had a fairly wide circle of friends. There was a faint shadow over Liz's social life in that she couldn't join in enthusiastically when everyone else was talking about their work, but she had taken those she lived with into her confidence and told them that she worked for one of the intelligence agencies, so they protected her and didn't question it when they heard her telling casual acquaintances that she worked for a PR agency.

The secondment to Merseyside police came as a considerable jolt. Liz knew that at some stage, as part of the training programme, she would be sent off on attachment to learn how a provincial police force and its Special Branch worked, but she wasn't expecting it so soon. And Liverpool was alien territory to her – she had never been further north than Nottingham.

It was the period before the Peace Process had taken hold in Northern Ireland and she was one of a team collating intelligence on the threat from the Provisional IRA. Liverpool had an established community of Irish expats, many with nationalist sympathies and a few with actual links with the Provos. The Special Branch had some sources that from time to time provided useful intelligence, so she'd already had some dealings with Merseyside Special Branch officers and she had not much liked them. As she'd travelled up on the train to Liverpool that gloomy, showery day she was feeling nervous.

As it turned out she had good reason to be, but not because of the IRA. In the police headquarters' rectangular red office block near the docks, a gloomy middle-aged sergeant with a pencil behind his ear had sent her upstairs with a grunt and a jerk of his thumb. One floor up she found a large open-plan room with a dozen or so desks in untidy rows, about half of them occupied by men, some young, some middle-aged, some in shirtsleeves, some in leather jackets, some typing, some talking on the phone. Cigarette smoke hung in the air in a blue uncirculating haze.

Every man looked up as Liz came into the room. She asked where Detective Inspector Avery could be found, and one of them pointed to the back of the room where a small office had been partitioned off with opaque glass. As Liz walked through the rows of desks, someone gave a low wolf whistle. Liz tried not to react, but she felt herself blush.

She knocked on the door, and a gruff voice said, *Come in.* Opening the door, she found a wide-shouldered man in shirtsleeves, with a tie pulled down an inch or two from his collar. He looked close to retirement age, and had greying hair cut very short, though he had let his sideboards grow in some misguided youthful impulse.

Avery looked annoyed by her interruption. 'What can I do for you, miss?'

'DI Avery?' The man nodded. 'I'm here from Box 500,'

said Liz, using the acronym by which the police referred to MI5. 'My name's Liz Carlyle.'

He stared at her. 'You're Carlyle?' He sounded astonished. 'I was expecting a George Carlyle, or a John Carlyle, or even a Seamus Carlyle. But nobody said anything about a *Liz* Carlyle.' He was looking at her with distaste; Liz didn't know what to say. Avery suddenly added, 'I suppose you're a graduate.'

'Yes.' Never had she felt less proud of it.

'Good. You'll be used to reading then.' He pointed to three stacks of papers on a side table. 'You can start with them. I've got more important things to do than read bumf from the Home Office all day. Come back in the morning and you can tell me what's in it.'

After this welcome, Liz reckoned things would have to get better. She was wrong. By her third day she had acquired a nickname – Mata Hari – but not much else in the form of contact with her new workmates, whose initial curiosity was swiftly followed by the hazing rituals of an American college fraternity. The first morning when Liz went to the desk she had been allocated, she found a large cigar lying on the desk top. An hour later when she came back with a cup of muddy coffee from the vending machine in the hall, she found that someone had moved the cigar suggestively to the seat of her chair. While the men around her watched surreptitiously she broke the cigar in half and threw it in the wastepaper basket.

The next morning another cigar was in place. Again Liz threw it away, and this time she said loudly, without looking around, 'I hope you boys can put cigars on expenses. If this goes on, it's going to cost you a fortune.'

All week she ate lunch alone and saw no one after work. The only other woman in the office, the typist for DI Avery, was a middle-aged woman called Nellie who came in at exactly nine in the morning and left at precisely five at night. She had clearly never read Germaine Greer or heard of sister-solidarity; she made a point of ignoring Liz.

Not all the men joined in the harassment. Some just ignored her and one in particular was quite polite – McManus, a tall, sharp-featured detective sergeant who dressed better than the others.

The work itself was dull, a relentless progress through mind-bogglingly dense papers from the Home Office. Liz was desperate to get her teeth into something real; otherwise she would finish her secondment without knowing any more about how a police force ran than she had when she came. She resented Avery's using her as an intellectual dogsbody, covering his back in case some civil servant expected a response to one of the documents sent seemingly by the truckload from Whitehall and Scotland Yard.

The harassment persisted, though not any longer with cigars. Purvis, a tall man with a dimple in his chin, seemed particularly intent on making Liz feel unwelcome. 'Ask our new graduate colleague,' he would say when someone had a question at the weekly briefing meeting.

Liz ignored this as best she could, but it made for stressful working hours, and she wasn't sure how long she could put up with it in silence. Part of her was determined not to let these bastards get to her; another part wanted to run back to London. Then one morning she arrived to find a bundle of dirty shirts on her desk, with a note pinned to them. *Washed, ironed and folded by Thursday please.* She felt the eyes of the room upon her as she stood by her desk. Suddenly furious, she picked up the shirts, walked over to the open window and dumped them out into the alley below.

And then things changed – whether because she'd shown she'd had enough or because some of the men had begun to feel embarrassed, she never knew. As her third week in Liverpool was drawing to a close, she was sitting looking at what seemed an undiminished stack of type-script pages when McManus stopped beside her desk. 'That looks interesting,' he said, pointing at a Home Office circular on top of the pile.

She looked up at him warily. 'It's absolutely entrancing,' she said dryly. 'I'd be happy to tell you all about it.'

'No, thanks.' McManus paused for a moment, and she watched him as he seemed to be making up his mind about what to say next. He was a good-looking man – and he seemed to know it. Not my type, Liz told herself; her last boyfriend had been a gentle guitar player at Bristol. Besides, McManus must have been fifteen years older than she was. There was no way she was interested in him.

'Fancy joining us on a little mission?' he said lightly. 'Or are you chained to your desk?'

'I'm just following orders,' she said, nodding towards Avery's office.

'Boss is in Manchester today, so why don't you come along?'

She hesitated, but anything was better than reading any more bumf. 'OK. What is it?'

'I'll explain in the car.'

Outside they joined two detective constables, Cardew and Purvis, who looked surprised when McManus explained Liz would be joining them. He added, 'You boys go ahead. We'll see you there.'

Cardew, who Liz suspected had been the wolf whistler on her first appearance in the office, rolled his eyes.

McManus gave him a look and he and Purvis stomped off to their car.

McManus drove her in his black Range Rover away from the Docks and towards the eastern suburbs of the city. It was unseasonably warm and Liz put her window down as the evening turned from dusk to dark. The smoky yellow of sodium lights lined the streets in glowing dots. They climbed a bit and were going past a series of large institutional-looking buildings, a few modern but mostly Victorian. 'Where are we?' asked Liz.

'The university,' said McManus. After a pause, he added, 'I was there.'

'Really? What did you read?'

'Business studies. It seemed the practical thing to do. I'm a local lad – my dad was first-generation Paddy, and worked on the docks till they closed. I didn't know what I wanted to do; I just wanted to get out from his way of life.'

'Why did you join the police then?'

'Because I was bored by business.' He turned his head and gave a wry smile. 'If I'd stuck with it I'd have gone mad before I was thirty.'

Liz laughed, and McManus said, 'Where'd you grow up?'

She explained, and he said, 'Sounds very posh. Your dad a grandee?'

'No, he just worked for one.' This time McManus laughed. They were in the suburbs now, tree-lined streets with large detached houses. 'This is what I was aiming for,' he said, gesturing around them.

'Aren't you still?'

He shook his head. Liz said, 'What's changed?'

'It's called maintenance,' he said with a trace of bitterness. But then his tone changed and he was all business.

'I'm meeting an informant. He's just over from Belfast; the RUC's passed him on to us.'

'You sound doubtful.'

McManus nodded. 'I am. He's a tricky little sod.'

'How so?'

'His RUC handler said they were never sure how reliable his information was. They had doubts about his real allegiances – nothing they could put their finger on. He seemed to provide just enough to keep them interested but not enough to be really useful. They were pretty sure he could have given more if he'd wanted to. They've sent him over here to see what we make of him. He's supposed to be getting alongside the Provo sympathisers here.'

He pulled the car over and parked at the top of a rise. Down the street a little below them was a small precinct of shops. At the corner there was one still open; it had a retro neon sign Liz could just make out – it said *Café Noir*. McManus pointed at it. 'That wine bar's where we're going to meet. I'm going to stand by the door smoking and chummy will come past me and go in. I'll have a look round to check he's clean then join him – there's a little room in the back where we can talk. Purvis and Cardew are parked further along that street, watching my back from there. You can watch it as well from up here. I'm not expecting any bother. I'll leave the keys in case you need to move the car, but whatever you do, don't drive down the hill.'

'I thought—' Liz began to say, but McManus had already opened the door and was halfway out of the car.

He said, 'Won't be long.' And he slammed the door and began striding quickly down the hill towards the wine bar.

Liz sat there, fuming. The paper work in the office was bad enough, but having the promise of something real to do, only to have it snatched away, was worse. Why had McManus brought her here if it was only to leave her in the car while he met this informant? He already had two detectives watching his back – though it seemed a bit unprofessional to have them both in the same place – so he didn't need her as well. And what if she did see anything? She had no way of contacting him to warn him. Maybe he'd brought her along to find out more about her so that he could pass it on to the others. Yet he didn't seem that kind of man. So what exactly was he doing?

McManus had almost reached the wine bar now, and he stopped and casually lit a cigarette. He lounged by the entrance, studying the menu in the window. There was no sign of his contact, or anyone else – the street was deserted.

Then she heard footsteps on the pavement behind the car. Two sets. She grabbed her bag and rummaged through it, keeping her head down in case she was noticed sitting alone in a parked car and someone got the wrong idea. The footsteps had reached the car now, but thankfully they didn't slow down, just went on past. Slowly she lifted her head and saw two men wearing short leather jackets, jeans and trainers. They looked young and fit. She wondered if they were plainclothes policemen – but these two weren't Purvis and Cardew, and McManus hadn't mentioned any other backup.

A car came up towards her from down the hill, and as its headlights swept across the pavement she saw the two men suddenly stop and tuck themselves into some bushes growing at the front of someone's garden. The car went past and the two men continued down the hill. They didn't want to be seen; Liz wondered why. Unless they weren't police at all.

The two men stopped again and exchanged a few words. They were still only about forty yards ahead of Liz, and she watched as one of them crossed the street. The other one waited for a moment; he was out of the direct light of the street lamp but she could see him clearly enough. He had his hand behind his back and as he brought it round something glinted momentarily, and she caught on: it was a handgun. He held it for a moment then tucked it away under his jacket.

She hesitated. Was it a gun? Could they be plain-clothes police? If it was and they weren't, there was no time to waste. The two men were now halfway between her and McManus, still outside the wine bar. They would reach him in a couple of minutes.

Liz slid over behind the wheel and turned the keys in the ignition. The engine responded right away. She turned on the side lights and pulled out into the street, coasting down the hill. As she passed the two men, one on each side of the street, she tensed, half expecting them to fire at her. They were striding quickly now and the one on the right-hand pavement had pulled his gun and was carrying it in his hand openly.

As she passed them she suddenly switched on the head-lights full beam, blinding a van coming up the other way, and as she picked up speed she began hitting the horn so it sounded loudly in short warning beeps.

When she reached the wine bar she braked hard, coming to a sudden halt just in front of the entrance. She reckoned she was seventy or eighty yards in front of the men. McManus was looking startled. She pushed the button and the window on the passenger side came down. She yelled, 'Get in quick.'

'What the hell—?' he said.

'There's a couple of gunmen just behind me. For God's sake, get in.'

McManus looked over the top of the car back up the hill. The two men had stopped; they must have been uncertain what was happening. By now Purvis and Cardew had seen the commotion and came roaring up from the other direction.

'What's going on, Guv?'

McManus was shouting into the car radio, calling out an armed team. He broke off to yell at the two men, 'Up the hill. Two of them. Get up there now. See if you can follow them but hang back – one of them's got a gun, possibly both. Armed response is on the way. Keep in touch.'

'Park up there,' he said to Liz, pointing to a space in front of the line of shops.

'Shouldn't we help go after them?'

He shook his head. 'No. A gun fight's no place for you. Anyway, odds are they'll be gone. I need to wait here in case chummy shows. Though that seems a bit unlikely now.'

'You think he set you up?'

He nodded. 'Must have. Unless he's blown and they were after him. If he doesn't turn up we'll know which it is. Either way, he's not going to be any more use. I'd give you odds he's safely back in Ireland by now, thinking he's helped assassinate a Special Branch officer.'

They sat in silence then, too shaken to talk, McManus keeping his eyes on the street ahead, while Liz kept a lookout behind through the rear-view mirror. It must have been ten minutes before a car pulled up in front, and Cardew and Purvis got out.

Cardew came over and spoke through the open window of the passenger seat. 'No trace. The boys are out combing the streets but it looks as if they've got clean away. We don't know the car and we've got no description so there's not much chance. Jesus, Guv, we were wondering what the hell Mata Hari was doing, driving down like that.'

McManus stared at him. 'She was saving my life, Officer, while you were sitting picking your toes. And don't call her Mata Hari. Her name is Liz.'

6

WORD SPREAD QUICKLY IN the Special Branch
office that Liz had saved McManus's skin and the
atmosphere got a lot more friendly; even Nellie the typist
began to talk to her. When Avery stopped offloading
Whitehall's paperwork onto her and started asking her to
analyse the intelligence reports coming in from Belfast to
see if they threw up any leads to local activity, she felt that
at last she'd been accepted as someone who might have
something useful to contribute.

That wasn't all that changed. Looking back on it now,
she supposed it had been inevitable that after their run-in
with the IRA she and McManus would be drawn together.
Their shared danger formed a bond which at first made
them friends, and then, as if it were the most natural thing
in the world, something more than friends.

It didn't happen right away. McManus was cautious
about getting involved with the Spook, the woman from
MI5, and at first he was just cordial. Three days after the
drama of what they now all accepted had been an assassi-
nation attempt, he casually asked her to join him for a
drink – but when she walked into the pub she saw that
Purvis and Cardew were sitting at the table with him. A

week later he asked her again, this time on his own, but before he'd even got her a drink, he was called on his mobile and had to go – an informant had been arrested for benefits fraud and he had to sort things out.

A few days later she had left her car at a local garage for its MOT on her way to work and to her annoyance the garage had rung late in the afternoon to say the car wouldn't be ready until the next day. She was waiting for a bus down the street from the office when a man's voice called out, 'Want a lift?'

She turned, ready to tell the man to buzz off, when she saw it was McManus at the wheel of a smart Audi. He lifted his hands in mock-surrender. 'Don't shoot. It's only me.'

She laughed. 'What are you doing here?'

'Looking for damsels in distress. Hop in.'

'What happened to the Range Rover?' she asked as she got in.

'Strictly for operations,' he said, as he accelerated away. 'This one's mine. Now where are you going?'

When she told him he gave a little groan. 'That's a very respectable address.'

'Well, of course,' she replied with a grin. 'I'm a very respectable person. The lady who owns the house is the widow of some former contact of the Service. I don't know the details. I've got a couple of rooms on the top floor.'

'I bet she watches you like a hawk. That can't help your social life.'

Liz suppressed the temptation to ask, *What social life?*

'Tell you what,' said McManus, glancing sideways at Liz, 'why don't you come back to my place for a drink? Then I'll run you home,' he added quickly, as if he didn't want to scare her off.

He accelerated past a dawdling queue of cars, his eyes straight ahead. Liz considered what to say. She sensed her answer was going to make a big difference to her relationship with McManus, and she wasn't sure it was a step she wanted to take. But then she thought of what otherwise awaited her that evening in her flat – a quick glass of mediocre wine, a shallow bath (the hot water tank was minute), followed by a solitary microwaved supper, a little television, a couple of chapters of the disappointing thriller she was reading, and lights out. Not a very exciting prospect.

So she said, 'OK. Thanks.'

Looking back, she supposed the whole affair wasn't surprising. McManus was an attractive figure to a young woman. Good-looking, confident, mature – he could see Liz was pretty inexperienced and hadn't been around much and he enjoyed showing her the town. He knew Liverpool like the back of his hand: from the industrial wastelands to the newly fashionable dockland; from the gentility of its grandest suburbs to clubs so rough that even the bouncers were scared of the clientele; from fancy French restaurants where the city's famous footballers spent £1,500 on a bottle of wine they couldn't pronounce to the bingo hall where he said his mother had been a habituée. Wherever they went the proprietor knew the Special Branch detective, and treated him with respect.

Liz was less certain what McManus saw in her. She sometimes wondered if in other circumstances he would have given her a second look. Observing the admiring glances he attracted from women of all sorts, from restaurant cloakroom girls to the chic owner of an upmarket boutique, she knew that he could have had his choice of women. But circumstances were what they were, and the simple fact remained that she had probably saved his life. If his interest in her arose out of gratitude, Liz couldn't really object, since she was also grateful to him.

It was an intense affair, and for all the excitement of their social life, what really kept the two together was a mutual commitment to their work. Liz had already discovered a capacity for immersion in the job, and now that Avery had given her something substantial to do, she was interested and intent on doing it well. But she was nothing like McManus. As she quickly discovered, life for him was filtered through work. In the pubs and restaurants they visited, his conversations with the manager were information-gathering exercises. Even when they were most relaxed – a walk on the beach, a quiet meal in a country pub where no villain had ever set foot – McManus was alert, noticing anything out of the ordinary, any behaviour in the least bit strange. This was the first time Liz had experienced something that she later encountered often in her colleagues and indeed learned to practise herself, the acute awareness of one's surroundings of the true intelligence officer.

But she soon discovered that McManus's almost forensic attentiveness was focused not so much on intelligence gathering as on a righteous passion to sniff out wrongdoing and see it punished. He was a zero-tolerance police officer, openly disdainful of the way so many of the criminals he had hunted down wriggled free in their progress from arrest to the jury's verdict. The only time Liz saw McManus lose his temper was when the Crown Prosecution Service refused to prosecute the leader of a drug ring, a man called Pears whom McManus had pursued for years, because in their view there was insufficient evidence to secure a conviction.

If Liz sometimes found McManus's crusading spirit unsettling, she also admired it. Where some of his colleagues appeared quite happy to accept the odd freebie – drinks in a pub, a taxi ride home, free admission to a club – McManus wasn't: when one evening the owner of a local restaurant brought them two brandies at the end of their meal and said they were 'on the house', McManus insisted they be added to the bill. But with Liz he was relaxed; she found him caring, loving and warm. To her surprise he seemed happy to be open about their relationship, and made no effort to disguise it from their colleagues. She was startled but flattered when quite early on he asked her to think about moving into his flat, and though she didn't take that step she did find herself wondering how she could get her secondment to Liverpool extended.

They had been together for two months when things went suddenly wrong. They were in McManus's flat, an elegant one-bedroom pad high enough up in a new block to give a spectacular view over the Mersey. McManus was in a jubilant mood, and over a glass of wine he explained that Pears, the drug dealer, had been arrested again and this time the Crown Prosecution Service were going to prosecute.

'What changed?' asked Liz.

'New evidence,' said McManus.

'Really, what sort of evidence?' She was curious to know, since the CPS had previously complained that the available evidence was too circumstantial.

'A witness has come forward. He's prepared to say he saw Pears make a big sale.'

'That's excellent,' said Liz. 'Why did he come forward now? It must be a bit risky for him. Are you going to have to protect him?'

McManus shrugged. 'Maybe it was my appeal to his better nature – not that this particular little runt has one.' He paused and looked at Liz with a grin. 'Maybe it had something to do with letting him off another charge if he came good in this case.'

'A deal, in other words,' said Liz, starting to understand.

'If you want to call it that.'

'What else should I call it? The little runt, as you call him, has decided he's seen something because that way he gets off.'

'It may be a rough kind of justice, but believe me it's still justice. He would have seen Pears do other deals plenty of times.'

'But not this one?'

Again McManus shrugged, this time in acknowledgement. His jubilation was gone. He said defensively, 'What the hell. I didn't say it was ideal. But this way we'll get a result.'

Liz said, 'It's wrong. You know that.'

He looked at her and shook his head. 'Forget about it. More wine?'

'No, thanks. You haven't answered my question.'

'I didn't hear any question.' He'd got up and was pouring himself a glass of Chianti.

Liz said, 'You know what I mean. I know what you've done, and it's wrong.'

'Says who?' His voice was sharp now. 'Says Liz Carlyle, twenty-something trainee spook from London. The same Liz Carlyle who's never walked a beat, never made an arrest, never looked down the barrel of a gun held by some scumbag who'd as soon pull the trigger as sneeze. A Liz Carlyle who might be just a little out of her depth here.'

He had never spoken like this to her before. She said as

calmly as she could, 'It's not right, Jimmy. Not because little Liz Carlyle says so. It's not right because it just isn't. You can't go round making up evidence just because you're convinced someone is guilty. You can't be judge and jury; that's not your job.'

'Nice speech, Liz, but if we can't rely on the legal system, what else can we do? If I have to bend the rules to get this bastard, I will. It's the results that matter. Getting Pears off the streets and locked up where he belongs.'

'It's not some minor rules you're bending, it's the law. Here you are saying Pears can't stand above the law, but then where are *you* standing?'

McManus made a show of looking at his watch. 'Time's up,' he announced. 'Our booking's ten minutes from now. You better get your coat.'

The flippancy in this dismissal enraged Liz. 'I'll get my coat,' she snapped. 'And see myself out.'

They didn't speak for three days, each locked into their conviction that they were right. Finally Liz decided it was ridiculous to behave this way – she was never going to agree with what he'd done, and her whole view of the man had changed. But even if they weren't going to be lovers any more, it seemed ridiculous not to be on speaking terms, so towards the end of the day, when McManus came into the office and sat down at his desk, she went over.

'Fancy a drink?' she said lightly. Purvis at the desk next to them was pretending not to listen.

'Got a lot on,' McManus said tersely, without lifting his head from the papers he was reading.

'OK,' said Liz. The rebuff couldn't have been clearer.

She gave it a week, then tried again, and received the same short shrift. After that, they ignored each other, which made for a certain tension in the office, though nothing like it had been when she first arrived. She went back to spending the evenings boringly alone, now looking forward to the end of her Liverpool posting. She missed McManus – or she missed the man she had thought he was, though it gave her a sliver of comfort to know that that man did not exist.

When McManus left Liverpool on promotion to Greater Manchester, she barely noticed, so accustomed by then was she to not having him in her life. She was not invited to his leaving do, and he did not even bother to say goodbye. So she could only imagine his reaction when the drug dealer Pears was convicted and given eight years.

Then one morning she heard Purvis complaining that he'd paid more than he could afford for a second-hand Audi he'd bought from McManus when he'd left for Manchester. Liz's car was once again in the garage and suddenly she found herself offering to buy the Audi off Purvis for the same price he'd paid McManus. Purvis accepted with alacrity. Since she was never going to see or hear from McManus again, Liz reckoned this would be the legacy of their affair.

7

THE SKY WAS BLACK over the mountains as Miles
drove his SUV along the sandy road into the countryside. The Trade Minister, Baakrime, had said that he
would have something to tell Miles in a week, and the
previous day an invitation had arrived at the US Embassy
inviting him to lunch at the Minister's farm in the hills
outside Sana'a.

Miles's colleagues in Langley were waiting impatiently
for the payback on the cash that Baakrime had been given,
information they were sure the Minister was holding about
the sources of arms that were getting into the hands of
jihadis through Yemen.

But Miles was uncomfortable, nervous about this journey
away from comparative safety in the bustle of the town.
Minister Baakrime had fallen for his recruitment pitch
suspiciously quickly, taking the envelope of cash and promising information. But had he really agreed, or was this
invitation a trap either to kill Miles or expose him as a
foreign spy? He had consulted Langley overnight but they
were keen to get the information and prepared to take a
risk, so he was instructed to go to the meeting – and wear
a tracking device that would be monitored by a drone far

overhead. It wouldn't help if he was killed but might if he was kidnapped – small consolation.

Miles glanced uneasily at the darkening sky. The climate in Yemen, normally so hot and dry, could produce sudden short but heavy cloudbursts, and it looked as if that was exactly what was on the way.

Seconds later it arrived. Rain beat thunderously on the top of the car; the wipers sweeping at top speed from side to side of the windscreen had no effect and the glass ran with a stream of water thick with sand raised by the sudden wind and the force of the rain. Miles could see nothing. The fields of arable crops and fruit orchards that bordered the road disappeared from sight and he stopped the car where he was, in the middle of the single-track road, hoping no vehicle was coming the other way. If there was, he wouldn't see it and it wouldn't see him until it was upon him.

He sat sweating with heat and tension until suddenly the rain stopped, the wipers cleared away the sand and he could see the road again. It was more of a small river now and his wheels threw up a fountain of water on each side of the car as he drove slowly on. As the sun came out again, he saw in the distance the red walls of what he took to be his objective, the Minister's farm.

The carved wooden gates of the compound were open as Miles drove up. A young man in a white robe and a Western-style sports jacket saluted and waved him in through the gates, then walked across to open the car door as Miles parked against the wall beside a wet and muddy silver Mercedes with a two-digit licence plate – 12.

'Salaam aleikum. Come this way, sir.'

Miles followed the young man into a lofty hall. Sunlight glanced though small windows set high up in the walls, but below the room was in shade and at first Miles, coming in from the bright sunlight, could see little. As his eyes got used to the dim light he saw the rough stone walls, the red-tiled floor covered with rugs in subdued colours, and around the room ottomans and chairs covered with cushions and throws of bright silks. This was a very luxurious farmhouse.

'Sit down, sir. The Minister will be here shortly,' said the young man in unaccented English. He clicked his fingers and a servant appeared with a tray of glasses of fruit juice.

Miles sat on the edge of an ottoman, sipping a glass of pomegranate juice. His sense of unease grew as he waited, wondering what would happen next.

'My friend.' A loud voice echoed across the hall as Baakrime in a long white robe strode towards Miles, his hand held out. 'It is delightful to see you here. I must apologise for our weather. These rain storms blow up at this time of the year, but they are soon over. Unlike your hurricanes, they do little damage.' He pumped Miles's hand enthusiastically, setting up a sharp twingeing pain in his shoulder.

'I thought it best to meet here. It is safe and away from prying eyes. Everyone here is family or old servants of my family. The road you came along is watched by my people and the young man who met you is one of my sons. He is my secretary. He was at school in England and at Cambridge University. Do you know England?'

'Yes,' said Miles. 'I have worked in London.'

'London. I love that city.' The Minister rubbed his hands together. 'We go there every year. My wife enjoys the shopping. Oxford Street, Harrods. I come back a poor man.' He smiled and Miles smiled back. Baakrime's poverty was not to be taken seriously.

'But let us eat while we talk,' and the clapping of his hands produced two servants with trays of little dishes and jugs of more fruit juice. One tray was placed on a brass-topped table beside Miles and the other beside Baakrime. Glasses were filled and the servants withdrew.

'I am honoured to see you in my house,' Baakrime began. 'Sana'a is not a safe place for me to meet you. This is a dangerous time in my country. There is much discontent; the people are unsettled, the country is fragile. There are elements in Sana'a who want to overthrow the govern-ment and would like to be able to show we were pawns of the United States. In our desert regions, the jihadi groups have established strongholds. They are in league with groups in other countries and they want to kill us all.'

Miles nodded. 'Yes. These are disturbed times in the whole of this region.'

'You asked about weapons,' the Minister went on. 'They are everywhere. Where are they coming from? Iran, Paki-stan – all the places you would expect.' He paused to eat some things from the dishes.

'What do you know of arms from the United States or Europe?' Miles was anxious to come to the point and get away. In spite of the Minister's assurances of security, he felt exposed in this place with no backup.

'My friend, with the arms trade it is always difficult to know the origin. These people are masters at deceit – false invoices, changing documentation while a cargo is en route, and of course there are corrupt officials in every port and so much money to be made. The people who run this trade are very rich indeed – unlike in my country, where the poor are everywhere.'

He sipped his juice and looked at Miles over the rim of his glass.

There was silence. Miles ate some food. He felt sure there was more information to come, but it seemed to need some assistance. 'Yes. The poor. I hope our contribution helped a little.'

'Yes indeed, my friend. We are so grateful. But there is so much need.'

Miles felt in his pocket and produced an envelope. 'Let's hope this will satisfy some of it,' he said, placing the envelope carefully on the tray of dishes beside him.

Baakrime began to talk again as though there had been no interruption. 'Yes. The people who run this trade are very clever at disguising themselves. But I have heard that there is a main middleman for deals from Europe. They call him *Calibre*. His real name is never used. I hear that he is meeting the leader of a group of jihadis or rebels – I don't know what group or exactly who they are, though I understand they are being funded by al-Qaeda. The meeting is in Paris in the next week or so. It is to arrange a shipment. The delivery will come through Yemeni ports, I hear.'

Miles nodded and waited. His face was calm but he was excited. At last he had something for his money, though it was pretty vague and probably not anything that could be acted on.

But Baakrime had not finished. 'I will try to find out more about this meeting and if I do my secretary will get a message to you.' He stopped for a sip of juice. 'There is one more thing. It is generally thought that the arms that come via this route are for use in Arab countries, and that may be so, but I have heard that the man behind those deals, this *Calibre*, is using someone from England to help with this latest deal. The arms trade is a very tight-knit network, almost like a club, but it seems someone British is applying for membership.'

8

IT WAS EIGHT O'CLOCK in the evening and Liz was tidying up the kitchen after her supper. Unusually for her she'd been cooking. Martin was convinced that only French women knew how to cook and she had promised herself that next time he came to London for the weekend she was going to surprise him by producing the perfect soufflé. So she had been practising on herself and this evening she reckoned she'd cracked it. She had just eaten what she considered to be a masterly example – cheese and spinach soufflé à la mode de Carlyle. She was just wondering what to do with the half that remained, asking herself if it would be OK if she heated it up again for tomorrow night, when the phone rang. It was the Duty Officer.

'Evening, Liz. The Six Duty Officer has just rung with a message for you from Bruno Mackay,' he said. 'Would you join him and Geoffrey Fane at Grosvenor tomorrow morning at half past eight for a meeting with Mr Bokus? Apparently something urgent has just come in from Langley. He said you should bring an overnight bag.'

'Oh thanks,' said Liz. 'And did he say what I should put in it? Jeans and a T-shirt, a fur coat or a long black garment suitable for interviewing Arab sheiks?'

"Fraid that's all the message said.'

'OK. Thanks. I suppose I'll just have to use my initiative.'

'Good night then,' said the Duty Officer cheerily, and rang off.

At quarter past eight the following morning she was walking across Grosvenor Square towards the American Embassy, carrying an overnight bag, when she spotted Geoffrey Fane and Bruno Mackay getting out of a taxi. It was uncanny how similar they looked. Fane, his tall, slim, pinstriped figure, nowadays with a slight stoop that made him look even more heron-like than when he was younger. Bruno, equally tall and slim, equally elegantly clad, though his suit was finely checked rather than pinstriped and the colour lighter than Fane's navy blue. Bruno's shock of fair hair and deeply tanned face contrasted with Fane's pale skin and black hair, but they might have been, if not father and son, at least related. They certainly came out of the same mould.

'Good morning, Elizabeth,' said Fane as they all reached the steps up to the Embassy front door together. 'Glad to see you've come prepared,' he added, glancing at her bag.

'Good morning,' she replied, her heart sinking as she noticed that Bruno was carrying a black leather valise. It looked as though wherever she was going, he was going too.

In Andy Bokus's office in the CIA suite of rooms behind the locked and alarmed steel door in the Embassy, a plate of oversized bagels and cream cheese was set out on the table. 'Help yourselves to breakfast,' said Andy, waving his hand at the plate. 'Coffee's over there.'

Fane shuddered slightly at the sight of the bagels, and from the corner of her eye Liz caught Bokus's grin. Liz enjoyed watching Bokus and Fane playing a game with each other. It was a game that neither acknowledged but she suspected both understood. In Fane's presence Bokus played up his roots as a son of humble immigrants – his grandfather had been a coalminer in the Ukraine and his father had landed on Ellis Island at the age of sixteen with nothing but the clothes he stood up in. Bokus senior had ended up running a gas station in Ohio and making enough to put Andy through college. Andy was bright, or he wouldn't be where he now was, heading the CIA station in London. But he didn't like London and he didn't like most of the Britishers he met. And in particular he didn't like Fane, who struck him as snobbish, self-satisfied and devious. So to Fane, Bokus presented himself as rather stupid and very uncouth, hence the enormous bagels. Fane responded by shooting his cuffs and adopting an exaggeratedly public school drawl and a patronising manner.

How much of all this psychological drama Bruno was following Liz didn't know. He was contentedly munching a bagel, seemingly oblivious. But she knew that you could never tell with Bruno.

'Well, I've got things you folks need to know,' said Bokus. 'We'll go down to the Bubble.' The Bubble was the secure room in the bowels of the basement, purpose-built to foil any attempt at eavesdropping. It always struck Liz as strange and illogical that, as the main threat of eavesdropping in London must come from the British intelligence services, the Agency conducted its most sensitive conversations with the British in their most secure room.

The door of the windowless room closed with a pneumatic hiss behind them and they sat down on padded benches around a central table. The faint hum of the high-frequency-wave baffler had a rather soporific effect on Liz and she hoped that the hastily convened meeting was going to produce something worthwhile.

'Geoffrey, you and Bruno know something of what I'm going to say, but I'll just recap for Liz here. We recently sent an officer to Sana'a. He had one objective, to make a quick pitch to a highly placed official who'd been making it pretty obvious to the Commercial Counsellor – a State Department man – both that he was in the arms business and that he could be bought. So we sent young Miles Brookhaven. You all know him from his time here.' He grinned at Liz; she pretended not to notice. 'He made a quick pitch and it came good. The guy is now signed up. He's going to give us stuff on arms supplies going through Yemen, to rebels and jihadis. As you know we're particularly looking for anything coming out of Europe and the States.'

Fane shifted in his seat, unwrapping his long legs and crossing an ankle over a knee. He clearly found the narrow benches uncomfortable but, more importantly, he couldn't bear to let Andy Bokus talk for more than a few minutes without interrupting. 'I mentioned to Elizabeth that you thought young Brookhaven was making progress,' he said.

'Yes. He's done quite well.' He looked at Liz, 'You heard he had a rough time in his last posting? Quite badly injured.'

'Yes. I heard.' Liz was wondering when he was going to get on to whatever had brought them here.

'So,' said Bokus. 'What he's got from this new source – we're calling him *Donation* – is that there is a European arms dealer who is arranging supplies from somewhere in Eastern Europe, the old Soviet Union probably.' He paused for effect. No one spoke; they all knew there was more to come. 'We don't know what nationality the arms dealer is. They call him *Calibre*. But *Donation* says that he's using someone to help him ship the arms – a transport expert, I guess. And this expert is a Brit.'

'Are you sure this *Donation* isn't just telling Miles what he thinks he wants to hear?' said Liz after a moment. 'It all sounds a bit too pat.'

'Wait till you hear the rest,' said Bokus. 'He says that there's a meeting arranged between *Calibre* and a jihadi leader, tomorrow in Paris.'

'Big city, Paris,' said Bruno dreamily.

'In the Luxembourg Gardens,' Bokus went on. 'At twelve noon.'

'So that's where we're going,' said Liz, turning to Bruno.

'That's where you're going,' he replied with a grin. 'I'm going to Sana'a.'

9

JEAN PERLUE WAS EXCITED. He had been in the DCRI, the French equivalent of MI5, for just eighteen months and this was his first real surveillance operation. At the briefing the team had been told that an international arms dealer was going to meet a dangerous jihadi in the Luxembourg Gardens, and that it was vital that both of them were photographed and followed.

So at the age of only twenty-four Jean was engaged in counter-terrorist work of international importance. His instructions were to hang around, just inside the park gates on the Boulevard St Michel, looking natural and merging into the surroundings until he heard the controller, speaking through his earpiece, telling him to move.

But it was a frosty morning and his feet were very cold and he had been in place for more than an hour. He was running out of things to do to look natural. He'd bought a crêpe from the mobile cart parked outside the gates and eaten it slowly; he'd read a copy of *Le Monde* standing up until he knew the front page virtually by heart. Now he was stamping his feet and looking angrily at his watch, for the fourth time, as if he was waiting for a girlfriend who was late. Just as he was wondering what to do next, conscious that the crêpe seller was staring at him, he heard a voice in his ear.

'We have a possible for *Numéro Un*. Male, Caucasian, about forty-five to fifty, one hundred eighty centimetres, grey/brown hair, brown leather knee-length jacket.' The voice was Gustave Dolet's. Jean Perlue knew he was sitting with Michel Vallon in a Renault car parked in the Rue Gay-Lussac with a view of one of the other gates of the Gardens. 'He's heading into the Gardens now. Michel is going with him.'

Jean felt his throat constrict as his excitement rose. His cold feet were forgotten, as was the cover of waiting for a girlfriend. He peered eagerly in the direction of the action, hoping desperately that the target would come his way. This was better than a training exercise.

The thought had hardly entered his head when he heard, 'We have an Arab at the gates. He's nervous, looking around. I think he may be *Numéro Deux*. Thin, about twenty-five to thirty, white trainers, jeans, navy-blue sweater. He's in the Gardens now, heading west.'

'I have him,' came the hoarse voice of Rabinac. Rabinac had been one of his teachers on the course and had been known by all the students as Mr Croaky. 'They're walking towards each other and slowing down. I'll have to pass them.'

At that moment Jean Perlue, from his post by the Boulevard St Michel gates, saw them. They were walking together now, approaching a park bench. He saw Rabinac walk past as they sat down. Rabinac came on towards Jean and, without giving any sign of recognition, went through the gates, passed the crêpe seller and walked off along the Boulevard.

'I have eyeball,' said Perlue into his microphone, his voice rising in excitement. 'They're talking. The Arab has a piece of paper and the European is shaking his head. They're too far away for my camera to get a clear picture. I'll go closer.'

'Stay where you are,' came the urgent voice of the controller. 'Michel has photographed the targets.'

'I might be able to see the paper he's holding if I walk slowly.'

'On no account approach them,' ordered the controller, but Perlue was already on the move, heading diagonally across the grass towards the bench where the two men were sitting.

His headphones were silent now, but even if anyone had spoken he wouldn't have heard. He was sure he could get a perfect photograph of the men and the paper that was still in the Arab's hand. As he approached the bench, he was making a show of consulting his wristwatch, muttering, tapping it and shaking his wrist. When he reached the bench he smiled at the two men and leaning over them asked them if they had the right time. The European replied and Perlue thanked him and continued on down the path.

When he was a little distance away from the bench he heard the voice of Rabinac in his ear. 'You've blown it Perlue, you idiot. They're leaving.'

Suddenly the Luxembourg Gardens were full of move-ment and the headphones were busy as the surveillance team tried to get into position to follow the two men as they went off quickly in different directions. Now that it was pretty certain that Perlue had blown the surveillance operation, the controller was less concerned with the team being seen, more with keeping in contact with the targets.

Rabinac got up from the bench where he had been sitting, stretching and yawning as if still dozy from a good nap. The Arab was a good fifty metres past him now, heading down the avenue of trees towards the palace. Marcel Laperrière would be waiting there, ready to chuck away his newspaper and walk as a front tail, while Rabinac followed from behind.

But what about the other man? Perlue knew that if he had stayed at his post the European would be passing right in front of him now, but instead he was far away on the wrong side of the Gardens. He felt mortified at what he had done; he knew that in all likelihood he would be back on the training course the next day. That is if he wasn't sacked. He prayed that Gustave and Michel had had time to move their car closer to the entrance gate.

'Get back to your position, Perlue,' came the instruction from Control, and he walked quickly towards the Boulevard Saint Michel, seeing as he approached the gates that a large crowd had gathered on the pavement just outside the gardens. There must have been close to 200 people there. What was this about? Surely nothing he'd done had caused this. Then he saw that some kind of performance was under way just outside the gates. A juggler perhaps, or a mime. Someone good enough to capture the attention of a large audience.

Perlue was at the gate now, puffing a little. Breathlessly, he started to offer excuses for what he'd done, but the controller cut him short. There would be time for that later but now he wanted only to find the European. Perlue stared at the crowd, hoping that Gustave and Michel were across the street, also watching for him.

Control asked tersely, 'Anyone got sight of *Numéro Un?*'

'Can't spot him,' Gustave replied.

'Negative,' said Michel.

Perlue went out of the gates into the boulevard and saw

that the performance was by a couple of mimes, one male, one female. *Numéro Un* must be somewhere in the crowd. It was a motley mix of tourists, families, local residents, small children with their minders, and businessmen stopping to see what was going on. Jean Perlue looked for anyone whose face was turned away from the mimes, watching for a figure who was not interested in the performance but merely using it as cover.

He was desperate now to make up for his mistake and wanted above everything to be the one who found *Numéro Un*. He must be here somewhere – he couldn't have got past Gustave and Michel, could he? But everyone he could see had their eyes fixed intently on the two performers, though there were so many spectators that he couldn't properly inspect even half of them. It would have been easy for *Numéro Un* to insinuate himself into the middle of the crowd, and put himself out of sight of any of the watchers.

After five minutes, movement began in the crowd. Some of those on the edges started to drift off. The performance was coming to an end. The mimes came out among the spectators, each holding out a hat, bowing exaggeratedly when anyone dropped money in. They moved quickly, trying to catch people before they left. Perlue followed on behind them into the middle of the onlookers, but there was still no sign of *Numéro Un*.

On the other side of the boulevard he could see Gustave scanning the dispersing crowd; there was a strained look on his face, and it was obvious he was getting nowhere. But then neither was anyone else.

He looked behind him, in case *Numéro Un* had somehow slipped back into the park, but there was only a woman holding the hand of a small child, who was holding in his other hand the string of a fat pink pig balloon, which bobbed in the air above his head.

Jean Perlue turned back and saw that the crowd was getting smaller and smaller. He stared at each departing spectator, hoping against hope that he'd find *Numéro Un* among them. Some of them stared back, clearly wondering what was wrong with the young man with the drawn and anxious face. Like the sand seeping through an hourglass, his chances were inexorably running out, and finally only three or four people remained, chatting idly as the mimes picked up their props and pooled the money they had collected.

Suddenly the radio silence was broken and in his ear he heard the voice of Rabinac. 'We have *Numéro Deux*, just ahead of us. He's leaving the park. Do we pick him up?'

There was a pause. Control was consulting. 'No. Keep with him but if you think there's any danger of losing him, then pick him up. Gustave and Michel, get over there and help Rabinac and Marcel. There's nothing more to be done where you are. *Numéro Un* has given us the slip.' Then came the words Jean Perlue did not want to hear. 'Perlue. You come straight back to base.'

10

THERE WAS SILENCE IN the Control Room in the headquarters of the DCRI where Liz was sitting with her opposite number Isabelle Florian. They had just heard that not only had *Numéro Un* disappeared but Rabinac, Marcel and the others had also lost *Numéro Deux* in the crowd.

Isabelle ran her hands through her hair. 'I'm sorry, Liz,' she said. Her English was fluent. 'We should never have had that young man on the team.'

The control officer broke in: 'The trouble was that we had too many operations going on today and this one came in at short notice. Perlue passed all the training courses but it looks as though his temperament let him down in the excitement. I shall be sending him for retraining.'

'Never mind,' said Liz. 'It happens to us all sometimes.' Thank God Bruno wasn't here, she thought. He'd certainly have made some scathing remark that would have ruined Anglo/French cooperation for good.

Isabelle sighed and said, 'Well, let's hope we've got some decent photographs. They're just being printed up; let's go back to my office where we can have a cup of coffee and look at them.'

Liz had been working with Isabelle Florian on and off for several years now. When she had first heard that her opposite number in the French Service was a woman, she had expected to encounter an epitome of Parisian style. She had been pleasantly surprised to find that Isabelle, a woman a little older than Liz, was more given to wearing jeans, a sweater and flat shoes than high heels and an elegant black number. Her pleasantly weathered face was normally bare of make-up and her hair was usually tied back in a ponytail.

But as they walked back to Isabelle's office Liz couldn't help remarking on the change in Isabelle's appearance. Today she looked far more as Liz had originally imagined her. The jeans and sweater had been replaced by a black skirt and tights and a silk blouse the colour of ripe cherries. The ponytail had gone and her hair had been cut stylishly short.

When she complimented Isabelle, the Frenchwoman said, 'I never feel quite comfortable dressed up like this, but I've been promoted and they told me I had to dress the part. I have to go to more meetings and talk to government ministers and my bosses thought I looked too workmanlike.'

'Well. It suits you. Not that the other didn't,' added Liz hastily.

Isabelle smiled. 'And you, Liz. You look flourishing. How is our friend Martin?'

'Well, thank you. We've just been on holiday. The curious yellow shade of my face is the remains of a tan.'

Liz had first met Martin Seurat when she had been working with Isabelle on the case of a dissident Irish Republican group. The leader of the group had kidnapped one of Liz's colleagues, Dave Armstrong, and taken him to the South of France, where Martin Seurat had been instrumental in saving his life.

Liz now stood by the window in Isabelle's office, admiring the glimpse of the Eiffel Tower, which was just visible from the corner of the window. A girl came in clutching a sheaf of A4-sized photographs that she put down on Isabelle's desk, saying cheerfully, 'I think you'll be pleased with these.'

As she went out Isabelle said, 'Come and have a look, Liz. Let's hope they are some use.'

The two women leaned over the desk, their heads close together, looking at the picture on top of the pile. It was of *Numéro Un*, the European, as he walked towards the rendezvous with the Arab. At the same moment, Isabelle exclaimed, 'It can't be,' and Liz said, 'Isn't that . . .'

They were both staring at the picture in astonishment.

Isabelle nodded. 'Yes, it's Antoine Milraud.' A former officer of the DGSE, and a former friend and colleague of Martin Seurat, Milraud had been dismissed from the DGSE after an operation had gone disastrously wrong. Milraud was suspected of taking money that had gone missing from an arms deal, but he had disappeared before he could be prosecuted.

Martin Seurat had made it his mission to capture Milraud; he blamed him for having betrayed both their friendship and the Service they both worked for. It later became apparent that Milraud had used the money he'd stolen to launch his own career as an arms dealer, where he skirted the border of legality until he crossed it with a vengeance. The Irish Republican who had kidnapped Dave Armstrong had been one of his customers and Milraud had assisted in the kidnap.

That was several years ago, and Milraud hadn't been seen

in France since – though there had been a host of rumoured sightings, including one of his wife, Annette. Reliable reports had come in that Milraud had continued acting as a middleman for arms sales; he had been linked to major transactions in a range of conflict-torn territories from Central Africa to Chechnya.

'Why would he resurface in Paris now?' asked Liz. 'He's taking a hell of a risk.'

Isabelle pursed her lips, and started to push her hair back on one side, until she remembered that she no longer had long hair. Her hairdresser had told her that the style was chic for a woman of a certain age. Isabelle had liked the result, though she had bristled at being called 'a woman of a certain age'. She said to Liz, 'It must mean this is a big transaction. Only a lot of money would get Milraud to take such a risk.'

'Mmm,' said Liz, unconvinced. 'It still seems very strange to choose Paris when they could have met in any city in the world.'

Isabelle looked at Liz. She found her English colleague's habit of looking for hidden meanings unsettling. She added, 'I'll need to tell Martin.'

'Of course,' said Liz, though there was resignation in her voice.

Isabelle said hesitantly, 'Is he still so ... obsessed with Milraud?'

Liz sighed, and Isabelle added gently, 'It's understandable, Liz. The two of them worked closely together. That must make Milraud's betrayal very painful.'

'I know, but I had hoped he was getting over it. There's been no real sign of Milraud for several years. Just rumours and false leads. Martin used to jump at each one, but the last time there'd been a possible sighting he didn't seem to feel the need to go rushing off after it. I thought that was a good sign.'

'This is different, alas.' They looked through the sheaf of photographs. 'I'm afraid there can be no doubt. It is Milraud. Which makes it especially galling that he got away.'

Liz shrugged. 'These things happen.'

Isabelle admired her equanimity. Had their roles been reversed, she liked to think she would have stayed equally calm. But she wouldn't have bet on it. 'Anyway,' she replied. 'we will do our very best to find him. I'll get these photographs out straightaway. We'll check the airlines, the railway stations, the hotels. But I'm afraid he'll be long gone by now.'

Liz nodded. 'Unless you think there's anything I can do here, I need to be getting back to London. I want to send the pictures out to Bruno Mackay. He's gone out to Sana'a to join the CIA man there whose source gave us this lead. I'll send the pictures of *Numéro Deux* too. Maybe someone out there can identify him, though it's pretty unlikely. He could be absolutely anybody.' Then, seeming to sense Isabelle's gloom, Liz added, 'Cheer up, Isabelle. You may get a break. If Milraud was stupid enough to show up in the Luxembourg Gardens, he may have made some other mistakes as well.'

11

THREE HOURS LATER ISABELLE was still in the office, Liz having long gone. Isabelle would have liked her to stay longer, though she knew that there was nothing she could do by sticking around. She liked her English colleague, not least because she was a woman who seemed comfortable with herself. She was intelligent and very focused but she was also attractive and easy to get on with. Too many of Isabelle's female colleagues seemed so intent on proving to their male colleagues that they were their equals that they lost all femininity.

It also pleased her to see Liz so happy in her relationship with Martin Seurat, even if inevitably it made her a little jealous. Isabelle was divorced. Her former husband was a diplomat; their two careers just hadn't fitted together and Isabelle had not been prepared to give up hers for her marriage. And nowadays she worked such long and irregular hours that there didn't seem much prospect that she'd find a successor to him.

She was married to her work, she thought to herself, imagining her own obituary. How ghoulish – she decided to stop feeling sorry for herself and get on with finding Milraud.

Ten minutes later, as she was wishing for the hundredth

time she hadn't given up her beloved Gitanes Blondes, there was a knock on her door.

'*Entrez,*' said Isabelle mildly, thinking it was time she went home. Her young son was at her mother's apartment; he often spent the night there when Isabelle was working late. So often in fact that Isabelle sometimes wondered guiltily if he would grow up thinking he had two mothers. But it wasn't too late to collect him now.

Her assistant Madeline came in, looking unusually excited. 'I think we've found something. They have been checking the hotels of the inner arrondissements and they've discovered where Milraud was staying.'

'*Was?*'

'Yes. He checked out two hours ago. A place on the Rue Jacob. He must have gone back there when we lost him. He got the receptionist to call him a taxi.'

'Where was he going?'

'The taxi company can't reach the driver.' She saw the disappointment on Isabelle's face. 'There's more. We know the alias he's using. It's Pigot.'

'Pigot?'

'Yes.'

'I don't believe it.' It was almost the exact name of Milraud's Irish Republican customer – who had been gunned down attempting to escape from their hideout off the south coast of France. Calling himself after his dead colleague seemed a bad joke, unless Milraud was thumbing his nose at his pursuers.

Isabelle shook her head, trying to focus on what needed to be done. 'I want the airlines contacted, and we need to check car rental agencies and the train stations.'

Madeline said mildly, 'It's all under way.'

'Good,' said Isabelle. 'Could you ring my mother please?

Ask her if she'll keep Jean-Claude tonight. I'll be here a while yet.'

Five minutes later Madeline came in again. 'A Monsieur Pigot made a reservation on an Air France flight to Berlin. Business Class.'

'That's him all right,' said Isabelle. Milraud had always liked the best; Seurat had once told her that his expenses had been legendary in the DGSE. 'I want him arrested at the gate, and held at the airport until I get out there.'

'Too late. The flight took off from Charles De Gaulle twenty minutes ago.'

Damn. Another tantalisingly close miss. But this time she knew exactly where Milraud was. 'Get me the BfV on the phone – I want the Germans to be waiting for the plane when Milraud lands.'

'Anything else?'

'Yes. Book me on the first flight to Berlin in the morning.' She paused for a moment, thinking of something. 'Book two seats while you're at it.'

She examined her options. What should she ask the Germans to do? Arrest Milraud? Martin Seurat would be delighted to lay hands on him but Liz would be worried that the trail to her case would go cold as a result. Milraud would be sure to have some plausible story about his meeting in the Luxembourg Gardens. So put him under surveillance instead? But did she dare risk losing him again?

Minutes later she was on the phone to her opposite number in the BfV, Germany's security service, asking him to set up surveillance on an international arms dealer travelling under the name Pigot, who would land at Tegel in one hour. Photographs of the man were on their way. He was a former intelligence officer and highly surveillance-conscious.

Then she rang Martin Seurat.

12

Hans Anspach of the BfV stifled a yawn as the flight information line on the board at Tegel airport flipped over. Air France 1134 from Paris had landed. Anspach signalled to his colleague, Pieter Dimitz, who was coming back from the terminal's Starbucks with two cardboard cups of coffee in his hands. 'You'd better dump those,' he said.

The junior officer groaned. 'Don't tell me the flight's on time.'

'Yes. It's just landed. And I bet our man will be one of the first through. Control has just told me that the French say he has no checked baggage on board.'

Anspach had been halfway home when the call had come, telling him to go to Tegel airport where a French arms dealer called Pigot would land at ten minutes past nine. Anspach and his hastily put together team were to follow Pigot wherever he went and stay with him till they were told to stand down. No reason was given at this stage, though according to the French he was likely to be alert for surveillance.

That probably means they screwed up and he saw them, thought Anspach grumpily. He was missing seeing his son's school play and he was going to get hell from his wife when he eventually got home.

Sitting inconspicuously in a small interview room just behind the passport control desks, Gunter Beckerman was waiting for a buzzer to alert him that Pigot was at the passport desk. He would send a warning to Anspach's phone, before following Pigot through Customs and into the Arrivals Hall.

There Anspach and Dimitz were taking up their positions. Dimitz wore a dark blue suit and had now put on a peaked cap. Holding a sign reading *Herr Rossbach*, he went to stand alongside the waiting chauffeurs next to the exit point from Customs.

Anspach stood further back at a newsstand, idly examining a copy of *Der Spiegel*. As he turned the pages he kept a deceptively casual eye on everyone emerging into the Hall. He wasn't relying on Beckerman's call to tell him the suspect was coming through, for it was perfectly possible that Monsieur Pigot might now have a different name, and a different passport, from those he had used to board in Paris.

His phone vibrated and he glanced down at its screen. *Coming now. Brown leather coat*, read the message attached to a photograph of a man in a leather coat and roll-neck sweater, carrying a laptop bag on one shoulder.

And then, not thirty seconds later, he spotted him.

Pigot was medium height, broad-shouldered, dressed in the smart casual clothes of a businessman. But, unlike a visiting businessman, he wasn't carrying a suit bag, only the laptop case hanging from a shoulder strap. He was walking quickly – though not so quickly as to call attention to himself – and heading towards the far exit, under the sign for taxis. Anspach followed, knowing both Dimitz and Beckerman were behind him.

Outside, the sky was pitch-black, but the pavement was eerily illuminated by the series of sodium lights lining the front of the terminal's façade. Anspach saw his quarry standing in the taxi queue, which was short this late at night. He waited until Dimitz passed him, no longer wearing his peaked chauffeur's hat. Then both men got into the back of a Mercedes saloon parked by the kerb in which the final member of the team had been sitting in the driver's seat. He'd prevented vigilant security and parking staff from having it towed away by waving his security pass at them.

From the car they watched Pigot enter a taxi. When it drove off they followed. Beckerman, having joined the taxi queue two behind Pigot, was in another taxi, not far behind. The convoy headed off on Route 11 for the centre of Berlin.

Ten minutes later a message flashed up on Anspach's phone. 'Booking in name of Pigot made two days ago at Westin Grand Hotel, Unter den Linden. 3 nights, arriving yesterday. Await further inquiries.'

'What do they mean, "Await further inquiries"?' muttered Anspach. 'How can we await anything? We're right behind the guy,' and he tapped furiously on his phone.

Twenty minutes later as they drove, still in convoy, into the centre of Berlin, Anspach's phone vibrated again. 'A Madame Pigot checked out of Westin Grand this pm. No forwarding address. No trace so far of any other booking in central hotels in name of Pigot.'

'Don't lose that cab,' said Anspach to the driver. 'We don't know where the hell we're going now.'

'Well, we'll be on Unter den Linden in a minute,' he replied. 'So perhaps he's rebooked.'

The lights were bright along the pavements of Unter den Linden, traditionally Berlin's most glamorous avenue, but the atmosphere was marred by a darkened construction site running all the way down the street's centre, where work was going on to connect the subway between the former west and east sectors of the city. The beautiful trees were virtually invisible behind the boards and railings; what could be seen of them was covered in white dust that each day's excavations threw up.

'If he gets out here and crosses the road we'll lose him behind the hoardings,' said Dimitz.

'It depends if he's spotted us,' grunted Anspach.

But the taxi containing Pigot didn't stop. It drove on at a stately pace down Unter den Linden until it turned off into a small quiet square and drew up in front of the Hotel Schmitzkopf, an ornate six-storey building with little balconies and flower boxes, an oasis of nineteenth-century solidity amid the city's East German decrepitude and its obsession with new build. This was a hotel designed for comfort rather than style. *We have seen it all before*, the hotel's stone façade seemed to say. *Fads come and go, but the Hotel Schmitzkopf remains the same.*

Warned by a text from Beckerman in his taxi, Anspach and Dimitz had stopped their Mercedes further up Unter den Linden, behind a skip that was half full of broken asphalt. They waited fifteen minutes, then Anspach got out. He turned into the square, climbed the steps to the glass and oak door of the hotel and went into the ground-floor lobby, where at this late hour the soft sofas and chintz-covered armchairs were unoccupied.

At the reception desk a young blonde woman in a smart black suit gave a welcoming smile from behind a large bowl of wrapped sweets. Her face fell slightly when Anspach produced a card identifying him as a government official and asked for the manager.

'He's on his break,' the girl said hesitantly. 'Do you want me to fetch him for you, sir?'

'That won't be necessary. Tell me – a man came in a few minutes ago and checked in. A Herr Pigot, if I'm not mistaken.'

'No, sir,' said the girl. 'That was Herr Pliska. He's a Polish gentleman. He and his wife are in Room 403. She arrived this afternoon. We have no guest called Pigot and no booking in that name.'

'Oh,' said Anspach. Then, after a pause while he absorbed the new information he said, 'I must have made a mistake. Got the wrong hotel. Please don't mention to anyone that I was inquiring for Herr Pigot. It's a matter of national security,' he added solemnly.

'Certainly not, sir,' the girl replied, wide-eyed. 'Shall I let you know if Herr Pigot turns up?'

'Please do,' replied Anspach. 'Here is a card with a number to ring,' and he handed her an official-looking card with no name on it and a telephone number that didn't exist.

13

'WHAT THE HELL'S GOING on?' Annette Milraud got up from the chair where she had been watching TV as soon as Milraud walked into the hotel room. 'Why did you tell me to change hotels and names? Did something happen in Paris?'

She paused as Milraud dropped his bag onto the floor and sat down on the bed. He was tired. Tired of life on the run. He'd always known that things would be difficult when he cheated his old employer, the DGSE, and went underground. But he'd thought that eventually some sort of steady state would emerge, allowing him to live without constantly looking over his shoulder.

He'd been wrong. His old employer had not forgotten him. And everywhere he went he'd been conscious that somewhere in the shadows they were there, waiting to pounce if he gave them the smallest chance. There had been financial rewards greater than anything he had ever enjoyed before, but with them went a total lack of peace of mind.

Annette was always angry these days, always nagging. He was taking too many risks, she said, but he had tried to explain that it was only because he took risks that he could make the kind of money he did and she could live in the style she demanded. Risk and money were linked like uneasy soulmates, bonded as unhappily as . . . Milraud and Annette.

They had been together seventeen years, married for fifteen of them. At first, they had been very happy. He enjoyed his work at the DGSE and she was content with their life in the prosperous Parisian suburbs, such a far cry from her humble origins in Toulon in the south of France. He realised later that her single goal then had been to have children, and that compared with this nothing else mattered.

It was when, after every kind of test, the doctors had finally told them that having a family simply wasn't going to happen, that Annette's dissatisfaction had begun. It was as if money had replaced children as her objective, and making the kind of money she had in mind was no more likely for Milraud as an officer in the DGSE than having children with his wife.

Then an operation to bust an arms deal had gone wrong, through an untimely intervention by the Swiss authorities. For a few hours the money at the heart of the deal had floated in a kind of no man's land between the dealer and the buyer. It was there for the asking, and before anyone had thought to reclaim it, Milraud had seen his chance – and taken it.

And since then money had led to the pursuit of more money – and more trouble. He had left the Service under a cloud that soon turned into a criminal investigation and a warrant for his arrest. He had fled France, escaping by the skin of his teeth, with Interpol fast on his heels. In the years that followed, his new business dealing in arms had become global. He had set up shop in Venezuela, where he had made certain arrangements that he felt confident would keep him safely out of the reach of Interpol and the European and American intelligence services. From there he ventured forth carefully, using a multitude of different passports, and usually to countries where there was no danger of extradition – certain Central European countries, the Middle East, parts of Asia, other South American countries. This trip to Western Europe was an exception and, as he was now realising, a mistake.

Now Annette was looking at him with irritation. 'Go and get a shower and change. I've hung your clothes up in the wardrobe. Let's get out of this stuffy old hotel and get some dinner. I've booked a table at a restaurant round the corner. You can tell me what happened while we eat.'

When he came out of the bathroom, Annette was getting dressed. She had put on a chic, tight-fitting black dress, and was trying on necklaces. He recognised one of them, a heavy silver chain he had bought for her in Geneva. The others she had bought for herself, with his money.

'Which one?' she asked as he came out of the bathroom.

'Which one what?'

'Necklace, you idiot,' she said, half crossly, half affectionately. He noticed the small chicken wing flaps of skin under her arms. Annette was growing older and he couldn't offer her the certainty of a secure retirement.

She settled on a simple affair of thin gold strings braided together and turned for his approval. He nodded without looking at the necklace. 'I'm a bit tired,' he said.

'Of course you are, *chéri*.' She looked as if she would give him a hug for a moment, but the damp towel he'd wrapped around his middle put her off. 'I think some supper would be just the thing. I've been cooped up all day waiting for you and worrying. Go on, darling, put some clothes on.'

He shook his head and she stared at him. He said, 'I don't think we should go out tonight. In fact, I know we shouldn't go out tonight.'

'Why?' she demanded. 'This is the first time in months that I've been out of that violent, uncultured dump where you make us live, and now you say I have to stay in our hotel room?'

Milraud's shoulders slumped. Annette looked at him despairingly. 'I'm not asking to go dancing, Antoine; just a decent meal in a restaurant where the food isn't Spanish. I thought that was the whole point of my joining you here in Germany.'

'It was.'

'Then what's changed?'

He sighed. 'I think they may be onto me.'

Annette looked at him, disbelieving. 'Who's they?' she demanded.

He shrugged his shoulders. 'Does it matter? The French – it could be our old friend Martin Seurat. Or the English. Or any number of countries. It doesn't really matter. This is Western Europe, not South America. Countries here cooperate.'

'What makes you think they've spotted you?'

'I can't be sure, but I had a meeting in Paris, in the Luxembourg Gardens. Somebody interrupted us – a young man. There was something odd about him, so we broke off the meeting. I haven't been able to make contact since.'

'Why didn't you call me when it happened? I wouldn't have come.'

'It was too late by then and you were already en route. That's why I told you to change the hotel and use the other passport. If they did spot me, they'll have a picture, and it won't have taken them too long to trace where I was staying in Paris, to get the name I was using and from that discover the flight I took to Berlin. As long as you left no trace at the last hotel of where you were going, then we should be OK for twenty-four hours or so – long enough for the meeting tomorrow. It's critical I attend that; if it goes well there will be other larger deals, and then we'll have enough money to retire somewhere nice and not to have to go on taking all these risks.'

Annette was shaking her head. 'I told you not to go to Paris. But would you listen? Of course not. You seemed to get pleasure from thumbing your nose at your old colleagues – even if it meant both of us ending up in prison. How could you?'

She looked on the verge of angry tears, but Milraud had seen this display often enough before to feel unmoved. It was a bit rich of Annette to complain about their being forced to live in Venezuela in one breath, then in the next to moan about the risks.

He said patiently, 'I am doing my best, Annette. And if it comes good ... Believe me, there's a lot of money at stake or I wouldn't have taken these risks.'

'But what if they are already onto you? What if they picked you up when you got here?'

It was a possibility he didn't want to face and certainly one he didn't want to discuss with Annette. 'I'm sure we've got at least twenty-four hours. Time for me to make this deal and get us out of here.'

'To go where?' Annette said, in a whine, her voice like a distant but approaching siren.

'Just in case they're watching the airports, I think we should take the train to Poland. If we don't hang about there, we should be safe to fly back home.'

'Home? You call Caracas home?' The sirens in her voice were at full blast now.

'It's home for now, Annette, and at least it's safe. The point is, if things go well tomorrow, then we can start to think about living somewhere else.' He raised a hand to stave her off before she could get started. 'No, not Paris, that's true. But somewhere better than Caracas. A place where you can feel you're back in civilisation.'

'Like where? You said yourself all the Western services are on the same side.'

He sometimes forgot how quick his wife was. He said, slightly faltering, 'I thought we might try South Africa.'

She stared at him, then laughed disdainfully. 'Cape Town here we come, eh? Well I can't see that's much better than where we are now. Believe me, if that's the only choice on offer, you'd better just buy one ticket. I'll come back to Europe and take my chances.'

He didn't respond to this; after all, it was not a new threat. He inched along the bed and reached for the phone on the bedside table. 'So what do you want from room service?'

14

'WHAT ARE WE WAITING for?' Martin Seurat demanded.

Isabelle sighed. Martin had seemed edgy throughout the flight from Paris. Normally a calm man, he had barely sat still, crossing and uncrossing his legs, folding and unfolding a copy of *Le Monde*. Isabelle had tried to divert him by asking about his daughter, now studying at the Sorbonne and the apple of her father's eye, but he had cut off the conversation and stared moodily out of the plane window.

Now sitting in the BfV conference room with Isabelle and the German investigating officer, his tension was even more obvious. She sensed that Martin's excitement at the prospect of finally getting his hands on Antoine Milraud was dwarfed by his fear of letting the man slip through his fingers.

Seurat went on, 'We know where Milraud is, so why don't we arrest him at once? If we hang around he'll disappear again. We don't know whether he saw the surveillance last night but he obviously suspected something in Paris. It sounds as if his wife, Annette, has joined him here; he must have contacted her, told her to change hotels, and to use a different name. He's clearly thinking we're not far behind him. There's no problem with the warrant, so let's get on with it before they vanish.'

The German said mildly, 'We can do that, of course. If that's what you want.' He looked pointedly at Isabelle, as if to say, *This is your problem, not mine.*

'Martin, you know as well as I do that we are not the only people interested in Milraud,' said Isabelle. 'And we've only found him at all because of the information we got from the British. At the very least, we need to consult them before making an arrest.'

Seurat was shaking his head, more from frustration than disagreement. He looked at the German. 'Is that what you think?'

The German frowned and shrugged his shoulders. He was a youthful-looking man, a classic German with light blonde hair and pinkish skin which was turning red as he tried to follow the argument between his two French visitors. 'Well, as I said, it's really up to you. We have no information against the man but the warrant is outstanding, and the request to help came from your country.' He paused. 'The matter is complicated by the fact that he is not alone.'

Seurat said impatiently. 'There's a warrant out for his wife as well. She's helped that bastard every step of the way.'

The German acknowledged this with a nod, but said firmly, 'Nevertheless, since other countries' services are involved, I would feel more comfortable knowing they agreed with the action we decide to take.'

Seurat looked exasperated, but when he turned to Isabelle there was resignation in his eyes. 'All right. Ring London. Let's talk to Liz.'

*

Liz Carlyle was at her desk in Thames House when the call came through from Berlin. She had heard about the German surveillance from Isabelle the previous evening, when she'd arrived back from Paris. So she knew that Milraud and Annette had changed names and hotels and that they must suspect that their pursuers were not far behind.

Now Isabelle explained the dilemma. 'Martin is keen to go in now and arrest the pair of them, but I felt we must consult you first. If we do arrest him he's most unlikely to talk about what he's doing here and you'll lose your lead to his contacts. What do you think, Liz?'

Martin Seurat was tapping his fingers on the top of the conference room table and he suddenly leant forward and spoke into the speakerphone. 'Liz, you know that Milraud has broken French law in too many ways to list. Larceny, kidnapping, conspiracy to murder. These aren't trivial offences. We at the DGSE want to see him extradited and put on trial, and who can blame us?'

Isabelle said, without looking at Martin, 'He's a big fish all right. And of course we have our national priorities. But perhaps we need to take a wider view.'

Isabelle sensed that Martin was bristling. He ignored her raised placatory hand, and said, with indignation in his voice, 'What you call our national priorities ignores the fact that Milraud has been involved in arms deals all over Europe. Indirectly, he's killed people on at least three continents. It also ignores the fact that Milraud was instrumental in kidnapping an MI5 officer in Northern Ireland, and bringing him to the south of France. If we hadn't moved in, I doubt very much that that officer would still be alive.'

Isabelle said calmly, 'But there may be other sharks

swimming with him that we can catch. That's what you think, Liz, as I understand it. And the Americans too. Is that not correct?'

To Isabelle's relief, Liz Carlyle broke in, her tone brisk but conciliatory. 'I have something to propose. But first let me ask our German colleague, are you confident of keeping Milraud under surveillance?'

Isabelle thought, can a fish swim? No intelligence officer worth his salt would say no to that question. Where was Liz going with this?

The German replied stiffly, 'Of course.'

'Good,' said Liz, 'then I advise the following: we keep tabs on Milraud, and obviously his wife as well. But if he goes off to meet anyone connected with his activities in Paris, it seems to me very unlikely that Annette will go with him. He wouldn't want to involve her or expose her to the risk. I'm sure she knows exactly how he makes his living, and we know that when he escaped from us in the south of France several years ago, it was with her help. But I can't believe she's actively involved in his deals, whatever they are.'

'So?' asked Seurat impatiently.

Liz said patiently, 'So, if he goes out and leaves her in the hotel, then that should be the time for you, Martin, to go in. After all, you know the woman well, don't you?'

'I do.'

'So you can work on her. You can explain that if she tells us who Milraud is working with, and helps us move up the ladder of this deal, then we can see that things don't go too hard on her. Or her husband.'

'I'm not prepared to promise that. I want things to go hard for the bastard.'

'Martin. It's up to you what you say. We all know you

won't have any influence over what happens to them when they're arrested.'

There was silence while all the participants considered this. At last Seurat stirred. Leaning towards the speaker on the table he said, 'All right, Liz. You win – you, and the Americans. But let's not lose him, OK? Nothing personal, but he's caused me a lot of trouble. I couldn't bear it if he had the chance to cause any more.'

15

T HE SCHWEIBER MANSION AT the eastern end of
Unter den Linden had once housed the private collection of Ernst Schweiber, a German manufacturer who
became fabulously wealthy in the late nineteenth century.
He and his sons after him had used their wealth to amass
an eclectic collection of paintings, furniture and *objets d'art*
from all over the world, which they had housed in their
grand baroque mansion. But the mansion had had the
misfortune to be in the path of the Red Army when it
arrived in Berlin in 1945.

The Schweiber family had by then been long dispersed,
some to other parts of Europe, some to their deaths in
concentration camps. By the time the Russians arrived,
part of the collection had already been removed by the
Nazis. What remained was taken as booty by the conquer-
ors, some of it to find its way eventually into galleries and
museums in Moscow and Leningrad.

After the Berlin Wall went up, the Schweiber Mansion
found itself in East Berlin, no longer grand but grimy,
broken-windowed and pocked by shell holes. The house
became home to a department of the Stasi and was feared
and avoided as far as possible by East Berliners. As part of

the restoration of East Berlin, the building had fairly recently been renovated to something of its former grandeur. But now, instead of sitting in an avenue of equally grand mansions, it rested uneasily between two glass-fronted office blocks, surprising the tourists who came to see what was at least a part of the Schweiber Collection, gathered together again from around the world and returned to Berlin after much diplomacy and haggling.

If Hans Anspach had known about the diplomacy and haggling, he would probably not have thought it worthwhile. He was gazing at a rather gruesome painting of someone being flayed alive. But in any case his mind was not on the art, for though the headphones he was wearing looked like those the museum supplied to visitors who wanted a commentary as they toured its collection, what he was hearing through them had nothing to do with art.

'Still here,' came from Beckerman, who was a few rooms away. Taking a couple of casual-looking steps, Anspach could see, through an arch, the back of Antoine Milraud's head. The Frenchman was standing with half a dozen other visitors in front of a Corot which had lately made the news – to the embarrassment of the German authorities, it was now thought not to have been part of the Schweiber collection at all but to have been plundered by Field Marshal Göring from a French aristocrat in Burgundy, whose descendants were threatening to sue for its return. Beckerman added, 'No movement.'

It had been easy enough to follow Milraud to the gallery. He had left the hotel half an hour ago, dressed in a white roll-neck sweater and a grey tweed jacket. He had walked, without looking around, straight down Unter den Linden, then fifty metres along a side street to the Schweiber

Collection. With two teams of three on his tail, there had been no chance of losing him, and with the museum busy but not too crowded, it was simple enough to keep tabs on the man as he wandered through the ground-floor rooms.

He had been in the building over half an hour now, and there had seemed no particular rhyme or reason to his progress. He had looked at paintings and porcelain and classical sculptures. To Anspach's experienced eye, he seemed to be killing time rather than appreciating the objects.

But the Corot was holding his attention far longer than anything else had. Was he waiting for someone? Was this the meeting point? Anspach edged into the next gallery, from where he could get a wider view of the room where Milraud stood.

He noticed the black man as soon as he walked into Milraud's gallery. Berlin was full of students from Africa, but this man was no student – he was tall, slim and beautifully dressed in a tailored grey wool suit, a cream silk shirt, and a tie. The fact that he was probably the only man in the gallery wearing a tie would have made it remarkable enough, but this was clearly a designer tie, broad, silky, with a brightly coloured pattern. His figure was elegant but his height and broad shoulders suggested there was strength behind the smooth façade.

The man didn't glance in Milraud's direction; he moved towards the far wall, where a group of young Chinese tourists stood giggling in front of a large nude. As Anspach watched, he saw Beckerman stroll in from the other gallery; he had joined the back of a tour group that gathered briefly at the Corot before moving in Anspach's direction. The group, with Beckerman in tow, walked into the gallery where Anspach stood and gathered at another picture.

Anspach glanced again in Milraud's direction. The Chinese had moved on from the nude, but where was the black man? Then he spotted him; he had been hidden by another group listening to an English-speaking guide. Now he walked up to the Corot and stood next to Milraud, with only a foot or two of space between them. Both were examining the Corot as if they were experts, and when the Frenchman turned his head slightly Anspach could see the two men were talking.

He drew back until he was out of sight, then looking down he said softly into his microphone: 'We have contact. Newcomer. Black male. One hundred eighty-five centimetres tall, slim, smart grey suit.'

The two men stayed standing, side by side, until suddenly the black man turned and walked out of the room. Milraud waited a few minutes then left the room too, going quickly towards the museum's exit. As he left the building he headed off in the direction of his hotel, watched by Anspach, who had joined Dimitz in an unmarked car parked in the car park outside the building. Three spaces away a second car was parked containing two more officers of the BfV; a third team member was busy buying a newspaper from a kiosk outside the entrance of the museum.

'We'll take the Newcomer; you take the main man,' ordered Anspach on the car's radio. 'When you've housed him at the hotel, come and help us. If he goes somewhere else, stick with him.'

Anspach settled down to wait for the black man he'd labelled Newcomer, and a few minutes later he emerged, with Beckerman fifteen metres behind him, examining a map of Berlin with apparent concentration. Anspach waited until Newcomer had walked a couple of hundred metres away from Unter den Linden, towards a shopping district, busy on a Saturday morning. When it got hard to see him in the crowd on the pavements, Anspach nodded at Dimitz, who started up the car and drove in the direction their target had gone. They could see Beckerman, struggling to keep up with Newcomer, who was striding quickly past the shops as if on his way to keep an urgent appointment.

They drove past both men, and Dimitz pulled up, just short of a pedestrian-only area. Anspach hopped out, waved to Dimitz as if to thank him for the lift, and walked swiftly into Nadelhoff's department store, an old-fashioned emporium that was adjusting badly to its new concrete and glass quarters. Inside he loitered on the ground floor, looking at men's shirts near the front windows, waiting for Newcomer to walk past. When he did, Anspach abandoned the shirts and left Nadelhoff's, just in time to see his target disappear through the swing doors of a shopping centre – six stories of small independent shops known collectively as the Boutique Mall. Whoever this elegant black man was, he seemed to know his way around this part of Berlin.

Anspach spoke into the mike under his lapel. 'He's gone into the Boutique Mall. I'll try and keep with him in there; park the car and come round to cover the rear entrance. Beckerman, watch the front. Control: get the other team over here as soon as they've seen their target home.'

Anspach spotted his target easily enough as soon as he went into the Mall. He was in a record shop on the ground floor, leafing through CDs. Anspach walked past and went into a shop opposite; from there he could see the door of the record shop.

He was beginning to feel desperately exposed but he didn't want to call in either of the other two to take his place for fear of leaving the exits unmonitored. The black man was taking his time – or was he killing time? He had twice looked at his watch but he went on flipping through CDs.

Then he moved, suddenly and quickly, heading straight for the atrium in the centre of the Mall. If he had clocked Anspach he didn't show it; he walked fast, looking straight ahead, and by the time Anspach was out of the shop, he had crossed the atrium and was striding down the aisle leading to the rear exit.

'Dimitz, target coming your way. He's yours,' he said into his mike. He was hanging back now to avoid detection if his target should look back. He gave it a good sixty seconds, then said into his mike, 'Have you got him?'

The reply was a grunt.

'Which way is he going?'

'He's not "going". The bastard's just standing on the kerb.'

'Any cabs around?'

'No. If he wanted one there's a taxi rank that he walked right past.'

So what was he doing? Waiting to see if he was being tailed? Possibly, but there were better ways to shake off surveillance, or even just to see if it was there. Waiting in one spot wouldn't do the trick, since the watchers didn't have to show themselves.

Anspach decided he should risk a closer look. He had reached the rear entrance and could see the black man now, across the street, staring into the window of a women's shoe shop. It seemed contrived, unnatural. Was he using the window to spot surveillance? Anspach had a premonition. 'Dimitz, quick get the car.'

'I'm in it already. Just round the corner.'

87

'Come and pick me up.'

But it was too late. There was a whoosh of an approaching car – a black Mercedes limousine, with tinted windows – the screech of brakes, and in an instant the black man had disappeared into the back seat, slamming the door behind him. The Mercedes executed a three-point turn at the expert hands of an invisible driver, then accelerated away down the street.

By then Anspach had his phone in his hand, and its camera snapped and snapped again. 'Dimitz, where the hell are you?' he shouted into his mike, not caring now if he was overheard.

'I'm stuck. There's a rubbish truck in front of me and I can't get round.'

16

A NSPACH STRODE ROUND THE corner into a caco-phony of car horns. Dimitz was sitting at the wheel of his car, at the head of a line of stationary cars, all blowing their horns at the garbage truck blocking their way.

'What in heaven's name is going on?' shouted Anspach.

'The driver's in that café and he won't come out.'

'I'll get him out fast enough,' said Anspach, and headed into the café waving a card identifying him as on special government business. In seconds he was out again, shouting at a couple of men in yellow jackets who had come out of the café. They got into the rubbish truck and drove it off up the street. By then Beckerman had joined his colleagues in the car.

'I've passed the registration number of the Mercedes to Control and he's asking the traffic police to look out for it,' said Anspach. 'We've got no reason to stop him, unless Traffic can get them for exceeding the speed limit, but at least we should get a fix on where he's going.'

'I got some good photographs of both of them in the gallery,' said Beckerman. 'I swear that was no chance meeting. They were discussing something. It was an RV.'

'Yeah. And I think that black fellow clocked us, at

least by the end. That was a very smooth getaway,' added Anspach.

'Where to, boss?' asked Dimitz.

Anspach snorted. 'God knows. We'll join up with the other team and hope Traffic get lucky.'

And they did – up to a point. Ten minutes later a report came in that a traffic patrol car had spotted the Mercedes heading north on the E26 near Westend. Unfortunately the patrol car had been going in the other direction.

A quick conference with Control sent both teams off to Tegel airport, where the BfV officers and the police and immigration officials were all alerted to look out for a tall, elegantly dressed black man, and to note his passport details and where he was heading.

Tegel was crowded when Anspach and his team arrived. They had to push past long queues of passengers at the departure desks in the hexagonal International Terminal A to reach the office where the airport team had their base. There was no news of their target. He had not been observed going through security or passport checks at Departure and no sightings of the Mercedes had been reported by police outside the terminal.

But Anspach wasn't going to give up; he found a ticketing supervisor, and with the man by his side, slowly worked his way along the lines of check-in desks – British Airways, Lufthansa, Delta and all the other airlines running international flights from the airport, showing the desk clerks the clearest picture he had of the dozens taken by Beckerman in the Schweiber Museum. As each desk clerk peered at the tiny image on the mobile phone's screen they responded with a shake of the head.

As he was working his way along the desks he heard

Beckerman's voice through his earpiece say, 'They've seen the car at Terminal D.'

'What's Terminal D?' he asked the supervisor, who was still with him.

'It's Air Berlin – domestic flights.'

He looked at the man, puzzled. 'Domestic flights?' Surely their target wasn't going somewhere else in Germany.

The man added, 'Private jets use it as well.'

'How do I get there?'

'Not easily. There's a bus . . .' the man started to explain, but Anspach was already racing for the terminal doors, shouting into his mike for Beckerman to pick him up.

At Terminal D they were directed to the far end of the departures hall. There they found one small counter manned by a middle-aged woman in a blue suit and forage cap who greeted them with a smile.

'*Guten Tag*,' she said, 'and how may I help you today?'

'Have you seen this man?' asked Anspach, thrusting the mobile phone in front of her face.

Taken aback, the woman paused. 'Our clients expect confidentiality, Herr . . .?'

'Anspach.' He brought out his card – official-looking, special government business, it breathed authority.

The woman's eyes widened. 'Yes, I have seen this gentleman.'

'Where is he flying to?'

'Rotterdam.'

'When is he leaving?'

She looked at Anspach with mild surprise. 'His plane took off ten minutes ago.'

17

Martin Seurat knew he had to work fast. He'd been waiting, hidden from view by a pillar in the lobby of the hotel, and as soon as he'd seen Milraud leave he had come upstairs. But if Milraud had only gone out for a paper or to get some fresh air, then he would be back soon, and before that Seurat had to make his pitch.

He had no idea how Annette would react when he turned up at the door of her room. Once, they had known each other very well. In the DGSE, officers worked in small teams, often abroad and in stressful circumstances, and they got to know each other intimately. He and Milraud had worked together on and off for over a decade, and despite some fundamental differences in personality – Martin was quieter, more analytical, focused on getting the job done; Milraud was flamboyant, sometimes inspired, sometimes simply erratic – they had grown to trust each other. Whenever they could, they liked to socialise together and to include their wives, who could easily feel ignored and left out because of the secret nature of the work their husbands did.

Annette Milraud had been a lively young woman then, apparently carefree, without any children. She loved the good things of life: the Milraud apartment was beautifully furnished, her clothes expensive and stylish – enough so that Seurat's wife used to wonder enviously how she could afford it all on the salary of a DGSE officer. Once a week Annette ran a little market stall in the Marais where she sold jewellery, some antique, some that she'd made herself and some just rather pretty junk that she had picked up for practically nothing. She was always wearing three or four of the more flamboyant rings from her stock when they met. It was difficult to believe that the stall brought in enough extra money to finance her lifestyle.

When the four of them got together for an evening, Annette drank more than any of them, smoked incessantly, and liked to dance. She had the kind of loud, extravagant *joie de vivre* that hinted at dissatisfaction or even desperation lying not far beneath. Seurat's wife had got on with her well enough, though she'd never trusted her in the way her husband trusted Antoine Milraud, and she had made it clear that she didn't want to see the Milrauds too often.

Now Seurat knocked on the door of Room 403, taking care that he could not be seen through the spyhole. He heard nothing at first, then there were steps inside the room. '*Oui?*' a woman's voice called out.

He replied in accented English, hoping she would think he was a concierge. 'I have a message for you, Madame.'

'A message?' She sounded suspicious. 'Put it under the door.'

He sighed – it had never been easy to hoodwink Annette. He said quite loudly, in French now, 'Come on, Annette, open the door.'

'Who is that?' He could hear the surprise in her voice.

'It's Martin Seurat.'

There was no reply for a moment. Then the door opened

a crack, held on its chain. Annette stared out at him, surprise replaced by hostility.

'What the hell do you want?' she demanded.

'If you let me in, I'll explain.' When she hesitated he added, 'I need to talk to you alone, Annette. Before Monsieur Pliska gets back.' He could see her flinch at the name. 'We know what name you're using, and the one Antoine used in Paris – Pigot. If need be we can even find out the one you used before that.'

'If you know so much, why do you want to talk to me?'

'Because you can help us. And help Antoine. You don't need me to tell you how much trouble he's in.'

Annette stared at him, as if considering what to do, then she suddenly closed the door. For a moment Seurat thought that would be it. But the door opened again, and she stood there, looking angry. 'I suppose you'd better come in,' she said.

Annette had obviously been packing. Two suitcases lay open on the floor and a smaller Vuitton bag was on the bed.

'Going already?' asked Seurat. 'You've only just arrived.'

Annette shrugged. 'That was the plan,' she said.

'Mind if I sit down?' said Seurat, taking one of the two armchairs. 'Whether you go and where you go is going to be up to you, Annette. If you help me you at least may be able to go wherever you like. Don't cooperate and you'll be seeing the inside of a French prison before long.'

'The Germans may have something to say about that.'

Seurat shook his head. 'I don't think so. They'll accept a European arrest warrant, and there's more than enough evidence behind it. You have aided and abetted your husband, a man who's facing charges on everything from illegal arms dealing to kidnapping.'

'What do you want me to do? You know I would never

betray Antoine,' she said defiantly, gesturing to emphasise the point. Seurat noticed that nowadays she limited herself to two rings – but both looked a good deal more valuable than in the days of the market stall.

'I'm not asking you to betray him; I'm asking you to help him. And you can do that by helping me.'

She looked at him sardonically. 'That sounds unlikely. How does it work?'

'He listens to you, Annette. You know he does. He thinks all the rest of us are fools and you and he are the only clever ones.'

Annette grimaced. 'I'm not sure he'd include me, not these days. He'd tell you I'm always whining. Anyway, I don't see how I can help you. I don't know the details of Antoine's business. I never have. He's an old-fashioned Frenchman that way.'

Seurat eyed her sceptically but she returned his look with a stare of her own, as if daring him not to believe her. He was confident she knew more than she was letting on, but her true value lay in her influence over Milraud, not in any information she might have about his activities. He said, 'I believe you. But a judge might not – you're in this up to your neck, as I'm sure you know. But if you cooperate – and more importantly if you get Antoine to cooperate – there's still a chance you can lead a normal life again.'

It was her turn to look sceptical, so he went on: 'I mean it. I'm not saying Antoine won't have to serve time in prison, he will – and you may too – but perhaps for less time than otherwise. To be quite clear, what I'm saying is that Antoine can help himself by cooperating and you can help him and yourself by persuading him. Life in prison won't be pleasant, but I can't imagine life on the run is much fun either.'

'It's had its moments.'

'Where do you call home these days?'

She shrugged. He said, 'Come on, Annette, we're already checking with the airlines for passengers called Pliska. I'll know all your recent movements soon enough.'

She hesitated, then said sourly, 'Caracas. We have a flat there.'

'Good God. I don't imagine that's the safest place for a woman left on her own a lot of the time, as I imagine you are.'

'Venezuela's a very beautiful country,' she replied defensively.

'I should think it needs to be – to compensate for all the other disadvantages.'

Annette laughed out loud. A good sign, thought Seurat; he had always been able to make her laugh in the past. He went on, 'The good news is that you won't be going back there for a while. The bad news is that it could be a long, long while. That's up to you.'

'So what do you want me to do?'

'Encourage Antoine to work with us. That's all.'

She was still thinking about this when there was the sound of footsteps in the corridor, then a card was inserted in the lock and the door swung open. Antoine Milraud walked into the room. When he saw Seurat he didn't seem surprised.

'So it's you on my tail, is it? I wondered who had stirred up the Germans. I knew we'd meet again one day.'

Seurat had to admire the man's sangfroid: Milraud had always been nerveless, even in the most hair-raising situations. But then Seurat supposed you had to be if you were going to live on the run. He looked at his former colleague, the man who had been his trusted friend and had become his nemesis, haunting his dreams, filling his head with thoughts of revenge, and said, 'I doubt this is how you envisaged our meeting.'

Milraud shrugged, and sat down heavily. 'Some days life is a bowl of cherries; some days the bowl holds only a few stones. I knew someone was onto me, but I congratulate you on your efficiency. I was hoping I was a few hours ahead.'

He started to reach into his jacket pocket, but Seurat put up a warning hand. 'Don't even think of doing something stupid. I'm armed and downstairs in the lobby there are two members of the local police and an officer of the BfV.'

'I was going for a cigarette actually,' said Milraud, bringing out a pack of *Disque Bleus* and a gold lighter. He inhaled greedily, then blew out a long funnelling plume of smoke. 'So, what happens now?'

Seurat outlined the position. If Milraud cooperated Seurat would do everything he could to get a reduction in his sentence. There was no point in pretending that Milraud wouldn't be serving time, and some hefty time at that, but equally, his assistance, if it led to other convictions, would be taken into account by the court. If he didn't cooperate, then he could expect the maximum sentence. Seurat said softly, 'I think we're talking twenty years.'

Milraud nodded and stubbed out his cigarette. 'That was very well put, Martin. You haven't lost your touch for clarity. But I have to say I doubt there's much really that you will be able to do for me. I've rubbed too many noses in the dirt. Even if your offer is sincere – and I have no reason to doubt that it is,' he said with a wry smile, 'I have to question your ability to see it through. I'm cooked, as the Americans like to say, though if I take my punishment like a man I will have a chance of breathing free air again some day. If I squeal, then I have very little chance at all.'

'So you won't cooperate?'

'Regretfully, no. Believe me, the sort of people I work with are not the kind one wishes to annoy.'

'What a pity,' said Seurat. It was clear to him that Milraud was far more scared of his arms-dealing associates than he was of the French authorities. Seurat decided it was time to play his trump card, and hoped that Annette would play her role. He said firmly, 'In that case you leave me no choice. I will have you placed under arrest . . . and Annette as well.'

'Annette?' Milraud's voice rose in alarm. 'Why Annette? She's done nothing.'

'On the contrary, she's helped you virtually every step of the way. Beginning with your escape from France. It's a serious offence and she will do serious time.' He paused to let this sink in, then added, 'I think I can guarantee ten years minimum.'

Milraud stared at him, his eyes widening in shock. There was a loud gasp. Annette had her hand over her mouth and she was shaking her head almost theatrically in disbelief.

Whether the appalled look on her face was genuine or not, it was doing the trick. Milraud stood up and rushed to her, throwing a comforting arm around her shoulders. 'It's all right, *chérie*.'

Annette started to cry, tears the size of raindrops rolling down both cheeks, her sobs growing louder despite her husband's efforts to console her. 'Ten years,' she wailed, as Seurat watched, mentally giving her performance five stars.

His arm still around Annette, Milraud looked at Seurat with undisguised hatred. 'I tell you, she has nothing to do with my affairs, and I don't believe you have any evidence that she has. So leave her out of this.'

'It's too late for that, Antoine. As for evidence, don't

worry: we have a strong case – for starters, just travelling on a false passport will get her behind bars. You should have thought of that before you had her fly from Caracas.'

Annette had moved away from her husband's embrace and sat down on the bed, where she began to rock backwards and forwards, still sobbing heavily. When Milraud moved towards her she pushed him away, and Milraud's face fell.

He turned to Seurat angrily. 'What would it take for you to drop charges against her?'

'The truth. All of it. Let's start with why you came to Berlin.'

18

BACK IN THAMES HOUSE in London Liz Carlyle was feeling out of sorts. An investigation with which she was vitally concerned was unravelling without her and she didn't like it. She was happiest when she was at the centre of events; watching other people take the decisions and viewing the action from far away was not how she liked things to be.

She had been unimpressed by the surveillance efforts of the French, and from what she had heard of the Berlin operation it hadn't been much better. 'A4 could knock that lot into a cocked hat,' she'd said to Peggy Kinsolving.

Geoffrey Fane had been unusually quiet too, and there had been no response from Bruno Mackay in Sana'a, after she'd sent him the French surveillance pictures of the young Arab in the Luxembourg Gardens. She wondered if MI6 were doing something they were not telling her about.

To make matters worse, she was anxious about Martin Seurat. She knew how obsessed he was with Antoine Milraud. She knew how personally he had taken the betrayal, and she was worried that he might not be able to keep his cool when faced with Milraud again.

In spite of all her frustration, some progress had been

made in London. Peggy had managed to put together details of the route taken by the private jet boarded by Milraud's contact, the elegant black man, at Tegel airport in Berlin. The Germans had not asked for any special monitoring of the flight as they had no case against the passenger, so Peggy had worked from the records, something she loved doing.

'Smart plane,' she observed. 'Pilatus PC-12, registered in Russia. Even hiring that costs a bomb. We're dealing with real money here.'

The plane had landed in Rotterdam to refuel and taken off straight away, heading for Prestwick Airport. No one had disembarked at Rotterdam. Twenty minutes into the flight, the pilot had requested permission to divert to a small private airfield in North Wales. Inquiries at the airfield afterwards by the local Special Branch had established that the plane had indeed landed there; that one passenger had got out and had been picked up by a private car. No one had asked to see his passport. The duty desk clerk had been confused and had thought that the plane had flown from Prestwick, and yes, the manager of the airport thought that the passenger might have been a tall black man, and no, nobody had noted the registration number of the car.

'I can't believe the sloppiness at that airport,' said Peggy. 'Special Branch is reporting them to the Civil Aviation Authority. I hope they lose their licence.'

'If they've got one,' observed Liz.

Peggy had also circulated the photographs taken in the Schweiber Museum to Special Branches across the UK, with a request for any information about the black man. No replies had been received so far.

The arrival of a detailed report from Martin Seurat of

his interview with the Milrauds in the Berlin hotel room gave Liz something to focus on. It was clear that her concerns that Martin might be hindered by his personal animosity towards Milraud had not been realised. In fact, it had probably helped him in being quite ruthless in using Annette's fear of prison to get Milraud to agree to cooperate.

The report was followed by a phone call from Martin, who reported that the Germans had agreed to release the Milrauds into his custody and he was about to leave Berlin for Paris in the company of a small posse of French and German police and security officers.

'Where are you going to take them?'

'I've arranged a safe house in Montreuil.'

'Montreuil? I thought that was a fashionable holiday resort. Why so posh?'

'Not that one. This one's a suburb of Paris. Not posh at all.'

'Good. I wouldn't like to think of the Milrauds living it up at your taxpayers' expense.'

'Can you come over tomorrow? I think we should hook him in firmly to what you want him to do without giving him too much time to think about it.'

'All right. I'll let you know if there's any problem; otherwise you can expect me by lunchtime.'

Liz put the phone down thoughtfully. She and Martin had been close now for more than two years. So close that he had made it very clear the previous year that he would have liked her to give up her job and come to Paris to live with him. From her reaction he had realised that that had been a mistake. Her job was an essential part of Liz's being and without it she could never be happy, even with him. Since then he had been talking about leaving his own job in the DGSE and looking for some other form of work. Liz wondered whether, now that he had finally caught Antoine Milraud, the man who had obsessed him for so long, he might actually decide to do it. She wasn't sure that would be a good idea for him or, she had to admit, for her either.

She was sometimes concerned that there could be a conflict of interest when they found themselves working closely together on a case, as now, but so far they had managed to keep their personal relationship and their work in separate compartments. She knew that her bosses had their eye on the situation and that she needed to be scrupulously professional if she were not to be moved onto other work. Yet now here she was, going to Paris to take over the handling of Milraud. She planned to use him to flush out whatever was going on, and she had to take the lead, because the intelligence so far, such as it was, was pointing to the UK.

Martin met her at the Gare du Nord and they drove to Montreuil, where they found Antoine Milraud waiting in the living room of a nondescript stucco bungalow. He had a young DGSE officer called Thibault and a couple of tough-looking guards for company. Little had been spent on the décor of the bungalow – a few battered-looking chairs, a much-used coffee table and a frayed sofa furnished the sitting room and the walls were enlivened by gaudy reproductions of Impressionist paintings. I wonder who buys this sort of stuff in the first place thought Liz, hoping that the kitchen was equipped rather more expansively – with perhaps a pâté and a bottle of Chablis in the fridge.

Milraud had dressed up for the occasion. In his smart wool jacket, open-necked shirt and polished loafers, he looked more like a successful film director or the owner of a trendy gallery than a renegade intelligence officer.

Liz gazed coldly at the elegant figure who stood up to greet her. She ignored the hand he held out and did not respond to his 'Good morning, Madame'. This was a man who had not only destroyed the peace of mind of the man she loved but had worked alongside a psychopathic killer to kidnap her colleague Dave Armstrong and hold him for days in a damp cellar; a man she had last seen as a shadowy figure in the darkness on a French holiday island, escaping capture and leaving his partner to die in a hail of bullets. She was glad to see him confined in this charmless room, but she would rather have seen him in prison. In the present circumstances she had no option but to work with him, but she certainly wasn't going to treat him with any warmth.

The young officer came in with a cafetière of coffee and three small cups, then quickly withdrew. Milraud fidgeted nervously on the sofa. As soon as Martin had handed out the cups, Liz said abruptly, 'Let's get started. As you know I'm from MI5 and I'm going to ask you some questions about your recent activities. Firstly I'd like to know why you were in Berlin.'

She knew from Martin that Milraud's English was excellent, almost idiomatic, yet she wondered whether he would pretend not to understand her, and he was giving her a questioning look. But then he said, 'Has Martin not told you what I've said already? I'm surprised; I thought you two were close,' he added.

Liz ignored this. 'Of course he has. But I want to hear it from the horse's mouth.'

He nodded. 'As you wish. As I told Martin, I was in Berlin to act as a liaison – the venue was not of my own choosing. I know you are aware of my earlier meeting in the Luxembourg Gardens – this was to follow up my instructions from that.'

'Whose instructions?'

Milraud put both hands up and shrugged, in the universal sign for *who knows?* He said, 'He is Arab, he is young, he is anti-establishment. To me that means the rebels of the Arab Spring. Other than that, I have no idea.'

'Do you often do business with anonymous contacts?'

Milraud gave her a patronising smile. 'Of course. I doubt I know the real name of any of my customers, Madame.'

'Why did this mysterious person send you to Berlin?'

Milraud looked at her as if checking to see that she was minimally intelligent.

'To meet the black man in the Schweiber Museum?'

'Yes.'

'And what is *his* name?'

'Smith,' said Milraud without batting an eye. Then he added, 'Perhaps it was Jones.'

Liz sighed. 'All right, let's forget about names for the moment. What was he going to do for you?'

Milraud was silent. 'I don't know,' he said at last.

Liz looked at Milraud, waiting. Then he said, 'I've never seen him before. I don't know him.'

'Then what were you talking about?'

'He was setting up another meeting. For tomorrow. He wanted to make sure we weren't being watched yesterday. I didn't think I was, then I went back to the hotel and found Martin talking with my wife. So I was wrong and the black man was right to be suspicious.'

Liz sat back in her chair. This didn't make any sense. Milraud seemed to be claiming that all these meetings were only to set up further meetings.

He saw her scepticism. 'I could still go to the next meeting tomorrow,' he offered. 'Then I might find out what it's all about.'

Not a big help, thought Liz, since the black man had left Germany and was presumably now somewhere in Britain. She wondered if Milraud knew this and was lying – if she accepted his offer, he would simply invent another rendezvous point, dutifully go there, then profess regretful surprise when the black man didn't show up.

Liz switched tack. 'What about the man from the Arab Spring? How were things left with him?'

Milraud looked at her blandly. 'He was not forthcoming. He only wanted assurance I could supply the weapons he wanted.'

'What kind of weapons?'

'Automatic rifles. In time he said they'd want more sophisticated armoury – RPGs, SAM missiles, you name it. But you have to walk before you can run, and at the moment it's basic infantry armaments he's looking for. Rifles, ammunition.'

'So what was agreed?'

'Nothing. I named a price, and he made a counter-proposal. As is usually the case, we settled somewhere in between. Then we aborted the meeting because we were being watched. The next step is for him to confirm the order – which in practice means a down payment of twenty-five per cent. Not unreasonable,' Milraud said with a hint of pride, and Liz realised he was enjoying talking about his trade. He wouldn't have had many opportunities to do so in recent years.

'How is he going to contact you?'

'If he contacts me at all, after that clumsy surveillance in Paris, it will be by email. Third party – a dummy box I've created. He'll ask for a meeting, though it won't read that way – on the surface, it will look like a misplaced request for a booking at a restaurant. The name of the restaurant will contain a link to another site – that site will contain coordinates which when I apply them to a pre-existing grid will give me the location, time and date of the meeting.'

'You told Martin this will be in the UK.'

'Yes. That is what the man told me in Paris before we aborted our meeting.'

'He didn't give you any sense of where in the UK?'

'No.' Milraud looked at her impatiently. 'I have already told Martin all this.'

She ignored him. 'When are you expecting an email?'

Milraud shrugged. 'I am working to my client's schedule, not my own. When it arrives, it arrives.'

Martin interjected. 'My colleague Thibault has taken charge of his laptop and will monitor all emails.'

'This better be right, Antoine,' said Liz, 'or any reassurance you have received, about how Annette will be treated will no longer be valid.'

Milraud looked at her wide-eyed. 'Do I take it you are in charge then?' He seemed surprised.

'As far as you're concerned I am.'

Milraud turned to Seurat, as if expecting him to dissent, but Seurat said simply, 'She's right, Antoine. She will be directing what you are to do.'

Milraud looked confused as he tried to take this in. At last he nodded again, and gave an ironic shrug. 'I am accustomed to it. Annette wears the trousers in my family too.'

19

'*D*ONATION WILL SEE US this evening,' said Miles Brookhaven, putting down the phone. 'I told his son I was bringing a colleague from the British Embassy and he didn't ask any questions. His son seems to be a sort of secretary for this so-called charity he runs. Well, he calls it a charity, but as far as I can see it's a kind of private fund-raising operation. God knows what shady deals they're doing. Anyway, we're to go out to his farm this evening.'

'A farm?' Bruno Mackay raised his eyebrows. 'How far away is it? I don't fancy a long drive in the dark in this place. I won't be at all popular with Geoffrey Fane if I end up as a kidnap victim.'

'It's not that far. About ten miles or so along a fairly decent road. It'll be dark when we come back, but *Donation* seems to have some sort of security operation set up to control who goes along that road, so it should be OK.'

Bruno Mackay was sitting in Miles Brookhaven's office in the American Embassy in Sana'a. The surveillance pictures from Paris were spread out on the table in front of them.

'I hope it's worth the journey,' said Bruno. 'I can't imagine they'll make much out of these photographs. I don't know why Liz Carlyle bothered sending them. The guy looks like thousands of young men you might meet anywhere from Algiers to Afghanistan.'

'Maybe he does, to you, but *Donation* or his son may recognise him – or know someone who will.'

'Let's hope so. Our French colleagues certainly seem to have messed up thoroughly in Paris. First they blew the surveillance and then they lost both of their targets.'

'I don't think it's a complete disaster. I've heard from Andy Bokus that they know the European who met this guy in Paris. He's called Milraud, a DGSE officer who left the Service and turned rogue.'

'Oh him. The French have been looking for him for years. He stole a lot of cash and set himself up as an arms dealer. If he's reappeared it will have set the cat among the pigeons. He used to work with Liz Carlyle's boyfriend Martin Seurat; Seurat's sworn to get him.'

'Well, apparently they have got him. They pinned him down in a hotel in Berlin and they're hoping to find out why he was meeting this guy in Paris' – he waved at the photograph of the young Arab – 'and what he went to Berlin for.'

Five hours later Miles Brookhaven was driving the Embassy SUV along the road through fields and small apple orchards. The sun was setting over the line of hills in a clear pink and red sky.

'No clouds tonight, thank God,' remarked Miles. 'Last time I came along here there was a downpour. I couldn't see a thing. Had to stop dead in the middle of the road.'

'Hmm,' said Bruno, who was sitting uneasily sideways in his seat, keeping an eye on the road behind them and looking from side to side.

'Don't worry,' said Miles. 'I'm sure it's OK. I told you, he's got this road monitored. It feels safe to me.'

'Hmm,' said Bruno again.

Miles drove on another few miles and then Bruno, who was peering out of the front windscreen, said, 'I thought you said there were no clouds tonight. What's that then?' He pointed to what looked like a small black cloud low in the sky ahead of them.

'It looks like smoke. It's just about where *Donation*'s compound is. Perhaps they're burning rubbish.' But as they got nearer the cloud seemed to separate itself and gradually it became a moving mass of birds.

'Vultures,' said Bruno. 'Something's died.'

'Probably a cow or a buffalo. We'll soon find out. We're less than a mile away from the farm now.'

As they came up to the walls of the compound, another cloud of flapping vultures rose up to join those circling in the sky. Miles turned the car to go under the arch and then slammed on the brakes.

'My God,' shouted Bruno. 'What the hell's that?' A body clad in what had been white robes was swinging in the arch, dangling from a rope round its neck. Its face was a raw mass of bloodied flesh and its eyes had been pecked out. The legs, swinging in mid-air, ended in shiny black leather shoes.

'It's *Donation*'s son.' Miles's voice shook.

'Turn round,' yelled Bruno. 'Let's get out of here.'

'*Donation* may be inside. He may need our help.'

'If he's in there,' said Bruno, 'he's long past our help. Can't you see? It's a warning. Go on, get out or we'll be next.'

Suddenly Miles jerked into action. With squealing tyres throwing up sand and stones he turned the car and drove off, back down the road they had come along.

Bruno was leaning forward now, holding on to the dashboard. 'I thought you said they had security on this road.'

'That's what *Donation* told me and I believed him. I thought they knew what they were doing. It all seemed very casual but I figured they were the best judge of what was safe. I bet it's that bloody French surveillance operation that's blown it. The guy in Paris knew he was being followed, so he knew there'd been a leak and they've traced it back to *Donation* and his son.'

They fell silent, each thinking over the implications of what had happened. Miles drove fast, bouncing the heavy car over the ruts in the road, while Bruno kept a sharp eye on the fields to each side. The light was fading now as Bruno turned to look over his shoulder at the road behind them.

'How much further?'

'About six miles.'

'Well, get a move on. There's company behind us.'

'I know. It came out of a field track just back there.'

A battered-looking pickup truck was approaching at high speed. As it got nearer two men in black balaclavas stood up in the back, each waving a heavy weapon in one hand.

Miles had his foot on the floor but the pickup truck was gaining on them. 'Hold on,' shouted Miles, 'I'm gonna knock them off,' and as the pickup drew alongside them, he turned the wheel of the SUV hard to the left.

But the truck driver had anticipated the manoeuvre and with a burst of acceleration managed to block their sideways move. There was a loud bang as metal hit metal, and the two vehicles each did a sweeping one-eighty and came to a halt side by side, slewed along the road.

The two armed men leapt down and pulled open Miles's door.

'Get out. Both of you,' said one in an accent straight from the streets of south London.

The two climbed out of the SUV, and the man with the London accent motioned with his rifle for them to move away from the car. 'Get down on your knees,' he ordered, and when Bruno hesitated he pointed the gun at his head. 'Get down, I said.'

As they knelt on the sandy road, Miles glanced at Bruno. He had clasped his hands behind his head and was staring straight ahead. Miles knew he was waiting for the shot. Then they'll shoot me, he thought. There was silence for a moment. A breeze had picked up, bringing a faint smell of petrol from the pickup truck. Behind them one of the men moved close; Miles could hear him breathing, noisily and fast. This is it, thought Miles, trying to come up with something meaningful for his final thought.

But then the Londoner spoke again. 'This is a warning. Keep out of our business and go home or you'll end up like that corpse at the farm. Now get back in that car and bugger off.'

And as Miles got slowly to his feet, he saw the man and his colleague leap back into their pickup truck. The engine started, the truck turned in a cloud of dust and drove back along the road the way it had come.

Miles stood with Bruno in the road for a moment, looking after the rapidly disappearing truck.

'What on earth was that all about?' said Bruno, his voice shaking very slightly. 'Why did they let us go?'

'Are you complaining?' asked Miles with a tremulous laugh. 'Perhaps they've got too much going on to want two dead diplomats on their hands.'

Bruno said, 'Maybe that's it. We've been lucky this time. Let's get the hell back to your Embassy.'

20

    'I NEED A DRINK,' said Miles as he parked the dusty
SUV in the car park underneath the US Embassy.
'Come on up. I've got a bottle of Scotch in my cupboard.'

As he was getting the bottle and glasses out, Miles's eye
fell on a piece of paper propped up on his desk. He read its
message out loud: *The Ambassador would like to see you in his
office as soon as you get back.*

Looking at Bruno he said, 'Something must have
happened. I have a regular meeting with him on Monday
mornings and he never asks to see me otherwise.'

'Surely he won't still be in his office at this hour,' said
Bruno. 'Sit down and drink up. You've deserved it.'

But Ambassador Thomas B. Rodgers III, not a man to leave
his post when there was still business to do, was at his desk.

'Come in, young man,' he called out as Miles appeared
in his outer office. 'I've had a complaint about you.'

Ambassador Rodgers was a State Department professional. Sana'a was a tough posting, potentially dangerous,
requiring diplomatic skills; not the sort of plum Embassy
that presidents gave as a reward to their business friends
and supporters. Thomas B. Rodgers had been round the

block a few times, served in more junior posts in some tough places, and now in his mid-fifties had made it to Ambassador. He was used to dealing with the CIA.

'I'm sorry to hear that, sir.' Miles's voice was calm but his heart lurched. He hadn't yet made up his mind what, if anything, he was going to say about the events of this evening. He knew for certain that if the Ambassador found out that not only had he nearly got himself kidnapped or killed, but that he had led a British colleague into the same danger, there'd be a request to Langley for his withdrawal. Yet surely the news couldn't have got back to the Embassy so quickly.

'It concerns Minister Baakrime. You told me that you were hoping to use him as a source of information on arms supplies. Well, you should know that your contact with him has been noticed by the Yemenis, and I've been warned that we should steer clear of him. Other members of the government don't trust him. He's been making too much money on the side.' He waved an exasperated hand. 'I know, I know, most of them are at it in one way or another, but he's been making more than other people.'

'I see,' said Miles, wondering what else the Ambassador had been told.

'I don't know how much you know about him, but apparently he's working with the Russians.'

'With the Russians?' Miles was taken off guard and his surprise showed. 'No. I didn't know that. What's he doing for them?'

'I wasn't told. But probably much the same as you were hoping he'd do for you. Whatever it is, he's visited the Caucasus twice in the past year. Dagestan apparently. God knows what for, but whatever it is it seems to be making Minister Baakrime a lot of money. I'd be grateful if you'd steer clear of him from now on. I think he may shortly find himself in prison.'

If he's not already dead, thought Miles, remembering the hideous sight of the Minister's son, dangling in the entrance to the farm.

21

I T WAS HARD WORK trying to extract any useful information from Milraud. It had needed frequent reminders from Martin that Annette's treatment depended on his cooperation to get him to fill in any of the details; even then he could only be described as a reluctant witness.

Eventually Liz had got him to admit that the Arab had got in touch with him via a contact in Yemen – a man who had put business his way before. He did not know his identity, he'd said, or who the Arab was – he never asked such questions. The request had been for comparatively small arms, as he'd said at the beginning, and he had been told these were for use by rebel groups in the Arab Spring countries. He had assumed this meant Syria, but he had not asked. It was not his concern. The Arab had said that the arms were to be delivered to Dagestan, one of the former Soviet republics, from where they would be moved on to their destination. He'd quoted an inflated price for the deal and there had been a bit of haggling, but he was very pleased with the final bargain they'd struck.

When Liz asked if he was not surprised that the delivery was to be to Dagestan, he'd said that nothing surprised him. He had both delivered arms to Dagestan before and bought arms there. When she asked more about the black man he'd met in Berlin, all he would say was that the Arab had asked him to meet the man – who he guessed must be arranging the onward shipment, though he couldn't be sure of this as the man was so jumpy they had had no significant conversation.

As Martin drove her to the Gare du Nord to catch the last Eurostar to London, Liz was mulling over all this.

'You know,' she said after a while, 'I don't believe a quarter of what Milraud said. The trouble is, I'm so tired I can't work it out.'

'I can't say I'm surprised to hear you say that. Milraud's not one to give up easily. It sounded unlikely to me too; I'm sure some vital parts are missing. I just don't believe he wanders around the world having meetings with people he doesn't know anything about. He wouldn't have lasted as long as he has, with me on his tail, if that's how he did business.'

'I know. And I can't understand why the Arab Spring rebels would want to buy small weapons at a high price from someone like him. Surely they are getting all they need from Iran and Hezbollah and the like.'

'Why don't you stay the night and we can talk about it in the morning?'

'I'd love to, but I can't. Peggy rang to say there was some new information about the black man. One of the Special Branches think they know who he is.'

'Let Peggy deal with it,' he said, as he stopped the car at the station.

She touched his hand on the wheel. 'No. I want to do it myself. I want to be sure Monsieur Milraud isn't going to get away with anything now we've got him. For your sake, as well as my own.'

She kissed him on the cheek, jumped out of the car and was gone into the station before he could say anything.

Liz got up early in the morning and was at work by eight. Peggy Kinsolving, another early riser, was already there at her desk in the open-plan office.

'Here's the number to call,' Peggy said, handing Liz a piece of paper. 'It's DS Halliday from Cheshire Special Branch. He said he's fairly sure he knows the black man.'

Halliday wasn't in his office until ten, but when he answered the phone he sounded cheerful and eager to help. 'I've had your photo. I'm pretty certain I know your guy. It looks like Lester Jackson, who owns a club in Wilmslow. I'll send you one of our pictures of him, so you can see what you think. He's well known to me and my colleagues.'

'Tell me more.'

'He's a tried and true bad guy, involved in trafficking drugs and women. But the frustrating thing is we've never managed to pin anything on him – not a single thing. The only trouble he's been in that I know of was years ago. Some teenage scrapes, and one arrest for burglary – but he was underage, and I don't think he even saw the inside of a young offenders' institution. He's never done time as an adult.'

'You say he owns a club. What sort of club?'

'It's called Slim's. In Wilmslow, which is in my bailiwick here in Cheshire. He gets quite a lot of the football fraternity in the restaurant and there's gambling and girls, and drugs, of course. Sometimes it gets a bit wild at the weekends but nothing too bad, just some young footballer drinking too much or snorting too much coke and getting involved with the paparazzi.

'There's an upstairs operation as well, with girls providing special services, as you might say, but we've had no complaints and we've never bothered them up to now. Recently Immigration have been sniffing around. They've a strong suspicion that some of the girls may have been trafficked, probably from Eastern Europe, and they think he may be selling women on, because his own upstairs operation isn't very big. Between you and me they're planning a raid pretty soon and I'm helping them. I've got my eye on one of the girls as a possible inside source. The club's in Cheshire, like I said, just inside our border, but Jackson lives in Greater Manchester's area. You should talk to them; they know him pretty well. How's he come across your radar anyway?'

Liz said cautiously, 'We're investigating a dodgy-looking arms deal on the Continent and it's possible he may be involved.'

'Guns? Jackson's crooked as a dog's hind leg, but as far as I know he's never sold weapons. Still, there's always a first time – he's not somebody who would turn down an opportunity.'

'If I wanted the Manchester angle who should I contact?'

'You should probably call the Deputy Head of Special Branch there.' His voice sounded unenthusiastic.

'Not the Head then?'

'No, he's new. It's his deputy who knows Jackson. He says he's been helpful in the past.'

'What. You mean he's a source?'

'I wouldn't go that far. But you're better off getting the story from him.'

Halliday sounded oddly wary and Liz decided not to press the point. 'OK, the Deputy Head it is. What's his name?'

'McManus. Do you want me to ring him first?'

'Not Jimmy McManus?' said Liz before she could stop herself.

'Yes. That's him. Do you know him?'

'No, not really,' she said, trying to recover from the surprise. 'I met him quite a time ago. I'll ring him myself,' she added, though her heart was sinking at the prospect.

When the photographs came through Liz looked at them carefully, trying not to jump to conclusions. Some had been taken in the street, some in what looked like a restaurant but was probably the club. But there wasn't any doubt – it was the same man. The same handsome face, with wide-set thin eyes, a sharp chin made sharper by the width of the high cheekbones. Afro-Caribbean, almost African but lighter-skinned, just the dark side of *café au lait*. Hair neatly cropped and, in all the pictures, very smartly dressed.

'What do you think?' asked Peggy, looking over Liz's shoulder, unwilling to hope for too much. 'Could it be our chap?'

'"Could be" is the understatement of all time. He's our man all right.'

'But do we have any real evidence he's one of the bad guys? Maybe he's just a respectable businessman holidaying in Berlin.'

'No. Milraud admitted he had a rendezvous with him and that the mysterious Arab set it up. What he hasn't told us is why he met him and what they said to each other – nothing, according to him, except to arrange another meeting, but I don't believe it. That's just one of the things he's holding back. So far we don't have anything on Mr Jackson, and the Germans couldn't hold him just for standing in front of a picture in a gallery, but I'm convinced he's in it up to his neck. A Mercedes that comes out of nowhere, a private jet that diverts to God knows where, and most of all the contact with Milraud – that's enough for me. And Halliday says he's a tried and true bad guy.'

She looked at Peggy, who seemed convinced. 'Now,' said Liz, looking pointedly at her phone, 'I've got someone else to ring to try and find out more.' And Peggy took the hint and left Liz alone to make the call.

22

'SPECIAL BRANCH. McMANUS SPEAKING.'

The voice was familiar, even after all these years, but it was more subdued, as if its owner had lost some vitality. Liz said brightly, 'Hello there, it's Liz Carlyle from MI5. I'm assuming I don't have to say "remember me?"'

There was a long pause, followed by the quick sharp laugh she remembered well. 'You can say that again. Hello, Liz. I take it this is a business call.'

You bet it is, she thought firmly. 'I sent round a photograph recently asking for information. I'm surprised I didn't hear from you. It's been identified as one Lester Jackson. Apparently you know the man.'

There was another, shorter pause.

'Yes, I do. I didn't see your photograph. What's he gone and done now?'

'I was hoping you'd tell me. Has he got form?'

'Strictly speaking no. But this isn't Little Lord Fauntleroy you're asking about. Why are you looking at him?'

'He's cropped up possibly in contact with someone we're investigating on the Continent,' she said cautiously. 'We're trying to work out what role he might be playing.'

There was another pause, then McManus said, 'I would

have thought the Continent was a step too far for our friend Jackson.'

'Oh really. Why's that?'

'Frankly, this guy is not the sharpest knife in the box. He's home-grown and strictly a small-time villain. On his own patch he does OK, and most of his business is legit – his club has its dodgy angles but the restaurant's not bad. To tell you the truth, there're a few shenanigans that go on upstairs, but nothing to get excited about. I'm surprised to find him showing up on your radar.'

'Your colleagues over in Cheshire seem to take a different view.'

'You must mean Halliday.' McManus gave a derisory snort. 'He's a young man who gets a bit over-excited. Not much goes on in Cheshire and he's got a bee in his bonnet about the club. He's cross that he's never managed to get anything on Jackson.'

'He said Jackson was a source of yours.'

'Is that what he called him?' McManus laughed, but there was nothing amused about its tone. 'Listen, the guy's helped me out on a few occasions, pointed me the right way when I was bringing down the coke traffickers in this town. He's done enough for us that we leave him alone.'

I get it, thought Liz angrily. Let Jackson traffic in women in return for helping out once in a while with drugs. Drugs got the headlines, while prostitution was just seen as a necessary evil – however many lives it ruined, however many women it kept in a kind of slavery. 'So why was he in Berlin then?' she asked. Immediately the words were out of her mouth she wished she hadn't been so specific.

'I haven't a clue. But believe me, if he's got himself tangled up in something big-time, Jackson is not playing a large role in it. He's small beer, Liz. Honestly.'

'OK. Thanks for letting me know.'

She paused for a second, feeling awkward. Then McManus said, his voice softening, 'It's been a long time. So how goes life for you?'

'Good, thanks. Same employer, as you can see.'

McManus laughed. 'I always had you down as a lifer. You had the talent, and the commitment. I wouldn't be surprised if you end up running the whole shebang one day.'

'Don't count on it.' McManus had always been a charmer when he wanted to be. 'But what about you? You must like Manchester if you're still there.'

'Like? I don't know about that.' His voice was flatter now. 'It's a living. I can't complain.'

'Oh.' It wasn't the answer she'd expected. 'Well, I'd better get moving; we've got our weekly brief in a minute. Thanks for the info.'

'Any time.'

She didn't like leaving it like this. She said, wanting to give the conversation a better ending, 'I may have to come up to your part of the world. If I do, I'll drop in and say hello.'

'You do that. It would be good to see you again.' Then he added, 'Just don't make a special trip on account of Lester Jackson. Take my word for it, the guy's nothing for you to worry about.'

Putting the phone down, Liz felt troubled by the conversation. She stood up and went over to the window, looking down as a small tug chugged along the river. The Thames was lifeless-looking and grey under the overcast sky of late autumn. His account of Lester Jackson just hadn't rung true. 'Small beer; not the sharpest knife in the box' did not describe the elegantly dressed man who, according to the

Germans, had strolled into the Schweiber Museum, had conducted quite clever counter-surveillance, had been whisked off the street by a Mercedes, picked up by a private plane and collected by yet another limousine from a private airfield.

Why had McManus tried to downplay Jackson's importance? Come to that, why had he not responded to the photograph Peggy had circulated to all Special Branches? He must have received it and known very well who it was.

She thought back to the McManus she had known years ago and the reason she had split up with him. Then he had been prepared to bend the rules in his pursuit of criminals who he was convinced were guilty, even when he couldn't prove it. Was he now bending the rules in pursuit of something else? His own interests perhaps?

And McManus had exhibited all the verbal tics of the practised liar – 'honestly', 'believe me', 'to tell you the truth', and 'frankly'. She realised that she didn't believe a word he'd said about Lester Jackson, and now she was worried that in talking to him she had given too much away.

23

KATYA KNEW ALL ABOUT the police in her country – they were armed and violent and sometimes if you paid them enough they would go away – but she didn't know about the British police. People said they were different, but those were normal people, people who were in the country legally, people with the right stamps in their passports, people who had genuine passports. Not people like her for whom the smallest brush with the authorities could mean disaster.

So when a young man knocked at the door of the house where she rented a room and said he was a policeman, an icy panic gripped her. He flashed an identity card so quickly that she couldn't have seen it even if her eyes had been working properly. She'd been woken by his knock and was still half asleep as well as scared.

'Detective Sergeant Halliday,' he said. 'Can I come in?' and before she could say anything he pushed past her and went into the lounge. The three other girls who lived in the house had all gone out to work. They had nine-to-five jobs, but Katya got home at four o'clock in the morning and usually slept till the early afternoon.

The lounge was in a mess. One of the girls slept there on

the sofa and she'd left her clothes and underwear scattered on the floor. Halliday sat down on the one chair while Katya stood in the doorway in her nightclothes and nervously waited for him to say something.

'I expect you know what this is about, love,' he said with a smile that was only superficially friendly. He seemed young to be a detective; his hair was spiky and shiny with wax, like the kids she saw sometimes on her way home, coming out of the clubs.

She didn't say anything and he laughed. 'Come on, Katya. Speak to me.'

'Just tell me what you want,' she said, not that she had much doubt. He must know she was there illegally, without proper papers, and she feared the worst – deportation back to Dagestan, the country she had been so happy to leave. But if he'd come to arrest her, why was he on his own? It seemed odd.

'I'm interested in your place of work.'

'Slim's?'

'That's right, love. You work upstairs, don't you?'

'Yes.'

'Funny kind of place, Slim's. I mean, it's a club downstairs, full of respectable citizens having dinner and a drink or two and a dance. But if someone wants a special dessert they can get it upstairs.'

Katya said nothing, wondering what he was getting at. She didn't know whether what went on upstairs in Slim's was legal or not, all she knew was that neither she nor any of the girls who worked there had the right papers. But if he was inquiring into what went on in the club, why had he come to her? She didn't run the place. Whatever he wanted, she wished he'd get on with it. But his next remark gave her a shock. 'How well do you know Mr Jackson?'

She shrugged. 'He is there most nights, but he doesn't often speak to the staff.'

Halliday sneered. 'Oh, so he's too grand to talk to the people who help make him rich.'

She didn't reply; the less she said the better. She must do nothing to rouse his interest and then he might go away. She knew Jackson, of course, but as a daunting presence rather than as someone you could talk to. He was the owner of the club, with the power to hire and fire. But it was more than that – he owned them, the girls, and she had no doubt that he was behind the operation that brought them into the country.

The girls in the upstairs room at Slim's were stunners – the prettiest girls their home country had to offer. Katya was proud of this, since part of her job was selecting the girls who got brought over. For that, she had to travel to Dagestan from time to time, and when she did she used a false passport that was given to her for the journey, then taken away. It said she was Bulgarian. The girls she recruited came to the UK in a lorry; she knew that from talking to them when they got here. The other part of her job was managing the girls once they arrived.

There was an air of menace about the man Jackson; behind his stylish clothes and cool manner she sensed a brutality that scared her. The other girls saw it too, though as far as she knew he had never hurt any of them.

There was another strange thing about him. In Katya's experience any owner would have occasionally sampled the goods; that was a right that came with the territory. But not Jackson; he never talked to any of the girls, let alone touched them, and he only occasionally had a word with Katya, just to check that the customers were happy and that there had been no complaints. There never had been and he seemed satisfied, but she still found him frightening.

Halliday's breezy manner had changed. His voice sounded ominous when he said, 'Your employer is about to find himself brought down a peg or two.'

'Oh?' said Katya.

'Yes. And you're going to help me do it.'

24

The two men sat in a dimly lit alcove on the raised dais at the back of the dining room. Slim's, named after Joe Slim, the Manchester United footballer who'd started the club eight years earlier, was in Wilmslow, ten miles or so south of Manchester. It was said that the Aston Martin dealership in Wilmslow sold the highest number of Aston Martins in the UK, so affluent was the local lifestyle. The room was crowded this evening, loud with music and the raised voices of a group of young men and girls at a long table. One of the two men looked around and smiled in satisfaction at the packed tables.

He was the owner, a tall black man known as Jackson. No one at the club ever used his first name. Jackson had acquired the club after Joe Slim was found, early one morning, face down in the Manchester Ship Canal. It was generally assumed that he had fallen in from the towpath while he was drunk, but no one seemed to know why he was down there and no witnesses had ever come forward.

Jackson dressed as smartly as his well-heeled clients, and tonight he wore an elegant blue suit, a cream-coloured woven shirt, and a subtly patterned Hermès tie. His companion was less flashy but his suit looked equally pricey; he had the air of a successful self-made business-man – the kind of man who paid in cash from a roll of banknotes held by a silver money clip.

'Good trip then?' asked the man who looked like a businessman.

Jackson gave him a quizzical look, then seemed to decide the question was innocent enough. 'Not bad. Though I had a spot of bother with the locals. I don't know what sparked them off but they seemed to be wondering what this uppity nigger was doing over there.' Jackson chuckled. 'They didn't find out though.'

'What were you doing over there? Was it business?'

Jackson laughed sarcastically. 'I wasn't in Berlin for my health, man. I was chasing up a new opportunity.'

'German girls?'

Jackson shook his head. 'I'm getting tired of that line of work – too many hassles. I'm thinking of branching out a bit.'

When he didn't elaborate, the other man said, 'Well, it must have been important if you took a chance like that.'

'What chance?'

The other man shrugged. 'You don't want to get Euro-pean police forces on your tail. They can be a bit nasty. Just watch out if you're up to something dodgy over there.'

Jackson said nothing at first. Then, 'I don't know if it was the police. I didn't see any uniforms.'

The other man said, 'But you got out all right?'

Jackson looked amused. 'I'm here, aren't I?'

'It looks that way to me,' said the other man. His role there was hard to place. He didn't act like a customer; he was too self-confident to be a dependant; yet the black man didn't seem the type to have friends.

'Anyway,' said Jackson, 'when are they coming?'

The businessman looked at his watch. 'Any time now.'

And as if in response, the maître d' came up to their table, looking agitated. 'Mr Jackson,' he said breathlessly. 'There are Immigration officers outside the back door. They're asking for you.'

Jackson raised his eyes but didn't seem surprised. 'Thank you, Émile.'

The maître d' went on, 'They have police officers with them. They say they want to check the papers of the girls.'

Jackson looked at his companion, who also didn't seem surprised by Émile's news. Jackson said to him, 'You better excuse me. I like to leave by the front door of the places I own.' He turned to Émile. 'This gentleman's my guest, so put our dinner on the house tab.'

'Of course, Mr Jackson. But what should I tell the police?'

'Tell them if they want to see me they need to make an appointment. Like my guest here,' he added with a smile. And then, without any show of haste, Jackson was out of the front door of the club in ten seconds, leaving Émile to deal with the officers of the law. Jackson's guest remained seated at the table, and after a moment signalled for a waiter and calmly ordered a large cognac.

25

SHE HAD SEEN HALLIDAY twice and each time he had pumped her about the upstairs operation at Slim's. She'd explained that she didn't know any details of the business; once a week Khoury, the accountant, showed up, and sat in the little room next to the cloakroom, where he went through all the tabs the girls had handed in. But he didn't talk to Katya about the business, and she certainly didn't know the turnover figures. She only knew that none of the girls, even the desperate ones, dared to try and skim any of the money. They handed it all over. That's how scared they were of Mr Jackson.

At their second meeting, Halliday had told her about the coming raid. 'Not a word to anyone,' he'd said. 'They'll be picking up the girls, and that'll include you. But don't worry – I'll see you right.'

And he had been true to his word – too true for Katya's liking. The police and Immigration officers had come in the back entrance, quite politely. This had seemed curious to her – she'd expected something like the movies, with armed officers breaking down the door, waving guns and shouting as they forced their way in. But instead they had waited outside, only four of them, in plain clothes, while the bouncer had called Émile, the maitre d' of the restaurant, who had come back and let them in.

It had all been tidily done, and despite the initial panic of the upstairs customers – that early in the evening, there had only been one group of stag-night revellers and a sad-looking man who said his wife had recently died – it was soon clear that the police were only interested in the accountant's room, where one of them had gone right away, and in the employees. None of them was English, of course, and none of them had papers as far as Katya knew – not a National Insurance card, a driving licence, or anything at all.

There had been seven girls working that night, including Katya (though her job was to supervise the goings on, not participate), and they had all been escorted out to the police van while Émile had wrung his hands and promised that he would have them out as soon as he could locate the club's lawyer.

It hadn't been quite that easy – by three in the morning there had still been no sign of the lawyer, and until the preliminary hearing scheduled for noon there didn't seem much chance of any of them getting released. It didn't matter much, since they were in a long row of adjacent cells, and the girls – however frightened they really were – took things in good part, calling out to each other, whistling to keep their spirits up, even briefly having a sing-along, until the duty sergeant came along and told them to pipe down. After which they curled up on their respective bunks and settled in for the night.

Which made Katya's release so noticeable, since alone among the seven of them she got called, by the same duty sergeant, and brought out from the cell. 'You're free to go,' the officer said grumpily, giving her back the small hand-bag she'd been made to hand over when they'd booked her and the other girls.

'What about my friends?'

'What about them?'

'Aren't they getting out too?'

The duty sergeant shook his head. 'Not as far as I know. What's the problem – do you want to go back to your cell?'

It would have been better if she had, Katya reflected, as she opened the front door to her home. Her housemates were still asleep and she crept in quietly. It wasn't that much later – or earlier depending on your time frame – than her usual return home after the club's closing.

She was worried about being the only one released. It must have been Halliday's doing, she decided. Hadn't he told her he would look after her? But she wished he hadn't done it this way. The other girls were bound to wonder what set her apart. They were loyal to her, but only up to a point. She did her best to look after them, and she could protect them from the drunks or abusers or the ones who didn't want to pay. But there was no disguising the nature of the operation upstairs in Slim's, and any girl who thought her duties stopped at serving drinks didn't last long – which meant an ignominious return to Dagestan, since none of them had papers that would enable them to find a proper job.

Katya knew this, since she had come to the UK origi-nally by the same route and found herself in the same posi-tion. Back in Dagestan the offer had seemed irresistible: *Come and be a hostess in a deluxe club in glamorous Manchester. Earn five times the wage you are earning now. Meet interesting powerful people and live a life of Western luxury.*

She knew the come-on lines by heart now, since she used them herself when she was sent home to recruit new girls. Occasionally when she was interviewing a girl who seemed particularly sweet and likeable, she tried to hint that perhaps the job wouldn't be quite what it seemed; that maybe the girl should have a long think about what was on offer before accepting. But Dagestan was dire; no one under the age of thirty could see their future in a positive light, and the girls she saw didn't want to know that the West was not the land of milk and honey; that men could be just as exploitative in Manchester as in Makhachkala; that the money on offer would go mainly to pay the rent charged for their squalid shared rooms, or in 'fees' for nebulous services to the owner of Slim's.

Now she hesitated for a moment in the hall, wondering if she should have a cup of tea, then decided to go upstairs. Normally she would head straight to bed, but she felt grimy after her time in the cells, and went and ran a bath, closing the bathroom door so as not to wake the other girls in the house. She was pleasantly surprised to see that Michele, the French girl who always had a bath late at night, had for once cleaned the bath after using it.

Katya lay and soaked for a while, wondering if by now the other girls had been let out. She hoped so, as otherwise she knew they would be wondering why Katya had been released. And if word got round it would be certain to be picked up by Émile – he was cat-like, that man, always lurking nearby, avid for gossip. And Émile would never keep news like that to himself, which meant he would tell ... Katya shuddered, and quickly got out of the bath.

She managed to fall asleep, half waking when the other residents of the little house got up and went to work, then falling asleep again. When she finally rose it was just past noon.

Downstairs the kitchen was in its usual post-breakfast disarray – used cereal bowls and half-drunk mugs of tea and coffee. She opened the back door to air the place and started tidying up – her housemates were younger than Katya, and, just as at work, she looked after them. Maybe someday she'd have her own children to look after, but in the meantime she did not mind looking after girls younger and less worldly than herself. Michele in particular seemed in need of sisterly advice, especially when she expressed interest in ditching her boring secretarial job and coming to work at Slim's, something Katya had so far managed to steer her away from.

She had just finished with the leftover dishes when she heard the postman push the mail through the letter box slot. No point rushing to see it; bills and more bills would be lying on the mat. But a minute later she thought she heard a tap at the front door, so this time she left the kitchen and went out into the hall. She opened the front door, but there was nobody there – she must have imagined the noise. Then she bent down and picked up the post, examining it as she walked back to the kitchen. There was one envelope for her, which she was opening when she came into the kitchen again, not paying much attention. It took a moment to notice the man now sitting at the kitchen table, and she jumped when she saw him.

'You startled me,' she said, feeling flustered at first, then fearful as she realised who it was.

'Did I now?' said Lester Jackson mildly. 'Maybe you were expecting the police instead of me.'

'Why would I be expecting them?' Katya managed to say.

Jackson shrugged. 'There has to be someone in the force you're friends with. Seeing as you were the first one sprung last night. Why don't you sit down and tell me who your friend is?'

He gestured at the chair next to him, and Katya stiffened. 'I would, Mr Jackson, but I have to go out now . . .'

Jackson was smiling as he shook his head. 'I don't think so. Sit down, Katya,' and there was something so steely in his voice that reluctantly she did.

'Now,' Jackson continued, his voice mild again. 'Was it DCI Lansley or DCI Robertson? Or is it your friend from Special Branch – maybe Detective Halliday?'

When the French girl Michele came back from work later that day she was surprised to find the front door of the house unlocked. She went in and called out for Katya, who was usually at home at this time, getting dressed for work at the club. Michele didn't care what Katya said; Slim's sounded fun, and a thousand times more exciting than her own job, typing the correspondence of a fat and unsuccessful property developer. She was going to tackle Katya again about it; Michele knew she was attractive enough to work at Slim's – it was only the older woman who was standing in her way.

'Katya,' she called out, but there was no reply. Funny that, thought Michele, as she walked towards the kitchen at the back of the house. She couldn't remember the last time Katya wasn't at home when she came back from work.

And sure enough, Katya was at home – and in the kitchen too. It was when Michele found her that the screaming started.

26

DINNER ALONE. GOD KNOWS, Martin was used to it, but it seemed strange to have seen Liz only so briefly in Paris, considering how close they had become. He knew that she found it awkward to be working so closely with him, and particularly to be the cause of delaying what she knew Martin had been working for years to achieve, the trial and conviction of Antoine Milraud. He saw that she had been relieved to go straight back to London the other evening after seeing Milraud, and though he understood the reason why, it made him sad.

He hoped the slight chill in their relationship was only temporary. Even in the fog that seemed to distort everything connected with Milraud, he knew that Liz promised a happy life ahead and Milraud only represented the past.

He was annoyed when the phone rang on the table in his study and broke into his reverie. It turned out to be his young colleague from the safe house in Montreuil, Jacques Thibault.

'Yes? What is it?' he asked sharply.

'He's had an email.'

Seurat was alert now. 'What did it say?'

'It's calling him to another meeting – in London. It's

encoded in the form he described when your British colleague was here. He says it's from the Arab.'

So Liz was right, and the UK connection was proving key. 'When's the meeting and where?'

'Two days from now. We're working out exactly where but I wanted to tell you straightaway. The instructions are in the form of coordinates disguised as sports scores. As soon as we've unzipped it, I'll let you know.'

'Do you know the time?'

'Four o'clock in the afternoon.'

Dusk at this time of year, which would make surveillance of the meeting more difficult. 'I'll let London know. Contact me as soon as you've worked out all the details.'

'OK. I'll get back to you shortly.'

Young Thibault was a computer genius, a real geek, thought Martin. Let's hope he can get more out of that message than the time and place of the meeting.

27

WHEN THE ALL-CLEAR CAME through from the A4 team looking for counter-surveillance, Milraud was let out of the car. He walked along Regent's Park Road, and turned left through the open gate of Primrose Hill Park. Eight pairs of eyes watched him go.

The light was fading now after a bright late-autumn day. It was 3.45 in the afternoon and it would be practically dark by 4.30 at this time of the year. Maureen Hayes, sitting in an apparently closed up and deserted park-keepers' shed, was observing Milraud's progress across the park. His light-coloured raincoat made him easy to spot as he sat down on a bench at the top of the hill. She didn't envy him sitting out there on this chilly evening.

His was the only bench occupied; the wind was getting up and everyone else in the park seemed to be hurrying home. A woman in a fake fur coat was dawdling along, holding a little plastic bag in one hand and apparently urging the terrier she had on an extending lead to do his business so they could leave. Three small boys in school uniform went out of the gate chattering, one holding a football under his arm. A faint aroma of burning leaves seeped through the wooden slats of Maureen's hut.

For a second the setting sun caught a window of one of the tall glass buildings somewhere in the City to the south, and a flash of brilliance lit up Milraud's figure, sitting alone at the top of the hill, and momentarily blinded Maureen as she peered at him through her binoculars.

When she could see again, she noticed several people were walking into the park through the same gate Milraud had used. Perhaps an underground train had just come in or maybe they'd got off a bus. Then, as she watched, a young man separated from the others and turned up the path that led to the seat where Milraud still waited.

Could this be Zara, as Milraud's Arab contact was now codenamed? She had been told to expect a tall, thin young Arab, dressed scruffily like a student. But this young man was wearing a dark business suit and carrying a briefcase and a rolled-up copy of the *Evening Standard*. He was tall and thin all right, and dark-skinned, but he looked more like a City worker returning to his flat in this expensive part of London than a student or a jihadi.

The man was passing Milraud without a glance, when he suddenly stopped, and seemed to be admiring the view. To Maureen's practised eye he was looking for signs of surveillance. Then he stepped behind Milraud's bench and seemed to be rubbing his hands up and down the Frenchman's back. Maureen stared at them through her binoculars, thinking that in other circumstances this would look like some kind of gay encounter.

The newcomer slowly circled around the bench and sat down at the far end from Milraud. There was a pause and the two men seemed to be talking. Then Milraud got up and took off his raincoat, folding it and laying it on the bench. Again the smart young man appeared to be stroking Milraud's body, his chest this time. Whatever was going on? After a short time, Milraud got up, put his rain-coat on again and the two men conversed, apparently calmly. After a further ten minutes, the young man stood up and walked away down the hill, in the opposite direction from which he had come, and Milraud retraced his steps to the waiting car.

As Zara headed for the far gate, Maureen alerted the Ops Room, and as he left the park six of Maureen's colleagues were on his tail.

28

L IZ HAD HAD A bit of a struggle persuading the Home Office that she had enough on Lester Jackson to justify a warrant to intercept his communications. On the face of it, a small-time Manchester club owner with no criminal record, let alone any proved involvement in terrorist-related activity, did not present any threat to national security. She had argued strongly that his covert contact with Milraud, a man well known to the French as an arms supplier, in an apparent plot to supply weapons to a group of jihadis, justified the warrant. Eventually she had won the day, but the warrant was to be reviewed after two weeks and if by then no information indicating a national security threat had emerged, it would be cancelled. She had come away from the meeting in Whitehall feeling disgruntled. Two weeks was a very short time in which to prove anything.

She was reading the first transcripts when her phone buzzed – an internal call. She picked it up, impatient at the interruption.

'Liz, you'd better come down.' It was Wally Woods in the A4 Operations room.

'What's happened?'

'Your Zara operation. The meeting took place and we've

got the Frenchman back safely in our custody. That's all OK, but we're following Zara and I need to know how you want us to handle it.'

'Give me five minutes?'

'Make it three.'

She rang off and looked at the transcripts again. At 16:45 the day before, Jackson had taken a call on his mobile. The caller had been located two thousand miles away, though they still hadn't tracked the signal down specifically. The conversation had been in English, with the caller speaking fluently but with what sounded like a Russian accent. The transcript read:

CALLER: It's Tag here.

JACKSON: What's the state of play?

CALLER: It's ready to go.

JACKSON: There may be some more to come. But for now, have you got everything?

CALLER: Yeah, all of it.

JACKSON: Twenty pieces?

CALLER: (Impatiently) Yes, yes. They all look good to me, though I'm no expert.

JACKSON: Can you confirm the route?

CALLER: Same as last time.

JACKSON: Why not a different port?

CALLER: That's up to me, my friend. Once I deliver, the shipment's all yours. Until then it's my worry.

JACKSON: Have you got a date?

CALLER: Not yet, but it won't be long now. We have some snow so it is hard to be more specific than that.

JACKSON: I need 12 hours' warning.

CALLER: I can do better than that – I'll give you 24.

JACKSON: OK, I'll hold you to that.

Liz shook her head, trying to make sense of it, then got up and walked to the lifts in the centre of Thames House. As she went, she thought about the transcript. Given Jackson's background, it would be fair to assume the conversation was about human trafficking – the goods being East European women shipped over on a lorry for service in places like Slim's.

But something was wrong with that – Liz simply didn't believe twenty would be coming in one shipment, one lorry perhaps. Not to work at Slim's at any rate, where Halliday had explained only half a dozen women were on the game upstairs in the club. And even if Jackson was involved in trafficking women for other places, *twenty pieces* seemed an improbably large number at one time and an odd term ('pieces') to use, even if the caller was not speaking in his native language and was trying to be discreet. And wasn't it rather strange to say he was no expert, if he was talking about women?

So what on earth was Jackson importing? If it was guns, why only twenty, if they were then going to be re-sent to . . . God knows where? Was this what Milraud had been talking to him about?

She pondered all this as she walked along to the A4 Ops Room. Inside Wally Woods and two colleagues sat, headphones on, in front of a row of TV monitors. Wally was talking into the microphone on the desk and waved her to the battered old leather sofa just inside the door that was kept specially for visiting case officers. The Ops Room was Wally's domain and no one was welcome when an operation was going on except by invitation.

'Which side of Pentonville Road?' he asked the microphone.

Over the speaker a voice Liz recognised as Daley, a

veteran surveillance officer, replied, 'South side and walking fast.'

'I have him,' said another voice, more muffled.

Wally kept his eye on the screen but spoke to Liz. 'This
Zara's led us a pretty dance. He walked all the way to Great
Portland Street station and went into the Tube. We had to
rush in there, but then the bugger came out again and
caught a bus.'

'Do you think he saw you?'

Wally shook his head. 'Don't think so. You told us to
take extra care and we have. I just think he's been trained,
and he's being extra careful too.'

'Where did he get off?'

'In Euston Road, by the British Library. He hung
about for a bit – I think he wanted to see who else got off
the bus. None of us was on it – I've got three cars on this
so he was easy enough to follow. It must be the only time
in my life I've been grateful for the traffic on the Euston
Road.'

As they spoke, video pictures appeared on one of the TV
screens of Zara walking up the Pentonville Road, just past
King's Cross. It was a hazy picture, taken through the
window of one of the surveillance cars, but Liz could
clearly see the tall, dark-suited figure striding along the
pavement. She watched as it turned and moved towards
the entrance of a large building set back from the road. A
group of young people were talking by the front door.

Maureen Hayes's voice came through the speaker. 'Zara
entering a building. It looks like some sort of college.
Groups of young people outside.'

Wally replied, 'Send Tia up to check it out.'

And as Liz watched, a young woman in a hooded jacket
and headscarf walked to the front of the building. She

threaded her way through the groups of chattering young people, went up the steps and inside.

She was gone about five minutes, and when she came out she said, 'It's called Dinwiddy House.'

Wally turned to Liz, who shrugged. Tia was saying, 'It's a hostel for students at London University. Most of them are at SOAS – School of African and Oriental Studies.'

It made sense. Zara was young, Middle Eastern, like any number of SOAS students.

'Any sign of Zara?' asked Wally.

'No. There's a common room and bar on the ground floor but I couldn't see him in there, though it was pretty crowded and I might have missed him. But I think he went upstairs. That's where their rooms are.'

Wally turned his swivel chair to face Liz. 'You want us to ask around a bit? Try and find out if he lives there?'

Liz shook her head. 'Too risky, especially if he comes downstairs again when you're asking questions. But I'd like an eye kept overnight, just in case he's only visiting. Maybe he's got a girlfriend there. Can you do that?'

Wally nodded. 'It'll be another team but I'll make sure they're well briefed. What do you want us to do if he leaves? Follow him?'

Liz nodded. 'Yes, please. And keep Peggy posted. I've got to go out now to debrief Milraud.' She stood up. 'Thanks, Wally. That's a great help. Now I've got some chance of finding out who this Zara is.'

Two hours later, after Peggy had made a series of urgent phone calls resulting in a senior university administrator being rooted out of his home to consult the file in his office, Liz knew. Zara did indeed live in the hostel known as Dinwiddy House, and was studying for a Masters degree in International Relations at SOAS. He was a Yemeni called Samara and was in the UK on a temporary students' visa. The address given on his visa application and supplied to the college was in Sana'a, the capital of Yemen. He hadn't drawn himself to the attention of the college authorities in any way and a search of the records in MI5 and MI6 came up 'No Trace'. But then, thought Liz ruefully, if this guy was any good, that's what you'd expect.

29

The Royal Standard Hotel was in an undistin-guished street between Victoria Station and Buckingham Palace. Though it billed itself as 'situated in the shadow of Buckingham Palace', it was in fact much nearer to Victoria Station. An anonymous sort of place, part of a small chain, it provided everything a mid-level businessman or official visiting London might require: wi-fi, cable TV with 'adult' films, in-room tea and coffee, minibar and even an ironing board and iron. All of its 361 rooms were furnished identically, and carpeted and upholstered in variations on the colour theme of beige and maroon.

All in all it was the sort of place where people could come and go without anyone taking much notice. Which is why, a few years ago, Liz Carlyle's colleagues had identified it as perfect for the sort of rendezvous they occasionally needed to conduct. The manager had been recruited as what was called a 'facilities agent', to provide a room or rooms as required, without asking any questions about who might occupy them or what might go on in them. In return he received a present at Christmas and the satisfaction of knowing that he was helping Her Majesty's Government.

On this occasion, two pairs of interconnecting rooms had been booked on different floors. In one of the pair on the eighth floor, Liz Carlyle was sitting, waiting for Dicky Soames, the burly A4 officer and member of the team 'minding' Milraud while he was in London, to produce his charge, so she could find out what had happened at the meeting on Primrose Hill.

There was a light tap on the door and a deep cockney voice said, 'Here we are. OK to come in?' Milraud entered followed closely by Soames, who closed the door firmly behind him and put the lock on.

'I'll be next door, if you want anything,' said Soames, and he went into the other room leaving the intercommunicating door slightly ajar.

Liz motioned the Frenchman to one of the two chairs. She thought how tired and strained he looked. Much more so than when she'd first met him in the safe house in Montreuil.

'Would you like something to drink?' she asked. 'There's tea or coffee, or a drink from the minibar if you'd prefer.'

Milraud shook his head. '*Non, merci,*' he said shortly. He had kept on his mackintosh, and he looked chilled, even though it was warm in the room.

Liz switched the kettle on, and as she waited for it to boil, she pointed out of the window at the coloured lights strung across the street. 'Christmas starts earlier every year,' she said cheerfully. Milraud glanced out and nodded, but he seemed a million miles away. Liz took her time making coffee for herself and chatting inconsequentially, hoping to relax the man a little.

She sipped her coffee and winced. 'You made the right decision,' she said, but Milraud's smile was perfunctory. He was clearly impatient for the debrief to begin.

'So how did it go?' asked Liz, sitting down at last.

Milraud shrugged. 'Much as expected.'

'Was he concerned about security? I mean, since your Paris meeting was aborted because of the surveillance.'

Milraud sat up. 'Yes. He was worried that I might have been followed and he checked me out for a microphone. I assured him he need not worry; that I was once an intelligence officer and I know about these things.' He gave a wry smile. 'I explained that I had gone to Paris and Berlin under different passports and I was at least twelve hours ahead of anyone hunting me.' He grimaced; they both knew Milraud had thought this himself.

'Do you think he suspects you?'

'In his position I certainly would – I never trust my customers, so why should they trust me? But when he pressed me about being spotted in Paris, I told him I had as much right to worry about him as he had about me. That shut him up.'

'So after that, what did you discuss? He called the meeting, didn't he? What did he want to say to you?'

'He wanted to add to his order. That was for firearms, as you know.'

'What else does he want?'

'It's a bit surprising. He wants grenades – two dozen of them.'

'Really?' Liz was astonished. The whole business seemed surprising, as it was generally assumed that the jihadi groups fighting in the Arab Spring countries had no difficulty acquiring weapons from their supporters, but this requirement was even more unexpected.

'That's right. And then the oddest thing of all – he wants more ammunition for the weapons he'd ordered. Not more weapons; just more ammunition. Twenty thousand rounds.'

'*Twenty thousand*?' Liz could not contain her astonishment. It sounded as if Zara was equipping an infantry battalion. And why so much ammunition for only twenty weapons?

'I agree it doesn't make sense, unless he already has a lot of weapons at his disposal. But I didn't have that impression from our first meeting. It's quite peculiar.'

Milraud looked uneasy; Liz sensed there was something on his mind. She waited, but he said no more. Eventually she asked, 'Let's come back again to this black man you met in Berlin. What did he want?'

'I was asked to meet him. I was told he wanted to see who was involved in the deal. I was told he has not done this type of business before.'

'What did he say?'

'Almost nothing. He just asked about my business – how long I'd been supplying, what parts of the world I supplied, that sort of thing.'

'What did you tell him?'

'Very little, but it seemed to satisfy him. Then he rushed off. He was very jumpy.'

He still looked uncomfortable. Then he shrugged and returned to the subject of the meeting with Zara. 'Anyway, I wasn't sure how you wanted me to play it today. So I told him that I would check if I could get the goods he wanted in time and get back to him. He pressed me, so I had to promise to let him know tomorrow.'

'How are you to do that?'

'By email.'

She knew from Seurat that the French were in control of the email traffic.

Milraud asked, 'What do you want me to say?'

'Can you supply the extra things he wants in time?'

153

'Yes. I only have to email my supplier.'

'Where is he?'

'In Bulgaria.'

Liz didn't hesitate. 'Do it then and tell him you can fulfil the supplementary order. But also tell him you need to know precisely where and how it should be delivered. Press him for details.'

She looked at Milraud intently. He might have been surprised by Zara's request, but she was certain he was holding something back. It didn't make sense that he knew nothing about Jackson. Milraud was acting as if Jackson was Zara's contact and he had nothing to do with him, but she was sure that wasn't the case. Maybe if young Thibault over in Paris could hack into their back email exchanges the full truth would emerge – and a lot sooner than if she waited for Milraud to come clean.

30

IT WAS ALMOST EIGHT when Liz left the hotel. Milraud would be spending the night there in the other pair of interconnecting rooms, under the watchful eye of Dicky Soames and his colleagues, before returning to Paris with them as close escorts. There was no way Liz was going to be responsible for losing the man whom Martin Seurat had spent so many years hunting.

In the dark, Thames House looked like a lit-up half-filled egg box: unoccupied offices were dark, but enough officers worked late hours to dot the heavy masonry façade with the lights of their midnight oil. In her office Liz found a handwritten slip from Peggy: *Halliday rang. Said call him any time. He has news.*

When she reached Halliday there was the background noise of a raucous party going on. 'Hang on a minute,' he shouted. Gradually the noise subsided, until she could hear only traffic whizzing past in the background, tyres wet from rain. Halliday must have stepped outside from whatever club he was visiting. 'Sorry about that,' he said.

'It's Liz Carlyle; I got a message to ring you. But I don't want to interrupt the party.'

'I'm working, believe it or not. I'm drinking vodka and tonic without the vodka, and waiting for the barman to offer to sell me three grams of coke. I thought I'd better take your call outside. I've got some news for you. Not good, I'm afraid.'

'What's happened?'

'We raided Slim's with Immigration – that's the club owned by Lester Jackson. We arrested half a dozen girls working upstairs – they were "hostesses" but they were doing more than serving drinks. All from somewhere in Eastern Europe most likely but they didn't have a set of papers between them.

'Normally that would have been enough to close the place down, and maybe let me squeeze our high-flying friend Mr Jackson a bit. But he wasn't there and he didn't seem to care, and I now know why. He had a leading brief go to the lock-up by breakfast time, and bob's your uncle, it turned out all the girls had proper papers and valid passports – the solicitor claimed he'd been holding them on the girls' behalf.'

'What sort of passports?'

'Bulgarian – every one. And now that it's in the EU that means they can work here, come and go as they please. Not that I believe for a minute their papers were kosher. None of those girls speaks Bulgarian.'

'How do you know? Do you speak it?'

Halliday laughed. 'No. But one of the cleaners at the police station is from Sofia. She said the girls couldn't understand a word she said.'

'But you had to let them go anyway?'

'Yes. No choice. They're all living in Manchester, so it's not up to me. I would have tried to work the prostitution angle, but Manchester SB couldn't be bothered. These days it's hard to convict unless you show the girls involved are either under duress or illegal immigrants. None of the girls would make a complaint so we couldn't do either.'

'Too bad,' said Liz, though she wasn't very surprised. Jackson seemed unlikely to jeopardise his club by laying himself open to a single police raid.

Halliday paused and Liz heard the sound of a bus passing. As it died down Halliday went on, 'That isn't good news, but there's worse to come. I had a source in the club – an older woman who functioned as a kind of "mother" to the working girls. Name of Katya.'

'You "had" a source?'

'Katya was found strangled in the kitchen of her digs two mornings ago. The uniform thought it was a burglary gone wrong but it doesn't ring true to me. There was no sign of forced entry, nothing taken. One of her flatmates found her when she came home from work.'

'Do you see a connection with the club?'

'Yes I do, not that I can prove it.' He hesitated, then finally said, 'The thing is, when we arrested the girls we took Katya in, too. But she was released hours before the others were. I don't know why – she was the only one sprung early. It would have looked peculiar. I didn't ask for her to be let go, that's for sure.'

Liz sensed he was very upset by this. She said encouragingly, 'Maybe Forensics will find something.'

'I don't think so. The killer was very careful. Her place was in the Greater Manchester area and the CID guys there have made it a low priority.'

'Why's that?'

'Either because they reckon it's a one-off and won't lead anywhere, or because they know where it leads and have been warned off.'

'What does that mean?' She didn't like the sound of it at all.

'Ask your friend in Manchester Special Branch.'

He's not my friend, thought Liz, but there was no point in saying this. She asked, 'This woman Katya, did she have a Bulgarian passport too?'

'I don't know what passport she had, but I know she wasn't from Bulgaria.'

'Then where was she from?'

'One of those funny ex-Soviet countries – the ones that end in "stan". Hers was called Dagestan. At least that's what she told me. Never heard of it myself. Have you?'

'Yes,' said Liz flatly. She had heard of it quite recently. 'Listen, I wonder if you can help me with something.'

'Just say the word,' said Halliday so breezily that Liz wondered whether perhaps there had been some vodka in his tonic after all.

'You remember I told you that we'd learned that Jackson was connected to an arms dealer.'

'Yes, I do.'

'Well, we've now had confirmation that he's involved.' She hesitated, then decided she had to trust him – so far at least, he had been completely straight with her, unlike her old friend McManus. 'I think there might be a connection between his role in this arms deal we're investigating and his usual business at the club – bringing in the women, I mean.'

'What kind of connection?'

'Not sure yet.' Liz was working largely on intuition now; she couldn't give Halliday any specifics because she didn't have any. She went on, 'That's where you could be of help. Can you keep an even closer eye than usual on what goes on at Slim's?'

'Yeah, I can do that. But what am I looking for?'

'I know it sounds rather pathetic but I can't actually tell you. Anything that looks stranger than usual. It's about bringing stuff into the country. Importing stuff that could be arms but it probably wouldn't look like that.'

'If you seriously think he's into weaponry, it would probably be wise to run it by Manchester SB, just to be diplomatic.'

'Do you have to? I thought you said Slim's was on your patch?'

There was a pause, then Halliday said, 'No, I don't have to if you're not going to.' He gave a short laugh. 'I see you don't trust McManus either.'

The overnight team outside Dinwiddy House had had a busier time than expected. At twenty past seven in the evening Zara had emerged, dressed now in a black hoody and jeans and carrying a small backpack. He had walked to Euston Station and after collecting a ticket from a pre-paid ticket machine, boarded a train for Manchester Piccadilly. Two of the team had accompanied him, while the Ops Room had dispatched another team to Manchester to be ready to meet the train, in case he stayed on all the way to Manchester.

Which he did. At Manchester the original team handed him over to the new team, which went with him, first on the metro to Manchester Victoria station and then on a local train, from which he got off at Eccles.

By this time it was past eleven o'clock and Liz in bed was on a conference call link to the Ops Room in Thames House. 'Eccles,' she said. 'What on earth can he be going there for? Does anyone know anything about Eccles?'

Peggy, in her flat in Muswell Hill, a few miles further

north from Liz, was in on the call and also searching the internet. 'Eccles is part of Salford, about four miles from Manchester. The interesting thing is that it has quite a large Yemeni community. There have been Yemenis in Eccles since the 1940s,' she read out from a website. 'Large numbers came in in the 1950s. There's a Yemeni Community Association. Perhaps he has friends there.'

Meanwhile the team in Manchester was reporting that they had followed Zara to a small terraced house, No. 31 Ashby Road. The door had been opened by a lady, probably in her late sixties, in traditional Muslim dress, who had kissed Zara and welcomed him into the house. They hoped Liz did not require overnight watch on the house, as it was a very quiet neighbourhood and therefore it would be difficult to remain unobserved. Liz had agreed that they could stand down for the night; it seemed most unlikely that anything was imminent. She and Peggy would meet in Thames House at seven in the morning and decide what to do next about Zara.

31

Miles woke up slightly hungover, the after-effect of a long evening at the French Embassy, and discovered that his mobile phone was ringing. 'Hello,' he said tentatively; the screen read 'number unknown'.

'Ah, the croaky voice of a man who's had a good night out.'

It was Bruno Mackay. At the best of times, Miles felt a mild antipathy towards his British Intelligence counterpart, and right now there was a jauntiness about the man he could do without.

'What can I do for you, Bruno?' he said shortly.

'I've had a communiqué from London. It seems there's been some progress. Better if we talk face to face, old man? I'll see you at Sharim's café in an hour.'

Miles made it in fifty minutes, feeling slightly revived after a long shower and a shave. He drove cautiously into the old city, keeping an eye on his rear-view mirror; after their experience on the road from *Donation*'s farm, he felt that his car might be a marked vehicle. Parking in a Diplomatic parking bay, under the eye of a policeman, he walked along the pavement until he saw the wide awning of Sharim's – and Bruno, in a white cotton jacket and pink tie, sitting at an outside table.

Miles joined him. Bruno gave a commanding wave and a waiter scurried over with a fresh pot of coffee and a cup for Miles, who watched while the man poured out the syrupy local brew. Miles added two sugar cubes from the little clay pot on the table. As he stirred them in with a tiny wooden spoon, he said to Bruno, 'So what's the news?'

'London's identified the guy they sent the photographs of. The one at the meet in the Luxembourg Gardens that we were going to ask *Donation* about. His name is Samara and he's Yemeni. He's doing a Master's degree at London University, the School of Oriental and African Studies, SOAS we call it. On the surface he looks perfectly legit. Only quite obviously he's not. I've been asked to check out his credentials here, and I thought you might be able to help me.'

Why? wondered Miles, but then Bruno said, 'You're a bit better placed to ask, I think. If you get my drift.'

And Miles now understood. Official Yemeni–American relations were blossoming. A cynic might say that the United States was propping up a weak local government to further its own interests, but for whatever reason, a request for help from the American Embassy was likely to get a quicker, more favourable reaction than if the Brits had asked.

'It may take me a little while,' Miles said.

'Not a problem, old boy. We've got a couple of hours on London as it is. They'll still be fast asleep.'

Miles's contact was a middle-level officer in the Yemeni Intelligence Service called Arack, who had been a graduate student at the University of Southern California. It was never entirely clear what he had studied there, and he seemed to know the beaches north of Santa Monica rather better than the classrooms of USC. But he was a useful contact, since the Yemeni bureaucracy was both legendarily cumbersome and unreceptive to foreign approaches, and Arack was always willing to help the Americans, provided the request was relatively easy to fulfil and his reward readily forthcoming. He was known to Miles and his colleagues, semi-derisorily, as 'Sweet Tooth' because of his love of sugary cakes and desserts, which made payment for his services unusually easy.

Miles and Arack met now for coffee and a baklava-like concoction in a café near the Yemeni Ministry of Defence. Arack listened sympathetically while Miles explained what he was looking for. 'We just want confirmation that the personal details we have for this student are correct and that he is known to your authorities and is in London legitimately.'

'Is there any reason to think he is not?' asked Arack mildly.

'No,' said Miles, though it didn't take a genius to realise there had to be a question about the 'student', or else Miles wouldn't be checking him out. 'It's just a formality.'

Arack nodded, happy to hear that this was not something he would have to call to the attention of his superiors. 'Naturally births and deaths are registered here, as they are in the United States, and there is a department for that purpose. But you might find its office difficult to navigate. Let me make a few calls and get back to you. Give me the details please, and I would be grateful if you could ask the waiter to come over.'

Arack rang Miles just before dinner. There was a shortage of eligible Western women in Sana'a and Miles was about to have dinner with one of them – a new shapely secretary called, appropriately, Marilyn, who had come out to work in the Embassy the month before. He waited impatiently as Arack went through the standard Middle Eastern formalities, applied rigorously even to a phone call. How was Miles? As if they hadn't met five hours before. Was not the weather good this day, and would it not be fine throughout the evening? At last Arack came to the point, though even then he spoke elliptically. 'I am afraid I have surprising news for you, my friend.'

'Really?'

'We have no record of this man, you see.'

'What do you mean?'

'Just what I have said. There is no birth certificate, no record of an education and no passport.'

'Could the name be spelled differently?'

'I have pursued all possible variants. More important, the residential address you say this fellow gave in Sana'a does exist but . . . it is a bicycle shop. I can assure you, there is no citizen with the particulars you supplied.'

Miles mind was no longer on his date with Marilyn. 'OK. Thank you for checking this for me.'

'My pleasure. I wish you luck finding this gentleman. But I can assure you, it will not be in the Yemen.'

Damn, thought Miles as he put down the phone, then picked it up to cancel his date. He hoped Marilyn wouldn't be too disappointed – though he was, especially since he realised there would be a further call to make. It looked like he would be having dinner with Bruno Mackay instead.

32

SINCE PEGGY KINSOLVING HAD joined MI5, and particularly since she had been working with Liz Carlyle, she had found out a lot of things about herself that she didn't know. At school and university she had been a quiet, studious, and rather shy girl. She loved acquiring information, categorising it, sorting it out so she could access it and apply her considerable intelligence and her almost photographic memory to it.

These were the qualities that had taken her from her grammar school in the north of England to Oxford, where as predicted she had obtained a good 2:1 degree. No one, including Peggy herself, had ever thought she had the intellectual confidence and verve that makes a first-class scholar.

Her social life at university had followed the same cautious pattern. She had joined a few societies of the intellectual type and one day, showing much daring, she had gone with a friend to a meeting of the college dramatic society, who were looking for backstage staff. Everyone in the society, it seemed, wanted to be on the stage and in the limelight, and no one was prepared to do the behind-the-scenes work. Peggy thought that job would suit her very well, and it did. She brought her formidable information-sorting skills to organising the props, the scenery, the sound effects; eventually she became completely indispensable to any performance.

She would stand in the wings, noticing every detail, knowing everyone's part better than they did themselves and making sure that at least from a technical point of view the performance was perfect. She loved the drama but only from behind the scenes. She could never be persuaded to take even the smallest role on the stage. The thought of appearing before an audience petrified her.

Satisfied with her 2:1 and pursuing what she thought was her métier, Peggy had taken a job in a small research library, working on sorting and cataloguing the papers of an obscure female Victorian novelist. But after a couple of years she had begun to find the work dull and unsatisfying, and her social life in a small town where she knew no one was practically non-existent.

So when she saw an advertisement for a research post in a government department in London, with some hesitation she applied and found herself working as a research assistant in MI6. A chance secondment to MI5 a few years later led to her working with Liz Carlyle. At first her work had been purely research, but Liz had seen something in her young assistant that made her think there was more to Peggy than met the eye, and she had gradually encouraged her to take on a more upfront role.

At first Liz had given her some simple interviews to do, then she had moved her on to situations where Peggy had to play a role, to pretend to be someone other than an MI5 officer.

This was when they both realised that Peggy had a penchant for acting a part. Though she would still rather die than go on stage and act before an audience, put in a one-to-one situation she could convincingly present herself as anything from a housewife to a hedge-fund manager – and enjoy doing it.

Today she was an electoral registration officer. She'd dressed primly: a mid-length blue skirt, matching tights, sensible shoes, and dark paisley shirt under a navy blue blazer. She carried a clipboard and pen, and with her glasses firmly in place on her nose looked entirely like the local authority bureaucrat she was pretending to be.

At two o'clock that afternoon she knocked on the door of 29 Ashby Road. Most of the area seemed to be lived in by Muslim families, but she knew from the electoral register that this house was occupied by a Mrs Margaret Donovan. The door was opened by a large red-faced woman whom she guessed to be in her early seventies.

'What can I do for you, luv?'

'Mrs Donovan, is it?' asked Peggy, and she explained that she was from the electoral office, confirming the names of the occupants of voting age in each house along the street.

'Wasn't there someone here a few months ago about that?' the woman asked.

Peggy sighed. 'Probably. There seems to be a lot of duplication in this job. I've only been at it three weeks, but you're not the first one to tell me it's all been done before.'

The woman smiled sympathetically, and just then the phone in the hall rang. 'I'd better get that,' she said. Peggy started to make her excuses but Mrs Donovan waved her in. 'Come inside and close the door before you catch your death.' While she went to the phone, Peggy waited patiently in the hall. The woman wasn't long. 'Bloody tele sales,' she announced, coming back into the hall.

'They are a nuisance,' said Peggy, shivering slightly. It

was a raw day outside, and in her anxiety to look authentic she had not put enough clothes on. The weather had been hovering between autumn and winter for several days, but today for the first time you could sense the months of real cold ahead.

'You look like you're freezing, dearie. Come into the kitchen and have a cuppa and warm yourself.'

Peggy didn't even pretend to protest, foreseeing a golden opportunity to gossip about the neighbours. As the kettle warmed on the gas hob, she looked around the room, which had family photographs all along the top of a sideboard. 'Your children?' she offered.

'All five of them. Grown up now,' the woman added sadly, 'and my poor Leonard gone ten years now. Still, mustn't grumble.'

'Have you been in this house a long time then?'

Mrs Donovan gave a little laugh. 'Each one of my children was born and raised here. It will be forty years come October.'

'Gosh,' said Peggy appreciatively. 'I suppose the neighbourhood's changed a bit since then.'

The woman gave Peggy a sideways look. 'Not for the worse,' she said firmly.

'Not at all,' said Peggy. 'I can see that. It looks a fine street to me.'

The woman relaxed. 'It's just that so many left when the Asians came. Not me, mind; I wasn't going anywhere. I always said, there's good and bad – white, black, and all the in-betweens. Why should I up sticks if people treat me right? Who cares what colour they are?'

'Who indeed?' said Peggy, taken aback by the old woman's almost aggressive tolerance and the implication that she – Peggy – might not agree.

The old lady went to the stove and poured boiling water from the kettle into two waiting mugs. 'Milk?' she asked and Peggy nodded. When she brought the mugs over she pushed the sugar bowl along the kitchen table, and Peggy shook her head and pushed it back.

They sipped in quiet contentment for a moment. Then Peggy said casually, 'You've got good neighbours then?'

'The best,' Mrs Donovan declared. 'The Desais live on that side,' she said, and proceeded to talk about the Hindu family next door. Peggy nodded as the old woman took her through three generations of Desai family tree, little realising that her listener was entirely uninterested in them, and was only waiting for her to talk about her neighbours on the other side.

Peggy's cup had been refilled by the time she felt able to ask about the other neighbouring family. 'Mrs Atiyah,' Mrs Donovan said, and her face seemed to light up. 'Isn't it a lovely name?'

'Very pretty. What kind of name is it?'

'The family was from Yemen, luv. What we used to call Aden before they went and got themselves independent. Though then there was a lot of trouble, and that's when the Atiyahs moved here.'

This time Peggy paid close attention while Mrs Donovan went through the generations of Atiyahs. Mr Atiyah senior had passed away several years before, leaving Mrs A solitary in the house, though she had two daughters (and five grandchildren) living nearby, and almost every day one of them paid a visit on their mother. 'She's seventy-two next March, not that she looks a day over seventy if you ask me yourself.'

'It's nice she's got daughters to look after her,' said Peggy, resisting the temptation to finish her tea, since she couldn't be sure she would be offered another refill. 'Though I suppose she would have liked a son as well.'

'Oh she's got a son, all right. He's the youngest child and the apple of her eye. And Mrs A spoils him rotten. You'd think he was still a schoolboy from the way he lets his mum take care of him – I've seen him lug his laundry home for her to do, and him living all the way down in London.'

'He's got no family then?'

Mrs Donovan shook her head. 'No, he's still a student. If you ask me, it's all very well everyone going to university these days, but sometimes they carry it on too long. Mika is twenty-six if he's a day. By that age my Leonard had been working for ten years, yet this lad's still at his books.' She shook her head uncomprehendingly. 'My nephew Arnold—' she started to say, but Peggy cut in quickly to impede the diversion. 'Do you reckon his mum minds? I mean, his being a student and all?'

For a moment the old lady looked confused, as if her nephew Arnold was being discussed, then she realised Peggy was talking about the Atiyah boy and she shook her head decisively. 'No, his mum thinks the sun shines out of that boy's eyes. Even when it's grey and overcast outside.' She gave a little chuckle.

'They say Middle Eastern lads are very dutiful sons.'

The woman gave a little harrumph, and Peggy realised she didn't like her neighbour's son much. She said nothing but waited patiently, and sure enough there was more to come. 'Like I say, the boy's been spoilt. Why, last year he said he wanted to go back to his homeland – he meant Yemen – and his mum coughed up the air fare. What was the point, I ask you? He's born and bred British just like you and me, so why start pretending you're not? Never go backwards, that's my motto.'

'Maybe he wanted to explore his roots. Like that programme on the TV.'

'I can't see him sobbing over his great-grandmother like what's-his-name did. He's a hard little bugger, our Mika.'

'Did he like it in Yemen?'

Mrs Donovan shrugged. 'I didn't think it was my business to ask. Mrs A knows I don't approve of the boy – he's not polite, at least not to the likes of an old lady like me.'

'Really?' said Peggy, trying to sound indignant.

'Not since he went to the Middle East. He hardly says hello when he sees me.'

'Are they a very religious family?'

Mrs Donovan paused, as if she had never thought about this before, and said reflectively, 'The old man was, but not Mrs A. Since he died I don't think she goes to the mosque much. And when one of her daughters married an English bloke, she didn't bat an eye.'

'And Mika?'

She shrugged, and looked at the mugs on the table. Peggy realised she was in danger of outstaying her welcome; the old lady liked to talk, but on her own terms, and that didn't seem to include answering too many of a stranger's questions. Peggy got up from her chair. 'Golly, what you've said has been so interesting I could stay and listen all day. But duty calls, and I have to get back to work. Thanks so much for the tea, Mrs Donovan.'

'Call me Maggie, dear.'

'Right, Maggie. You've been very helpful.'

'Have I?' asked Maggie, and her face was suddenly cheerful again. 'That's kind of you to say, luv, though I don't see how.'

'I'll just leave you this,' said Peggy, putting a small printed leaflet on the kitchen table. 'It explains about the

Electoral Registration process and it's got my phone number on it in case there's anything you want to inquire about.'

'Thanks, luv,' said Mrs Donovan, picking up the leaflet and putting it on the sideboard beside the photographs.

33

M ARTIN SEURAT LOOKED MOODILY out of the window of his office in the headquarters of the DGSE, France's external intelligence service. He occupied a small room in a corner of one of the white stone buildings just off the Boulevard Mortier on the outskirts of Paris. Outside, the gravelled courtyard had darkened to the colour of slate from the rain that had come down in a short heavy burst earlier that morning. The sky had stayed overcast, with no hint of sun, and now the wind was picking up. It all seemed like a plot by winter to hurry things along, thought Seurat, who every year wanted to hibernate at this season and wake up only when the clocks changed in spring.

He couldn't quite understand why he was feeling so low. After all, he had achieved his ambition of capturing his old colleague Antoine Milraud, the man who had betrayed his friendship and his trust. Why wasn't he feeling elated?

He supposed the trouble was that he did not yet have the pleasure of seeing the man in court, answering for his crimes. That pleasure had to wait until the operation in Britain was concluded. But he wasn't directing that operation; he was having to leave that to Liz Carlyle, since it was happening on her turf. So at present he had only a minor role to play, keeping Annette sweet and monitoring the arrangements at the safe house in Montreuil.

He could hear the noise of workmen moving furniture around across the passage. He'd left his door open, and occasionally he saw one of the workmen passing by, carrying a chair or a cupboard. A colleague had returned from a posting in Taiwan and was moving into the vacant office. Funnily enough, that very room across the passage used to be Antoine Milraud's office. Seurat had spent many an hour there, talking with his old friend and colleague, sometimes cracking open a bottle of Bordeaux if they had stayed working late enough to deserve a glass or two, talking quietly until the phone would ring and – Seurat could hear her voice from the other side of the room – Annette would demand to know when Antoine was coming home and did he really expect his dinner to be waiting when he did?

Annette was not so chirpy now, living with a guard in the small flat the Service kept in the Fifth Arrondissement, while her husband twiddled his thumbs in the Montreuil bungalow not far away from this office. Seurat had talked to Liz that morning and heard her account of her debriefing of Milraud in London. Both had agreed that he was still holding something back, and only superficially cooperating. Whatever it was the man was not saying was bound to be important, or why keep it secret? Maybe it was something that reflected badly on him. But why would he bother, considering the mess he was already in? Liz thought it most likely to concern Lester Jackson's role in the whole affair, and Martin did not disagree.

The problem was there didn't seem any obvious way to

prise more information out of Milraud. He'd already been threatened with the prosecution of Annette, and had folded accordingly. They could always threaten him again, but to what end? Putting Annette in prison wasn't going to tell them anything more about Lester Jackson or the young Arab whom Seurat still thought of as Zara. And in any case, after a while repeated threats failed to frighten, as if the ferocious dog barking from inside a house turned out, when the front door was opened, to be a chihuahua.

'Monsieur?'

The voice was gentle but Seurat was startled none the less. Looking up, he found a young man in the doorway. At first he thought he must be one of the moving men, but no, this fellow had longish hair and wore a cotton jacket and chinos. He looked like a student rather than a workman.

'What is it?'

'Forgive me, Monsieur. I am Jacques Thibault. I have been helping out with Antoine Milraud.'

Seurat stared at Thibault; he seemed very young to be guarding his ex-colleague. Then he remembered. 'Ah, of course. You are the computer genius.'

Thibault gave a modest shrug. 'You are too kind.'

'How goes it? Anything more to report?'

'In fact, yes. As you know, I have control of Monsieur Milraud's laptop and I read all his emails. That includes the recent communiqué asking him to come to London. He claims he wiped all the earlier emails on security grounds. What he doesn't realise is that I have been working hard to find them nonetheless.'

Seurat saw the importance of this immediately. 'And have you?' he asked eagerly.

'Only up to a point. I am sure you are familiar with reverse engineering.'

'I think so. You go backwards to reconstruct a trail. It's especially useful to see how something began, isn't it?'

'In a sense.' Thibault had lost his air of diffidence and had come into the office, sitting down when Seurat pointed to the empty leather chair across from his desk. 'But I would argue that it is most valuable when something has been destroyed rather than built.'

'Really?' said Seurat, trying to be patient.

Thibault nodded vigorously. 'Suppose you are confronted with a brick house and want to see how it came to that state: through reverse engineering you gradually work your way back until the walls have come down and the first foundations are about to be poured – the bricks for the walls may not even have been delivered. Now that is a beautiful process in its own way, but it doesn't tell you much if what you want to learn about is the finished house.'

Seurat nodded politely at this elaborate metaphor, but privately he wondered what point Thibault was trying to make. If Thibault sensed his doubts he gave no sign of it, and continued: 'Think about it this way – what if this finished brick house is destroyed? Accidentally or on purpose, it doesn't matter. Either way all the information you want is lost, irretrievably. Unless' – and he started to smile – 'you could reverse-engineer the act of destruction, slowly work your way back from the present position of crumbled walls and masonry dust to the house in its former glory.'

'You can do this with Milraud's emails?'

'Yes.' Thibault was sure of his ground, his voice entirely confident. 'Not the whole house at first, more like one of its rooms. But in time I am certain it can all be reconstructed.'

'Do we know anything yet?'

'We do, but I don't know how much of it is of value. The first exchange occurred when Milraud was in South America. I am not quite sure where.'

Caracas, thought Seurat, and motioned for Thibault to continue. He said, 'I can be more precise about the sender of the email, however. His message came from Yemen. Not far outside the city of Sana'a.'

'Hang on a minute. Was the sender the same person in England who's contacted him recently?'

'Yes, well, at least it is the same email address.'

Liz had told Seurat about Peggy Kinsolving's fact-finding mission to the northern town of Eccles. Atiyah, apparently the real name of the young Arab they'd been calling Zara, had visited Yemen within the last year according to the neighbour. It all fitted. 'What about more recent communications?' he asked Thibault.

The young boffin shook his head. 'Not yet. There is a large gap to be filled between these first exchanges and the last email, which we've already seen. I am confident of filling in this gap, but it will take some time.'

'Oh,' said Seurat, sounding disappointed. Thibault was obviously elated to have recovered even a small part of what had been deleted, but if it didn't actually tell them much then there didn't seem any reason to get excited.

Thibault said, 'I will send you the transcripts of what I have managed to disinter.'

Seurat wondered if there was any point in passing this on to Liz. Probably not; the 'breakthrough' hadn't amounted to much.

Thibault shifted in his armchair, ready to depart. Then he said, 'There is one other thing that may be of interest. It's a reference in the very first email from Yemen to the man who made the introduction to Milraud.'

Seurat was suddenly alert. 'Does it give his name?'

'No, because he was careful not to use it. But does sound as if the man is a senior person in the government. Possibly a minister, I can't tell exactly.'

34

M ILES BROOKHAVEN WAS USED to working in the
Middle East, but each year as winter hove onto
the horizon he thought fondly of home. He had just been
reading a letter from his mother, describing the Thanks-
giving dinner she was planning in the small town in
upstate New York where she lived. It would soon be
snowing there, with icy winds coming in over the Great
Lakes from Canada.

It all seemed a very long way away from this café in Sana'a
where he was sitting at an outside table under a hot Yemeni
sun, watching as Arack used his fork to attack a second
helping of pistachio and syrup-laden pastry. CIA HQ back
in Langley must have seen some odd expense claims over
the years, everything from 'booze and babes' to a legendary
purchase of a racehorse, but Miles couldn't imagine what
they would think of the three-figure bill he was planning to
submit for the purchase of Yemeni patisserie.

Not that he had much to show for it in return: Arack
seemed as mystified by the disappearance of Baakrime as
Miles was. Arack said between mouthfuls, 'No one knows
anything. I made up an excuse to ring his office at the
Ministry. It's quite obvious that his secretary doesn't have

a clue where he is. My own Minister's secretary was trying to contact him to find out if he was coming to a meeting just two days ago, but no one could say whether he was coming or not.'

He looked contemplatively at his fork. Noticing a vestigial smear of cream on one of its tines, he licked it clean, then said, 'His son has disappeared as well, you know. That is also a mystery. He worked for the Minister's charity but no one there seems to know where he is either.'

'That's interesting. What do *you* think it's all about?' asked Miles. He couldn't prevent his mind recalling the bloodied, white-robed corpse, whose shiny black shoes seemed to make the mental image even more gruesome.

Arack shrugged, and looked over at the waiter, who fortunately for Miles's expense account was occupied serving another table. He said, 'Someone must know something. You have to remember what kind of man Baakrime is.'

'How do you mean?'

'He's rich, he's powerful; inevitably, he has enemies. Maybe something has frightened him enough to go into hiding. And that would also frighten anyone who knows his whereabouts. All one can do is keep asking, though it requires care in order not to make people suspicious.' Arack's face suddenly broadened into a smile. He had caught the waiter's eye.

Two nights later, Miles left the embassy after attending a reception given by Ambassador Rodgers for what he called 'a visiting fireman' – in this case, a natural gas producer from Monroe, Louisiana. It was a three-line whip for most of the Embassy staff, and the trade representatives of other missions and embassies had also been invited. The party was never going to be a barrel of laughs, but Miles didn't mind – among the other conscripts was the voluptuous Marilyn.

But when Marilyn cut him dead in the embassy foyer and went instead to talk to the other secretaries, Miles realised she was still cross with him for cancelling their dinner date. His disappointment turned to annoyance when a little while later he saw her with Bruno Mackay, who seemed to be putting something into his phone – probably her number, thought Miles jealously.

Miles compensated for Marilyn's snub by having three glasses of wine, which meant he left the party feeling mellow. He lived in an apartment in the old quarter of the city, and he drove there in the dark with extra caution. Since the events on the road from Baakrime's farm he had changed the car he drove, but he still felt uneasy driving at night, even in the city.

He parked in the underground car park of his apartment block. As he slammed and locked the car door his eye caught a movement behind a car two spaces along the row. His stomach lurched and he stood still, keeping the car between himself and whoever was there, alert for what might happen next.

Then a figure emerged into the light, and after a second or two Miles recognised Minister Baakrime. Standing just fifteen feet away under the yellowish glow of the car park lights he was a changed figure. The finery of his office apparel – silk ties, handmade shoes from London – was all gone. He wore a brown canvas jacket with side pockets, and unpressed cotton trousers; he looked utterly nondescript, which must have been his intention, though no doubt it galled him.

'What are you doing—' Miles began to ask, but Baakrime put an urgent finger to his lips, then beckoned him into the shadows in the corner of the car park. 'Quiet, my friend. I do not want to be seen by anyone.'

'I've been looking for you,' whispered Miles.

Baakrime gave a melancholy smile. 'You are not the only one.'

'Why have you disappeared?'

'I had no choice.' His voice was hoarse. 'My son was murdered. That was a warning to me that I would be next.'

'I am sorry for your loss,' said Miles. There was no point in saying that he had seen the body of the young man. 'Who did it? Who's after you?'

'I know their identity, and it will be of great interest to your country and the British. But I cannot stay in Yemen much longer; I want to emigrate to America. I think I have information to earn that right; I have been of considerable assistance to you in the past and I have more to tell.'

Miles said nothing while he digested this. His estimate of Baakrime was that he was a wily old crook who had probably got what he deserved, though what had happened to his son could not be wished on anyone. It was not as if the Minister had been helping the United States out of the goodness of his heart: each time he'd imparted any information he had been well paid for it. There was no question of giving him free passage into America and, as he no doubt hoped, a pension to live on when he got there. Those who held the purse strings in Washington would never authorise it unless he had a lot more to offer.

Miles spoke carefully now. 'You have been a valuable friend to my country, but I think you will admit your efforts have always been rewarded. In the end we are all in business, even if our goods are information. I need to know what more you have to offer before I can put your proposal to my superiors. I need to know a lot more about these people. Why are they hunting for you, where do they come from, what are their plans? If you can tell me that, then maybe I can help you.'

Baakrime didn't reply at first. He exhaled noisily, wiped at his thinning hair impatiently, then looked around. He was less agitated now, but his shoulders were slumped; clearly Miles had not told him what he had been hoping to hear. At last he spoke, 'Very well. I see the position, even if I regret it. I will tell you what I know, though I want guarantees of protection – until you arrange for me to go to America. Is that agreed?'

'There's only so much I can do in Yemen. Once you have left this country I can guarantee your safety. Until then, I can only give advice.'

Baakrime thought about this, his lips pursed. 'It will have to do for now,' he said grudgingly. Then he added reluctantly, 'The man attending the meeting in Paris is not working for the rebels of the Arab Spring. He is working for jihadis. Ones that are based here in Yemen.'

He looked at Miles as if he had handed him a gift of unexpected value, but Miles shook his head, to show that he would have to do better than this. 'We already know that. We have learned a lot more since you alerted us to the meeting in Paris.'

If the Yemeni was disappointed he didn't show it, but like a magician whose rabbit has failed to impress, simply produced another one. 'Of course, but I doubt you know much about these jihadis. You see, they are not Yemeni, they are British.'

Miles remembered the British voice in the armed gang who had forced him and Bruno Mackay off the road. 'Believe it or not, I did know that too. But tell me more.'

'Do you know their plans?'

'Which plans?'

'Ah,' said Baakrime, 'I thought not. These British men are here only temporarily. Soon they will be returning to their country, with a small stop in Paris. I don't think they're going there to see the Eiffel Tower.' He laughed. 'And when they get to England I don't think they'll be training to become lawyers.'

'What are they going to do?' Miles demanded. Baakrime didn't reply. Miles insisted: 'What are these men planning to do?'

'It's not entirely clear,' said Baakrime, which to Miles meant either he didn't know or he was holding the information as a bargaining chip. The latter seemed most likely when he said, 'I believe I can find out.' He paused, then added, 'If . . .'

'If you can tell me when these men are going to Paris and what they are planning to do in England, then I think I may be able to help you. It will take forty-eight hours and the information will need to be checked.'

Baakrime said slowly, 'Forty-eight hours is a long time in my position.'

'You've made it this far; what's a few more days? Get me the information I want and then I'll set everything up. How long will it take you?'

'I will meet you tomorrow at this time, but not here.'

'I have a small place I keep as a safe house,' said Miles and he gave him an address in the old city. 'Come there tomorrow but be sure you are not followed.'

'Trust me, my friend. I still have a few friends who look after me.'

35

A T EIGHT O'CLOCK THE following morning Liz
Carlyle, Geoffrey Fane and Andy Bokus were sitting
in the basement secure room in the Grosvenor Square
Embassy. Each had in front of them a copy of the message
that had come in overnight from Miles Brookhaven in
Sana'a, describing his meeting with Baakrime in the car
park.

'Well,' said Bokus, looking at his two British visitors,
'I've been in touch with Langley overnight. We don't want
this *Donation* guy, so it's up to you. Are you prepared to
have him?'

'Come now, Andy,' said Fane in his most patronising
tone. 'I know it's early in the morning and you may well
have been up half the night, but let's just talk about this
for a minute. As I read what Baakrime said to Brookhaven,
it's the US he wants to go to. He made no mention of
the UK.'

'He wants to get out of there before someone tops him,
and I don't suppose for a minute he's going to turn down a
passage to London. It seems to me that it's you who stand
to benefit from whatever he has to say. He's talking about
British jihadis, not American, so it's your side who should

bear the cost. That's what I've advised Langley and they agree.'

There was silence for a moment. Geoffrey Fane was leaning forward on the bench with his elbows on the table and his fingertips together. Liz Carlyle knew that any meeting between these two had to begin with some sort of ritual sparring match, and she was used to biding her time until the first bout was over. It looked as though it was, so she said, 'I think you'll agree, Andy, that it's crucial that we find out what *Donation* knows about these British jihadis he's talking about. It seems to me that Miles has asked him all the right questions. What we don't yet know is whether he can answer them. It's far too early to consider giving him asylum, let alone accepting him as a defector.'

'It's easy for you to say that, sitting here in London,' replied Bokus testily. 'The guy wants an answer and he's expecting Miles to give him one. Can he get out of the country or not? That's what he wants to know. Miles may not be able to get him to spill his guts if he can't give him the assurance he wants.'

'I hear what you say,' said Fane, 'but you and Langley seem to have made your mind up that the answer's No. It's just as much in your interests as ours to find out what these jihadis are planning to do. They may be British, but how do we know they're not planning an attack on a US target? Maybe it's the Embassy here. You won't look so clever if your colleagues get blown up.'

'Give it a break, Geoffrey. Our security is better than a bunch of home-grown jihadis can breach, and you know it.'

Round two over, thought Liz as Fane turned to her. And asked, 'Is your Service prepared to sponsor this character at the Defector subcommittee?'

Liz knew that doing that would mean making a case that *Donation* was likely to have information, or had already given information so valuable to the UK that he should be accepted as a defector with all the expenditure of cash and resource that that implied.

'Not as things stand now,' she replied. 'They'd never accept it. I'm afraid I think we will have to rely on Miles to extract whatever information *Donation* has, while making no promises about his future.'

'He's going to love that as a brief,' grunted Bokus.

'Have you any better idea?' asked Fane.

'I'm sure he'll do it perfectly,' said Liz with a charming smile. I hope so, she thought to herself. If not, all we're left with is the Jackson end of this puzzle and whatever we can get out of Antoine Milraud.

'OK,' said Bokus with a shrug. 'I'll let Miles have the good news.'

36

IT WAS AN UNPREPOSSESSING kind of place – just a
small room with a little kitchen and a lavatory on the
first floor above a minimarket in the old city. But it was
safe. The minimarket was owned and run by the father of a
longstanding and trusted CIA contact who lived in
Virginia. Access to the upstairs was through the shop and
under the watchful eye of its owner.

Miles and Bruno Mackay sat on a scruffy sofa gloomily
contemplating a bottle of scotch and three glasses lined up
on a low table in front of them. They'd read the instructions that had come in from Bokus earlier in the day.

'God knows how they expect us to get the story out of
him when we've got nothing to offer in return,' Miles had
said angrily.

'I know. I sometimes wonder if our lords and masters
have forgotten what it's like at the sharp end, dealing with
real people. String him along, they say, cheerfully, till he's
told you all he knows, then we'll think about whether it's
good enough and if not we'll throw him back to whoever's
hunting him.'

They'd made their plan: who was to start the conversation, who was to say what and when, and now they sat in

silence waiting for the concealed buzzer that would indicate that their visitor was in the shop. Silence; just the sound of shopping going on downstairs and the ring of the till as purchases were made.

Time passed. Miles looked at his watch for the third time. The Yemeni was now half an hour late. They both knew not to expect punctuality in this part of the world, but how long should they wait?

'I'm having a drink,' said Bruno suddenly. He unscrewed the cap on the whisky bottle and poured out two generous slugs, slopping in some water from a jug.

Miles was brooding over the fact that Marilyn had sent him an email, asking if he would be her guest at a small chamber concert hosted by the Ambassador's wife that evening. Though he wasn't especially interested in classical music, he was still interested in Marilyn, but he'd had to decline the invitation because of this meeting. Not being able to tell her the truth about his evening plans, he'd had to give her a vague excuse, and from her reaction he'd sensed that that had been his last chance. If Baakrime wasn't going to turn up it would be all the more galling.

'He's not coming,' said Bruno, another half-hour and another drink later. 'Let's pack up and go and get some dinner.'

'OK but we'd better let London know first.'

'Yes. Liz Carlyle is going to be pretty fed up that we haven't got any information about these British jihadis.'

Miles slept badly, dreaming of a sailing expedition from his childhood when they had run aground off Nantucket. In real life no one had been hurt; in his dream, inexplicably someone had drowned, lost in the shoals after the boat overturned in the incoming tide. He woke in a sweat at three in the morning, then turned on the BBC World Service, which eventually lulled him back to sleep shortly before dawn.

At the Embassy he found a message from the Ambassador's secretary, summoning him to see Rodgers. He went along anxiously, thinking he must have been spotted meeting Baakrime two days before, and wondering how to explain this violation of the Ambassador's orders to stay well away from the Minister. But he found the Ambassador unaccountably good-humoured, honouring Miles with a beneficent smile as he entered his office. 'Miles, Miles, how good to see you. All going well?'

'Yes, sir,' Miles said cautiously, wondering what was coming next.

'I've got some news. You remember our conversation about Minister Baakrime?'

'Yes,' said Miles.

'Well, you don't have to worry about him any more.'

'Oh. What's happened?' He felt a sense of dread. Had Baakrime been right to fear for his safety? He should have done more to protect him.

The Ambassador didn't answer him directly. 'Yes, you won't have to avoid that gentleman any more.'

Miles stared at Rodgers, unable to pretend he was anything but horrified. 'Is he—'

Rodgers nodded. 'Yep. The Yemeni government has informed me this morning that Mr Baakrime is currently a resident of Moscow, courtesy of an Aeroflot flight he caught yesterday in Istanbul. Fine by me, I have to say, though the Yemenis are not at all amused. They reckon he took twenty-five million bucks of government money with him. I bet the Russians won't let him keep a dime of it. What do you know about that?'

Far more than you, thought Miles, wondering what Bokus was going to say when he learned that Baakrime had not needed any of the US government's money – he was perfectly capable of paying his own way.

37

THERE HAD BEEN NO further emails to Milraud from the young jihadi Zara in the UK. When Seurat pressed him Milraud merely shrugged, and said that when he'd met the young Arab both in Paris and Primrose Hill he had not been given a schedule for his next communication. Milraud's insouciance infuriated Seurat, but he did his best not to show it – he didn't want to give his former colleague the satisfaction of seeing him get angry, when getting angry wouldn't do any good.

But he needed to move things forward. Liz had told him that the Americans' source in Yemen, the government Minister who had started this whole operation going, had now fled the country; she had also told him of MI5's discovery that Zara, far from being the Yemeni student he claimed, was a native-born Briton. It was quite possible that whatever Zara was plotting could be well advanced, which made it crucial to find out what else Milraud knew. He clearly wasn't going to volunteer information, so Seurat had to find some way to lever it out of him. He knew Milraud well enough to know that threats and confrontation would get him nowhere, so he fell back on his ace card – Annette.

He arranged to meet her at a café near the Seine, a few streets from the Musée d'Orsay. The café straddled an intersection of two streets that met at right angles; its outside tables allowed a clear view of both the pedestrians and the cars that drove past. When Annette arrived, accompanied by her two guards, Milraud had been sitting for fifteen minutes, and was satisfied that he would recognise any returning cars or pedestrians that might indicate surveillance. The coast seemed to be clear, as he expected it to be.

As Annette sat down, her two guards took up positions at a nearby table. The waiter came over and she ordered a large Campari and soda before asking Seurat, 'To what do I owe the privilege of being let out of my cage?'

'I thought you might enjoy a little outing.' He knew that Annette was allowed out once a day for a stroll, but only when accompanied by her armed escorts. Meeting Seurat here, she could at least enjoy the pretence of being an ordinary Parisian.

'Come, come, Martin,' she said. 'We both know your concern for my welfare is strictly professional. You never cared a damn about me.'

'That's not true at all—' Martin protested.

Annette dismissed this with a curt wave of her hand. 'Even if you did regard me as a friend back then, you are not going to let that affect you now. So tell me what you want from this tête-à-tête.'

Seurat said nothing while the waiter was putting Annette's drink on the table. The two guards, alert and watchful, weren't even pretending to talk to each other; they were scanning the comings and goings at the café tables and in the street. When the waiter had left, Seurat said quietly, 'Antoine is holding back on us, Annette. I don't know if he's actually lied to us, but he certainly hasn't told us the whole truth.'

Annette lifted her drink and took a long swallow. Putting the glass down, she pursed her lips, as though considering what to say.

Seurat sighed. 'I haven't got time for games, Annette. If Antoine is concealing information, it will come out sooner or later, and then things will go very hard for him. And you.'

'You've already made that clear.' She reached into her bag and brought out a packet of cigarettes – Russian Sobranies. She lit one with a wafer-thin gold lighter from Cartier – he remembered Milraud showing it to him after he had bought it for Annette's Christmas present years ago. A reminder of more innocent times.

He said, 'Yes, but what I haven't told you is what Antoine has got himself involved in. This isn't a normal kind of arms deal we are talking about.'

'No?' Annette said neutrally, but she was tapping the fingers of one hand on the Formica tabletop, and Martin sensed her curiosity.

'No, it's much worse than that. Your husband would like to think he's supplying arms to freedom fighters in the Arab Spring, but that's not the real situation and I think he knows it. He's helping to arm terrorists – al-Qaeda supporters.'

Annette frowned and shook her head. 'You've been listening to the Americans too much, Martin. They think anyone who doesn't agree with them is a terrorist – and that all Muslims are al-Qaeda supporters.'

'Don't pretend to be simple-minded. What I'm telling you is true. I can't be sure yet exactly how the weapons Antoine has agreed to supply to these people will be used, but it's not for any struggle against dictatorship, I can tell you. Antoine's buyer is a radical jihadi, whose sole purpose is to kill anyone who fits his distorted idea of an enemy of Islam. His mission is likely to be to murder as many people as possible. Innocent people, by any civilised standard.'

He was staring at Annette but her eyes avoided his face, gazing past him to the street outside. She took a deep drag of her cigarette, then slowly blew it out in a white trail that hung in a plume over the table. She tapped her milky pink nails on the table. 'Antoine is many things, Martin, most of them good. You may not approve of his life now, but he is as human as you are, in every essential way. I am sure he would never sell weapons to anyone like the man you are describing.'

'He may not have known at first, I grant you that. But I think he's guessed now and he's doing it just the same.'

'Can you prove it?'

'No. Not yet. But everything is pointing to the truth of what I'm saying.' He judged that it was better to be up-front with Annette; if he misled her she would press him until that became clear. 'What I do know without a doubt is that his customer is English, even if he's ethnically Arab. And why would an English citizen want twenty thousand rounds of ammunition – and it is even looking possible that it is to be delivered to England – unless he was planning a terrorist attack of some kind? It simply doesn't make sense if he's a "freedom fighter" in Yemen, does it?'

He could see she was taking this in, and beginning to waver from her previous defiance, so he turned the screw further. 'We don't know what his plans are, but we need to find out before there's a bloodbath. You wouldn't want to have that blood on Antoine's hands, would you?' He added more gently, 'Or on your own.'

'I'd like another drink,' Annette said loudly, and Seurat

signalled to the waiter. Annette sighed. 'You were always a persuasive bastard, Martin. Antoine used to come home and describe how the two of you had interrogated someone. You know my husband – he'd have been direct and aggressive. But he admired your method; he said you could charm the birds out of the trees.'

Seurat gave a non-committal shrug. Annette laughed. 'Still the modest one. That was something else Antoine admired.'

'There was a lot I admired in Antoine too,' said Martin.

'Yes, perhaps there was.' She sounded wistful. 'But not any more. I can see that in your eyes.'

'No. Not any more. Not after what he did. I took that as a personal betrayal.'

'Really?' She looked at him thoughtfully. 'I don't think I'd realised that – though I suppose I should have done. You were always so upright; nothing tempted you off the path of duty.' Her face looked sad and drawn as she sat quietly while the waiter brought her drink. When he had gone she sat up straight as though she had resolved something. 'So back to the beginning – what is it you want me to do?' she asked.

'Talk to Antoine. If you believe what I've told you about his client, and I think you do, then make him believe it too. Forget about jail sentences or clemency or anything like that; I'm not bargaining right now. I just don't believe Antoine would want to see dozens, maybe hundreds of innocent people massacred because he'd helped their killers.'

38

MILRAUD WATCHED AS ANNETTE got up from the bed, dressed in a silk slip and nothing else. She took a cigarette from the packet on the bedside table, lit it with the Cartier lighter he had given her years ago, and then went to the window, where she stood staring down at the narrow street that snaked along until, just out of sight, it reached the Seine.

He sat up in the bed, so that his back was cushioned by the pillows that he'd propped against the headboard. He said softly, '*Chérie*, it is good to be with you.'

'Yes, my darling,' she said, but there was a hint of sadness in her voice and she didn't turn round.

He said, 'Martin is no fool, you know.'

Now she did turn round, and looked at him, her eyes filling with tears.

He went on, 'He let me come to see you because he knew how much I wanted to. Enough to tell him what he wants, in the hope that he will let us stay together.'

'Yes,' acknowledged Annette. 'But better this time together than no time at all.' She had been surprised, sitting in the flat, reading an old paperback novel she had found on a shelf and trying to ignore the guard who was making tea in the kitchen, when Antoine had arrived. He told her that he had suddenly been told to grab his coat and go for a drive; he'd had no idea that he was being taken into Paris to see his wife. In a rare tactful act, the now-combined force of armed escorts had left them alone, though they were hovering nearby – in the hall outside the flat, on the ground floor with the concierge, and outside by the parked Mercedes that had chauffeured Antoine from Montreuil.

Milraud looked at his wife, still as attractive to him as she'd been when they'd first met some twenty years before. He tried not to think of what prison would do to her figure, and to her spirited approach to life. It would do the same to him, no doubt, but he had already resigned himself to a long spell behind bars.

'Are there important things you haven't told Martin?' she asked.

Milraud raised his eyes towards the ceiling. He assumed the flat was bugged, especially if they'd let him see Annette here. She understood, and came back to the bed, stopping to turn on the radio on the bedside table. The station was playing Edith Piaf and they both laughed as they heard the song in mid-flow – 'Je Ne Regrette Rien'.

Annette lay down next to Antoine and whispered, 'So are there?'

'Of course. But why are you asking now? Has Seurat put you up to this?' He only slightly lowered his voice; he didn't care if the microphone picked this up over the radio; he was angry that they were being manipulated.

She didn't waver, whispering right away, 'He says the people you are supplying are much worse than you realise. They're not rebels fighting in the Middle East. He said they're al-Qaeda or their equivalent, and they're planning a terrorist attack.'

Milraud shifted uneasily on the bed, moving an inch or two away from his wife. 'How does he know?' He realised he had not spent any time questioning the intentions of the young Arab he had first met in the Luxembourg Gardens. His initial introduction to the man had come from Minister Baakrime, whom he had dealt with often before. He had simply assumed that the Minister had either been bribed by Yemen's insurgents to help them get arms, or was actually a secret sympathiser with the rebels.

He realised now that he had been naïve, but what did it matter? He had never made judgements about his clients, and he had helped arm revolutionaries across most of the world. There was no telling which side was right and which wrong, and if someone in his trade tried to make those sort of judgements they'd soon go mad or out of business. These affairs often ended in a place no one had foreseen. Look at Iraq now, or Libya, or Syria.

He was about to say as much to Annette, when she put a firm finger to his lips. 'Listen to me, Antoine. Naturally, Martin wanted me to talk to you; of course he wants me to persuade you to tell him everything you know. I would never hide what he said from you. I don't think we have any choice. If you know more about what's going on, then you should tell me and I will tell Martin.'

'But then I have nothing left to bargain with.'

'We are in no position to bargain, *chéri*. But even if we were, I have to tell you that if Martin is telling the truth – and I think he is – then I don't want you to help these people. They are killers; they kill children and their mothers. They have no just cause, only hate.'

Milraud lay back, his head against the pillow, and stared

at the ceiling while he thought about this. Had Annette gone soft on him? It seemed improbable – if anything she had always been the tougher of the two of them, more businesslike, never very concerned about the morality of his trade. He knew she was scared of going to prison, but he also knew that she was very loyal to him – and her concern about what this young Yemeni, if that's what he was, was going to do with the weapons he was supplying was genuine. And he had to admit it did alarm him too – the thought of this character and his followers or colleagues killing dozens of innocents in Western Europe was appalling.

'OK,' he said at last, though he didn't look at his wife, but kept his eyes on the ceiling, as if addressing a deity or, he was pretty certain, the listening ears of his former colleagues in the DGSE. 'I'll tell him what I know. But it's not much.'

'I expect anything will help,' said Annette lightly.

Milraud turned on the bed and looked at her at last. 'The originator of the contact in Paris was a Yemeni minister. That's why I thought this was legit.' *Legit* struck him as a funny way to describe the transaction, but he knew Annette would understand what he meant – he had thought he was simply supplying one side of the innumerable civil wars that seemed to be proliferating all over the region.

'I understand. But now?'

'What Martin has told you could make sense. I haven't told him everything I know. I haven't told him exactly where the shipment is being assembled, though he knows the country. He doesn't know anything about the onward shipping arrangements. He knows there's a British person involved but he doesn't know that the order is now to be delivered to England. And he doesn't know that originally it was to go somewhere else.'

'Where?'

'Here,' he said simply. 'Paris.'

Annette looked shocked. 'So what changed?'

Milraud shrugged. 'I don't know. But if Martin's right about these people, it means the target's changed. Now it must be in Britain.'

39

THIS TIME THEY WERE to meet in Fane's office in the MI6 building at Vauxhall Cross. As she walked across Vauxhall Bridge from Thames House, leaning into the gusty wind that was blowing off the river, Liz recalled the email exchanges between Grosvenor Square and Vauxhall that had preceded this meeting. Their tone suggested that the encounter between Fane and Bokus was going to be as rough as the weather, and she was not looking forward to playing the role of peacemaker.

Fane's office was a spacious room, high up in one of the semicircular protuberances at the front of the building. Its two large windows had a commanding view of the Thames – to the right Parliament and the MI5 building on the north bank, and to the left across to Kensington and Chelsea and upriver to Hammersmith. Somehow Fane had managed to acquire the sort of antique official furniture usually only to be found in the Foreign Office, and he had added some oriental rugs and a table that he had inherited from his grandmother. The whole effect was of a country gentleman's study, and about as far as you could get from the bleak, functional office that Bokus inhabited in the American Embassy in Grosvenor Square.

Liz knew that Bokus never felt comfortable in Fane's office, and when she arrived he was standing by the windows, looking stiff and awkward. Fane's secretary, Daisy, followed her into the room with a pot of coffee on a silver tray with china cups and saucers. Bokus waved her away when she offered him a cup and sat down heavily in one of the chairs round the table.

'Let's get on with it,' he said as soon as Daisy had left the room.

Fane took the chair at the head of the table and gestured to Liz to sit down opposite Bokus. He took his time sipping his coffee before saying, 'Thank you for the email, Andy; I think we are all sorry to learn that your source *Donation* has left Yemen. And very surprised to learn that he has gone to Moscow. I for one was not aware that he was in touch with the Russians. Were you, Elizabeth?'

Liz did not reply, and Bokus broke in, 'Not Moscow. Our latest information is that he's gone to Dagestan. We don't know why. He may have arms-dealing contacts there, or maybe the Russians have shipped him off there to get him out of Russia. But it seems that somehow he's got himself mixed up with jihadis – and got on their bad side; I told you his son was murdered. This is a man used to playing both sides from the middle, only suddenly he was squeezed from either end. The Yemeni government was growing fed up with him; now the jihadis have as well. So he's done a runner. But instead of running our way, as he would have done if you'd been a bit quicker on your feet, he's gone in the other direction.'

Fane shook his head and said, 'You were handling *Donation* – we weren't. If *you'd* been prepared to take a risk and be a little more generous, then maybe we would have got something back. Instead, the bird's flown the coop and taken his information and his money with him.'

Liz was about to intervene, but as she drew in her breath to speak, Bokus snapped, 'You can blame us all you like, but it isn't the United States that's at risk from this arms deal he was telling us about. It's you, and you weren't willing to do anything to keep him sweet and find out what he knew.' Bokus looked angry enough to spit. 'As always, you expect us to bail you out, and if we don't, you scream bloody murder and say it's all our fault. But you can't pin this one on the Agency.'

Bokus sat back in his chair, his face red and his arms crossed over his stomach. Liz could see that Fane was taken aback by the American's aggression. She had long suspected that Bokus's usual front was a pose. The bluff, rough Yank who spoke in monosyllables was, she had always been pretty sure, put on for Fane's benefit – a kind of defence mechanism against the smooth English gentleman. A tirade like this from Bokus was unprecedented, and unique for its articulate delivery, which meant that it came from the heart and what they were seeing was the real Bokus behind the taciturn façade.

Since Fane looked as if he was gathering himself for a counter-offensive, Liz decided to intervene before things got totally out of hand. She said calmly, 'I think we need to move on. *Donation*'s gone, and we won't get any more from him, wherever he is. We need to focus now on what we've learned.'

'OK,' said Bokus. '*Donation* was only the middleman. The coalface is this guy Atiyah. He's the one you've got to worry about, and he's been operating right under your noses. He's a Brit, and you didn't know anything about him.'

'For God's sake,' broke in Fane, 'how is that supposed to be helpful? We've got a British citizen gone bad – is that a unique situation? You want to tell me how the American Somalis slipped through your nets? Or the Boston bombers? Two can play at that blame game, you know.'

Liz broke in, 'Or we can accept that we both face the same difficulties and work together to sort them out.'

Fane was silent and Bokus gave her a long stare, but her words seemed to have a calming effect. Bokus threw both hands up in a parody of surrender. 'OK. But I didn't start this.'

'Oh no?' Fane said, ready to dive in again, until Liz gave him a look that could freeze stone. She continued quickly, 'Why don't we start with what we know?' Before either man could say anything at all, she added, 'Antoine Milraud the French arms dealer has decided to be a little more forthcoming. I'm not sure he's telling us everything he knows, but it's more than he was telling us before.'

'How'd you manage that?' asked Bokus. 'Feminine charm?' Liz was relieved to see him grin.

'It was the French, actually, who got him to talk.'

'Monsieur Seurat?' asked Fane.

Give it a rest, Geoffrey, thought Liz, doing her best to ignore him. 'The man Milraud met in Berlin, the black man in the museum, will be receiving a delivery of guns and ammunition in the next ten days or so, somewhere here in the UK. Originally the delivery was going to be in Paris.'

'So what's changed?' asked Bokus. Liz rather liked the way he was always happy to ask the obvious questions – whereas Fane would hold back, unwilling to admit there were things he didn't understand.

She said, 'It's looking increasingly likely that the arms aren't for use in the Middle East – why bring them all the way to France or Britain if they were? We don't know why at first it was Paris, but I'm now afraid they're intended for a terrorist attack and that it's going to take place here in Britain.' She noticed that both Bokus and Fane's eyes widened at this.

Fane said, 'You say "all the way to France or Britain" – where do we think these arms are coming from?'

'Milraud says it's Dagestan.'

'Where our friend *Donation* – Baakrime – is right now,' said Bokus.

Liz nodded. 'I doubt it's a coincidence.'

Bokus said, 'But he's unreachable there – for us and for you. Neither of us has any permanent post in Dagestan and we'd never get anyone in there in time to find out anything useful. If we're going to crack this open it's not going to be through Dagestan or Baakrime.'

'That's right,' Liz said firmly, determined that the question of who was to blame for Baakrime's flight from Yemen should not be reopened. 'But we still need Miles Brookhaven in Yemen on the case. If he can find out the identities of the British youths who went out to Yemen – the ones Baakrime said were planning on returning home for some purpose – then we can keep tabs on them if and when they come back into Europe.' Liz didn't really think Miles would be able to find out anything useful, but she felt it was important to keep the Americans on board. Which meant providing at least a pretence of a job for Miles Brookhaven to do in Yemen.

'That's if they haven't got new false documents,' said Bokus doubtfully.

She went on, 'We've got two potential sources of information here: the young man Atiyah, who's been the contact with Antoine Milraud – we've got twenty-four-hour surveillance on him. And this man Lester Jackson.'

'That's the black man from Berlin?' Fane asked.

'Yes. He owns a club just outside Manchester. He's well known to the local Special Branch, but it's all standard criminal stuff – drugs and the white slave trade. Since Jackson's shipped women, he'll know how to ship arms, I imagine. I bet he's being employed for his expertise in trafficking.'

'Trafficking from where?' asked Bokus.

'I wonder,' said Fane caustically.

Liz gave a resigned smile. 'Dagestan, of course,' she said. 'We know that at least one of the women in his club came from there. Anyway, we can't do much besides watch Atiyah for now – if we brought him in, it could blow the case without our finding out what he's planning to do. If he's been terrorist-trained in Yemen, he's not going to crack under questioning. We just have to hope he makes some kind of a mistake in the next week – you know, phone someone or send an incriminating email.'

'Why don't you turn him over to the Yemenis?' asked Bokus, and Fane laughed.

Liz shook her head in regret. 'I wish we could. But there's the small matter of his being a British citizen. So we'll watch him all right, but I think Jackson's a better bet. He's got no reason to think we suspect him – as far as he knows he got away in Berlin – but we know more about him than he realises.'

Fane said, 'Who's going to direct the operation to put the squeeze on this chap? Local Special Branch?' He sounded sceptical.

'No,' said Liz. 'It will be us. I'm going up to Manchester tomorrow.'

'Rather you than me,' said Fane, looking at the rain now lashing the windows and sounding pleased for the first time that day.

40

LIZ HAD DONE HER homework before she'd made an appointment to see the Chief Constable of Greater Manchester Police. She already knew that Greater Manchester was one of the largest police forces in Britain and she was expecting to find that the Chief Constable was one of the old school, a man who had risen through the ranks, man and boy a policeman, near to retirement and fiercely loyal to his colleagues and to the old style of policing.

What she found was that Chief Constable Richard Pearson was forty-seven years old, the youngest Chief Constable of any of the larger forces in England. He had degrees from Nottingham and Edinburgh Universities and a D.Phil. from Oxford and had been a part-time officer in the Territorial Army for a number of years. He had risen fast through the police ranks and had been in his present post only six months, appointed as part of a push from the Home Office for a new image for policing. He had previously spent two years as Chief Constable of the Cheshire force. With all this information filed away in her mind, Liz set off in quite cheerful mood on the train to Manchester, thinking that perhaps the interview with the Chief was going to be less tricky than she'd thought.

The Police HQ was a three-mile taxi ride from the station, on a smart new industrial estate, full of brick-and glass buildings dominated by the service industries. After signing the register in the large atrium and receiving a visitor's pass to hang round her neck, Liz waited, sitting on a sofa in front of a low table spread with newspapers and assorted police leaflets, one of which was covered with photographs of Manchester's most wanted criminals. She flicked through these with interest and was not in the least surprised to find that Lester Jackson was not among them. She was musing that he was probably worse than any of those whose mugshots were on display when a young female constable arrived to escort her to the Chief's office on the top floor.

A tall, lean man with a shock of blonde hair got up from the desk as she was shown into the room and came forward with a big smile and a hand held out. As she shook it Liz said, 'Thank you for seeing me at such short notice.'

'It sounded important.'

'It is,' she said as they sat down in easy chairs in a corner of the room. 'We're working on a counter-terrorism case that involves a young British man of Yemeni origin. His mother lives in Eccles.'

'That's part of our Salford West Division,' said the Chief.

'He doesn't live there. He's a student at SOAS in London – though he's told the college he's from Yemen and he's given them false identity details. But he's Eccles born and bred and he comes home periodically.'

Pearson gave a half-smile. 'I suppose even terrorists have mothers. Do you have a name for this chap?'

'We do. His name is Atiyah. We call him Zara and we'll

be briefing your counter-terrorist team as things develop. But Zara is not the reason I'm here to see you.'

Liz paused but Pearson said nothing. She went on, 'We believe that Zara is due to receive a shipment of guns and ammunition from abroad – it's coming from one of the ex-Soviet republics – Dagestan. We're not sure exactly when but believe it will arrive in the next week or so – as part of a delivery to a middleman in Manchester, who we think regularly receives shipments through this route as part of a criminal business.'

'Does the middleman have a name?'

'Lester Jackson. He owns a club called Slim's in Wilmslow – it's a combination of flash restaurant, small-time casino and brothel.'

The Chief Constable nodded. 'I know all about Jackson and Slim's. I was Chief in Cheshire before I came here. But I wouldn't have associated him with terrorism.'

'No, I understand. And I don't think he is directly involved in terrorism. I think he's just making some extra cash by adding the weapons to one of his regular deliveries. I very much doubt if he realises all the consequences of what he's involved in.'

'How did he get drawn into this?'

'I think it must be through his transport contact in Dagestan. It's complicated, but the whole affair seems to have originated with a corrupt government minister in Sana'a in Yemen. We think he has been buying weapons in Dagestan and selling them on at a huge profit to whoever will buy them. He seems to have agreed to supply a bunch of jihadis – and Zara is one of them. At first we thought they were going to use them in the Arab Spring countries, but it's beginning to look as if they plan to use them here.'

'OK,' said the Chief slowly. 'I know you'll be keeping

our counter-terrorist team up to date with all this, but what did you particularly want to see me about? I get the feeling there's something else you haven't told me yet.'

Liz smiled. 'You're right – there is something else. As you said, Lester Jackson is well known to the Manchester and Cheshire forces. I gather he's never been arrested, and I'm told he's been helpful on more than one occasion. He's not actually a source, but one of your officers knows him pretty well.'

'Meaning?'

Liz paused, then said, 'This is where it gets difficult. What I mean is that your officer may know him too well. So I can't approach this officer in the normal way and ask for help with Jackson. In fact, I did speak to him on the phone to see what he knew about Jackson, and he gave me a cock-and-bull story – that Jackson was small beer of no possible interest to my Service. He was so dismissive that I didn't tell him that Jackson was suspected of being an accomplice to terrorists trying to bring arms into this country. To be quite honest with you, Mr Pearson, I just didn't trust the officer.'

'Are you trying to say that he is involved in some way with Lester Jackson?'

'Yes. I'm afraid I am,' said Liz. She could see Pearson starting to bristle. 'I should tell you,' she went on, now feeling very uncomfortable, 'that the officer in question is someone I used to know. It was a long time ago – in Liverpool where I was seconded to the Special Branch when I first joined the Service.' When Pearson looked at her curiously she said, 'The officer's name is James McManus. He's Deputy Head of your Special Branch.'

To her surprise the defensiveness she had sensed building in the Chief Constable almost instantaneously disappeared. He nodded and his face grew friendly again, and though it wouldn't have been right to say he was smiling, he somehow seemed relieved. 'Are you telling me you think McManus is involved with this arms delivery?' he asked.

'No. But I think he may be involved with Jackson in a way that isn't altogether . . . healthy.'

Pearson gave a snort. 'That's a generous way of putting it. What I think you really mean is that McManus is in Jackson's pocket, so you can't trust him to help you investigate.'

Liz said nothing and the Chief waved a dismissive hand. 'Don't worry about offending me. Forgive me if I seemed a bit chilly a moment ago – nobody in my job wants to hear that one of his senior officers isn't trusted. But in this case . . . you should know that you aren't the only one with questions about McManus.'

'Really?' She found herself half relieved and half upset, but all attention.

'Absolutely. McManus is one of our most senior officers, as you know, very experienced, with a record anyone would envy. He's popular, and said to be charming with the ladies,' he added, smiling at Liz.

She was too old to blush, and she looked straight back at Pearson, expressionless. He went on, 'But a few years ago, when I was still in Cheshire, I got the feeling that something wasn't right with McManus's relationship with Jackson. He wasn't my officer then, of course, but I did mention it to the Chief here in those days, Sir Charles Worthington. He was a very senior Chief Constable, not long to go to retirement, and frankly he was more interested in international policing and making trips all over the world than in running this Force. Anyway, for whatever reason he did nothing about it.

'But when I came here I realised that there were certain no-go areas for McManus – certain select villains he didn't want to pursue. One of them was certainly Lester Jackson. It is true that we do get the odd titbit supplied by Jackson, and McManus uses that to justify his relationship. But nothing ever substantial enough to make it right that Jackson is allowed to operate so freely from that club. And from what you're telling me he's now involving himself in even more serious crime.'

Liz listened intently as Pearson went on: 'For the last three months my Professional Standards Unit has been covertly investigating McManus. They've put together quite a significant file and we are just about ready to confront him with the evidence. We know now he's been taking money from Jackson – and others – to warn them of criminal investigations and keep the CID off their backs. His usual way of doing that is to claim they're acting as valuable Special Branch sources.'

Liz nodded, though part of her was deeply dismayed. 'Thank you for being so candid with me. As I told you, I knew Jimmy McManus more than ten years ago when I was very junior in the Service. He was kind to me when some of his colleagues were bullying me; for a time he and I were close. But our relationship ended when I thought he was being dishonest. He was convinced that a man he had been investigating was guilty of drug dealing. When the man was acquitted, Jimmy fitted him up by getting some-one to give false evidence against him in another case. I've no doubt the man *was* a drug dealer, and I suppose you could say that in one sense Jimmy was acting on the side of the angels in those days – certainly he thought he was, and he liked to call it "conviction policing". But I thought it was corrupt, and we fell out. Still, I never thought that he'd go over to the criminals' side and take money to protect them.'

The Chief nodded. 'In my experience, conviction policemen are dangerous people to have in a force. They can easily get disillusioned and cynical, and if they have a shaky moral compass in the first place they can become thoroughly crooked. I don't know enough about McManus's personal life to understand precisely what turned him bad, but something certainly has.'

Liz said, 'I'm afraid that what you've told me just makes my problem worse. McManus is in a unique position to give me an inside view of Jackson, but not if I can't trust him. The only other possible source of information I have on Jackson is a young DI in Cheshire called Halliday.'

'Oh yes,' interrupted Pearson. 'He's a good lad, though a bit green.'

'Yes. And he's nothing like as close to Jackson as McManus is. My problem is that we've seen enough to know that Jackson's very alert to surveillance, so I can't rely on that to find out when this delivery's due or where it's going to come into the country. But if I tell McManus what I know, he'll most likely leak it all to Jackson.'

The Chief Constable said, 'Yes. I can see the problem. We need to put pressure on McManus to get him to help, but we've got to do it in such a way that he doesn't tell Jackson what's going on. In other words, we've got to scare him rigid.'

The Chief thought for a moment, then said, 'Here's what I propose. I said we were just about ready to confront him with what we've learned in our investigation. Well, we'll bring that confrontation forward and we'll do it tomorrow morning. I'll make it quite clear to him that we have enough on him to prosecute him for corruption, and if he's convicted he's likely to get a good stretch in prison, which he'll know anyway.

'If you agree, I'd like to add that we have now learned that he may be involved in acts preparatory to the commission of terrorism. He won't know what I'm talking about so I'll tell him that you will be meeting him in the afternoon. You'll be seeking his help and what you'll be telling him is Top Secret. If he doesn't fully support you or if he leaks what you say, we'll throw the book at him and he'll be in prison for the rest of his life.'

'Right,' said Liz, her breath taken away by the Chief Constable's decisive response. 'That should sort it.'

'We'll have him in at eleven tomorrow. I'll tell him to be ready to see you at two pm, but I don't think I'll tell him who he'll be seeing – unless you want me to. Surprise sometimes helps on this sort of occasion. What do you think?'

'I agree,' said Liz weakly. The Chief Constable was well into his stride now.

'If you care to come here at about one o'clock I'll brief you on how it went before you see him. Does that suit you?'

'Yes. Thank you,' said Liz.

41

A T ONE O'CLOCK THE following day Liz was standing in the Chief Constable's office looking out of the
window. Pearson had not appeared and Liz was wondering
whether that meant the interview with McManus was
going well or badly.

She was feeling nervous, uncertain how McManus
would react when he found out that it was his old flame
Liz Carlyle who had come to put pressure on him. It
wouldn't take him long to work out that she would know
all about the accusations of corruption against him. Would
that make him more or less willing to cooperate?

As she was mulling this over, the door suddenly swung
open and the Chief Constable strode into the room. 'Good
afternoon,' he said cheerfully, shaking Liz's hand with a
firm grip. 'Sorry to keep you waiting. You must have been
wondering what was going on. Well, I'm pleased to say
that we've put the fear of God into him. He obviously had
no idea that we knew what he's been up to. I suppose he's
got away with it for so long under the last regime that he
hadn't noticed things have changed.

'He denied everything at first, of course, but when he
saw the amount of evidence my team has collected, he

went silent. I think he's scared enough now that you can be confident he'll cooperate with you. When I told him that he was at risk of a charge under the Terrorism Act if he leaked anything you were going to tell him, he went pale.

'So he's all yours now. He's been taken to get some lunch with one of my investigating officers; he'll be back at two. Is there anything you'd like to ask me?'

'I don't think so. Not at this stage. I take it he still doesn't know who he'll be meeting this afternoon?'

'Correct. I just told him it was someone from the Security Service.'

'Have you any free time later on so I could look in and tell you how it went?'

'I'll be in the building all afternoon, though I've got various appointments. But Constable Symes will find me if you come back here when you've finished.'

An hour later Liz was sitting at one end of a long table in a conference room two floors down in the Police HQ, waiting for McManus to arrive. She had resolved to keep the conversation strictly on the subject of Jackson and the arms delivery and not to get drawn into any reminiscing.

When McManus walked into the room his appearance shocked her. His face was gaunt and pale and he seemed to have shrunk since she last saw him on the stage at the conference in London. His eyes were cast down as he walked into the room, but when he looked up and recognised her, they flared with anger.

'So, it's you,' he said. 'I should have guessed it would be, after your phone call. I suppose you're the one that's been investigating me.'

'Sit down, Jimmy,' she said. 'Of course I haven't been investigating you. That's nonsense, as you know perfectly well. Whatever trouble you're in has nothing to do with me and I don't even know the details of what's gone on. I'm here for one reason only, and that is to get your help with a counter-terrorist investigation.'

'That's what the Chief said, but I don't know anything about any terrorists. I just deal with ordinary villains.'

'Deal' is the right word, thought Liz. But she went on, 'I want to ask you some questions about Lester Jackson. When I spoke to you on the phone, you told me he was just a small-time crook, not one of the real bad guys. If that ever was true, it's not true now. What I'm going to tell you is strictly Top Secret and you must keep it to yourself.'

'The Chief told me that already. I don't need a lecture from someone I bedded years ago.'

'There's no point in insulting me, Jimmy. It won't help you or the investigation. Let's get the business done without getting personal and then I can go away and leave you alone.'

'To my fate,' he responded bitterly.

'So, Lester Jackson. Our information is that he's got himself involved with a shipment of weapons and ammunition coming into the country for terrorist purposes.'

'I don't believe it. That sort of thing wouldn't interest him. He's not an extremist; he's not religious. Why would he want to get involved with terrorists?'

'For money, I should think. I'm not suggesting he is going to carry out a terrorist attack himself. I believe he regularly brings merchandise into the country covertly – girls, drugs, maybe other contraband as well. I also believe he has contacts in Dagestan, the ex-Soviet republic in Central Asia where weapons are easily available. What do you know about any of that?'

There was a pause while McManus shifted uncomfortably

in his chair and looked out of the window. Then he said, 'I suppose this conversation's being recorded?'

'Not as far as I know,' Liz replied.

'That doesn't mean a thing. I know that if Jackson finds out I've told you stuff about his business he'll kill me.'

'And if you don't tell me, the Chief will throw the book at you. So get on with it, Jimmy.'

McManus sighed and shuffled his feet. Then he said in a low voice, 'He has a contact with a man in Dagestan. He gets girls there and brings them in, hidden in lorries. He gets other stuff as well, drugs and legit stuff – cheap clothing that gets sold in the markets here. Some of the girls are for the club and some he sells on. It's not like proper trafficking,' he said defensively. 'Most of them know what they're coming here for, and they're so glad to get out of that hellhole that they don't mind. The ones who work at his club, Slim's, are treated fairly well. If they don't like it, they can go home, the way they came in. But most of them stay.'

'How did he get to know anyone in Dagestan?' asked Liz. 'It seems an unlikely place for him to have a contact.'

'It's someone who used to live in Manchester. I think he came in on political asylum from Chechnya when the war was on there. But I don't know much about him.'

'So he provides the goods and the transport for Jackson. What do you know about the way it's done? I mean the route, the name on the lorries, that kind of thing.'

'He told me once that they come through Turkey. I don't know what registration they have when they set off, but by the time they get here they have Bulgarian number plates and documents. I think they come into this country through different ports. I can't tell you more than that.'

'Come on, Jimmy. Do the lorries have a name on the

side? How do we recognise them? We're talking about weapons coming in for terrorists to use. You don't want to have the deaths of innocent people on your conscience, do you?'

'Along with all the other things, you mean.' He put his head in his hands and muttered, 'They're Mercedes, rigid sides like a box with double doors at the back. Not huge – medium-sized, long-distance lorries, I'd say. They're blue – a sort of royal blue, with a white stripe low down on the side, and they've got DSA written on the side in white capital letters with a big white flash in front of it – shaped like a tick in a kid's schoolbook. I don't know what the letters stand for, if you're about to ask.'

Liz wondered how he could give such a good description. What exactly was his relationship with Jackson's trucking operations? But she would leave that to the Chief Constable and his team to find out.

'So can you tell me where the lorries unload their cargoes?'

'He'll know it's me, if I tell you that. Who's going to protect me when he finds out? He'll get me – even if I'm in prison. I've had it now: if Jackson doesn't get me, Mr Clean, the new Chief Constable, will.' McManus got up from the table and went over to the window; he rested his forehead on the glass and rocked backwards and forwards, gently banging his head on the pane. 'I want protection,' he said, without turning round.

'It goes without saying, that as far as my Service is concerned your help will remain entirely confidential, but I can't give any undertakings about what will happen if Jackson is prosecuted. That's for the Chief Constable.'

Mc Manus snorted, and Liz continued, 'I'll tell the Chief how helpful you've been and I'm sure he'll arrange to have you looked after.'

'He'd be pleased if I was killed. It would save him the embarrassment.'

'Come on, Jimmy. You know that's not true. Just tell me what else you know and then we can get this over with.'

McManus sat down again, at the other end of the table from Liz and started to talk freely for the first time. It was as though something had clicked into position in his head.

'He's got four lockups – warehouses – on industrial estates. They're all off the ring road round the south side of Manchester, the M60. I could point them out on a map. There's one on the south-east side, near Denton, one near Stockport, the other two are up the south-west side, one near Sale and the other near Eccles. He reckons if one of them gets busted, he's still got the others. They're all in different names. You can get to all of them straight off the M60, without going anywhere near central Manchester. That's the attraction for him. The lorries always come in from ports on the south or the east coasts.'

'Thank you. That's just what I needed to know. Is there anything else you can tell me that will be helpful – we're trying to stop these weapons from getting into the hands of terrorists.'

He shook his head. He was knocking his wrist on the edge of the table. 'When I first knew you, Liz, I was determined to get the villains, whatever it took. The system just wasn't capable of punishing all the bastards I came across – too many were getting away with it. You said it wasn't the right way to go about it and I should have listened to you.' He added bitterly, 'I never thought I'd end up on the side of the bastards.'

He looked so drawn and despairing that Liz couldn't help feeling sorry for him. But she said nothing. She rang the bell attached to the underneath of the table to indicate that the interview was over. A uniformed sergeant came in to take McManus away. Liz didn't shake his hand, but just said, 'Goodbye, Jimmy. Thanks for your help.'

42

B Y HALF PAST FIVE Peggy, in Thames House, was talking to her contact in the Border Agency, passing on the description of the lorry that might contain the weapons. She asked for all ports to be alerted but stressed that it was most likely to turn up on the east or south coasts. 'Please let us know as soon as it's sighted, but we don't want it searched, or anything done to make the driver think he's under suspicion. We need it to get to its destination, because what we are most interested in are the people who will meet it there.'

'How are you going to keep tabs on it if we don't delay it?' asked the contact.

'I was just coming on to that,' Peggy replied. 'We want your people to put a marker on it, and that'll help us pick it up even if we miss it at the port. We'll be able to keep our distance as we follow it. Have they got the equipment at all the likely ports?'

'Yes.' But he sounded doubtful. 'That is provided it doesn't turn up somewhere very small.'

'No. Our expectation is that it'll be on a normal freight route.'

'What about the tunnel?'

'I suppose that's a possibility.'

'OK. I'll alert our people there as well.'

Peggy went to see Wally Woods, the chief A4 controller, responsible for the implementation of all surveillance requests. 'Just giving you early warning,' she said. 'It'll most likely be in the next week or so, and we may not know till it arrives at a port. The Border Agency will try to put a marker on. It'll be going up to the outskirts of Manchester. One of four possible destinations. I'll come down tomorrow and give you as much detail as we've got.'

Wally Woods grunted. 'I don't know where we'll find the manpower. We're chock-a-block already.' Wally liked Peggy but he reserved the right to be grumpy with case officers.

'Oh, Wally. Please do your best. Liz says it's really important,' said Peggy, knowing perfectly well that Wally would die in a ditch rather than let Liz Carlyle down.

Peggy's next call was to Ted Poyser. Known to everyone in the Service as Technical Ted, he was the head of its eavesdropping operations. Ted had joined MI5 from the army after a legendary career in some of the most dangerous spots in Northern Ireland at the height of the Troubles. He was getting on now and due to retire in a couple of years, so he left most of the sharp-end work to his younger colleagues, spending most of his time on planning and research.

Peggy found him at his bench in the basement workshops, surrounded, as he nearly always was, with strange-looking bits of electrical kit, wires and laptops, their screens showing changing patterns of wavy lines. Ted seemed to like to work in a clutter. Once a compulsive smoker, the smoking ban had turned him into a compulsive sweet-eater instead, and his bench was always littered with discarded sweet papers and mugs containing cold coffee dregs. As he never seemed to put on weight and no one had ever seen him eating a meal, it was widely rumoured that he lived on a diet of Werther's Originals washed down with coffee. Some of the younger intelligence officers called him 'Grandad' after the Werther's advertisements, but Peggy always addressed him as Ted. Even though Ted was nearly sixty now, he wore his hair, which was very black (unnaturally black, some said), in a ponytail, and he rode a flashy Harley-Davidson motorbike while wearing the latest in leather gear. No one, except probably Personnel, knew anything about his private life, and no one had ever met a partner, or even a friend.

Ted still liked to play an active part in the occasional, particularly interesting operation, and his eyes lit up when Peggy told him that she needed eavesdropping and cameras planted in four warehouses on the outskirts of Manchester, as part of an operation to prevent a group of jihadis taking delivery of guns and ammunition. By now one of the police officers from the Chief Constable's inquiry team had sent down the map coordinates for the warehouses, and also a description and approximate dimensions, all of which they must have got from McManus. By the time Peggy left him, Ted had summoned a Planning Team for first thing the following morning and was contentedly poring over maps.

Peggy went back to her office just in time to pick up a call from Liz, who had returned from Manchester and was back in her flat.

'How was it?' Peggy asked. 'It can't have been easy.'

'It wasn't – at first. He tried to embarrass me by making it personal. But in the end I found it rather sad. It seems such a pity that he's got himself into such a mess. And he really has. I don't know all the details, but it looks as though he's in pretty deep with some very unsavoury characters, and not just the one we're interested in. He's facing a long stretch in prison according to the Chief Constable. Whom I liked, by the way. He's young and seems very straight.'

'Thank goodness for that,' said Peggy.

'How have you got on?' asked Liz.

'I've alerted the Border Agency, Wally and Technical Ted. I got the coordinates through from Manchester, and Ted and his team are going up tomorrow.

'I've warned Wally and Borders that it could come in at any south or east coast port. Borders mentioned the tunnel and I asked them to warn them as well, though it's probably unlikely – they're much more alert there because of all the illegal immigrants. I'll get on to the French tomorrow to ask them to keep a lookout. It would be great if we could know when it's boarding the ferry on their side. The ferries to Harwich come from the Hook of Holland, so I'll get on to the Dutch as well tomorrow first thing.' She suddenly stopped, breathless.

'Go home, Peggy,' said Liz. 'You've done all you can for one day. You sound exhausted.'

So Peggy went home, but later that night she dreamed of lorryloads of guns arriving at darkened ports all round the coast – ports that she hadn't thought of – and driving off unwatched into the night.

43

P EGGY WAS ALWAYS EARLY for appointments. She
wished she wasn't, because it often meant standing
around for ages with cold feet, especially at railway stations
where there were never any empty seats in the waiting
areas. But she knew herself well enough to know that she
would always be the same. She just seemed to have a
chronic fear of being late. Today was no exception. She was
waiting at Paddington Station for Jacques Thibault, the
young computer wizard from the DGSE who was responsible for monitoring Antoine Milraud's computer.

With access to Milraud's computer and his password,
Thibault had been able to follow current communications
easily enough. He was also working hard to reconstruct
the archive of Milraud's previous exchanges with the
Yemeni middleman who had first introduced him to the
young Arab now known as Zara.

But it was taking time and the Yemeni middleman was
no longer responding to emails, as Thibault had found out
when he initiated messages purporting to come from
Milraud. *Expand the net* – that had been Seurat's instruction to Thibault, and Thibault had done his best. But efforts
to work his way into Zara's system had been balked by a

227

sophisticated firewall that Thibault quickly realised would take months, possibly years to break. And there was no question of that; Seurat had made clear that he wanted results yesterday. He had instructed Thibault to seek the help of the British, who were in any case the senior partners in this operation. Peggy in turn had passed the problem to her colleagues in GCHQ.

The day before, her contact in GCHQ had rung to say that they had got something and asked Peggy and her French colleague to come urgently for a meeting. So Peggy, early as ever, was stamping her feet and waiting for Thibault, who had caught an early Eurostar from Paris, to turn up at Paddington so they could catch the 10.15 train to Cheltenham.

Not for the first time she wondered why GCHQ had put itself in Cheltenham. It was such an awkward place to get to from London. It took at least two hours by train, and you had to change and get on an uncomfortable little local train for the last part of the journey. It was no better by car, she thought crossly as she looked at her watch again. It was still only five past ten, so there was nothing to worry about, she told herself, but she was still relieved to see the tall, slim figure of Jacques Thibault walking with long strides across the concourse towards her. She waved and he smiled back with a schoolboy grin that made Peggy feel quite motherly. With his longish, wavy hair, anorak and laptop bag over his shoulder, he looked about eighteen, though Peggy guessed he was probably more or less the same age as she was.

Thankfully for Peggy, whose French was not very advanced, Jacques Thibault had one English grandmother, which meant that he spoke fluent English, honed by annual visits as a boy to Granny Fairfax in her crumbling rectory in the Norfolk Broads. The train was crowded so they didn't talk much in any case. Peggy read the *Guardian* on her iPad while Thibault opened his laptop, plugged earphones into his ears and tapped away on the keyboard.

After they had changed to the local train for the final part of the journey, Peggy explained that they would be met at the station by Charlie Simmons, who had been working on Zara's communications. They would have a sandwich lunch in his office so not to waste any time. 'He said he had something urgent for us,' said Peggy. 'And he particularly wanted you to be here.'

'It's about Zara,' said Charlie as they sat down in his office, overlooking the walkway known as The Street, which ran round the GCHQ headquarters building, whose shape made it inevitable that it would be called 'The Doughnut'. 'We've been following his chat. There's a lot of it – he seems to have contacts all over the globe.'

'Yes,' said Thibault non-committally, munching a sandwich, his long body slouched in his chair.

'I can't say we've got very far,' Charlie Simmons went on. 'Most of the messages are encrypted; a few are not. They're pretty humdrum – Facebook messages to his friends, that sort of thing.'

'And the encrypted ones?' asked Thibault, in a voice without much hope. 'I know that even with supercomputers, it can take a lot of time to crack the latest kinds of coding.'

But Simmons surprised them now. 'Oh we've cracked that easily enough. Only Level Two. I'm about to send you the results, but I'm sure you'll agree they're disappointing. It's just a lot of jihadi chat-room stuff – nothing firm. It's as if they're egging each other on, but in the most general ways.'

Peggy was familiar enough with these kinds of jihadi

online discussions and she was sure that Thibault was too. Death to the West; death to the Jews; death to the Infidels. A kind of OCD with Death, but rarely much specific detail about how to bring these deaths about.

'Could he have inserted more secret information in these emails?' Thibault asked. 'I'm thinking of the odd coordinates in the emails Zara sent to Milraud. I wondered if it was something a bit like those old codes, the book codes and the one-time pads that needed some sort of external reference to translate them.'

'I don't think so,' Simmons said. He sounded cheerful, and Peggy wondered why, and why he had invited them urgently to come to Cheltenham. Maybe he was one of those oddballs who were happiest with bad news.

Thibault was obviously thinking the same thing. He asked bluntly, 'So nothing to report then after all?'

'On the contrary, I've got plenty to tell you. It just came as a bit of surprise. You see, it seems our Zara is something of a mother's boy.'

'So?' said Thibault, his impatience now undisguised.

Charlie Simmons wasn't going to be rushed. 'He goes home practically every other weekend. All the way up to Manchester.' He paused, then went on. 'And while he's home he's often online – like most students these days. He takes his laptop home with him, and engages in the usual correspondence. But then something else happens, and here's the funny thing.'

'What's that?'

'His mother goes online as well.'

'His mother?'

'So it seems. It's a Gmail account in her name, and the recipients – on the surface at least – are other ladies who appear to be of Middle Eastern origin and of a certain age.'

'I don't get it.' Thibault was sitting up now.

'Neither did I. But then I had a closer look. The PC his mother apparently uses only comes to life when Zara's at home. The rest of the time it's in deep hibernation mode. I mean deep – I bet the old lady doesn't even know how to turn it on. Not surprising; it would be odder if the old lady were actually internet-savvy. I think it's pretty clear she's not. Zara's using her machine, and the people he's talking to are doing the same thing – using some unlikely dummy as the supposed sender of the emails.'

'That sounds clever,' said Peggy.

'And simple,' added Thibault.

'Yes. So simple I almost overlooked it. We could have wasted half the firepower of GCHQ on this and got absolutely nowhere, when the answer was staring us in the face. Though if you read the emails you'd be none the wiser. A recipe for tabbouleh. A discussion of how best to cook lamb shanks, with an awful lot of talk about whether it should be four and a half hours or three days. Food is the usual topic, which means numbers – one hundred and fifty grams of couscous, ninety minutes simmering etc.'

'So have you broken this food code?' Peggy was awestruck by the almost basic ingenuity of this. A circle of middle-aged Middle Eastern women, babbling about cooking techniques and recipes and food shops – perfect cover for what she assumed were in fact lethal instructions and commands.

'Pretty much. I'll spare you the details, but basically, every time numbers get used they have to be prefixed by something to indicate what they're referring to – is it time, or quantities or the geographical coordinates of a place?'

'Can't the prefix be in the numbers themselves?' asked Thibault, leaning forward, his elbows on the table, his hands supporting his chin.

'They could be, but then too often they would be the same. The repetition would be suspicious. Anyway, I've made enough progress to want to let you know.'

Oh gosh, thought Peggy. Simmons has made a breakthrough, but it's still only conceptual. He's brought us all the way here to tell us that he's cracked the code, but he doesn't know what the decoded material actually means. It was the classic folly of cryptanalysts the world over – fantastic excitement when they cracked a code, as if that were the be-all and end-all. If code breakers had run Bletchley rather than worked in it, the Germans would have won the War.

'I congratulate you,' Thibault said gravely. 'You have done remarkable work. Please keep me posted with any results that come from it.' He reached for his coat. 'I need to be getting back now.'

'What?' Simmons suddenly was almost shouting. 'It's the results I've brought you here about. Don't you want to know them? You should. There are five conspirators heading for Paris – they're going to meet up with an associate of Zara's called Michel Ramdani. He lives in Paris. He's going to send the five men on to England – it's not clear how they'll be travelling but he's responsible for the arrangements.'

'When are they due to arrive in Paris?' asked Peggy, reaching for her notebook.

'The day after tomorrow. I'd better tell you Ramdani's address. It seems that's where this little conclave is supposed to meet.'

44

IT WAS HALF PAST eleven, dark, windy and pouring with rain, when a small convoy set off from Greater Manchester police headquarters. There were six black Range Rovers with tinted windows. In one was Technical Ted and two colleagues, in a second, three more from Thames House. Both of their vehicles had an assortment of oddly shaped bags and holdalls in the back. In the other four were eight police officers, two in each vehicle, but only one of each pair was recognisable from the word 'POLICE' on the front and back of his black pullover. All the other men wore anonymous dark clothes.

The cars stayed in convoy as they joined the southbound M60, Manchester's ring road. Some miles on, at a junction marked Denton, one of the Thames House cars and two of the police cars peeled off, while the other three kept on the M60, circling the south of Manchester until they reached the turning for Eccles, where they too left the motorway and at a small roundabout headed into an industrial estate, led by one of the police cars. Ted, who was in the passenger seat of the Thames House vehicle, was talking to one of his colleagues in the other convoy.

'All's going fine here,' he was hearing. 'No problem with

the alarm. It's just the usual Chubb as we'd been told. The whole place is quiet as the grave. There's nothing in here but empty wine crates and cardboard cartons, doesn't look as though it's been used for ages. We've put in three mikes and we're doing two cameras; Frankie's just working on the first one now. Then we'll be testing it back to the Ops Room and we should be off to the next place in less than an hour.'

'Sounds good,' said Ted. 'We've just arrived at our first stop, so let's hope it's as easy.'

The three cars pulled up on a square of tarmac outside a large metal warehouse which stood on its own, separated by at least fifty metres of grass and weeds from the next building on the narrow road. The wind was rattling the structure, making it reverberate like a drum. Dim lights on tall concrete lamp posts weakly illuminated the road and the front of the warehouse. One of the police officers came across to Ted's car.

'There's resident security on this estate. They'll be holed up in their hut on the other side. We've warned them we're doing a search here and told them to keep away. If they come out, leave them to us.'

Ted nodded. 'Suits us. We'll be inside and we'll stay there unless you alert us to get out.'

The policeman nodded, and as he did they both saw the lights of a car across the estate.

'Looks as though they're out of their box,' said Ted. 'Over to you.' And as he turned away, one of the police cars drove off in the direction of the headlights.

By this time the small door to the side of the roller door was open and Ted's two colleagues were inside. They had rigged up a couple of lights which showed that the interior of the warehouse was partitioned along one side, forming what seemed, judging by the doors, to be three separate rooms and leaving a large open space in which a lorry or several cars could be parked. It was not what Ted had been expecting. He opened one of the doors and found a room with four bunk beds in a row, very close to each other. The next room was a very small shower room with a lavatory and wash basin, and in the final room, which was a primitive kitchen, there was a pile of boxes, some open, some taped up, all of which seemed to be full of bedding – duvets, pillows and towels.

'Looks like he's expecting visitors,' said Ted.

'Or maybe he's had visitors,' replied Ted's colleague Alfie, who had come in behind him, clutching a drill. 'Some of this stuff has been used.'

'We're going to need six cameras to cover this lot,' said Alfie, 'so we'd better get going. We need to fit four mikes as well.'

'OK. While you do that I'll get onto the others and see how they're getting on. This is going to take longer than we thought.'

The other team had just arrived at their second target, the warehouse on the industrial estate near Stockport, and reported back over a mobile phone. 'Looks as though he uses this one as a store for his club. It feels quite used, as though people have been in recently. There's restaurant-type tables and chairs, boxes of glasses and china and crates of wine and beer.'

'Yeah. Well, that makes sense. It's the one nearest his club. Stick in a couple of mikes and cameras and make sure you leave it as found. Then get out asap, just in case anyone turns up. We've got him under control but he must have staff who go there to get stuff, though probably not in the middle of the night – let's hope not anyway. Then let me know when you're finished, as it may be best for you to do the last one. This one's a bit complicated and we're going to be here some time.'

As he finished speaking, one of the policemen came in.

'We've just had the alert that Jackson's leaving the club. It's about the time he usually leaves so I don't think there's anything to be worried about. We've got a static surveillance near his house and they'll report in when he gets there. And we've got a team trailing him just in case he comes this way.'

. 'Thanks. We'll be at least another couple of hours, so let's hope he goes comfortably to bed. Do the others know? They're nearer him than we are.'

'Yes. Everyone's been warned.'

It was four thirty by the time Ted and his colleagues were ready to leave the warehouse near Eccles, having fixed and tested enough mikes and cameras to provide comprehensive coverage of all the rooms, including the bathroom and the open garage space. There had been no more interest from the security guards, who had been told firmly by the police officers that they would never work in the security business again if they spoke a word in the wrong place. Jackson had gone straight home and apparently gone to bed; his lights were out.

It was still pitch-dark and raining as the little convoy left the industrial estate. The other team had taken on the fourth target, the warehouse near Sale, but were finding it less straightforward than their other two and they were still there.

'There's something not right with this lock,' they had reported when they'd arrived. 'It's wired up to something. Could be some sort of a remote alarm.'

'Well, for God's sake go carefully,' Ted had replied. 'Liz

Carlyle and that little Peggy'll kill us if we cock it up. Send us a photograph.'

And with advice from Ted, sitting on the edge of one of the bunk beds and working from a greatly enlarged photograph on his laptop screen, they had managed to disable what was indeed a remote alarm that would have triggered an alert somewhere, possibly in Jackson's bedroom, if they hadn't noticed it. Once safely inside they had found that this building too had been partitioned down one side, to make what was in fact a set of offices. The three rooms contained desks and chairs and carpets and heaters and a number of large locked filing cabinets.

'Do you want us to open them?'

'No.' Ted made the decision without consulting anyone. 'Leave them alone. We can look at them another time when we've got someone with us who can make sense of what's in them. Just do the mikes and cameras and then get the hell out. It's getting late.'

45

'You look tired.' Liz was watching Martin Seurat closely as they sat in the restaurant.

He started to deny it but then smiled, 'I am a bit,' he acknowledged.

'Small wonder,' she said, and signalled to the waiter to come and take their order.

It had been a long day, especially for Martin – he would have got up in the dark to catch the first Eurostar from Paris, arriving at St Pancras as most people were on their way to work. He'd taken the tube to Westminster and joined the hordes of civil servants heading for their desks in the government offices around Whitehall. Liz had given him coffee in the Thames House canteen, then they'd gone upstairs for the first of the day's meetings, a catch-up with Peggy. The three of them had sat in Liz's office while Peggy pulled together the different strands of the investigation so far. She described what had been found at Jackson's four lockup warehouses the previous night.

'It looks as though he's been using one of them to store his most confidential papers,' she said. 'That was the one with the tamper alarm on the lock and all the locked filing cabinets. The police are going to want to have a look at them when this bit of the operation is over. The only other interesting one is the one near Eccles. That looked as though it had been used for sleeping in, presumably for some of the girls he brings in. But there is space in any of them for a lorry to be parked, so if the guns are coming in concealed in one of his deliveries, they could arrive at any of the four warehouses. We've fitted them all with mikes and cameras so we should be able to see and hear what's going on. We just have to hope that we get enough warning to be able to do something about it.'

'What about the lorry that's supposed to be coming soon from Dagestan?' asked Seurat. 'Any more news on that?'

'Well, we've got the description from McManus of the type of lorry we're looking for, its colour and the name on the side. So if it's the same as usual, we should get warning from the port when it arrives. I'm hoping we might hear from across the Channel – I've alerted all the likely ports in Holland, Belgium and France.'

'It's possible we may hear something on Jackson's phone, but it's been very quiet,' Liz added. 'They're too cunning to risk phone chatter.'

'You seem to have that side of things pretty well covered,' said Martin. 'Well done.'

Peggy smiled, looking pleased.

Then they'd moved on to what Thibault and GCHQ had discovered about the jihadis. Martin said, 'It seems fairly clear that a group of Yemeni-based, English-born terrorists are heading towards England, stopping in Paris to rendezvous.' He explained that the flat of the Parisian radical Ramdani, which was going to be the meeting place, was already under surveillance by Isabelle Florian's people.

Martin went on to say that they hadn't been able to get

eavesdropping inside the flat because it was in a tenement building occupied by a mixture of immigrant families and old people who had been there for years. No one was going to be able to enter or leave the flat without being observed.

At this point he paused and looked at Liz. 'We need to settle the key issue.'

'What's that?' asked Liz.

'Are we going to arrest these people when they arrive at this flat in Paris, or are we going to keep them under surveillance and let them come on to you?'

'I've discussed this with DG and he's talked it through with the Home Secretary and the Chief Constable in Manchester. The Home Secretary wanted us to ask your colleagues to make arrests. She said that we couldn't take the risk of allowing a gang of jihadis into the country when we might not be able to keep them under our control. But DG pointed out that there may be nothing for your colleagues to hold them on, particularly if they carry no weapons. They may well have perfectly valid documents. So she's agreed that you should just follow and watch and hand them on to us. We need to know what they're planning to do before we act.'

Martin nodded. 'I was hoping you'd say that. That is the view of Isabelle and the Interior Ministry, and my own Service agrees. But we do have to remember that there's always the chance, however good the surveillance, that they could give us the slip between Paris and Britain.'

'We just have to take that chance. If we detain them now, we have nothing to charge them with – even in France, they'll be out within days. Besides, there's every chance that others are joining them in the UK – not just Zara. If we grab this bunch the others may find out, and then we'll never locate them.'

Martin was smiling now. 'Clear, as ever. Let's hope the others think so too.'

'Frankly,' said Liz, 'it doesn't much matter if they don't, now we have the Home Secretary's agreement.'

'The others' had been Geoffrey Fane and the CIA Head of Station Andy Bokus. Bokus was already in Fane's office when Liz and Seurat arrived, and judging from the chilly silence they were not enjoying each other's company.

When Liz introduced Seurat, Bokus merely grunted and looked grumpily out of the window, as if he wished he were somewhere else.

'Cheer up, Andy,' said Fane. 'You'll find life south of the river isn't all that bad' – a reference to the impending move of the US Embassy from Grosvenor Square to a new, more isolated but thought to be safer, location in Wandsworth.

Liz noticed that the CIA man was losing weight, though not much – his suit was a little looser at the shoulders than it once would have been, but his buttoned-up jacket did his bulging midriff no favours.

They'd all sat down and waited awkwardly while Daisy brought in a tray of coffee.

'Don't bother, Daisy,' said Liz. 'I'll pour it out.' As she reached forward to pour out the coffee, she'd noticed that Bokus was already drumming his thumbs on the arms of his chair impatiently.

When the coffee was poured, Fane said, 'Elizabeth, why don't you bring us all up to date?'

Liz had been startled by how rude the two men were being to Martin. Bokus hadn't even acknowledged his presence when she'd introduced him and now Fane was behaving as if he wasn't there. But she made no comment and proceeded to summarise the situation. When she finished there was a heavy silence.

Bokus said gruffly, 'You mean to tell me, you got five bad guys – I mean *really* bad guys – right within your sights, and you want to let them come on here to do God knows what?' He was staring at Liz and sounded incredulous.

'We don't have any intention of letting them do anything. Nor do the French.'

'No. We certainly do not,' said Martin Seurat.

Bokus ignored him – it was Liz he was going for. He said in the folksy voice Liz had always been wary of, 'Listen, I'm just a country boy from Ohio. Sometimes I get a little lost if anything gets too complicated. But we used to say back home that a bird in the hand beats two birds in the bush any old day.'

'Did you really say that?' Seurat asked with feigned innocence, and Liz just managed not to laugh. She noted that Fane was staying quiet.

For a brief moment Bokus's eyes flashed, but he stuck to his Huck Finn persona. 'We sure did,' he said, still looking only at Liz. 'And I'm thinking it applies here pretty well. Why risk losing these guys if we can pick 'em up easier than a bird dog grabs a grouse?'

'Why indeed?' muttered Fane.

Liz was about to reply when Seurat broke in. He said simply, 'Here is why.' He looked at Bokus with a steeliness Liz had never seen before. 'The initial information in this case came from you, the Americans. Believe me, we are all grateful for that. And then, the focus shifted to here in the United Kingdom – this man Jackson appeared, and we learned that these British Yemenis are on their way to this country, almost certainly to commit an atrocity.

'But the fact remains, they are meeting first in Paris.

And we believe they were originally considering Paris as the target of their operation – whatever this operation is.'

'Not any more—' Bokus started to say. Seurat held up a hand and the American stopped.

'Hear me out, Monsieur. My point is that Paris has already featured in this case – this is where Zara and the arms dealer Milraud met, and where I fear the other side first suspected they had been observed.'

'Whose fault was that?' Bokus demanded.

'Ours. Not all of us share the American infallibility. In any case, Paris is now again the focal point of this operation and of our cooperation.' He looked around at them all. 'Naturally, we need to respect each other's point of view and to take dissenting opinions into account. But you will appreciate that since this part of the operation is taking place on French soil, then we – the French – must make the final decisions about it. So, since you are asking' – which, thought Liz, no one was – 'I must tell you that I agree with our colleagues here. We will not arrest the jihadis who are meeting in this apartment, and instead we will follow them to their exit point which we all believe will be the UK border.'

Seurat took a deep breath. 'I am sorry if you are not in accord with this, Mr Bokus. And I know that you think this will be the weak decision of another one of those cheese-eating surrender monkeys. But it is the monkeys' decision nonetheless.'

This speech had produced a startled silence in the room. Even Bokus had looked embarrassed in the face of Martin's eloquence. When Liz seized the opportunity to say that the Home Secretary, the DG and the Chief Constable of Greater Manchester police had all agreed to let the operation run to the UK, no one had anything more to say and the meeting had broken up in a chilly atmosphere of recrimination.

Now the waiter arrived and Liz said, 'So what do you want to eat, my cheese-eating friend?'

Seurat laughed. 'I'll just have a starter, I think. They will feed me on the train.'

'Somehow after an hour with Andy Bokus, I don't feel very hungry either – just a starter will do me too. But I need a glass of wine.'

When the waiter had left, Seurat sat back and sighed. 'You OK?' asked Liz.

He smiled. 'Yes. That was just a sigh of relief. A day I am glad is over. Though I will be happier when tomorrow is over as well.'

'Are you worried about it?'

Seurat shrugged. 'No more than I would be normally. Isabelle and her people are in charge, and I have every confidence in them. Thibault seems quite sure that what GCHQ have told him is right. He says it all makes perfect sense. It should be fine, and with any luck they will all be in the UK the day after tomorrow. Then it's your problem,' he said, with a smile.

'Thanks a lot,' said Liz with an affectionate grin. Martin seemed more like his old self now, and she was relieved to see it. His put-down of Bokus hadn't bothered her one bit – in fact, she'd loved it. It was such a change from the catlike way Geoffrey Fane danced around their American colleague. Though it had been direct, it had also been controlled, with no sign of the irritability Martin had been showing recently about Milraud.

Their food arrived, and they ate quickly, talking now of anything but work. Liz told him how her mother, whom he had met several times, had thought about giving up work at the nursery garden she ran, and how her partner Edward had dissuaded her since he rightly sensed she'd go mad if she didn't have enough to do. And Martin talked about his daughter; he was worried about what she'd do after she graduated from the Sorbonne.

It was funny, thought Liz, that when things had been tense between them they had not talked about personal affairs at all; now she felt they were back on their old intimate footing again and it made her happy.

She said, a little reluctantly, 'Tomorrow, will you be there?'

Seurat raised his eyebrows. 'At Ramdani's flat? No. Only the surveillance will be there. I will be with Isabelle and we'll be sitting safe and sound in the DCRI HQ. Nothing to worry about.'

'Good,' she said, forcing a smile. She wished she felt less worried about this operation. She was used to the mix of apprehension and excitement that came just before the action, but somehow this time it felt different. She reached across the table and held Martin's hand. 'There's a train at the crack of dawn, you know.'

He tilted his head back and smiled. 'And how tempting it is. But I should go back tonight.' He shook his head. 'I'd never forgive myself if something went wrong tomorrow and I wasn't there.'

'But you said there was nothing to worry about.' Liz kicked herself for letting her concern show.

Martin put one of his hands on top of hers and looked into her eyes. 'There isn't. But I just feel I need to be there. You'd feel the same, wouldn't you?'

'Of course I would. You're quite right.'

Martin looked at her. 'It'll soon be over.'

'I hope so.'

'And when it is, I was thinking . . .'

'Yes?' asked Liz.

Martin was smiling. 'You remember the hotel in the hills near Toulon?'

'How could I forget?' They had begun their affair there. She remembered the flowers in the garden of the small auberge where they had stayed as spring arrived.

'I thought a few days there would not go amiss.'

'*D'accord*,' said Liz. 'I'd like that very much.'

'Good,' said Martin. 'I'd like it too. Because I love you very much, Miss Liz Carlyle.' And then, as if embarrassed by his display of emotion, he signalled furiously to the waiter for the bill.

46

'I T's AT MOMENTS LIKE this,' Isabelle Florian declared, 'that I miss cigarettes the most.'

She gave Seurat a wry smile, and he nodded. 'I know. Anything is better than the waiting.'

Not for the first time, Seurat thought how fortunate he was to have Isabelle as his counterpart at the domestic intelligence Service. Relations between the DGSE and the DCRI were almost always tense, fuelled by the same kind of competition that seemed to affect domestic and external intelligence services the world over. But whereas Liz had to put up with the know-it-all patronising of Geoffrey Fane, Seurat had long ago established an excellent relationship with Isabelle, one based on mutual respect and by now a genuine liking for each other.

They sat in the operations room in the building that housed the DCRI. It was a windowless and low-ceilinged space, with a series of desk consoles ranged in a half-circle at one end to face a row of large screens that hung from the wall. At the moment just two of them were active. One screen showed a distant shot of the entrance to a tall grim-looking tower block, and the other, its picture obviously coming from a concealed fixed camera, showed the length of a passageway with one open side. You could clearly see the doors of individual flats that ran off the passage; the one in the centre of the picture belonged to the flat of the suspect, Ramdani. But there was no sign of anyone moving in either of these camera views.

At the centre console Alex Carnier, a veteran DCRI Operations control officer, struggled to suppress a yawn. He had a headphone set dangling loosely around his neck, and on the desk in front of him a microphone sat on its stand. He was directing the surveillance operation, but seemed happy enough to have Isabelle and Martin Seurat watching him work.

He turned his head to Isabelle and said, 'They're late.'

She shrugged. 'You said that five minutes ago. They could turn up at any time. What do you want me to do? Ask them to hurry up?'

Carnier gave a grin full of yellow teeth; unlike Isabelle, he pretty clearly hadn't given up cigarettes. The new regulations banning smoking in public buildings applied here too; Seurat thought it must have been hell for a twenty-a-day man.

'It's only been half an hour,' said Seurat mildly. 'There may be some reason for the delay.' Though Thibault had been very specific: the latest decoded email had said four o'clock sharp for the rendezvous at the flat.

Carnier brushed his greying hair back with one hand, then leaned forward and spoke into the microphone. 'Team Three, anything alive out there?' he asked, more in hope than expectation.

There was the crackle of a car radio, then a voice replied dully, '*Rien.*'

Isabelle had explained to Martin that there were six

teams, each of three people, on the operation. Most of them were in cars, parked safely out of sight, though there would also be a few surveillance officers on foot around Ramdani's tower block, which along with half a dozen other relics of some bright city planner's 'vision' in the 1970s sat on the edge of Seine-Saint-Denis, one of the constellation towns just north-east of Paris. It was all public housing, now inhabited overwhelmingly by first- and second-generation immigrants. Seurat often wondered whose idea it had been to create these hellholes so far away from the rest of the city's life. Or perhaps that had been the rationale: to deposit the North Africans who'd flocked to France in the aftermath of the Algerian war out of sight of the public face of the city, known the world over for its elegance.

Isabelle said, 'Martin, if you want some coffee there's a machine down the hall.'

'It's broken,' said Carnier. 'But there's a café on the corner.'

'I'm fine,' said Martin. Sod's law said that if he went out now the jihadis would show up.

But three hours later there was still no sign of them. Not that there had been any sign of Ramdani either. The surveillance had begun the day before, with only one team, but Ramdani hadn't left his flat in that time. A light in the front room suggested that he was there, but it had stayed on all night and that, taken with the failure of the others to arrive, meant that his presence in the flat was now open to question. Seurat said as much to Isabelle.

'I know,' she said. 'That's worrying me too. What if they changed plans and are meeting somewhere else?'

'It doesn't seem likely or we'd have seen Ramdani leave his flat. Thibault says GCHQ will notify him immediately if there's any change of plan.'

'Still, I'd like to make sure. Alex,' she said, turning to Carnier, 'I'd like to establish if Ramdani is actually in the flat. Any ideas?'

Twenty minutes later they watched on the screen a young man walking along the corridor of the tower block. He wore a parka and trainers, and carried a sheaf of flyers advertising a local takeaway pizza joint. Carnier said his name was Philippe, and that he had been with the DCRI for less than a year. 'But he's good,' Carnier said. 'He wanted to be an actor but he got tired of waiting at tables to pay his rent.'

They watched as Philippe began at the far end, ringing the buzzer of each flat one by one. Most of the doors were answered, sometimes by small children, always with the chain on, and Philippe would give them one of the pamphlets, then move on to the next apartment.

When he got to Ramdani's door he paused, and looked around. The corridor was empty as he rang the buzzer. He waited a good thirty seconds but no one answered, so he buzzed again. Still nothing. Philippe knelt down and looked through the letter box, then he stood up and moved over to peer through the small window to the side of the door of the flat. His voice came over the speaker on Carnier's desk, saying quietly, 'Nothing doing. And no sign of him through the window. I can see into the living room.'

Carnier said, 'Are you sure the buzzer's working? Maybe you should knock.'

'I can hear the buzzer from outside. The walls of this place are paper-thin.'

'Maybe he's in the shower – or asleep. Try knocking.'

So this time Philippe knocked on the door as well as

pushing the buzzer again. 'That's enough,' said Isabelle. 'He'll alert the neighbours and they'll think it strange he's so persistent.'

But it was too late, the door to the next apartment opened and an old lady with a walking stick came out, remonstrating furiously. As Philippe beat a hasty retreat, Carnier gave a laugh. The old lady was still shouting at him as he reached the far exit of the corridor by the lifts.

'Well,' said Isabelle. 'At least we've learned his neighbour's nosy. Could be useful.'

'She was as mad as a hornet,' Philippe said when he got downstairs and left the building. 'She told me that if her neighbour wanted a pizza he would have answered the door. I asked if she'd seen him recently.'

'And?'

'She said . . .' and he hesitated.

Seurat and Isabelle leaned forward to hear. Carnier snapped impatiently, '*What* did she say?'

'She said I should piss off.'

Carnier looked at Isabelle. 'What do you think?'

'I don't think he's in there.'

She looked at Seurat. He thought she was probably right. He knew what he wanted to happen next, but it was risky. Liz would never forgive them if they blew the whole operation. He waited for Isabelle to speak – this was her operation after all, even if it came at his instigation. In one sense he was only a privileged guest here.

Isabelle said, 'I think we should go in and have a look.'

Carnier said, 'You sure? What happens if Ramdani comes back while we're in there?'

'We'll put people outside to stop him coming in. We tell him that a smell of gas has been reported and we're required to check it out for safety reasons. So no one is allowed into the building while we do that. If he goes away your people will follow him, Alex.'

'And if the others turn up?'

'We tell them the same thing. They have to wait till the all-clear is given. I hope none of that happens, but I think it's a chance we have to take. It doesn't make any sense that the meet didn't take place. Ramdani wouldn't have had much time to change the plans, so it would have to have been a change from the other end. But whatever's happened, we're now out of touch with the jihadis – that's worrying, to say the least. I'm hoping there may be something in the flat that indicates what they're up to.'

As Carnier digested this, he looked at Seurat, who stayed silent – Isabelle had just decided to do what he'd been hoping she would, but it was certainly risky and he wondered what Liz would have done.

Finally, Carnier shrugged. 'OK. I'll set it up.'

Isabelle nodded. 'We'll need the locksmith – I don't want any doors broken down. The idea of this is to keep it as quiet as possible. A discreet entry, a quick search by officers with concealed weapons to make sure he's not there, then I'll go in.'

'I'll come with you,' said Seurat immediately. Carnier looked at him dubiously. Isabelle said quickly, 'It's all right, Alex. Martin knows more than anyone else what we're looking for.'

47

THE SKY WAS PITCH-BLACK now, and the corridor was only dimly lit by the few bulbs that were working. Seurat could just make out the two armed officers who were to go in first in case Ramdani was there. They were wearing fluorescent yellow jackets with 'GAZ' written on the back. One of them carried a bag, its contents not usual for a gas fitter.

Their instructions were to get inside the flat as quickly and quietly as they could and to avoid, if at all possible, attracting the attention of the other inhabitants in the block. The previous summer had seen three nights of rioting at this estate, which had started when the arrest of a drug dealer had gone wrong and a child had been shot. The last thing Isabelle wanted was anything to happen that might make trouble flare up again, alert Ramdani and the jihadis and send them off on another tack.

As the 'gas men' approached the door of Ramdani's flat, Seurat and Isabelle waited at the end of the corridor. It was dinner time and quiet except for the sound of television coming from the flats. At each end of the corridor two more men in yellow GAZ jackets stood ready to detain anyone who tried to come along the corridor.

The first policeman rang the buzzer and knocked on the door. They all waited tensely in silence, and suddenly a door opened. But it was not the one to Ramdani's flat. An old lady came out of the next apartment; Isabelle groaned.

'Who the hell are you?' the old lady was demanding. She had her stick with her and waved it threateningly at the men standing by Ramdani's door.

'It's perfectly all right, Madame,' said the senior of the men politely. 'Just go back inside, if you don't mind. We've had a report of a smell of gas coming from this flat and we need to go inside to investigate. It is probably nothing serious but we need to check. Do you know whether your neighbour is in?'

'I've no idea where he is,' she said. 'It's not my business to keep track of my neighbours. But if he's not answering the door, I suppose he's out. What are you going to do – break his door down?'

'No, Madame, there'll be no need for that,' replied the 'gas man', soothingly. 'Now if you'd just like to go inside out of the cold, we'll check it out. I don't think there's any problem but better safe than sorry.' And he ushered her gently back inside her flat and waited until she closed the door.

There was a sigh of relief from the end of the corridor as Isabelle let out her pent-up breath. 'He did well,' said Seurat. 'That old lady reminds me of my grandmother. Terribly nosy, absolutely fearless, and won't take any nonsense from anyone.'

The man with the bag started work on the lock. It took him only seconds to have the door open and the two officers went inside. Isabelle and Seurat went up to the front door but they waited outside by the door as the armed officers went through the apartment. After a few minutes they came back to the external corridor. 'The place is empty.'

'All right, thank you very much,' Isabelle said. 'Stay here please. I don't think we'll be very long, and then you can go and tell the old lady that everything's fine. Hopefully she'll forget about us.' In her grey parka and jeans Isabelle cut an unremarkable figure, but she was clearly in charge. 'All right, Martin? Time to have a look around, eh?'

They started in the living room at the front of the flat. There were thin curtains hanging at the window but they were not drawn. An unshaded bulb hanging from the centre of the ceiling was switched on. The room was tidy but minimally furnished with a threadbare sofa, one grubby armchair that had a rip in the fabric on its back, and a low table marked by the rings of mugs and glasses, on which was a two-day-old copy of *Libération* and a newspaper in Arabic.

The centre of the floor was covered by a faded carpet, the floorboards visible round the edges, and there was an electric fan heater in one corner that wasn't plugged in. There were no cupboards, desks or anything else that might contain papers, and no laptop or other electronic device. A new-looking television set on a stand in one corner of the room was the only thing that looked as if it had cost any significant sum.

Down the corridor, back towards the front door, was a small kitchen. There were cupboards above and below a worktop on one side of the room; the officers had left them open. Seurat peered in at their small collection of tins, cereal boxes, small bags of flour and sugar, a carton of salt, and an old jam jar full of couscous. The fridge was almost empty – wilted stalks of celery, three eggs in a little rack, a half-full milk carton and a chunk of hard cheese that looked as though it had been there for a good long time.

'If this guy was expecting visitors he hasn't exactly stocked up to feed them,' Seurat said.

Isabelle was examining the oven and grill. 'Thank God it's gas,' she said. 'I suddenly wondered if these flats only had electricity.'

Opposite the kitchen was a small bathroom. There was a bath with a shower over it and a plastic shower curtain. It was bone-dry. No one had taken a shower or a bath for a long time. The sink was streaked with the detritus of Ramdani's last shave – little black hairs that studded the basin like steel filings. On the porcelain top a razor lay carelessly askew, next to a can of shaving foam, its cap off. Seurat opened the mirrored front of the small bathroom cabinet and saw one stick of roll-on deodorant, a box of plasters, a pair of tweezers and an opened pack of razor blades.

'Looks as though he doesn't have a beard,' was Seurat's comment.

Behind him Isabelle was pulling at the wooden slats on the side of the bath, but they wouldn't give. She said, 'I don't think he's hiding under there. Not if he ever planned on coming out.'

Seurat snorted. 'I have to say, this all seems unnecessarily grim. I don't have any clear picture of Ramdani, but this flat barely feels lived in.'

'I know what you mean. After three days here any sane man would jump off the balcony outside. I bet he hasn't been here long. And wasn't planning to stay much longer.'

Seurat nodded. 'But where has he gone? And why isn't he here now? I don't get it.'

'Come on. Don't let's hang about. There's still the bedroom to check.'

The bedroom did nothing to lift their spirits. It held a double bed, and a cheap-looking desk with four drawers, containing a few pens and pencils, some rubber bands, paper clips and a lot of dust but no paper. A metal chair, a small bedside table on which sat a little lamp and nothing else, and a built-in cupboard that contained one empty suitcase completed the furnishings.

'Honestly,' said Seurat, gazing at the paltry contents of the room, 'this could be a doss house. Do we know anything about this guy?'

'Not much,' admitted Isabelle. 'We're working on it, but for now we've only official records. We couldn't exactly ask around here if we didn't want him scared off.'

'So what do we know?'

'He's a native Parisian – Yemeni mother, French father. The father is not in evidence, and the mother is dead. Ramdani grew up half a mile from here. He's twenty-five, and when he left school he went and lived in Yemen for a few years – at least that's what Immigration say; if he went anywhere else it didn't get stamped in his passport. He's on benefits now, but used to work in a little bar down the street – again, we didn't want to ask questions; I got this from the Office of Employment.' She added a little defensively, 'We can find out a lot more than that, of course. But at this stage discretion seemed to be preferable to a lot of inquiries.'

Seurat sighed, looking around the dismal room. 'I'm just frustrated the jihadis didn't arrive. And this guy seems to have disappeared and left virtually no sign of himself. Your people are sure he couldn't have got past them somehow?'

'Absolutely. We've had the camera up for thirty-six hours. No one's been out of this flat – or in. You've seen for yourself there's no other way out. And if he were hiding in here, we'd have found him by now. There isn't room to swing a cat in this place. He must have left before we started watching. That's the only explanation, isn't it?' she added, since she wasn't sure Seurat was paying attention to what she was saying.

He wasn't. He had gone over to one corner of the room and was looking up at the ceiling, where there was a square metal grating.

'What is it?' asked Isabelle, slightly annoyed. Martin was always so inquisitive, she thought, even when it just wasted time.

'It must be some kind of central heating system. There are no radiators in this place and it's not freezing cold,' he said, purposely misunderstanding her.

'What about it? The officers will have checked that out.'

'Maybe. But maybe not.' He picked up the metal chair and put it under the grating. 'There are no screws in this. How do you think it stays in place?'

'Heaven knows. It probably rests on a ledge. Can't you see?'

As he stood on the chair the cover was only inches above his upraised hand. He reached up and gently pushed. One corner of the grating lifted and then dropped back into place. He pushed again with both hands and the entire square cover lifted up and he was able to move it over to rest on the inside of the ceiling. He stared up into the hole above his head. He poked one arm through until it disappeared into the gap, and felt around in the blackness. Then he climbed down.

'Find anything?' asked Isabelle sarcastically. She shared Seurat's frustration, but couldn't see the point of what he was doing now.

'Not yet.' He reached into his pocket and took out a small metal torch. Then he repositioned the chair to place it directly below the opening in the ceiling and climbed back onto it again.

'You're not thinking of going up there, are you? Let the officers do it. They're younger than you.'

'Don't worry – if anyone's going to have to crawl along a shaft it won't be me. I just want to take a look to see where it goes.'

He hoisted both arms up into the gap, holding his torch in his teeth, and leaned his elbows on the ceiling. Then before Isabelle could protest Seurat pulled himself straight up into the air until his head disappeared into the opening. He's strong, thought Isabelle admiringly despite herself, for inwardly she thought this was all a waste of time.

'Come on down, Martin,' she said, staring at his legs hanging in the air. He must have replied, but his voice was muffled by the surrounding walls of the shaft.

'What did you say?' Isabelle half shouted, and just then he dropped back down again, missing the chair and falling onto the floor with a thud.

'Are you all right?' Isabelle was standing over him and held out a hand. But he sat up, shook his head and said, 'I'm fine. My arms suddenly gave way.'

'I told you it was a job for a younger man,' she said unsympathetically. 'What's up there anyway?'

'There's a duct, quite wide. You could crawl along it if you were slim – and young,' he added with a smile. 'It must run along the top of all the flats in this corridor. I can't swear to it, but I thought I heard something moving up there.'

'It was probably rats. Or the pipes heating up.'

'Mmm. Perhaps. We need to find out exactly where it goes. There may be an exit he could have used.'

'Why would he want to go out that way?'

'He may have spotted the surveillance and put two and two together.'

'Yes, and he may have invisible powers too,' she replied caustically.

'But don't you see? That would explain why the others didn't show. He may have warned them.'

'I don't believe it,' said Isabelle. 'We've been very careful.'

Martin shrugged. 'Well, whatever. But the duct's certainly a possible way out – and in as well. Do you think we can get a plan of where it goes?'

'I'm sure we can from the building management company. But I can't see much point in doing it now. There's nothing here to help us learn what the jihadis are planning to do, or where they are. And if you're right and Ramdani saw the surveillance, he's probably not coming back. If we stay here much longer we're going to have the old lady next door coming out to find out what's going on. I think we ought to leave now and get the "gas men" to tell the old lady that everything's fine. Then we can get the plans tomorrow and see whether it's worth sending someone to explore the ducting.'

Although he hated leaving the job unfinished, Seurat couldn't think of any reason to object to Isabelle's plan, so they put everything back as it was in the flat and went towards the front door where the two officers were waiting in the passage.

They closed the door behind them and Isabelle and Martin Seurat began to walk off down the corridor as the officer rang the old lady's bell. Nothing happened. So he rang again and put his ear to the door, listening for her. Then the officer called out to Isabelle, 'I think you should come.'

'What is it?' she said as she and Seurat walked back.

'Listen.'

Isabelle bent down and opened the letter box. She could hear a gasping, choking sound.

She said, 'I think she's ill. Sounds like a heart attack. Open the door.'

The lock was no more difficult than the one on the flat next door and within seconds the door was open. Martin elbowed Isabelle out of the way and went in first. He's acting as if the old bird is his grandmother, Isabelle thought with amusement.

The flat had exactly the same layout as the one next door and the sounds were coming from behind the closed door to the living room in front. Martin pushed the door open and saw the old lady standing up, held on her feet by a thin, dark young man. He had one arm round her neck and with his other hand he was pushing a revolver hard into the side of her throat. The old lady's eyes were open but only the whites were showing; her mouth was slack and saliva was dribbling out and down her chin. Her skin was a bluish white and there was a raw, rattling noise coming from her open mouth.

'Let her go,' shouted Martin. 'Can't you see? You're suffocating her.'

The young man, whom Isabelle recognised from the photos as Ramdani, tightened his grip on the old lady's throat, and pointed his pistol at Martin. He didn't look much more than twenty years old, thought Isabelle, and he looked frantic.

'Stop it!' Martin commanded. 'She's choking. She can't breathe.'

Isabelle added, trying to sound calm, 'Put the gun down. We don't want anyone to get hurt. And let the lady go.'

The man stared at Isabelle, and for a moment she thought that her words had got through to him. Martin must have thought so too, for he took a step forward and extended his hand. 'Just give me the gun.'

Ramdani relaxed his grip on the old lady's throat, but instead of handing over the gun, he held his arm straight out and fired.

Isabelle watched in horror as the shot hit Martin square in the chest, its force knocking him to his knees. Immediately one of the armed officers behind her raised his own weapon and fired back.

Ramdani's face creased in agonised surprise. He dropped the gun as his legs gave way, and he knocked down the old lady as he fell.

There were three bodies on the floor now, but only one of them was moving. The old lady was gasping and shuddering, the other two were still. One of the officers was on his phone calling for backup and medical assistance, Isabelle was kneeling on the floor, holding Martin's head up, his blood running over her hands and down his jacket. She was shouting, 'Martin, Martin,' but he didn't respond and she knew that he was dead.

Later Isabelle could only dimly recall the sequence of events that followed the shootings. Looking back she realised that she had acted automatically to try to prevent a public furore. She had sent the officers in their GAZ jackets outside to explain to interested bystanders, attracted by the ambulance and the presence of the police, that there had been a gas emergency, and that an old lady had had a heart attack, but the emergency was over and the old lady was still alive and was going to hospital.

She had insisted that the bodies of Martin and the young man, presumably Ramdani, once they had been formally declared dead, be left where they were until the middle of the night, when they could be taken out secretly.

She had stayed, at first sitting on the floor beside Martin, tears running down her cheeks, then sitting in the kitchen making the dreadful but necessary phone calls. Throughout this, some of her colleagues had thoroughly searched the old lady's flat. It was obvious how Ramdani had got in. The grating in the bedroom was off and there was a gaping hole in the ceiling. Why he had chosen her flat no one could explain, unless he had gone into the ducting when he heard the knocking on his door and thought he could hide there. Or perhaps he had heard Seurat come up into the crawl space, and panicked. He might have thought it would be safe to hide in the old lady's flat, or possibly he'd thought he could escape through her front door, until he'd realised that the officers were outside in the corridor. When they'd broken in, he must have intended to use her as a shield for his escape.

By the time the medical team returned to remove the bodies, Isabelle was back in the living room sitting beside Martin. Before Ramdani was taken out, she ordered a policeman to search his body thoroughly. She was glad she did – in a trouser pocket they found a folded train schedule. It was for the Eurostar from Paris's Gare du Nord to London.

Watching as Martin was zipped into a bag and taken away, Isabelle thought how unnecessary his death was, and cursed herself for letting him push ahead of her as they came into the flat. Like the grandmother he had been telling her about, and like the old lady who had now been taken despite her protests to hospital, Martin had been absolutely fearless. And curious, fatally curious.

The only good thing to come out of this whole dreadful night, she told herself, was that it was now pretty certain that the terrorists were heading for England.

48

A T THE SAFE FLAT in Paris, Annette Milraud was in
the kitchen making a late supper. Her husband
Antoine was with her. Martin Seurat had decided to move
Antoine from the Montreuil house to share the flat, judging that he was likely to cooperate more if he was with his
wife than if they were kept separated. As well as the guards,
Jacques Thibault was there this evening too. He was monitoring Milraud's laptop and phone for any messages from
Zara or the contact in Dagestan – any communication at
all that might throw light on what might happen next. If
need be, he could immediately ask Milraud to explain.

Annette poked her head round the sitting-room door.
'Would you like to join us for supper?'

'No, thanks,' said Thibault. 'I'll stay here.'

As well as Milraud's laptop, he kept checking his own
for any news of the operation at Ramdani's flat. From the
kitchen he could hear the low murmur of the Milrauds'
conversation. Once Annette gave out a loud groan, and he
heard Antoine say, 'It will be all right, I promise.'

It was about eleven o'clock when the landline phone rang.
Thibault picked it up, thinking with relief it must be Isabelle

at last. But it was a man's voice. He identified himself as a senior police officer. 'Am I speaking to Monsieur Thibault?'

'Yes,' said Jacques, warily, wondering why on earth a police officer had his name and this number.

'I have been asked to ring you by Madame Isabelle Florian.'

'Is she all right?' asked Thibault.

'Yes. But she wished me to tell you that there has been some shooting at a flat in Seine-Saint-Denis. The occupant of an apartment has been shot dead.'

The policeman seemed to hesitate and Thibault sensed that there was more to come. 'Is he the only casualty?'

The policeman said slowly, 'One other person was shot. He is also dead, alas.'

'I'm sorry,' said Thibault, thinking it must be some poor policeman who had gone first into the flat. Thibault barely registered what the caller said next – 'A Monsieur Martin Seurat from your Service, I believe' – but then the words sank in.

'Martin Seurat? Are you sure?'

'Positive, Monsieur. He was dead when he reached the hospital. I am so very sorry.'

In the background Thibault heard Annette clearing the table in the kitchen. He thanked the policeman for calling and hung up. He would learn the details later on; right now, he was too stunned to take in much more than the death of a senior officer of the DGSE.

'What's wrong?' Milraud was in the doorway to the kitchen, eyeing him suspiciously.

Thibault stared back at him. 'There's been a shooting.'

'Where?' Milraud asked, bewildered. Milraud had not been told anything about Ramdani or the anticipated arrival in Paris of the group of jihadis, but that didn't stop Thibault's mounting anger.

'In a tower block The wrong man got shot. Martin Seurat is dead.'

'What?'

'I said Seurat is dead.'

A plate shattered on the floor in the kitchen. A moment later Annette appeared in the doorway. 'What did you say?'

'I think you heard me.'

She looked at Thibault with disbelief, her arms outstretched. For once Antoine didn't try to comfort her but sat down heavily in one of the sitting-room chairs. He was clearly stunned, one hand on his forehead, his head bowed.

'But why?' asked Annette, as tears began to trickle from her eyes.

Thibault sensed that she must have had feelings for Seurat. He said, 'I don't know the details. Obviously something went badly wrong.' He stared angrily at Milraud.

Annette was crying openly now. 'But this is too dreadful.'

'I know,' said Thibault in a cold voice.

Milraud looked up. 'How can that have happened? I never imagined anything like this.'

'Oh no?' said Thibault. 'What did you think was going to happen when you met that Arab in the Luxembourg Gardens? What did you think would result from your meeting in Berlin? Did you think it was all just a harmless game?'

Milraud said, 'Martin was my colleague for years. Whatever our later differences, he and I were once very close.'

Thibault looked at him incredulously. 'You talk as if you were old pals who sadly no longer saw each other. We all know your story – they use you as a case history of betrayal in the Ethics lecture when we join the Service. So don't try to whitewash your past; it just dirties the name of a man who was widely admired. One who died trying to prevent the harm you were encouraging.'

Milraud sat up. 'You are blaming me for his death? I've told you everything I know.'

'No doubt.' Thibault shook his head in contempt. 'What a pity you couldn't have done it earlier.'

Ten minutes later Thibault sat gazing at the screen of his laptop but not seeing it. He could not have tolerated any more talking with either Milraud, but thankfully they had withdrawn to their bedroom. There was no one for him to phone: Isabelle would be busy for hours now, or she wouldn't have asked a police officer to break the news.

Then his mobile phone bleeped and the screen lit up. It was a text message from Peggy in London:

Charlie has just unzipped message: expected party in Paris cancelled. Group delayed leaving Yemen, now going straight on to UK. Ramdani to make own way and join them there. Sorry so late in letting you know. Problem with decoding. Peggy.

He stared blankly at the screen now, trying to still a surge of nausea. Perhaps if there hadn't been a decoding problem and the message had come through earlier, Martin Seurat would still be alive.

49

L IZ WAS LYING ON her bed in her Kentish Town flat, shoes off but still fully dressed. Isabelle had promised to let her know as soon as there was news of the group of jihadis, due to arrive at four o'clock at the flat in Paris. But she had heard nothing before she left work at seven and still nothing three hours later, by which time she had stretched out on her bed, with both her phones beside her. She was half asleep when her landline started ringing. She sat up and grabbed the handset.

'Hello.'

'Liz, it's Peggy.'

'Oh, Peggy. I thought you might be Isabelle. Have you heard anything from Paris?'

'No. But it will have been a no-show. That's probably why they haven't rung. I've just heard from Charlie Simmons. There's been a message in the cooking code. It was sent this morning but it's taken him ages to decrypt because it was full of mistakes. He thinks whoever sent it didn't properly understand the rules and it was badly encoded. Anyway he's managed to get into it and apparently it says that they're not going to Paris after all. They're coming straight on to Britain. I'm just about to text Jacques

Thibault. They must all have been wondering why no one turned up at the flat. They were probably hanging on, hoping they were just late.'

'Yes, but I'm surprised they didn't let us know that no one had appeared. I wonder what they've been doing. I'm going to ring Isabelle now to see what's going on.'

'OK. While you do that I'll text Jacques. Then I think we need to warn A4 that Zara might be on the move soon. Because if his friends are on the way here, they may arrive tonight, and he's the only angle we've got on them.'

'Yes, and when I've spoken to Isabelle, or Martin if I can't get her, I'll warn the Manchester Counter-Terrorist Group that we may have some action for them soon. Our friends may well be heading for one of those warehouses.'

Liz put the phone down and was just about to pick it up again to ring Isabelle when her mobile suddenly came to life.

'Liz, it's Isabelle.'

'Hello. We've been wondering where you were. I gather no one turned up. You've must have had a rather boring evening.'

There was a pause. Then Isabelle said, 'Well, actually that's not quite true.'

'Why? What happened?'

'It's true the people we expected didn't show – but we were puzzled why and we decided to search the flat to see if there were any clues to what was going on, and our man didn't seem to be there. But he was there – he was hiding in the next-door flat and, Liz, I'm so sorry . . .' Her voice crumpled.

'What is it? What's happened?'

She could hear Isabelle sucking her breath in, trying to

pull herself together. Then she managed to say, 'Martin, he was shot.'

'Shot?'

'Liz, I am so sorry. Martin is dead.'

Liz went ice-cold. She didn't want to believe what she'd heard. She took a deep breath, trying to control herself, and said as calmly as she could, 'What happened?'

While Isabelle explained, Liz tried to focus, to listen. But the words ran like noisy flowing water in the background while one brutal fact kept occupying the foreground – Martin was dead. Isabelle was explaining that when the jihadis hadn't shown up, she and Martin had taken a gamble and gone in, hoping to find evidence of what was being plotted. Martin had been curious, Isabelle explained – and Liz thought, *damn Martin, he was always curious*.

And it was here Liz completely tuned out, not wanting to hear the details of the death of the man she loved. Isabelle was still talking as a thousand images flashed through Liz's head: of her first meeting with Martin at the DGSE's old-fashioned headquarters on the outskirts of Paris; of Martin down at Bowerbridge, her family home, and the way he had taken to the place – so quintessentially English, he'd said; and of how Martin had chuckled when he'd seen the childhood relics Liz still kept in her bedroom there – the rosettes from gymkhanas, the watercolours she had liked to paint as a girl, and the photograph taken by her father as she stood gap-toothed and beaming and no more than nine years old, holding perhaps the titchiest fish ever to be yanked (and that with some grownup help) from the waters of the river Nadder.

All this came at her in a concentrated rush, which made her smile momentarily – though each time she had a loving image of him the grim news of his death intervened, and her memories fell away like waves hitting an unexpected reef.

She became aware that Isabelle was no longer talking. Liz did her best to pull herself together. She said mechanically, 'Thanks, Isabelle, for letting me know.'

'Liz, did you hear what I said? I said I thought you would want to come over.'

'Of course. Should I be arranging things?'

There was an awkward pause, and Liz suddenly realised that she had no real position in this. She hadn't been Martin's wife, not even legally his partner; officially, she had no real status in Martin's life at all.

She asked Isabelle, 'Have you told Mimi?' Martin's daughter.

'Not yet.'

'Or Claudette?' Martin's ex-wife, who lived in the Brittany countryside. It had not been a happy divorce – she had left Martin for an old boyfriend – but lately they had re-established speaking terms and could discuss their daughter civilly enough. Martin's bitterness at his wife's desertion had obviously been intense, but she remembered now how once as they were having coffee after dinner, he'd explained that since Liz had come into his life, his anger with his ex-wife had evaporated.

'No, I haven't called her yet. Listen, Liz, give me half an hour and I will phone you back. But remember one thing. You were the most important person in Martin's life.'

'It's kind of you to say that, Isabelle.' She was doing her very best not to sob but her eyes filled with tears.

'I'm not just saying it to be kind – he told me often enough.'

*

271

It was long after midnight when Isabelle called again. In the intervening time Liz had got up and made coffee, checked her diary for appointments the next day, rung Peggy and told her the news and that she'd be in Paris tomorrow, then asked her to tell DG about Martin. She went online and booked a ticket on the Eurostar, then put a few things in an overnight bag, just in case. Finally, having run out of diversions, she collapsed in an armchair in her sitting room. She sat still for several minutes, slowly composing herself. She didn't actually want to think any more about Martin just now – it was too painful. But quite unbidden, the memory of their last meeting came back to her, and she thought of his words – *Because I love you very much, Miss Liz Carlyle.* And suddenly she started to cry, then cried and cried until she could cry no more.

When her tears were utterly exhausted, she got up and went to the bathroom and washed her face. As she dried it the phone rang.

It was Isabelle again. 'I have reached Mimi and Claudette, Liz.'

'I hope they are all right.' She had little sense of Claudette. Early on in their relationship it had been clear that Martin didn't want to talk about his ex in any detail, something that Liz had always been grateful for, since it meant there were no shadows hanging over them.

'Well, Claudette was shocked, of course. I don't know if you ever met her.'

'No, I didn't.'

'She likes to control things in her life, Liz, so the unexpected tends to throw her at first, then she reasserts control, if you understand.'

'Yes,' said Liz, but she wasn't sure what Isabelle was getting at.

'At first she decided there must be a funeral right away. I explained that couldn't happen. Because of the circumstances there will have to be a post-mortem and there may be an inquiry, though it will be secret of course. Everything is being done to make sure there is no publicity – at present anyway – as we don't want to alert Zara and his friends. And I told Claudette you should be consulted.'

'Thank you,' Liz said mechanically. She didn't really feel able to cope with all this at present.

'She didn't like that – not because it was you, Liz; she has no axe to grind, but because she always wants to decide everything herself. But she did say she would be happy to have you attend the service.'

'That's big of her,' said Liz. Then she took a deep breath and forced herself to focus. 'I don't think there's much family, Isabelle. Martin's parents are both dead and he was an only child. My real concern is what Mimi wants. It's her wishes we should follow here.'

Liz had only met the girl once. Martin's relations with his daughter had been strained after the divorce; living with her mother, Mimi had not surprisingly sided with her in what had been an angry parental split. But since coming to Paris to attend the Sorbonne, she had begun to see her father regularly, and relations had improved immeasurably. When Liz had met her, not in Martin's flat but on the neutral ground of a café, conversation had been polite but strained at first.

Then Martin had excused himself to make a phone call and Liz had admired Mimi's new pair of boots, and suddenly they had begun to talk freely about all sorts of things – clothes, films, and why they hated cigarette smoke and were glad Martin had given up, and whether Paris was rainier than London – and their conversation was so spontaneous and friendly that when Martin had come back from making his call, he felt (as he said affectionately to Liz later that evening) that he was almost surplus to requirements.

Now Isabelle said, 'Actually, I have just come off the phone to Mimi – that's why I am so late ringing you again. Her mother broke the news to her, and of course she is distraught. I'd given Claudette my number and Mimi must have got it from her. At first, she wanted all the details of her father's death. To tell you the truth, I ducked that, Liz. I hope you think that was the right thing to do.'

'Yes,' said Liz, thinking that she didn't know the details either. She hadn't been listening when Isabelle was telling her what had happened. 'She'll learn all about it in due course,' she said, thinking, *So will I.*

'She wanted to make sure you'd been told, but she didn't have your number. I think she was relieved to learn that I'd already been in touch. She said she hoped you would come over right away. She'll take this very hard but I'm sure your presence here would be a great comfort.'

'I will,' said Liz. 'I'll be on the Eurostar that gets in at quarter past ten. But I don't really know Mimi at all.'

'I'll send a car to meet you and take you to the flat. Right now you are the one link to her father. She said that the last time she saw Martin he told her he hoped to marry you. He told her everyone has a true love in their life but not everyone is lucky enough to find them. He said he was one of the lucky ones.'

50

PEGGY KINSOLVING LIKED TO wake early – one of the best things in life was having a job she was eager to get to. In her earlier incarnation as a librarian, there had been mornings when she could barely get out of bed, especially in the dark winter months, but ever since she'd joined MI5 there had never been any problem about getting up.

This morning, however, she was fast asleep when her alarm rang at 6.30. After Liz's phone call telling her the dreadful news from Paris she had just sat in a chair for half an hour, everything spinning in her head. She hadn't been able to make up her mind whether she should ring DG straightaway or wait until morning. Should she ring Geoffrey Fane? She seemed to be immobilised, as if all the stuffing had been knocked out of her.

Then suddenly she had pulled herself together. What would Liz do in my shoes? she'd thought. Well, she wouldn't be sitting here like this. Peggy had long ago observed that the worse the situation, the more calmly Liz behaved, and she had drawn strength from Liz's cool efficiency. Well now, she said to herself, I must do the same. So she'd grabbed the phone, dialled DG's PA and passed on the news. 'He'll want to know now,' was the advice, so

Peggy had rung him. DG had asked for an update on the operation and had told her that she must be the main liaison with Manchester Police until Liz was able to take over again. She'd then rung the Duty Officer at Vauxhall Cross and given him the barest account of what had happened to pass on to Geoffrey Fane. She had decided to leave informing Andy Bokus until morning. Having done all that, she began to feel better about herself and got into bed. But it was past two o'clock and her mind was racing. She was thinking what she must do in the morning; how awful Liz must be feeling; whatever could have happened in Paris – and so it went on until she fell asleep at about five o'clock, only to be woken an hour and a half later.

When she got to Thames House, Peggy found that word had already spread about Martin Seurat's death. A few colleagues asked her what had happened, but she didn't know any more than they did. As more people arrived for work, they were also greeted with the news. Soon an almost palpable gloom settled over the open-plan office where Peggy had her desk. Liz was a very popular colleague, much admired by the younger officers. It was widely known that her partner was a DGSE officer whom she'd met when she was posted to Northern Ireland, and that an operation there had ended violently in the South of France. Some people knew that Martin Seurat had saved the life of Dave Armstrong, one of their colleagues, who had been kidnapped. So Seurat was something of a hero in the Counter-Terrorist branch, even though not many people had met him.

When everyone had arrived for work Peggy told them all that Martin had been killed in Paris in the course of the operation they were working on; that Liz had gone to Paris and would be getting a full briefing but at present she could not tell them exactly what had happened. DG had asked her, she explained, to stand in for Liz until she was back. She was going to move into Liz's office for the time being and she'd asked for her calls to be put through to Liz's extension. If anything relevant came through to any of them they were to come in and tell her immediately. She might well be going up to Manchester very soon. Then she went into Liz's office, closed the door and set about trying to get to grips with what was going on.

An hour later she felt like a salesman who'd made the rounds but come back with an empty order book. She had begun by calling Charlie Simmons at GCHQ. He'd had the news of Seurat's death by now, and sounded very subdued. There had been no further email traffic to or from Zara since the email had come in announcing that the meeting in Paris had been cancelled. He explained again that the reason why it had taken so long to unzip that message was that it seemed to have been sent by someone who was not familiar with the code. 'This may mean that those who usually send the messages are not there,' he said.

'That makes sense,' said Peggy. 'Presumably the messages are usually sent by the people who are on their way here. But they must be communicating somehow or how are they going to meet up with Zara?'

'However they are doing it, we're not onto it. Perhaps they made all the arrangements in advance and don't need to communicate.'

'Maybe so,' said Peggy, but she was sceptical. The silence seemed ominous.

Next she checked in with A4 and was told that Zara was acting like a model student, attending lectures, working in the library. 'Completely normal,' said the Duty Controller. Too normal, thought Peggy, sceptical again.

Finally she checked with her contact at the Border Agency. He was in constant contact with their counterparts on the Continent and no vehicle of the description she had given him had been reported crossing the Channel or the North Sea. Peggy asked, 'What if the vehicle were coming in a roundabout way?'

'How do you mean?'

'Say from much further away than the usual Channel ports. Like Scandinavia – ferries from Norway come here, don't they?'

'Sure, though that wouldn't help them escape detection. There isn't a port within five hundred miles east of here that hasn't been given the details of the vehicle we're looking for. And just to be safe, we circulated them to Ireland too. In fact, unless this lorry's coming from Brazil you don't have anything to worry about. If it sails, we'll know.'

'All right,' said Peggy, tempted to ask him to cover Brazil as well, but even she could see that was absurd. 'Thank you,' she added, realising that perhaps she had been a bit rude. She was getting very tense. It wasn't just the aftermath of Seurat's death and the absence of sleep, it was the absence of developments. No news was usually good news, but right now Peggy wanted something to happen.

51

IT HAD BEEN A really tedious few days. Maureen Hayes had wanted to take the week as holiday because her son was home on leave from Afghanistan, but she'd been told she had to work. Wally Woods, her A4 controller, had said that they needed all the resource they could muster to cover what was thought to be a developing terrorist plot.

But so far nothing had happened. The target Maureen and her team were covering, Zara, had gone reliably as clockwork every day of the week from his hostel, Dinwiddy House, to SOAS, where he had attended lectures, sat working in the library and drunk coffee in the snack bar with other students. He did not seem to have any close friends whom he met regularly but he chatted in a friendly enough way to whoever was around. She and her team had been unable to get near enough to overhear any of his conversations but everything looked perfectly natural. Then at about five or six in the evening, he had left the university area and gone back to Dinwiddy House, where, according to her overnight shift colleagues, he had stayed until the following morning. If he was plotting a terrorist outrage, thought Maureen, he must be doing it from his room, as there were no outward signs of a conspiracy.

Today was Friday, and at the early morning briefing before they took over the surveillance, she and her team had been told to be extra-vigilant. Something that had happened the previous day in Paris had led the desk officers to think that a group of possibly up to six people would be arriving in Britain, if they were not already here, and Zara would be meeting up with them. They were thought to be intending to carry out some form of terrorist attack, but what, where and when was not known. It was vital, they had been told, that if Zara broke his routine or met a group of people who had not been seen before, they reported at once; and above all that they did not lose him.

So Maureen and her team were very alert this morning, and rather disappointed when Zara came out at the usual time and headed off to SOAS just the same as on all the previous days. Marcus Washington went into the building and reported that Zara was in a lecture. After the lecture he went to the library, where he was reported by Marcus, by then sitting two places away from him, to be concentrating on a large book from which he was taking notes. Just before twelve noon, he looked at his watch, packed up his things, returned the book to the desk and came out of the library.

'On the move,' said Marcus quietly into his microphone as Zara left the library to be picked up by Maureen and her partner, Duff Wells, as he came down the steps.

'Having an early lunch,' reported Maureen to the Control Room. But instead of heading off to the snack bar where he usually went at lunchtime, Zara walked quickly out into Tottenham Court Road, ran straight across, narrowly avoiding being run over by a bus, and headed fast towards Goodge Street underground station.

'He's doing anti-surveillance,' reported Maureen as Wells,

who had anticipated the move and was already on the other side of the road, went into the station ahead of Zara. Maureen caught up, arriving at the station as Zara and Wells with a small group of passengers were waiting for the lift to take them to the platforms. Maureen, Wells and Zara, with about fifteen other people, piled into the ancient lift, which creaked its way down and juddered to a halt at platform level. Zara was first out, hurrying along the tunnel to the southbound platform.

'Doesn't look as though he's going to see his mum,' reported Maureen. 'Euston is north.'

Then began a short tour of the underground system as Zara, with Maureen and Wells accompanying him, went south on the Northern Line to Tottenham Court Road, west on the Central Line to Oxford Circus and finally back north on the Victoria Line to Euston, where he took the exit for the mainline station. Each time he changed trains he hung back and tried to be the last onto the train, but Maureen and Duff Wells knew all about that anti-surveillance ploy and, helped by the crowded platforms, one or other of them managed to board the train after him without drawing attention to themselves.

Half an hour later, as Maureen, now ahead of Zara, emerged up the stairs from the underground onto the concourse of Euston Station, she was relieved to see another colleague, Fred Watson, standing in the crowd in front of the departure board.

As she followed Zara towards the booking hall and watched from the door as he collected a ticket from the fast ticket machine, she heard Fred talking to the Control Room. 'There's a Manchester train at one o'clock; we'll go with him if he catches it. Gets there at seven minutes past three.'

'OK,' came back from Wally Woods. 'I'm alerting the police to meet the train at all the stops. I'll get a team out to meet you in Manchester. Keep us posted.'

Back in the main concourse Zara joined the crowd in front of the departure board, where he stood waiting, watched from different directions by the three pairs of eyes of the A4 team.

As soon as the platform for the 13.00 train to Manchester Piccadilly flashed up on the board, Duff Wells moved fast, ahead of the crowd, towards Platform 5 and Fred Watson followed, more casually. Maureen stayed in the concourse waiting for Zara to move too. But Zara didn't move. Maureen muttered into her microphone, 'Watch out for a last-minute rush. He's still here and he's very alert for surveillance.' At 12.55 Zara was still on the concourse.

Then suddenly he moved fast, out of the concourse, towards the platforms. 'On the move,' said Maureen. She was trying to keep up with him, but she lost sight of him in the crowd of people now rushing to get seats on another train. 'Control lost,' she shouted as she ran towards the platforms.

Fred and Duff were still waiting at the top of the ramp leading down to platform 5, but there was just a trickle of latecomers now and Zara was not among them.

'Pretty sure we haven't missed him.' It was Duff Wells. 'Fred got here before anyone else. Between us we've clocked everyone who got on.'

As Maureen ran up to join them, Wally Woods said, 'Try the next train', over their headphones. 'Thirteen-oh-three, Platform seven, for Birmingham.'

'I'll wait here till this train leaves in case he's just delaying,' panted Maureen as Duff and Fred set off running to Platform 7 where the stragglers were still boarding. Duff waited at the end while Fred sprinted along the platform, scanning the passengers without much hope of seeing his target, but then near the far end of the platform he spotted Zara, just about to get onto the train.

'Got him,' he shouted. 'Second carriage. I'm boarding now.' Duff joined a chattering group of grey-haired men dressed in walking clothes who were getting into a carriage in the middle of the train. Last to arrive was Maureen, clambering into the final carriage, just before the doors were locked and the guard signalled the driver to go. She stood leaning on the door, gasping for breath, her heart pumping at twice its normal speed. I'm getting too old for this, she thought to herself.

'Phew,' she heard Fred say. 'That was a close one. But we're still with him. I've got eyeball. He's just three rows in front of me.'

'OK,' said Wally from Thames House Control Room. 'Well done.'

'The train stops at Rugby, Coventry and Birmingham International; Birmingham New Street is the last stop,' continued Fred.

'Get off where he does, but I'll try to get the police to be at the stops along the way – I'm hoping they'll be able to take him on if he gets off before New Street. I'll get our teams to meet you at New Street in case that's where he's going.'

Rugby and Coventry came and went and it wasn't until Birmingham International was announced that Zara got up and joined the line of passengers waiting to get off the train.

What on earth is he up to? wondered Maureen. Don't say he's going to a conference – not after all this trouble.

But it wasn't to the Conference Centre he was heading.

As soon as he left the train, he made a beeline for the Skyrail to the airport and got on the first train that came in, with the A4 team in hot pursuit.

'What do you want us to do if he checks in for a flight?' asked Maureen.

Wally replied, 'You'll have to let him go. But get all the details.'

But at the airport Zara didn't go to the departure hall; he went instead to the arrivals hall, and straight to the Hertz car-hire desk.

'He's hiring a car. We've got no wheels so we'll have to let him go or hire one ourselves.'

'Get the number and make of the car and we'll pick him up on the road. There's a police team coming out now to join you.'

As the A4 team watched, Zara hired a dark blue Ford S Max and drove off, heading for the airport exit.

While Wally Woods in London passed the target to the police surveillance teams, Maureen and her colleagues went off in different directions to get some lunch in the airport cafés. By the time she had finished a not very enticing salad, Maureen heard over her headphones that Zara's car had been picked up by the cameras, heading towards the M6 Toll. That was a silly choice if he's trying to avoid surveillance, she thought. He'll be on camera all the way.

52

PEGGY HAD BEEN STARING out of the window, feeling as sluggish as the Thames at low tide, when the phone on Liz's desk rang.

'Hi, Border Agency here. I think we have something for you.'

'Where?'

'Hook of Holland. They called five minutes ago. There's a Stena Line ferry leaving for Harwich at fourteen thirty their time; that's half past one here, so fairly soon. Scheduled arrival time at Harwich is twenty hundred hours, British time. The lorry came in just before the deadline – they have to be quayside sixty minutes before sailing. It's got the markings you're looking for, though it's carrying Turkish registration plates.' He read out the registration number. 'Just one driver, Turkish passport, name of Deniz Keskin, date of birth thirtieth October 1963.'

'I bet that's a false passport. If that's our lorry it's come from Dagestan and he's not Turkish. What's it carrying?'

'Mattresses. Lots of mattresses, according to the manifest.'

Plus a few other things, thought Peggy. And she asked, 'Has anyone looked inside?'

'No. The Dutch are giving it a bit of space – as we requested. You said don't scare them off.'

'That's right.'

'It was weighed – all the vehicles are, so that can't have aroused suspicion; it was apparently normal weight for its declared load. But it's hard to tell much without looking inside. We can have Customs search it when it arrives if you want. Easy enough to do.'

'No, thanks. We don't want to risk alerting them at this stage. But please ask them to try and put the marker on as it goes through.'

As Peggy put the phone down she was hoping she'd taken the right decision. It was a big risk to allow into the country a lorry that she was pretty sure was carrying weapons, detonators and heaven knew what else, intended for a group of jihadis who had gone off the map and could be anywhere in the country. But she didn't have much time to worry about it. As soon as she put the phone down, she picked it up again and rang Wally Woods in the A4 Control room.

'Hi, Liz.'

'No, it's Peggy. Liz is out today.'

'Oh?'

Obviously the news from Paris hadn't percolated to the A4 control room. Peggy said, 'I'm running the op until Liz gets back. I've just heard news of our lorry from the Border Agency. It's on board the Stena ferry at the Hook of Holland coming to Harwich.' She passed on the details she'd been given. 'They're going to get the marker on at Harwich.'

'OK. We'll be there. You still reckon it's headed for one of those warehouses?'

'Yes. But we don't know which one. If I learn anything else I'll let you know. Anything new on Zara?'

'Yes. He's made a move. I was just about to pick up the phone to tell Liz when you rang. Is she OK by the way? It's not like her to leave her post just as things start hotting up.'

'Yes. She's fine but someone close to her has died.' She hoped she'd said enough and not too much.

'Oh. I'm sorry to hear that,' said Wally and went on, 'Zara took a train to Birmingham.'

'Birmingham?'

'Yeah. He's doing anti-surveillance but not all that cleverly. He took the Skyrail from the train to the airport and now he's in a hire car. Last seen heading towards the M6.'

'Oh God. Have you lost him?' asked Peggy, thinking of the lorryload of weapons she had just agreed to let into the country.

'No. Not as you might say "lost". We're not with him at the moment but we know roughly where he is and what car he's in, so the police teams will be behind him soon. He'll be on the cameras, and if he takes the M6 or the Toll, he'll be snapped every few hundred yards. And we can always stop him at the Toll gate if we need to. The paying system can break down for a bit.'

He must be heading towards Manchester, thought Peggy. Nothing else makes sense.

'Our team is ready to join in in case he goes off the M6 up a minor road,' went on Wally. 'Don't worry, Peggy. I think we can cope with little Mr Zara whatever he does.'

'He may be picking up some others somewhere.'

'Yeah. That occurred to us. He's hired a big enough car.'

'You've got all the addresses he might be going to, haven't you?' asked Peggy anxiously. 'The four warehouses and his mother's house.'

'Relax, Peggy. We've got it all in the brief. And we're in touch with Manchester CT Unit.'

'OK, Wally, thanks. Keep me posted please. I'll be on my mobile.'

'You going somewhere?'

'Yes. I'm going up to Manchester to liaise with the police. I'll be in the Ops Room up there.'

There was no point in hanging around in London. Not with both Zara and the lorry apparently heading for Manchester. So Peggy went back to the open-plan office and told the others where she would be, then headed out of Thames House and hailed a passing taxi. As she leaned back in her seat, she pulled out her mobile. The last thing Liz probably needed now was a phone call, but knowing Liz she would be wondering what was going on and, after all, she had asked Peggy to keep her informed. So Peggy sent her a text:

Off to Manchester – lorry and Z on their way.
The other package's whereabouts still unknown.
Hope you are all right. PK

She hoped Liz wouldn't be away too long. She wasn't at all sure that she could fill her shoes.

53

PEGGY MADE IT TO Euston with just enough time to
buy a ticket. The train to Manchester was packed but
she managed to find a seat that wasn't booked, though she
had to ask a rude young man to move his coat and briefcase so that she could sit down. As the train pulled out of
the station she closed her eyes and rehearsed in her mind
everything that had happened and what she thought was
about to happen. She was worried that they had seen no
trace of the jihadis. Where were they? Were they travelling
together or separately? Perhaps they were on the train.
Perhaps they didn't exist. Had they all misinterpreted the
intelligence? And if they did exist and were on their way to
meet Zara, what was it they were planning to do?

She was relieved that Manchester Police had set up an
Ops Room. The responsibility to prevent whatever was
planned no longer lay entirely on her shoulders. The police
were now in charge of the action and she was their adviser.

Her thoughts drifted to Paris and to Liz. She wondered
what she was doing and how she was getting on. What
had happened in Paris the previous evening and why had
Martin been shot? She tried to imagine the chain of events
but she couldn't make any sense of it.

When the refreshment trolley came through the carriage she realised she was starving. She had had no lunch and hardly any sleep the night before. She bought a sandwich and a black coffee and began to feel a bit better. She tried to relax, watching the reflections in the window and the bright lights of occasional stations. She had a feeling she wouldn't be relaxing again for a while.

There was a long queue for taxis at Manchester Piccadilly Station, and when Peggy eventually got to the front and the cab drove off, she remarked to the driver how busy the place seemed. He laughed. 'It's the pop concert.'

'Who's playing?'

He named a boy band Peggy had only vaguely heard of and added, 'It'll be worse tomorrow. There's another performance *and* the match – United's playing City at Old Trafford. There'll be gridlock, so I think I'll stay at home.'

At Police HQ Peggy signed in at the front desk. 'Third floor,' she was told. 'They're expecting you.'

When the lift doors opened she found a tall, youngish-looking police officer waiting for her. It took a minute before she realised who it was.

'I'm Richard Pearson, the Chief Constable. You must be Peggy.'

'Yes,' replied Peggy, rather breathlessly. 'Good evening.'

'I wanted to meet you to say how pleased we are to have you with us – but also how sorry I was about the sad events in Paris. I don't know exactly what happened but I understand that Liz Carlyle has lost someone close to her. Please pass on my sympathy when you see her.'

'Thank you,' said Peggy, very surprised. 'None of us knows the details, but Liz has gone over there and I expect she'll have heard the full story by now. It seems that the group of jihadis changed their plans. They seem to have bypassed Paris and now we think they're coming straight here. Your people will be more up to date than me – I've been on the train for the last couple of hours.'

'Yes,' replied the Chief Constable. 'There have been some developments. Let me take you into the Ops Room and introduce you. The officer in charge is Chief Super-intendent George Lazarus, Head of our Counter-Terrorist Unit. He'll brief you on what's going on.'

He led her down a corridor and into a large, brightly lit room. A big square table with chairs around it filled one end, and at the other a line of eight or ten desks, each with a computer, a phone and headphones, faced a wall of screens. A large digital clock on the wall showed 8.27 pm.

The desks were all occupied; there was a mix of men and women, some in uniform, some in plain clothes, some talk-ing on the phone, some tapping on keyboards, some sitting back in their chairs. The atmosphere seemed busy but calm.

The Chief Constable introduced Peggy to Chief Super-intendent Lazarus. Then with a quick, 'Let me know, George, as soon as anything starts to happen,' he left.

'Come and sit down and have a cup of coffee and a bun and I'll tell you what's going on. Then I'll introduce you to the team,' said Lazarus, shepherding Peggy to the table. He was a big man, with large hands and feet. He quite dwarfed Peggy. As they sat down he picked up a paper from the table. 'There was a call for you from Thames House Duty Officer about half an hour ago. He said that someone rang on one of your agent lines and asked you to ring back. Here's the number.'

'OK, thanks,' said Peggy, taking the slip of paper and glancing at it before putting it in her pocket. 'I'll ring them later.'

'Right then,' said Lazarus. 'The situation at present is that the Stena ferry carrying the lorry should be just about in to Harwich. The lorry will be allowed through Customs with no fuss, as you requested, and a marker will be put on covertly as it goes through. We have surveillance waiting to go with it wherever it goes. If it comes up here, as we expect, it should arrive any time from two o'clock onwards, provided it doesn't stop or get lost. Zara in his hire car has arrived at his mum's house in Eccles. We have three teams of A4 there, but they're having to stand off a bit as the area is difficult for surveillance. They are doing drive-bys and Zara's rental car is still there outside Mum's house. If he goes out they should pick him up. My only worry is if he leaves over the garden wall, but that's unlikely if he's going to make contact with the lorry. He didn't seem aware of surveillance. I gather he led your lot a bit of a dance on the way here, so he probably thinks he's clean now.

'I'm sure you're briefed on McManus,' he went on. 'Well, he's working with us now. He's got no choice,' and he smiled grimly. 'He's been told that if he doesn't hear from Jackson, he's to drop by the club at about twelve thirty and try and find him. If Jackson's going to meet the lorry he should make a move any time from one o'clock onwards. We've got an armed team standing by and we're going to conceal a couple of surveillance officers by the entrances to each of the industrial estates to warn us of who's coming in. We've got all the comms and the cameras coming in to us here, so this is Mission Control,' he said with a grin. 'But what I want to know from you is what's happened to your band of terrorists. I gather they didn't turn up in Paris.'

'No,' said Peggy 'but we're pretty sure they're out there somewhere and intending to meet up with Zara. What we don't know is what they're planning to do.'

'Well, let's hope we find out before they do it,' said Lazarus, sucking his breath in through his teeth with a faint hiss. 'Now come and meet the people.'

They walked side by side across to the desks. At the first desk was Lazarus's deputy, a balding man with a pate that gleamed in the bleaching glare of the overhead strip lighting. His headphones were hanging round his neck. Lazarus said, 'Andy's got all the surveillance comms on his desk. What's happening at the moment, Andy?'

'Not a lot,' was the reply. 'The ship's just docked.' Andy turned a knob and the sound of the A4 teams at Harwich, talking to each other and to A4 control, floated into the room.

Peggy and Lazarus moved along the line of desks meeting all the officers. A young woman Detective Sergeant, Emily something, was monitoring the cameras that Technical Ted and his team had placed at the warehouses. 'Do we know yet which warehouse they'll be going to?' she asked Peggy.

'No. 'Fraid not,' Peggy replied. 'Could be any of them. The one in Denton seems to hold all the paperwork of Lester Jackson's club, but the one in Eccles has beds.'

'Let's have a look, Emily,' said Lazarus. She leaned forward and clicked her mouse. Suddenly the screens on the bank of monitors on the wall cleared, replaced a moment later by views of the warehouses. Two were old brick buildings that looked pretty run-down; the Denton facility was a long, hangar-like building and the Eccles one was a large aluminium shed that was indistinguishable from those dotting the outskirts of every town in England.

Technical Ted and his team had put cameras inside and outside each warehouse, and Emily panned through the pictures from each.

A curly-haired man called Ames who had his head-phones on sat up quickly and raised his hand.

'Yes?' said Lazarus.

'McManus has heard from Lester Jackson. Jackson wants to meet him at Slim's at midnight. McManus wants to know if he should go.'

No one said anything for a moment. To Peggy's surprise she saw they were all looking at her. Yes, she thought, it was a question for her to answer.

'He should go. Definitely,' she said. 'I don't know why Jackson wants McManus there, but it gives us an opportunity to know where Jackson is while we wait for the lorry.'

Ames said, 'Jackson may suspect McManus.'

'Good point.' It was Lazarus now, giving his view. 'But we'll have to take that risk. It would only create more suspicion if McManus refused to meet him.'

'But what if Jackson doesn't go to the warehouse?' asked Ames.

'If Jackson leaves the club, McManus should tell us right away.'

Ames asked, 'Should he follow him?'

Lazarus turned to Peggy again. 'No,' she said. 'Far too risky. But at least we'll know from McManus when Jackson's on the move. Probably just as the lorry arrives. Or at least we hope so.'

54

S LIM'S CLUB WAS FULL. On a week night the customers were beginning to drift home by midnight, but this
was Friday, and people seemed happy to stay out late.
McManus found a space at the very end of the car park
and walked back towards the club's entrance. He could
hear the loud music from the dance floor while he was still
fifty yards away. He nodded at the bouncers standing by
the front door and went through into the restaurant,
surprised to find that most of the tables were still
occupied.

Lester Jackson, in an elegant dark suit with cream shirt
and crimson tie, was sitting in his usual place against the
back wall. He nodded almost imperceptibly when he saw
McManus, who walked over and joined him, sliding in
behind the table to sit on the banquette next to his host.

'Bang on time,' said Jackson without looking at McManus.

'Have you ever known me to be late?' The waiter came to
the table. McManus saw that Jackson was drinking his usual
fizzy water with a slice of lime. 'Whisky and soda,' McManus
said, thinking it would look odd if he ordered anything other
than his usual. 'So what's happening?' he asked casually.

Jackson didn't answer at once. He was looking around

the room, as if counting heads – or the money the heads would bring in. He took a small sip of his water and said, 'I got a nice little deal proceeding.'

'That's good,' said McManus, as if it had nothing to do with him.

'Big delivery. From abroad.'

'Girls?'

Jackson shrugged and pulled one of his cuffs. 'And then some. I could use a little help with this one.'

McManus said nothing. The waiter came back with his drink, and he took a large swallow, then put his glass down. 'I've been meaning to speak to you.'

'Oh yeah?'

'I'm going to be retiring soon.'

'Retiring? You ain't that old, man.' Jackson's voice had suddenly lost its polish.

'My pension says I am.' McManus tried a smile. 'Things are going to change.'

'How's that?'

'Well, once I'm no longer working I'm not going to be much use to you, am I? It's not like I'll know what's going on.'

Jackson looked amused. 'You'll still know plenty as far as I'm concerned. And you'll know how to find out what you don't know. Your buddies will still be working in the department, won't they?'

McManus didn't say anything. He sensed this was not the time to push the story of his retirement.

Jackson said, 'You're gonna help me tonight, aren't you? Or you getting cold feet in your old age? Looking for your bus pass maybe.'

'I'm OK,' said McManus resolutely. 'What is it you need me for?'

'I got a dude collecting something from me, only I haven't done business with him before. I want backup – in case he gets some odd idea of lifting one over me. I just need you to be there. Right?'

'Since when did you need extra firepower? I know you're carrying.' He gestured at Jackson's jacket. 'I'm not. What use am I going to be if things get rough? Or are you expecting me to arrest him?'

'It's not about shooting – or arresting. I just want you there. OK?' It was not really a question; the expression on Jackson's face was telling McManus it had better be OK.

'Where are we going?'

'Not far.'

'How far? I haven't got much petrol in my car. I'll need to fill up.'

Jackson gave him a thoughtful look. 'You won't need it. I'll drive you.'

'When do you want to leave?'

'Now is not too soon.'

McManus nodded and stood up. 'OK, let me have a slash first and then we can go.'

'Do it later.'

'What do you mean?'

Jackson stared at him expressionlessly. 'I said, do it later.'

'Can't a man go to the bog?'

'Sure you can,' said Jackson, relenting. 'But leave your phone behind.'

'Why?'

'Why do you think?'

'What's the matter? Don't you trust me?' McManus demanded, trying to put outrage in his voice.

Jackson looked amused. 'I trust you, Jimmy, as much as I

trust anyone.' He paused. 'Which means I don't trust you at all.'

McManus shrugged. 'OK then. I can wait. Let's go.'

Outside it was suddenly cold; frost was settling on the bonnets of the vehicles in the car park. McManus said, 'If it's not far I'll follow you. Then I can go straight home after.' He started to head for his car, but Jackson put a hand on his arm.

'Whoa. You're coming with me.' He pointed to the sleek silver Audi coupé he kept in a special slot reserved for him.

'How do I get home then?'

'I give you a lift or drive you back here for your car. But I need you with me.'

By now McManus was scared. It was clear from the way Jackson was behaving that he didn't trust him, so why did he want McManus to go with him? It didn't make any sense unless he wanted to use him as cover for whatever he was up to. They'd told him at headquarters, when they'd accused him of corruption, that the only way of avoiding a very long stretch was to help them get Jackson behind bars. They'd said that if he didn't cooperate he'd find himself charged with abetting terrorism, because Jackson had got himself involved with a bunch of jihadis. They'd said they were expecting something to go down tonight and he was supposed to warn them if Jackson moved out of the club, but with Jackson being so suspicious, he wasn't going to be able to do that. His only hope was that when they got wherever they were going he might get a chance to send a text to say where he was.

'Here,' said Jackson curtly, handing him the car keys, 'You drive.' He took out his phone. 'I'm turning this off for safety's sake. Give me yours and I'll turn that off too.'

55

ANDY, THE BALD MAN, yawned loudly. It was almost one o'clock. On the table was a litter of paper plates covered with crumbs, curling sandwiches, sausage rolls and other delicacies provided by the canteen, together with several Thermos jugs of coffee. They had monitored the lorry's progress for more than four hours as it had worked its way across country from the east coast, come up the M1, then, as if drawn by a magnet, moved west towards Manchester. It had been tailed the whole way by A4 teams.

'Any news of McManus?' The Chief Constable had been looking in from time to time during the evening, but now he'd sat down at the table, looking as if he had come to stay. He had been told earlier in the evening about McManus's text message.

Lazarus shook his head. 'No, sir. And his phone's switched off. As is Jackson's. They may still be at the club, but we don't know for sure.'

'Something coming through now,' Emily, the Detective Sergeant, announced. 'It's the Eccles estate.'

On one of the monitors a misty picture came up, showing a stretch of road, some bushes and the outline of a car in the distance, coming towards the camera. Officers Field-ing and Pierce from Manchester Police's CT unit were lying hidden in a shallow ditch that ran along the edge of the estate on the east side. A couple of their colleagues were in similar positions at the west entrance. While Pierce kept a lookout, Fielding lay on his belly and watched through the special nightscope of a videocam recorder he had perched on a low tripod. The feed from Fielding's camera, displayed on the screen in the Ops Room, showed an Audi coupé slowing as it turned off the approach road into the estate, then driving away from the camera on one of the estate's narrow roads.

In the Ops Room, Emily said, 'That's Jackson's car.'

'But where's McManus?' asked Peggy.

There was no sign of any other vehicle. Andy was talk-ing into his microphone, and he suddenly held up a hand. He flicked a switch and his conversation was audible on the speaker.

'Picture's clear enough,' said Andy. 'How many in the car?'

Pierce spoke from the ditch at the estate. 'Two guys. A black guy – I think it was Jackson. And a white driver. Mid-fifties maybe. Clean-cut.'

'Thanks.'

The Chief Constable asked, 'You reckon that's McManus?'

'Has to be,' said Lazarus. 'Otherwise he would have called us.'

'Jackson's no fool,' said Emily. 'He'll be keeping a close eye on everyone around him, and being extra-careful. I'm sure that's why his phone's off and probably why McManus's is off as well.'

They watched the monitor anxiously. From the perimeter where Fielding and Pierce were hidden, you couldn't see the Jackson warehouse, and the cameras in the warehouse – one on its exterior, the others inside – had so far shown no movement.

Suddenly the camera outside the warehouse came to life as a light went on, and the vast front door of the warehouse began to lift up slowly. Two figures were visible, standing just outside the building.

'Is that McManus?' Peggy asked.

'Yes,' said a new voice in the room. 'That's him all right.'

All heads turned to the door. It was Liz Carlyle, standing just inside the room, wearing her overcoat. Peggy leapt up, knocking her chair over. 'Liz.' The relief in her voice was clear. 'I didn't expect you back tonight. How are you?'

It had been a hard day by any measure, and it wasn't going to be over any time soon. But at least she would be concentrating now on something that didn't drain her emotions, something that called on her professional skills rather than her feelings.

She'd had plenty of time on the journey back to mull over her day's hurried trip to Paris: Isabelle meeting her at the Gare du Nord; the conversation and the tears on the drive out to Martin's flat; the realisation, when she stood in the sitting room and looked out of the window at the Square opposite, the trees bare of leaves now on this raw day, of just how much of her life, her emotions and, as she had thought, her future lay there.

Foolishly Liz had imagined she could collect all her belongings in a suitcase and take them back with her, but it took less than five minutes in the flat to recognise just how many clothes, books and odds and ends she had accumulated over the few years of her relationship with Martin. After the flat there had been a brief meeting with

Claudette, Martin's ex-wife, who had been civil, if not exactly cordial. And finally a tearful hour with Mimi, Martin's adored daughter.

There had been no reason to stay longer, since she would be coming back again soon – for the funeral, for the gathering of her possessions, and (this she had promised the girl) to spend some more time with Mimi. So she had headed back to the station and caught a late afternoon Eurostar back to London. She'd gone to her flat, planning to leave the operation in Manchester to the police, but after an hour at home she'd felt so desolate and restless that when eventually she'd checked her mobile and seen the text from Peggy announcing that she was leaving for Manchester, she had decided that she would go to join her.

She'd managed to get what must have been about the last seat on the packed train by travelling first class; she'd fallen briefly asleep, waited in a long queue for a taxi, and now here she was, slightly dazzled in the brightly lit Ops Room but relieved to be able to focus on something that had nothing to do with Martin Seurat and the grief that flooded through her in unpredictable waves.

Peggy said, 'Zara's been at his mother's house in Eccles. We've just heard from the A4 team there that he's gone out. He's in the car he rented in Birmingham.'

'Are they still with him?'

'Yes.'

'Here's the lorry,' Andy announced as the grey, wavy picture from the night-vision camera at the gate appeared on the screen again. The images from the camera outside the warehouse were showing on another screen. The lorry drove into the picture, made an enormous 180-degree turn, and stopped, facing out on the hard standing where

Jackson and McManus stood waiting. Jackson waved it backwards and the lorry reversed slowly into the warehouse, gave a belch of exhaust, and stopped.

Jackson and McManus went in and attention in the Ops Room switched to the pictures from the cameras inside the warehouse. After a moment the driver jumped down from the cab. He was a short, stocky man in a thick dark pea jacket.

'You made it at last,' said Jackson, his voice clearly audible in the Ops Room.

'Ya. That was one good long hell of a drive.' His English was heavily accented and quite difficult to make out on the microphones. 'We had to stop a lot for fuel.'

'I bet you did,' said Jackson knowingly. 'Everything all right with the cargo?'

'Yeah. You want to see?'

The man made to go for the rear of the lorry, but Jackson put up a hand. 'Wait a minute. Tell me about the journey. Any problems?'

'The journey? It was difficult, especially in Germany. Snow has come early this year.'

'I'm not asking about the weather. I meant, when you got to Harwich. Were you stopped at Customs? Have they been through the cargo?'

'No. I expected them to open the doors, but they didn't.'

Jackson turned to McManus, who was standing beside him, before turning back to the driver and asking, 'Do they usually look inside?'

'Always. In my experience. But not tonight.'

'I don't like the sound of that.'

McManus said, 'Could just be shortage of staff, weight of traffic, Christmas spirit – anything. I wouldn't read much into it. And he got here, didn't he?'

Jackson's eyes stayed on McManus. 'Yeah, but what I'm wondering is if anyone else came along for the ride.'

The three men in the warehouse now moved outside to the tarmac forecourt, and all the microphone could pick up was the faint sound of voices.

'What are they waiting for?' asked Andy. He sounded cross.

Before anyone could answer, the three men started walking back into the warehouse. The driver was gesturing at the back of the lorry. 'I should open it up now?' His voice came through loudly.

'Not yet,' said Jackson curtly.

The driver was insistent. 'I have done. Let me unload and then I can be gone. I have mattresses to go to Glasgow by tomorrow. And there is a breathing cargo here that needs some air.'

Jackson laughed harshly. '"A breathing cargo". I like that. Don't you, Jimmy?'

McManus shrugged. 'I hope you haven't dragged me out here for a bunch of tarts.'

'You'll see soon enough.' And Jackson walked to the front of the warehouse again, while McManus stood still, half in shadow, and the lorry driver lit a cigarette.

Back in the Ops Room, Emily asked, 'Why doesn't he want the lorry opened up?'

'Because the main customer hasn't arrived,' said Liz.

'If he ever does,' said Andy.

'He will. Zara's come all the way from London,' Liz said. 'I don't think it's just to see his mum.'

Fielding's camera had picked up another car coming into the estate, a dark Ford S Max. Peggy looked at Liz. 'That's the car Zara hired.'

Thirty seconds later, as the S Max appeared on the monitor parking on the tarmac outside Jackson's warehouse, Lazarus was on the radio to the armed police team. 'Target has arrived.' Turning to Liz, he said, 'Time to go in?'

'I think we should wait a bit.'

'You sure? If the guns are in the lorry we'll find them. We can strip the bloody thing down to nuts and bolts if we have to.'

'We still don't know where the others are.'

'You think they're coming to the warehouse?'

'Possibly. I'd like to hear what Zara and Jackson say to each other.'

'I make Jackson as just the middleman.'

'I think you're right, but don't we need to hear them make the transaction if we're going to be sure of a successful prosecution? Otherwise we haven't got much to stick on Zara. He can say he's come to collect mattresses, and without more evidence a jury might give him the benefit of the doubt.'

The Chief Constable broke in. 'We'll take the risk, George. Bring the armed team forward but hold off going in for a bit.'

Lazarus nodded and radioed some orders.

56

WHAT THE HELL IS happening now, thought McManus as he stood at the door of the warehouse and watched the dark-coloured car pull up. He hadn't believed Liz Carlyle when she'd told him that Jackson had got himself involved with a bunch of jihadis, but there was something going on here that was out of the run of Jackson's usual style. Who was this 'customer' who'd arrived and what was he collecting?

He wondered how much Liz Carlyle and the team back at HQ really knew about the situation. If they'd known tonight would be dangerous, they should have warned him. When Jackson had asked him to meet up at Slim's, there had been no reason for him to think there could be trouble brewing; it was only when Jackson had insisted on taking away his mobile phone that he'd grown worried. Without his phone, and without a gun, he felt doubly exposed.

They should have issued him with a weapon if they were putting him into a potentially violent situation, McManus thought angrily. But he knew the Chief Constable would never have authorised that, given the accusations against him. Not that the 'customer' who had just arrived looked very menacing. OK, he was Middle Eastern-looking, but he was slightly built, not much more than five feet nine, and looked more like a student, in his jeans, trainers and roll-neck sweater underneath a parka, than a jihadi terrorist. McManus hadn't wanted to believe Liz Carlyle's claims of a jihadi threat, and part of him still didn't. And even if this guy was a fanatic, intent on slaughtering innocents, there wasn't much he could do about it. Not when Jackson had his phone – and a gun.

Now Jackson signalled for McManus to follow him. They walked out to the tarmac in front, where the new arrival stood by his car, watching warily as Jackson and McManus approached.

'Good timing,' said Jackson. He gestured at the lorry. 'Your goods have just shown up.'

'Who's this guy?' the man demanded, pointing at McManus.

'My business associate,' said Jackson. McManus took a step back and kept his hands loose by his side. If he was supposed to be the heavy then he'd better act like one.

'You were supposed to come alone.' For all his youthful appearance, the man spoke with authority and without any signs of nerves. He's been trained, thought McManus.

Jackson seemed to sense this too. 'I'm sorry, man, but I didn't think it mattered.'

The young guy shook his head. 'I can see you're new to this. Rule Number One: no surprises. Understood?'

Jackson nodded reluctantly. It was clear now to McManus who was running the show, and it wasn't Jackson.

They walked together into the building, where the lorry driver was stubbing out a cigarette with the heel of his shoe. 'OK please to open up?' the driver asked.

Jackson shook his head. 'Not yet.' He turned to McManus and gestured at the new arrival. 'I'll be back in a minute. Give our friend a coffee, will you? There's a machine in the kitchen over there.' He pointed towards the end door in the partition at the side of the warehouse.

The Middle Eastern-looking guy said sharply, 'I don't want coffee. What's the hold-up?'

'Don't worry: I just want to have a look around outside,' said Jackson. 'Can't be too careful, can we? Then we'll get down to business.' And Jackson walked out of the warehouse before anyone could object.

McManus turned towards the other man. 'What's your name, mate?'

'Whatever,' the man said impatiently, his eyes following Jackson.

'All right, "Whatever" – are you sure you don't want coffee?'

In the Ops Room Peggy asked, 'What's Jackson doing?'

Lazarus looked at Andy, who said, 'Can't see him. He's out of camera range.'

'Perhaps he's gone to have a pee,' said Emily.

Nobody laughed. The atmosphere in the room had tautened with Jackson's sudden disappearance from view.

Lazarus said, 'Andy, get me Team Three.'

A moment later Andy said, 'On the line now.'

'Yes?' a disembodied voice came over the loudspeaker.

'Jackson's outside the warehouse. Don't know where he is – out of camera range. Hold your position until we know where he is.'

There was a pause. 'Do my best. But I've got two men closing in now.'

The Chief Constable looked at Liz and winced.

*

The lorry driver was growing agitated, which didn't improve his English. 'Doors to open,' he was insisting.

McManus shook his head. 'Not yet. The man will be back any time now.' The Middle Eastern guy was standing by the front of the warehouse, looking out. McManus had given up efforts to make conversation.

'Not waiting,' the driver said, going to the back of the lorry.

McManus took three strides and caught up with him as the driver was reaching for the steel handles of the twin back doors. He put a hand on the man's shoulder. 'The boss will be back in a minute,' he said firmly. 'So cool it.'

The driver stepped back from the lorry door. He shook his head. 'I am not liking this.'

'You'll survive,' said McManus. Out of the corner of his eye he saw something move outside, and then Jackson came back inside the warehouse, a tense expression on his face.

'He wants to open the lorry.' It was McManus speaking.

'Yeah, well, we got bigger problems. There's a car down the road that wasn't there before.'

'So? Lots of people must come in and out of here.'

'At three in the morning? I don't think so.' He stared at McManus. 'You wouldn't know anything about it, would you, Jimmy?'

'Me? Why would I?'

'You tell me. First you say you're retiring, then you try to duck out of driving over here with me. And you didn't like it when I took your phone. Who are you working for tonight?'

'I didn't realise I was working. You said could I lend a hand, and here I am. What's this about anyway?' He pointed over at the Middle Eastern customer who was watching them from the front of the warehouse.

'Never mind him,' Jackson said curtly. He seemed to have made up his mind. 'Here's what we're going to do. We'll open the doors and let the cargo out. I want you to take them into that room – I've got beds in there, and they can spend the rest of the night here. While you doss them down I'll finish up with my customer here. Got that?'

'OK.' McManus was thinking hard about his options, which seemed dismayingly limited. If there were police outside and they raided now, how was it going to look? They'd never believe he'd been forced into giving up his phone; they'd assume he'd been trying to double-cross them. Yet it was equally clear Jackson wasn't going to let him out of his sight – not long enough to get away, at any rate – and Jackson had a gun . . .

Jackson turned to the driver, 'Go on. Open up.' Then he looked back at McManus. 'Just try something now,' he said, his voice full of menace, 'and it will be the last thing you ever do try.'

'What on earth?' asked Peggy as they watched the monitor. The back doors of the lorry had been opened, and a pile of mattresses dragged out by the driver and chucked onto the warehouse floor. Now down a step at the back of the HGV came one, two, three, and finally a fourth woman.

They were all bedraggled, thin with matted blonde hair, and each clutched a suitcase. In spite of their winter coats and trousers, they looked frozen and they screwed up their eyes, dazzled by the light. They looked to be in their twenties – except for the last one, whom Liz watched with a growing sense of outrage: the girl could not have been more than sixteen years old.

Once out of the lorry, they huddled together in a little circle, clearly apprehensive about their new surroundings. The youngest was shivering uncontrollably, and one of the other women put an arm around her shoulder.

Jackson stepped forward. 'Welcome to England and the Jackson Hotel. You'll be spending the rest of the night here. My associate Mr McManus will show you to your quarters.'

The oldest-looking of the women stepped forward. 'We have not eaten for twelve hours,' she said. 'We're hungry.'

Jackson was unfazed. 'You'll have to wait till breakfast.' He made a show of looking at his watch. 'That won't be long now. So why don't you all get some sleep?'

McManus ushered the women towards the side of the warehouse, a plan starting to form in his mind. As he led the women along the partition towards the door into the so-called bedroom, he looked over his shoulder and saw Jackson and the driver conferring at the back of the lorry, while the young Middle Eastern guy stood by looking impatient. It wasn't going to take them long to locate the cargo in the lorry and bring it out; McManus would probably have less than a minute. But it might be time enough.

When they reached the first door in the partition, the girls stopped and looked back at him for directions. He nodded and indicated that they should open the door. He then stood in the doorway and watched as the girls put down their suitcases in the small spaces between the bunk beds. One of them opened the door into the tiny bathroom next door. He felt sorry for them in this comfortless place after their long journey in the back of the lorry.

'There's a kitchen next door,' he said. 'You can make some coffee.' From his position at the door in the partition, he looked back at the lorry. There was no sign of Jackson or the other two. They must all be inside the vehicle.

McManus walked fast back towards the front of the warehouse. As he passed by the lorry, he paused, listening carefully, then he set off, running fast towards the warehouse door.

McManus had gone out of sight of the internal camera as he'd taken the women towards the bedroom, and the attention of the watchers in the Ops Room had focused on Jackson as he clambered into the back of the lorry with the driver and Zara. As they all watched there was silence in the room. Liz now thought it was improbable that the other jihadis would be appearing, and she was willing Zara to get on and retrieve his 'goods' from the lorry, so they could send the armed team in to arrest him and Jackson.

Suddenly at the bottom of the screen a figure appeared, walking quickly towards the front of the warehouse. 'It's McManus,' Lazarus exclaimed just as the figure broke into a run, his shoes slapping noisily on the warehouse's concrete floor.

The outside camera took over, showing McManus as he reached the tarmac forecourt and ran out into the road. He was raising his arms and shouting, so loudly that in the Ops Room his voice came through clearly. 'Don't shoot, don't shoot,' he yelled. 'I'm police. DI McManus.' Fifty yards or so ahead of him an armed policeman had emerged from the undergrowth, holding an assault rifle aimed at McManus.

There was the flat crack of a gunshot and McManus half turned, clutching his stomach with both hands, stumbled, and fell. He lay motionless on his side. In the glare of the outside security lights the camera showed a small pool forming next to the inert figure; like a leak from a broken pipe the little pool gradually got bigger and began to trickle along the road.

'Oh God,' said Peggy as the policeman in a bullet-proof vest came slowly forward, his rifle still held high.

Liz looked on in disbelief. Had this policeman shot McManus, an unarmed man? Then at the side of the picture, she saw Jackson standing just outside the warehouse, a gun in his right hand.

Jackson must have seen the policeman at that moment, because he lifted his arm, aimed and fired. The same flat crack split the air, but now almost simultaneously there was a second noise – this time a burst of metallic-sounding gunfire. Jackson spun around, tottered for two steps and fell to his knees. One hand was still clutching his gun, but the other was pressed against his gut. He tried to stand again, but could only make it into a low crouch. He lifted the hand from his stomach and stared at it with a mixed expression of awe and disbelief; it was coated in blood.

He turned awkwardly on his heels to face the approaching policeman, who was shouting at him to drop the gun and stay where he was. But Jackson paid no attention; defiantly he managed to struggle to his feet and point his gun in the policeman's direction. There was the sound of another burst of fire, then silence. This time Jackson dropped for good.

57

PEOPLE ALWAYS SAID OLD people went to bed early, and Mrs Donovan wouldn't argue with that. Ever since the nine o'clock news on TV had moved to ten she'd never watched it. Nowadays she went to bed at half past nine and listened to the ten o'clock news on the radio.

But what people didn't understand was that just because you went to bed early, it didn't mean you *slept*. Every night she woke up, uncertain and hazy, lifting her head off the pillow to see the bright red illuminated numbers on the clock on her bedside table. They might say 12:30, or 2:17, or – when she was lucky – 5:45. Rare was the night she managed as much as four hours' continuous sleep; rarer still those where she slept through until dawn.

Tonight was no different. It was four o'clock and she was sitting at the kitchen table with a cup of milky tea, a biscuit and a copy of the *Sun*, which her grandson Michael had left behind.

She had put the telephone on the table within arm's reach, but it remained defiantly silent. She wasn't going to use it herself, because though she was accustomed to being up at this ungodly hour (the experts all said it was better to get up than lie in bed twisting and turning), she knew that

not many other people were. Old as she was, Mrs Donovan hadn't lost many of her marbles – she might keep odd
hours, but she knew what was and wasn't usual.

She'd tried to tell them about it earlier in the evening.
Someone had said they'd ring her back, but they hadn't.
She'd never believed for a moment that that girl who had
shown up really was from Electoral Registration. But she
had liked the look of her and she'd kept her leaflet with the
phone number, behind the little cactus plant that Michael
had given to her.

She couldn't have said quite who that girl did work for,
but she was sure it was something to do with those thrill-
ers she liked to watch when they were on the TV early
enough in the evening. 'Spooks', that's what they were
called. She was one of them, Mrs Donovan was sure. She
knew she was right because the number on the leaflet was
a London number. Why would the electoral registration
office for Eccles have a London telephone number?

She wouldn't have noticed any of this – or rung the
number – if things hadn't suddenly grown very peculiar
next door. Mrs Atiyah had come round three days before,
to say that she was going to visit her sister down in Croydon. Would Mrs D mind keeping an eye out for her cat
Domingo? He was a fat tabby with a scrunched ear from a
long-ago fight who liked to sleep in Mrs Atiyah's porch.
He wasn't actually the Atiyah cat – Domingo made it clear
he belonged to nobody – but the Yemeni woman was soft-
hearted and treated the animal like a favourite child. There
was always food for Domingo when he deigned to visit.

That was all fine, and Mrs Atiyah had gone off – Mrs D
had seen the minicab arrive two days before – but then this
morning the peculiar thing had happened. Just as she was
putting some Go-Cat in the bowl in her neighbour's porch,

with Domingo purring and rubbing himself against her legs, the front door had opened. She'd looked up, startled, expecting to see either Mrs Atiyah, back early, or one of her children. Instead a young man had stood there, Middle Eastern and bearded. He'd been just as startled as she was.

Mrs Donovan had stood up smiling, ready to introduce herself, pointing at Domingo to explain her presence. But the young man hadn't smiled or said a word, just gone back inside and firmly closed the door. Rude, Mrs Donovan had thought, but then later, back in her house, she had thought it also very odd. In that household, only Mrs Atiyah's son Mika was capable of that kind of behaviour, and it wasn't Mika who'd opened the door. So who was this stranger?

All day the question gnawed at her, competing with her usual instinct not to get involved, to leave things be, not to make a fuss. But she had been increasingly aware of something going on next door; of people – not just one surly young man, but others: someone playing the radio in the kitchen, while somebody else ran a bath, and someone came thumping down the stairs. You wouldn't have known, from the street, that anyone was there, since the curtains in front, both upstairs and down, were tightly drawn. It was only that the walls in these terrace houses were so thin that you always knew if there was anyone in.

If they were burgling the place in Mrs Atiyah's absence, it seemed a funny way of going about it; on the other hand, Mrs Atiyah would have mentioned it if she had invited people to use her house when she was away. And why would she have asked Mrs Donovan to feed Domingo if she had guests staying there?

Mrs Donovan was afraid of sticking her nose where it didn't belong. But what if these people were not in fact burglars, but something worse? Mrs Donovan was no coward, but neither was she a fool; she didn't think it would be sensible to go and knock on the door and ask who they were and what was going on. There wouldn't be much she could do if the strangers suddenly bundled her inside and . . . she didn't even want to think about it.

Then she had seen Mika, Mrs A's son, arrive. He'd parked outside and run into his mother's house, carrying a bag. Before Mrs Donovan could get to the door and go out to intercept him, he had gone inside, slamming the door.

He was driving a brand-new car from the look of it, a big one too, which struck Mrs Donovan as a bit much. These students were meant to be paying their own fees these days – weren't they always complaining about that? So how could Mika afford such a flashy car?

Finally Mrs Donovan decided that she needed to do something. She wondered again about whether she should knock on the door now Mika was back and ask him what was going on and whether his mother knew about all these people being there. But again she thought that wouldn't be wise. From the way he had rushed into the house, she didn't think she'd be welcome; the thought of the hostile young man she had seen that morning put her off the idea completely.

It was then she remembered her recent visitor who'd said she was from the electoral registration office. Whoever she really was, perhaps she could help. It had been evening by then, after six o'clock, so she wasn't sure if she'd still be there. But nowadays people seemed to work long hours and they all had these mobile phones, so she thought it worth giving it a try. She took the card down from the sideboard and dialled the number.

A woman's voice had answered, and thinking it was the girl she'd met, Mrs Donovan began to explain – until the woman interrupted. Once the confusion was sorted out, and Mrs Donovan had explained who she was trying to reach and why, the woman had promised to pass the message on. She'd said she'd be rung back right away. But nothing had happened.

It was nearly ten hours now since she'd rung. She'd seen Mika go out in his car, but the other people were still next door. She could hear them moving about even though it was the middle of the night. Mika had not come back; the car wasn't there. She'd been tempted to ring the number again but there probably wasn't any point.

Perhaps she was just being a silly old woman. Part of Mrs Donovan hoped she was, and that she was wrong in her suspicions of the people next door. I think I'll just forget about it, she thought, taking a sip of her now-tepid tea. I expect there's some innocent explanation and Mrs Atiyah will sort it out when she gets back. She yawned and stood up to go back to bed. Not that she would sleep.

58

I T TOOK EIGHTEEN MINUTES to reach the warehouse from Police HQ. They went in convoy, three cars in all. Chief Superintendent Lazarus stayed behind in the Ops Room to coordinate the operation. Liz drove with Chief Constable Pearson in his BMW; his driver, Tom, had turned the heater on high to melt the frost on the windows – the car had been standing outside waiting for the call to move and was cold inside as well as out.

At first there was no conversation in the car. They were listening to the radio transmissions as police cars converged on the industrial estate. Two ambulances were not far behind.

Then Pearson broke the silence. 'I wasn't expecting to see you here tonight.'

'Well—' she began, then found herself with nothing more to say. She hadn't expected to find herself here either. It seemed unreal. But she was grateful for the almost frantic sequence of events, since it kept her from thinking of the terrible happenings in Paris the night before. The night before? Incredibly it was only last night, even though it seemed to be days since she had first heard the news of Martin's murder.

Pearson said, 'I'm delighted that you're here. Don't get

me wrong, I think young Peggy is extremely good. But I know she was glad when you showed up.' He paused to listen to a burst of radio transmission then said, 'I think you're pretty remarkable, frankly, after the twenty-four hours you've had.'

'I wanted to see things through,' Liz said.

'Of course. But listen, if this gets too much for you at any point, just let me know. Tom will drive you back to Police HQ and sort you out with one of our guest rooms. Then you can pick things up again tomorrow.'

The driver nodded. 'I'll be with the car. Just let me know if you want to go.'

'That's kind of you, but honestly—'

Pearson lifted a hand to interrupt. 'Understood. Just remember if you change your mind, the offer holds.'

As they approached the trading estate they could see a ghoulish glow created by the dim sodium lights that lined the narrow strips of road and trailed off into the industrial enclave. Tom drove quickly, following the other two cars, turning right then left into a kind of cul de sac, at the end of which was a tarmac apron in front of a large metal warehouse. Scrubby grass and undergrowth filled the spaces between the warehouse and the adjacent buildings, derelict-looking brick and concrete workshops.

A lone policeman stood at the front of the tarmac, waving a flashlight to steer them around a small area which was marked by traffic cones. Behind the cones something lay on the ground covered by a tarpaulin sheet. With a jolt, Liz realised she was looking at McManus's dead body. They were now part of the drama that they'd been watching on the screens in the Ops Room. She felt as if she had stepped from the audience onto the stage.

Three police vans and an ambulance were already neatly parked and Tom pulled up beside them. Another two cars bringing Peggy and some more uniformed officers had just arrived. Liz and Pearson followed the policemen into the warehouse, stepping gingerly over Jackson's body, which was still lying in the entrance, also under a sheet,

Two members of the armed team were inside. One stood guard over Zara, who was handcuffed, sitting on a wooden crate. He was staring vacantly into space, pointedly ignoring the people around him. The other armed officer was trying to calm down the women, who had emerged from their tiny bedroom compartment at the side of the warehouse. The youngest was still shaking but now she was screaming too and tears were running down her face. Another, who seemed to be the oldest, was clawing at the arm of the policeman and shouting, 'Not to shoot.'

The policeman was trying to unhook her hands and saying, 'I'm not going to shoot you. You are quite safe here.'

But he was having no effect. The women were all clearly terrified and Liz couldn't blame them; two men had been shot dead nearby less than half an hour after their arrival. This was not what they thought they'd come to England for.

'Where's the lorry driver?' asked Liz, suddenly realising that someone was missing.

The armed policeman pointed to the cab. 'He locked himself in when the shooting started. I've been trying to coax him out, but he's scared to death.'

'At least we know where he is. We'll get to him in a minute,' said Chief Constable Pearson. 'First I want these women out of the way. Put them somewhere until we decide what to do with them.'

Peggy, who had come in behind Liz, stepped forward

and touched the arm of the woman who was clutching at the policeman.

'Come with me,' she said in a gentle voice. 'No one's going to hurt you. Let's go and see if we can make some coffee. Then I'll ask someone to get you something to eat.'

The woman let go of the policeman and grasped Peggy's hand. She looked at Peggy's face with frightened, anxious eyes, then after a moment she turned to the others and said something. It seemed to calm them, and then, like a mother hen, Peggy rounded up the little group and ushered them back towards the bedroom.

The armed policeman, the Chief Constable and Liz all watched in silence. A silence that was broken when one of the policemen came up to the group and asked, 'When we search the lorry, what are we looking for, sir?'

Pearson looked at Liz. She said, 'Guns and grenades. The firearms are probably a mix of assault rifles and hand-guns. And a lot of ammunition – they asked for twenty thousand rounds. That will take up a fair amount of space.'

Pearson said, 'I'm sure the driver knows where the cargo is hidden, so we should talk to him first. But whatever he says, take it slowly. I don't want anything going off because someone gets impatient.'

The other officer had joined them. 'I've frisked the suspect, sir,' he said, pointing to Zara. 'He wasn't armed.'

Liz asked, 'Was he carrying any ID?'

'No.'

'How about valuables? Any cash?'

'He only had a few quid in his pocket, but he had some-thing else worth a hell of a lot of money. A ticket for the derby tomorrow, at Old Trafford.' He handed the ticket to Liz. As she studied it, he added, 'They're like gold dust.'

Liz handed the ticket to Pearson, and said, 'We've dug

pretty deep into young Atiyah's past but I've never seen anything in the file about a love of football. Nor that he had the money to fund this sort of expense.' She turned to the policeman. 'Do you ever go to Old Trafford?'

'I've been known to attend a match,' he admitted.

'Do they search you when you go through the gates?'

'No. It wouldn't be practical. You've got sixty thousand people going in in a short time. The queues would go back for miles if they searched everyone. They tried it for the Olympics and it caused chaos.'

Pearson was looking on with growing apprehension. He said, 'It's cold enough now for everyone in the crowd to be bundled up. You could smuggle a weapon or a grenade in under an overcoat easily enough if there's no proper searching.'

'Exactly,' said Liz. 'And if you had six people in different parts of the stadium, then even if one got spotted you'd have five others who might not have been.'

The policeman said, 'To do what? Shoot Wayne Rooney?' He gave a weak laugh. 'And why do you say "six people"? The suspect only had the one ticket.'

Pearson didn't bother to explain. He saw what Liz was driving at, and he said, 'So the other jihadis must already have their tickets. Which means—'

'It means they've arrived and are holed up somewhere nearby.' Liz pointed towards the solitary figure of Atiyah, sitting in handcuffs on the wooden crate, then asked the policeman, 'Are you sure he didn't have anything else on him? Anything at all – a crumpled bus ticket, or a pocket comb. Anything.'

The officer shook his head. 'No, and he didn't say a word – he wouldn't even tell me his name. I don't think you'll get much out of him.'

Pearson said to Liz, 'Do you want to have a go here or wait until we take him back to headquarters?'

'Here please.' It was critical to try to get Atiyah to talk before he had time to collect his thoughts and invent a story – or just clam up and ask for a lawyer.

As Liz started to walk over to Atiyah, Peggy, who had come back from tending the Dagestan women, intercepted her. 'Could I have a word, Liz?' She held up her mobile phone. 'I've just had a message relayed from Thames House. It could be important.'

'Give me two minutes, Peggy. I need to talk to Zara urgently.' And she strode over and stood in front of Atiyah. He ignored her, continuing to stare out towards the parked cars on the hard standing in front of the warehouse.

Liz said, 'You all right? You didn't get hurt in the shooting?'

He didn't reply. His eyes remained focused on the distance, trance-like. For a moment Liz wondered if he was drugged, but then she remembered him from the video feed – he had been perfectly lively then, even aggressive. She said, 'Tell me if you got hurt; there are paramedics here now.' When he still didn't reply, Liz said softly, 'Mika, we know who you are.'

This time he blinked. For a moment Liz thought he was going to say something, but he didn't. She went on, 'We know the lorry has brought other things into the country, besides the women and the mattresses. We're going to start searching it in a minute or two. When we find what we're looking for, you'll be arrested.

'But that's not all we're searching for. I think you know that. At least five of your colleagues have entered the country from Yemen; I think they're supposed to meet you once you've collected the guns that are in the lorry. I didn't realise you were interested in football – are your colleagues going to the match too?'

He flinched slightly, then pursed his lips. Liz went on, 'I'm certain we'll be able to find them, especially if they show up at the match tomorrow.' She was watching him carefully. Without these guns, his comrades shouldn't be able to do much even if they made it inside the stadium next day – unless . . . And Liz shuddered at the thought. *Unless they already had other weapons.*

The only way to be sure was to find them. She suddenly hated the idea that Martin might have died for nothing; that despite the sacrifice of his life, and all their efforts, these terrorists might still manage to launch an attack. If only Zara could be made to talk. But looking at him she realised he was determined to give nothing away – he had adopted the same vacant stare again, as if transfixed.

Liz said, her voice hardening, 'Your colleagues will go down all right. But the big loser is going to be you, Mika, because you're the one we can tie to the guns we're about to find. We clocked you a long time ago, and you've been followed ever since. We watched your meeting in Primrose Hill, and the dealer you saw there is in custody in France. He's told us everything we need to put you away. I reckon you're facing thirty years. You might get out in time for the 2040 Olympics. Just think how old you'll be then.'

Liz gave a sigh. 'It's not as if you will have helped your cause very much, either. But there is a way you can help yourself, a way you could be out of prison in just a few years – you'd still have a life left. But, Mika, you have to tell us where the others are.'

Atiyah continued to sit impassively and Liz realised she was hitting a brick wall. He was obviously a fully signed up jihadi. This was his martyrdom and if she had said two

325

hundred years in prison instead of thirty, he would have been pleased. She made one last try: 'We're going to catch your colleagues anyway; it's just going to speed things up if you tell us where they are. Think about what I'm saying; soon it'll be too late for me to help you.'

Atiyah turned his head very slowly, and for the first time Liz felt hopeful that he might reply. His eyes met hers, and he held her gaze as his lips began to move. Then his mouth opened and he spat in her face.

Liz jerked back in surprise. She tried to collect herself, and wiped the spittle from her cheek with the sleeve of her coat. She was determined not to show her shock, or anger. She said calmly, 'If you help us, I promise you I will do everything in my power to help you.' A thought came suddenly into her head. She added, 'I'll also make sure your mother doesn't get dragged into this.'

Atiyah's eyes flared for an instant, and for a moment Liz thought he would spit at her again. But then he regained control, and his eyes resumed their opaque stare.

Liz turned round and saw that Pearson was waiting, standing halfway between her and the lorry. She shrugged as she walked towards him, leaving Atiyah in the care of his armed guard. Peggy was there too, waiting for her, and Liz remembered that she had something to tell her.

In the background, behind Pearson, three policemen had approached the lorry, gesturing to the driver to come out of the cab. One of them went round to the driver's side and climbed up on the step next to the door of the cab. He knocked on the glass and shouted through the window, 'Open up. We want to talk to you.'

The Chief Constable and Peggy turned round and Liz stopped and watched as the policeman, losing patience, shouted, 'Open up, or we'll have to smash the window.'

The driver was looking frightened – though suddenly Liz wondered if that was an act. She was about to shout a warning when she saw the man slide across the front seat of the cab to the passenger side. Opening the door, he leapt down just as two of the policemen came round the front of the lorry.

They were less than ten feet away when from the pocket of his pea jacket the driver drew out a small grenade. With his free hand he prised the pin off, then chucked the grenade underhand, like a child playing rounders.

The nearest policeman to him flinched and turned away with his arms holding his head. The grenade landed on the cement floor, just missing the policeman, then bounced high in the air, angled towards . . . towards Liz. She tensed, waiting for it to explode. There was nowhere to go and nothing she could do.

Then an outstretched arm, black-clad, with silver on its shoulder, reached out and grabbed the grenade as it started to come down. In one quick motion the arm then threw the grenade straight out of the open front of the warehouse.

It travelled twenty yards and hit with a sharp thump on the tarmac forecourt, where it promptly exploded. As dirt-coloured shards burst through the air, the noise of the explosion was astonishingly small, almost muffled. But it was followed by a series of sharp *pings* – the shrapnel was hitting the sides of the parked police cars.

Pearson ran to the front of the warehouse. 'Who's hit?' he shouted. But the two ambulance attendants had been shielded from the blast by one of the police cars. They looked dazed but unhurt. Tom, the Chief's driver, was the sole policeman outside, and he'd been in his car on the radio. He held a hand up to show he was OK.

Visibly relieved, Pearson came back into the warehouse, where the driver had been wrestled to the ground and handcuffed. As an armed policeman watched him, Atiyah at last showed some emotion – he was smiling broadly.

'Are you all right, Liz?' asked Pearson.

She nodded. 'Just surprised to be breathing. For a moment I was sure that was it.' She looked at Pearson. 'This is the first time I've had to thank anyone for saving my life. Thank you very much.'

'Pure instinct,' he said. 'I was in the Territorial Army and sometimes it seemed half our training was about dealing with incendiary devices and grenades. Never had to use it then.' He shook his head. 'And never thought I'd have to use it here. There must have been something wrong with that grenade, but thank God there was.'

Behind them they heard a quiet groan. Liz turned and saw Peggy squatting down against the side wall of the warehouse. She was holding her arm, which was bleeding badly just below the elbow.

'Were you hit?' Liz asked.

Peggy grimaced and slumped down, her back against the wall and her legs splayed out in front of her, flat on the floor. As Liz rushed to her, Pearson said, 'I'll get a paramedic.'

Liz crouched down next to Peggy. She saw at once that the wound was bad; shrapnel had ripped through the layers of sweater and shirt Peggy wore; there was a deep jagged cut in her forearm, which was bleeding profusely.

She saw Peggy's eyes glaze and start to shut. The girl was going into shock. 'Peggy!' Liz shouted, and the eyes fluttered open, stared vaguely at Liz, then shut again.

The paramedic had arrived and Liz stood up to get out of his way. As he examined Peggy's arm, she moaned in pain, and he took a syringe and vial out of his pack and injected something into Peggy's other arm. Morphine, Liz guessed; the pain of the shrapnel piece must be excruciating.

Two more paramedics arrived, carrying a stretcher between them. They carefully lifted Peggy onto it, then carried her towards one of the ambulances parked on the tarmac outside.

The medic who had injected Peggy looked at Liz. 'She should be fine, but we need to get her seen to properly right away – that's a nasty wound she's got. Do you want to come with us in the ambulance?'

Liz hesitated. She wanted to be with Peggy, but there was still everything to play for. She shook her head. 'I'm still needed here. But please keep me posted.'

Pearson was on his phone, but he rang off when he saw Liz. He said, 'We're going to have to make a decision about the match.'

She nodded. 'I know. It's your call of course, but I'm worried about these other jihadis. We just have no idea where they are or whether they have any weapons. I would hazard a guess that they haven't, but there are no guarantees. They might have access to some cache somewhere.'

'Yes. You're right. And if they do turn up at the match armed or carrying explosives of some kind, we can't be sure we'll be able to stop them getting in. We've got the seat number of Atiyah's ticket, but even if we searched everyone with a seat in the same block we might not catch them. They could have seats in any part of the ground.'

The Chief Constable was frowning. 'I'm beginning to think we have no option but to cancel the match. We can't take the risk. But if we do it's going to cause an immense furore. There'll be chaos on the streets, the media will have a field day, the Home Secretary will get drawn in and all of us including your Service will come in for a load of criticism. I need to speak to the Home Office before we do anything and you'll want to talk to your management too.'

Liz looked at her watch. It was now a quarter past five. 'I'll get on to the Duty Officer. DG will certainly want to be informed.'

Pearson looked round the warehouse. 'We're not needed here any more. We'll go back to HQ and set up a conference call and then everyone can have their say and get themselves prepared for the shit storm we're going to face. We can start the ball rolling while we drive back.'

59

AT SIX O'CLOCK THEY were in Pearson's corner office, joined now by Lazarus and several of Pearson's senior colleagues, called in to help plan what would be a major operation whatever was decided about cancelling the derby match. Outside it was still pitch-dark, and whenever Liz looked towards the windows she saw, reflected against the black sky, the dark-uniformed figures sitting round the conference table in the middle of the room.

Liz had rung the hospital from the car and learned that Peggy's condition was stable, but that they would soon be operating on the arm to remove the shrapnel, which had fragmented into a number of small pieces. Confident there was nothing she could do for Peggy at the moment, Liz was focused on the decision Pearson was going to have to make.

Reports had been called for from all police divisions for any sightings of a group of men acting suspiciously, but in the absence of any descriptions, no one was surprised that no reports had been received. Liz's colleagues in Thames House had been in touch with GCHQ, the DCRI in France and the UK Border Agency, but no new information was forthcoming. A4 and police surveillance teams were still out in the area – they all knew the urgency of the situation and would instantly have communicated news of any sightings.

From the speakerphone in the middle of the table an automated voice suddenly announced, 'Your call is ready to begin. All participants are now signed in.' Pearson took a deep breath and said, 'Good morning, everyone, I apologise for the uncivilised hour but we have an urgent decision to take in connection with the Zara Operation on which I think you are all briefed. Will you all please introduce yourselves?'

With the preliminaries over, Pearson outlined the situation, calmly summarising the dramatic events of the previous few hours. He concluded, 'We are confident that the target of this jihadi group is the derby match between Manchester United and Manchester City at Old Trafford this afternoon. We will of course continue to question Zara, but so far we've got nothing out of him, and I don't believe that will change. He's already asking for a lawyer. We have interdicted the arms imported for use in that attack, but the whereabouts of the group other than Zara is unknown and we do not know if they are armed or have access to arms. So a risk exists that they may attempt to proceed with the attack and that there may be casualties – possibly many.'

The gravelly tones of DG came through now. 'What security measures can you take at the ground that might help detect these people if they turn up? I'm assuming searching all the fans is impossible.'

'Yes. It would take too long and we don't have the manpower,' agreed Pearson. 'What I can do is double the number of officers patrolling the gates and the stands, and I can insert more plain-clothes officers into the crowd. Obviously we'll be closely monitoring the CCTV cameras too, but we have no descriptions of these jihadis and it's very likely we won't spot them until they start something.'

'The Home Secretary will wish to know what the law and order implications are if the match is cancelled at this short notice.' It was the Head of Counter-Terrorism at the Home Office.

'It won't surprise you, or her, that cancelling the match at this late hour will create plenty of problems on the street. Even if we announce cancellation now there will still be hundreds arriving in a short space of time, and we may have some violence when they find out the match is cancelled. The later we leave it to announce cancellation, the worse it will be. That's why need to decide now, I'm afraid.'

DG spoke again: 'Liz, what's your view of things? Do you have a recommendation?'

Liz was drawing in her breath to say that she thought the only safe option was to cancel the match, when Pearson's office door opened and a young uniformed policeman came in, looking nervous. Without saying a word he handed Liz a slip of paper. It read, *Most urgent call for you.* She started to shake her head, but something in the young officer's eyes made her change her mind.

'Excuse me,' she said, leaning towards the speakerphone. 'I've just been told there's a very urgent call for me. It may be relevant so I think I'd better take it.'

Liz was gone less than five minutes. When she came back into the room she walked straight up to the table and, still standing, leant towards the phone. 'I apologise for the interruption,' she said. 'You were asking my view a moment ago and I was about to recommend cancellation. But as a result of the phone conversation I've just had, I can now confidently recommend that we should let the match go ahead.'

As she paused to catch her breath, Pearson broke in. 'What's happened?'

'I've just been speaking to the lady who lives next door to Zara's mother. Zara was at the house early last night, before he went to the warehouse to collect the weapons.'

'Go on.' It was DG's voice.

'The neighbour told me that Mrs Atiyah is away, but when Mrs Atiyah told her she'd be gone for a few days she didn't say anything about anyone coming to stay. Yet the neighbour swears there are people in the house – she says she can hear them through the wall. And she actually saw one of them yesterday. It was a young man.'

Liz paused. No one spoke. 'I think they've got to be the jihadis. And they're still there now.'

60

L IZ HAD ALWAYS LOOKED forward to Christmas and enjoyed it, but not this year. She and Martin had planned to spend it in Paris, but after the funeral service and the day spent removing her belongings from Martin's flat, Paris was the last place she wanted to spend any more time, let alone the holidays.

She'd gone instead to Bowerbridge, her childhood home. Her mother and Edward Treglown, her mother's partner, had been doing their best to help her come to terms with Martin's death and she didn't want to hurt their feelings by refusing to join them for Christmas.

She had arrived on Christmas Eve afternoon and they had gone to the midnight service at the village church. Liz had been brought up an Anglican but she no longer believed in any sort of God, though she knew that the moral principles she tried to live by were firmly rooted in her Anglican upbringing. And in fact, the church service with its familiar words, its music and the carols she knew so well had proved oddly soothing.

Afterwards they had walked back through the estate that her father had managed for the then owners. She'd played there with the children of the big house when she was quite young and she knew every track and path. It was a clear starry night and frost was beginning to settle on the fields. So bright was the moon that they hardly needed their torches. As she walked, she thought about everything that had happened to her since the previous Christmas and wondered, not for the first time, whether the time had come to quit and find another job.

She had stayed on for Christmas Day, worried that the sadness she couldn't disguise might spoil the day, but by the evening she had eaten enough and drunk enough of Edward's favourite burgundy to dull the pain and they had spent a pleasant evening dozing in front of the fire and the TV. Then on Boxing Day they had joined a big lunch party at some neighbour's, where blessedly no one present had known anything about Liz's relationship with Martin or about his death, so all she had to do was dodge the usual questions about her job.

She left the next day, promising to try and come down for New Year's Eve, though she knew that both her mother and Edward understood that she wasn't going to make it. Wherever she was, Liz knew she was going to be in pain, and she thought it best to suffer alone – why spoil any more of the holidays for everybody else?

After an aimless evening in her flat, she went back to work the next day. She was used to the sense of anticlimax that came at the end of an operation, whatever the outcome, but this time grief redoubled her deflation. Yet she knew that immersion in work would be the one thing to get her through the coming days, so she was glad to be back at her desk.

The office was quiet, virtually empty of staff on her floor, though in pockets round the building people were work-ing as hard as ever. She rang the A4 Control Room to say thank you for all their efforts in following Zara on his anti-surveillance route to Eccles and the lorry from Harwich. Wally Woods answered.

'Happy New Year,' she said. 'Don't you ever have a holiday?'

'My work is my leisure,' he responded with a snort. 'We're in the middle of another drama now.'

On her return from Manchester, Liz had filed a brief report but knew she would have to supplement it. Not that there was much to add.

On that morning in Manchester when a half-conscious Peggy, just before surgery, had through sheer stubbornness insisted word must get through to Liz that Mrs Donovan had phoned the Thames House switchboard, it hadn't taken Einstein to see the link with Atiyah. Liz had called Mrs Donovan straight away.

She had expected a call that early would wake the old lady up, but quite the opposite proved to be the case. 'About time someone rang,' Maggie Donovan had said irritably. 'I haven't been able to sleep. I've been waiting for hours.' Then the old lady, still sharp as a tack, had told Liz about the visitors next door, and how Mrs Atiyah was away and hadn't said anything about people coming to stay.

Within half an hour, still in the moonless dark, a dozen armed police had filled the terraced street, blocking each end, climbing over garden walls and finally simultaneously breaking down the front and back doors and charging into the house. Inside they'd found the five associates of Mika Atiyah asleep on inflatable mattresses on the sitting room and bedroom floors. Caught off guard, they had been taken into custody without resistance. When they were questioned, they had all protested, claiming that they had come to Manchester to go to the football match with their friends. It hadn't taken much of a search of the house to find the little pile of tickets for the match, lying on top of a cupboard. But when they were asked to explain why the tickets were all for different parts of the ground, they became less vocal.

After it was discovered that each of them carried a Yemeni passport, even though they spoke in a variety of British regional accents and not one of them could understand the interpreter who was summoned to speak to them in Arabic, they'd refused to say anything at all. Not that that had helped them for long in concealing their identities, once the detailed inquiries were completed. They were all now in prison in Manchester, as was Mika Atiyah, on a variety of charges under the Counter-Terrorism Act.

The media had got hold of the fact that armed police had made arrests at a house in Eccles that were thought to be connected in some way with a shooting incident at a warehouse on an industrial estate off the M60, but so far it hadn't leaked out that a terrorist plot had been disrupted, or what the intended target had been. Jackson's death had gone unmourned in the Manchester metropolitan area, while the newspapers had been spare with the usual effusive eulogies for a murdered policeman – word seemed to have got round about McManus's less savoury activities.

And any sympathy Liz might have felt for her former lover disappeared when Halliday rang her. 'You know,' he said after congratulating Liz on the arrest of the terrorist suspects, 'I felt guilty that I was somehow responsible for the woman Katya's death – by tipping off Jackson accidentally somehow. But I've discovered it wasn't anything I'd done. McManus was in the police station the night Katya and the other girls were brought in. The desk sergeant told me it was McManus who got her released first – I guess to alert Jackson that she was an informer.'

On that night – really, very early morning – when the Atiyah house was being entered by armed police, a search party had been busy back in the warehouse. It had taken them almost three hours to find the weapons hidden in the lorry, and it would have taken longer than that but for a stray remark from one of the Dagestani women the police had begun to interview. She complained about how long the journey had taken. She said that the driver was forever stopping to fill up – yet he wouldn't let them out at the petrol stations to stretch their legs or go to the toilet. Since lorries of that size had enormous petrol tanks, this continual stopping for fuel seemed peculiar.

It was then that they checked the fuel tank itself, where they soon found that half of it had been fitted with a metal partition. In the newly created compartment they found twenty AK-47s wrapped in oilskins, grenades in metal containers, and box after box of ammunition clad in bubble wrap. It was an ingenious hiding place, and a stupid one, since a stray spark and some leaked petrol fumes could have set off the ammunition and blown the lorry sky-high.

Liz remained concerned about Peggy Kinsolving, whom the doctors had told to take six weeks' sick leave. Peggy had been through the mill, with fragments of shrapnel embedded deep in her arm. Some had chipped the bone, and it had required two bouts of surgery to remove them all and repair the bone. She'd been in Manchester Royal Infirmary for more than a week as they monitored her for shock and infection.

Liz had visited her just hours after the tumultuous

events at the warehouse had concluded with the arrest of the jihadis at the Atiyah house. She had found Peggy not long out of a first operation on her arm, propped up in bed and still looking dazed and shaken. A TV set on the wall of her room was showing the game between City and United. Liz sat down and they watched together in silence. As the camera panned around the stadium, which was packed to the rafters with noisy fans, waving, cheering and singing, they looked at each other. Liz voiced what they were both thinking.

'Look at them,' she said. 'Think what that would look like if Zara and his friends had got through. If they'd got those guns and grenades in there, into different parts of the stadium, they could have killed hundreds of people before anyone stopped them.'

The two were silent; wild cheering filled the room as a man in red scored a goal. 'I can't forgive myself for not checking the message Mrs Donovan left with the Thames House switchboard when I first got it. We could have picked up the terrorists hours earlier and arrested Zara before he ever came to the warehouse.'

'I'm not sure about that. We needed to have Zara go where the weapons were to have a good chance of prosecution. Anyway there's no point in beating yourself up. As it's turned out they *were* stopped. Thanks to you and everybody else working on this case, it didn't happen.'

'Yes,' replied Peggy, reaching out with her good arm for Liz's hand. 'And that includes Martin.'

Liz nodded, her eyes filling with tears.

Now, weeks later, there was still a lot more investigation to do both for the police and Liz's team before any trials could take place. Research into the young Atiyah's finances had unearthed a recent series of deposits into his bank account, totalling £177,000 – deposits which to Liz's fury, the particular branch had never thought to question, as if it were entirely normal for a student from Eccles to have that kind of money at his disposal. It had proved possible to trace the money to a Lebanese bank, which had so far been stubbornly slow to assist with British efforts to uncover the money's original source.

Following the spider web of connections from Atiyah back to his controllers in the Middle East was challenging and time-consuming, but Liz consoled herself that there was already ample evidence to prosecute Atiyah and his cohorts. Antoine Milraud, appalled by what his young customer had been planning to do, was cooperating fully with Isabelle Florian in Paris, and had agreed to give evidence in court.

Martin would have been pleased by this, Liz thought, as she stood up and went over to the window of her office. There had been a fall of snow the night before, but it was melting now, leaving a thin layer of slush on the pavement along the Embankment. The Thames was a dull grey and restless, with choppy waves stirred up by the winter wind. Martin had liked to tease her that the Seine was the superior river, and today she would have agreed.

Would she ever stop missing Martin? Even now she could only feel heartbreakingly alone in a world without him. His death had served some purpose, she knew. Had he not succeeded in flushing out Ramdani the terrorist would have warned his colleagues bound for England that they were blown. They would have melted away and Liz would still be searching for half a dozen lethal men. She couldn't make room for the thought that this was any kind of compensation for Martin's death – it wasn't – but at least it gave some meaning to it. He had been dedicated and professional to the end, and Martin would have been the first to scoff at any suggestion that he should have hesitated to act because of possible danger. He knew, just as Liz knew, that risk came with the job.

A knock on the open door of her office shook Liz from her reverie. 'Come in,' she said.

It was Geoffrey Fane, and for once he actually looked friendly, almost shy. 'Elizabeth,' he said awkwardly.

Liz smiled to herself. There was no point in getting cross; he really couldn't help it. 'Hello, Geoffrey,' she said. 'I actually do prefer Liz, you know.'

'Of course,' he said, coming into the room. Liz went back to her desk and sat down, motioning Fane to a chair. But he shook his head; unusually for him, he seemed to understand that his presence might not be entirely welcome. 'I just wanted to say how very sorry I was to hear about Martin Seurat. I know you two were close.' He paused, as if hearing his words and how lame they sounded.

'Thank you,' she said simply.

He gave a little cough. 'I gather you did stellar work up in Manchester.'

'It's kind of you to say that. A lot of things didn't go right.'

'Possibly, but when do they ever? And you did prevent the very worst happening. Well done.'

Is this why Fane had come? Liz wondered. Gentle commiseration followed by a pat on the back? She'd known him long enough to know there had to be some other agenda.

And so there was. Fane came right into the room now, sat down, straightened his long back and crossed a languid leg over one knee. This was the Geoffrey Fane she knew.

She watched him warily, waiting for what was to come. He said, 'I've got a bit of news actually.'

'Really?' She tried to look surprised.

'I had a meeting with our friend Andy Bokus yesterday. Not an altogether happy encounter, you could say. I pointed out that there was a missing link in this case, one that would have helped us a lot.'

'Baakrime.'

'That's right. The Minister,' Fane said, with the mild surprise he always showed when he found that Liz had got there too. 'He was both the instigator and the linchpin of this whole affair.'

'But currently unavailable.'

'So it would seem. Thanks to American cack-handedness. When they shilly-shallied he must have panicked and decided to throw in his lot with the Russians.'

'You said that to Bokus again?'

'In so many words.'

'That couldn't have gone down well.'

Fane gave a sly smile. Liz could see he was enjoying himself now.

'Actually, he had bigger things to worry about.'

'Oh?'

'Yes. It seems he's being moved on. Back to Langley.'

'I'd have thought he'd be pleased. Bokus never liked it here.'

'That's true. Or at least he never liked *us* – or to be even more precise, *me*.' Fane's grin now could only be described as wicked. 'But from his account, it sounded as if he was leaving under something of a cloud. No trumpets at the Langley gates when Andy reappears.'

'But what's he done wrong?'

'He's being blamed for Baakrime's disappearance.'

'Really? It was Miles Brookhaven out in Sana'a who was running Baakrime.'

'Ah, but it was Bokus who was giving him the line to take and Bokus who was pushing Miles to squeeze Baakrime.'

'I suppose so,' said Liz dubiously.

'And that's what provides the delicious irony – and what I suppose must gall Bokus the most.'

He paused, savouring his position as the fount of high-end gossip. Go on, spill the beans, Liz thought to herself, but she hesitated, knowing that Fane was longing to be asked. Finally curiosity prevailed. 'What delicious irony, Geoffrey?'

Pleased to be asked at last, Fane said, 'You see, they've already named the new Station Head for London. Usually, there's just the slightest lag – out of courtesy to the departing Head. Not this time.'

'Who is it?' But Fane was now laughing too hard to reply. 'Come on, Geoffrey, what's so funny?'

And at last he managed to croak, 'Miles Brookhaven.'

Liz stared at Fane, wondering if he was pulling her leg. It seemed too improbable to credit, until one looked at its natural symmetry. It was Miles who had first relayed the tip that arms were being sent to the UK, and Miles who had triggered the convoluted sequence of events that had ended – thank God – in a failed conspiracy to kill countless numbers of people.

So Miles's return to the UK somehow seemed entirely fitting. It was this – as well as the thought that she quite liked Miles, and was curious to learn what he was like after several years away – that meant Liz was glad to hear the news. Glad enough in fact to join Geoffrey Fane and find herself laughing too.